THE
END

MATS STRANDBERG

THE
END

Translation by Judith Kiros

Arctis · W1-Media, Inc. · Stamford

This is a work of fiction. Names, characters, places, and incidents are from the author's imaginations or are used fictitiously.

Arctis US

W1-Media, Inc.
Arctis
Stamford, CT, USA

Visit our website at www.w1-media.com
Author website at www.matsstrandberg.com

3 5 7 9 8 6 4 2

Library of Congress Control Number: 2020938378

ISBN 978-1-64690-006-0
eBook ISBN 978-1-64690-106-7
Translation by Judith Kiros
Cover design by Anders Timrén / Figures by Tuomo Parikka

Printed in Germany, European Union

PROLOGUE

The beginning of the end (May 27)

My legs feel oddly numb as I follow the stream of students into the hallway. There are people everywhere, and more and more phones ringing. Everyone's raising their voices, trying to be heard. Some people are already crying. But I can't feel a thing. It's as if I'm watching everything from afar. It doesn't bother me. I can even calmly come to the conclusion that this must be a defense mechanism, and I should be grateful for it.

Tilda picks up after the first ring.

"Are you at school?" I ask.

"No," she says. "I was on my way from the pool when I heard. I'm almost back home."

"I'm on my way."

"Hurry."

I promise her I will. Just before I end the call, I hear her let out a soft sob.

Farther down, in one of the other hallways, someone screams. I try to go online; it's too busy. Hampus says something to me, but I can't hear him.

As I pass a window, I feel the warmth of the day through my thin shirt. Out there, the sun is shining; the trees are almost unnaturally green. It's still early in the morning.

My first class had just started when the principal popped

his head into the classroom, waving at our math teacher, Mr. Andersson. They'd whispered in the hallway. I could see them when I leaned forward. The door to the classroom next to ours burst open. I heard footsteps and muffled voices. I stared down at the test Mr. Andersson had just handed over, the final one for the term. Phones started going off. My thoughts raced—*Terrorist attack? War?*—but I never could have guessed what Mr. Andersson would come back into the classroom to tell us. His hands shook as he polished his glasses, stalling for time.

I reach the lobby. Scan the crowd for Johannes. I can't see him anywhere. Around me, people are crying, loudly and openly. Seeing them just makes it all feel even more surreal. But there are others who seem to react more like me. Who've shut down. When I meet their eyes, it's like we're glimpsing each other in a dream.

Someone runs straight into me, a girl in a graduation cap. She drops everything in her arms. A closed laptop lands on the floor with a loud crack, and I hear something smash. Papers fan out across the floor. Pens roll across the tile.

"Shit, sorry," I say, bending down to help her.

But she's already gone. Only a trace of her sweet perfume lingers in the air.

I straighten up. Glance at the laptop. Feel a surge of panic. The voices around me fill the air, pressing against my eardrums, draining the air of oxygen. The lobby has never felt so small.

I make my way outside. It's full of voices, too, but at least it's easier to breathe out here. There isn't a cloud in the sky, only the azure emptiness above me.

It's out there.

The thought sneaks up on me, and I already know that the sky will never look the same to me again.

My phone vibrates in my hand. My mom Judette's face fills the screen.

Her new apartment is only a few blocks away from school. I start running, weaving between groups of students, the soles of my shoes slapping against the asphalt. Birds are chirping noisily. The air is full of right-before-summer-break smells: lilacs, damp grass, dust in the morning shade. A car's stopped, its rear wheel backed onto the curb, the radio blaring. I recognize the prime minister's voice but can't make out the words.

I run on. A dad is on his way to the playground with his daughter. He listens intently as she rambles about a robot that can transform into a cat. I look at the dad. Wonder if he knows what's happening. I hope not. I hope he'll stay blissfully ignorant for at least a few more minutes. They disappear out of sight as I turn the corner and see the antique pink three-story brick building and cross the parking lot, where the worn Toyota Judette bought last week is sitting.

The smell of the stairway is still unfamiliar to me. I climb the stairs two at a time until I reach the top floor, unlock the front door, and step into the hallway, which is still full of cardboard boxes. The television is on in the living room.

"Simon!" Judette shouts, getting up from the sofa. She's still in her bathrobe.

I turn to the TV, where a government press conference is taking place. Cameras are snapping. It looks as if the prime minister's been up all night.

"You've heard the news?" Judette asks, uncertain.

"Yeah."

She hugs me. That protective dream feeling threatens to dissolve. I want to stay in her arms. I want to feel small. I want her to promise me that everything is going to be all right, and I want to not give a shit that it would be the biggest lie ever told.

There's only one thing I want more than that.

"Stina's on her way," Judette says.

I pull away. "I have to go to Tilda's. Where are your car keys?"

"You can't drive by yourself," she says automatically.

"I'm pretty sure the police won't be checking people's licenses today."

As soon as the words pass my lips, the reality of what's happening hits. An abyss opens up, threatening to swallow me whole.

Judette lays a cool hand against my cheek. "Sweetie, I understand. But we need to be together, to talk about this."

"I'll be right back. I promise."

She opens her mouth to object, but I race back to the hall and find the car keys in the pocket of her jacket. Judette calls out behind me. My name's cut off as the front door slams shut. The keys jangle in my hand as I run down the stairs and back across the parking lot. Judette's still shouting from the balcony as I jump into the Toyota's driver's seat, buckle the seat belt, and start the engine. Pull out onto the road.

My heart is pounding so hard. I have pins and needles in my fingers, in my face. This is my first time driving alone. I shouldn't be driving at all right now.

My phone vibrates. Judette, of course. I put it on the passenger seat, where it continues to buzz like a small, furious animal. I drive along the railroad tracks, pass the train station. A crowd's gathered on the street outside. They're watching the skies. A couple of girls in their twenties are laughing hysterically.

I see something move out of the corner of my eye, and the tires squeal as I slam on the brakes. An old man glares at me from the crosswalk.

My phone vibrates again. My mom Stina is on the screen this time. I shift gears, carefully easing on the clutch and pressing down on the accelerator. The car jerks forward. I wish I could have taken Stina's automatic instead.

I force myself to focus. When I stop at a red light at the edge of the center of town, I see a woman leaning over her steering wheel on the other side of the intersection. It looks like she's crying. In the car next to hers, a man in a suit is staring blankly ahead. He doesn't seem to notice the light turning green. The cars behind him honk furiously. I keep driving, past the exit to the old industrial park, North Gate, continuing along the highway until I turn in to the row of houses where Tilda lives with her parents.

The flowers are blooming, and there are trampolines and colorful swing sets everywhere. Chalk hopscotch grids line the sidewalks.

The children who live here will never grow up.

The thought makes the muscles in my chest contract.

Emma is never going to . . .

I push away the thought about my sister.

I can finally see the white wooden house, one of the largest in the neighborhood. The red van with the FIRST KLAS, INC. logo is still parked in the driveway. On a regular morning, Tilda's dad would have left for work hours ago. Caroline's car is nowhere to be seen.

I park on the street. Leave my phone on the passenger's seat. Stina's calling me again.

Klas opens the door before I even ring the bell. He's wearing his stained work pants, the ones with reflective stripes. His arms, fat and muscular, burst from a tight T-shirt with the same company logo as the one on van stamped across the chest—a cartoon man holding a dripping cement trowel, grinning from underneath a jauntily angled cap. But the real Klas isn't smiling. He's pale beneath his stubble and his eyes bug out slightly, as if the pressure inside his head has ratcheted up.

"Hello, son," he says, and gives me one of his awkward hugs, slapping me hard on the back. "Good God, huh?"

"Yeah," I say. "Good God."

"They're saying three and a half months."

"Yeah."

We stand there awkwardly. I can feel the seconds ticking away, one after the other. How many seconds are three and a half months?

"She's in her room," Klas says at last.

I slip off my shoes near the door and run upstairs. The door to Tilda's room is open.

She's at the window. Sunlight makes the copper in her dark hair shimmer. She turns as I come in, looking at me with those pale eyes that change color depending on her surroundings, just like water.

"Everything looks so normal," she says.

"I know."

"And soon it'll all be gone."

I don't know how to respond.

Her open laptop is on the bed. A muted news broadcast is streaming. The American president stands by a podium in front of blue drapes. WHITE HOUSE CONFIRMS. It occurs to me that it's still the middle of the night over there. Quick glimpses from similar press conferences in Russia, England, Iran. They cut to an interview with the Secretary-General of the UN. I wonder what it's like in Dominica, if Judette's family are watching the same images.

"You're shaking," Tilda says quietly, stroking my newly shaved head.

I wake up, as if from a trance, and wrap my arms around her. Finally. She leans her forehead against my chest. Her hair is still damp, and I inhale the smell of chlorine and shampoo. Tilda's smell.

"It might not happen," she says. "It might just pass right by us. There's a small chance."

I don't want to say what I'm thinking. That they wouldn't have told us unless they were sure.

"Or they could come up with some way to fix it," she continues. "Maybe they'll ... build a giant trampoline or something."

I laugh. It comes out more like a sob. Maybe it is.

"I'm so fucking scared," she says.

"Me too."

Tilda looks up at me. She's so beautiful it hurts.

She can't die.

We kiss. The world outside disappears, shrinks until all that's left is our mouths, our bodies. Tilda locks the door carefully so that Klas won't hear it downstairs. I move behind her and unzip her hoodie, kiss her shoulders, tasting the chlorine that never leaves her skin completely, stroke her stomach under her white top. Then I remove that, too. Unhook her bra. I need to feel her skin against my own, as many square inches as possible.

She spreads her blanket across the floor, like we usually do when we aren't alone in the house. Tilda's bed is too loud.

"I didn't bring protection," I admit reluctantly as I get undressed.

"Does that even matter anymore?" Tilda says.

We look at each other. The world outside the room makes itself known again. I have to force it away, so I kiss her entire body, explore her like it's the first time.

Eventually, she grows impatient and pulls me close, throws her legs around my waist, leads me in.

Whenever one of us risks making too much noise, we silence each other with new kisses. Afterward, Tilda rests her head on my arm. Her back is to me, and she's breathing heavily. It sounds like she's drifted off. My eyes travel over the trophies and statues above the bed. Medals with pins pushed through their colorful ribbons. A clipping from the local paper. Tilda is wearing her swimming cap in the picture, laughing under a headline that calls her "up-and-coming."

Tilda's wall of inspiration is full of photos. Competitions all over the country. Swim camps in Denmark, Italy, the Netherlands. Her old friend Lucinda is in most of the pictures taken before last fall.

My eyes linger on a picture from last winter's St. Lucia Celebration. The hall, including the swimming pool, is black. Tilda is wearing a crown of candles on her head. The flames are reflected on the dark surface of the pool. She smiles like a maniac at the camera to hide how heavy the billowing robe is in the water. She never shows how much she sacrifices for this life, how much work goes into it maintaining it. I don't know anyone as determined as Tilda. She knows exactly where she's going. Me, I get good grades, but I still haven't figured out what I want to be. The endless number of options is paralyzing. How am I supposed to know what I want to do in ten years? In twenty? In fifty?

But I don't have to decide anymore.

The pins and needles are back.

Don't think about it.

I roll onto my side, putting my free arm around Tilda, and raise my head a little to kiss her cheek.

But she's not sleeping. She's watching the laptop on the bed. Notifications pour into the corner of the screen. Everyone wants to know where she is. If she's heard what's happening. The news shows pictures from rural India. Crying women stretch their arms out toward the sky.

I close my eyes.

"I love you," I say.

"Me too," says Tilda, without turning around.

THE END

NAME: LUCINDA
TELLUS # 0 392 811 002
POST 0001

I don't know a thing about whoever's reading this. I really mean *nothing*.

You might be a creature who looks like me. You might be something beyond my wildest imaginings.

In movies and on TV, extraterrestrials are almost always almost-people. Something derived from us, only with some small difference: Lizard skin. A pair of extra eyes on their foreheads. Tiny bodies with giant heads. Does any of that sound like you?

Can you even call it "extraterrestrial" when there's no more Earth?

Of course, the most likely scenario is that you don't exist. And if against all odds you do, how will you understand me? The TellUs app has a language key, a digital Rosetta stone encoded with a few hundred human languages. Hopefully, it makes it possible for you to read the diary entries we write, to decode all the audio files that transform into text before they're broadcast into space. But how are you supposed to understand anything *beyond* just the words? I mean, as I'm writing this, I've got a live broadcast playing in another window on my screen. The American president is giving a speech. (I don't even want to mention his name, that's how much I hate him. You'll hear enough about him from other people.) He's in the Oval Office in the White House, his hands folded on the desk in front of him, the American flag in the background. His opening line was "My fellow Americans." I can tell you these things, but what does it actually *tell* you? How do I explain how difficult it is to really believe what's going on? I still haven't gotten used to associating this scene with anything but thousands of movies and TV shows. In them, the presidents are usually handsome, dignified, reassuring. Everything the real president isn't. (These scenes are usually about aliens that have come to blow up Manhattan and then get thoroughly defeated. I apologize. We've usually assumed that you would want to colonize, enslave, or exterminate us. Probably because certain members of the human race have done this very thing to other members of the human race. I don't know if you study psychology, but around here, we call it "projecting.")

The president's speech confirms what all sensible people have understood by this summer. The final calculations have been made. There's no longer any room for doubt. In just over one month, it's all really over. We even have a specific time. September 16 at 4:12 a.m. (Swedish time), the comet called Foxworth enters the Earth's atmosphere. The air beneath it will become ten times hotter than the surface of the sun. Everything in the comet's path will be destroyed before it finally slams into the northwest coast of Africa, near the Canary Islands. The atmosphere will burn, and the sky will fill with light, brighter than anything we've ever seen. The shock wave will reach us in perfect silence, because it moves faster than the speed of sound. A couple of minutes after impact, the seas will turn into steam and the mountains will boil. Four billion years of evolution, suddenly gone. And there's nothing we can do about it.

That's not how the president chooses to put it. He doesn't talk about the details of how we're going to die, doesn't address the rumor that the Earth's crust might ripple and hurl us all into space.

Instead, he talks about "staying at home, being with your loved ones," and I wonder what that's like for all the people who haven't got "loved ones" to stay at home with.

It's been a couple of months since we found out the comet was coming—the news broke on May 27. The world hasn't been the same since. Everything we took for granted fell apart in just a few days. People stopped going to work. Schools shut down. The stock market collapsed. All trade ceased after just a few days. Money became useless. Travelers fought to get a seat on the last flights home. The roads were clogged with traffic.

The chaos was particularly bad during that period. New wars erupted out of nowhere, while old conflicts ended overnight. No one knew which rules applied anymore. And the worst of it happened in the places with the most social inequality. The oppressed masses had less to lose. They revolted. Occupied the palaces of the wealthy and plundered the luxury boutiques. In more democratic societies, it was easier for the citizens to stand united.

Here in Sweden, we've found our way back to some semblance of normalcy. Even though nothing is the same, surprisingly many things actually work.

Naturally, not everyone thinks Foxworth is going to hit us. One of the comet deniers is being interviewed on the news as I write this. He has that same impatient, ironic air they all seem to share—a preemptive *I told you so* attitude. And in some ways, I understand them. The fact that we haven't spotted a comet this size years before seems incredible. It's enormous, hundreds of miles across, but also dark and murky, and it came creeping up on us in such a far-flung orbit that the last time it closed in on us, there were no humans to notice it. It turns out that despite all our instruments and technological advancements, we haven't kept a close eye on the space around us. There's been a lot of debate about that this summer. *Who are we supposed to blame? Why didn't the scientists get more funding? Who is the guiltiest?* As if that matters anymore. The risk that a comet would exterminate us was so extremely improbable that no one took it seriously. On the other hand, the chance that life would evolve on this planet and that we'd become its rulers was even smaller. In an infinite universe with infinite possibilities, *everything* that happens is improbable.

If Foxworth had been discovered years ago, we could have directed a laser at it from Earth. That could have been enough to change the comet's trajectory. (Don't ask me how. It's got something to do with the gases inside it.) But by the time we found the comet, it was too late. Someone compared it to driving a car in a large open space: If another car comes at you from five hundred yards away, you can avoid a crash by turning the wheel slightly. But if you see the car only when it's right in front of you, you don't stand a chance.

There wasn't enough time to flee Earth, either. Our disaster movies usually end with us sending an ark into space if all else fails—a huge spaceship filled with thousands of people chosen to perpetuate the species. The reality turned out to be less impressive. One famous multibillionaire, despite the fact that his money's currently worthless, tried to organize an expedition to Mars. Even if he'd succeeded, ten people at most would have joined him, only to die slowly on our inhospitable neighboring planet. There weren't a lot of volunteers.

The comet deniers will probably keep denying it until 'the bitter end, believing that the rest of us are just gullible. They know the truth. This is PR intended to let the Americans "rescue us" at the last second. Or "fake news" from Russia designed to distract the world while they prepare an invasion.

Or it's a communist plot to crush the capitalist system. People believe whatever they want to believe. It's not like it's the first time. You should have seen how good we were at turning a blind eye to climate change. Earth has been ending for a while now.

At first, the comet's name was a combination of numbers and letters, but that felt entirely too impersonal for something that would end our existence. Now it's called Foxworth, after the woman at NASA who discovered it. I wonder what it feels like to have your name associated with something that's going to kill us all. She could have gone down in history. If there were anyone left to write history.

But I guess that's what I'm doing right now. Theoretically, anyway. TellUs is an attempt to hand over to other life-forms stories about Earth and what it was like to live here. I wonder how many TellUs users really believe that anyone is going to read what they write. Still, it's a way to pass the time. It gives you purpose. We need to believe that someone out there will know we were here.

What I write here is streamed to distant satellites that save our stories and send them out into space. When we're gone, the satellites will keep transmitting. At least, until they break or are hit by space junk or whatever. Despite everything, this might reach you. If you exist. And if you have the right equipment. If you're able to understand what I'm writing, or if you even care.

The same satellites will send out scientific facts about the planet, as well as coordinates of the places where we've tried to preserve our most famous works of art, books, and pieces of music, the DNA sequences of animals and humans—the seed vault that used to be at Svalbard (in a "doomsday bunker" that isn't sturdy enough for this doomsday). Everything is being packed into protective materials and lowered into mines far from the impact site. No one knows if it will work, but it seems to be the best we can do.

One day, you might be able to re-create a human in an alien lab. Or at least plant a few geraniums. That thought is supposed to make our deaths feel less meaningless.

I saw an interview with a few people who'd decided to move into the mine in Kiruna. They'll die buried underneath thousands of feet of molten rock. I can't imagine a worse way to go.

Do you know when you're going to die?

Humans have always known that we're going to die one day, but never precisely *when*. Not like this, not the very second.

Maybe you're wondering why I'm not panicking. I *am* scared. More scared than I might seem. But I think I'm less scared than a lot of other people. And the worst thing—the thing I can't tell anyone other than you—is that a part of me is relieved. Well, maybe not relieved. That's not the right word. But it's not entirely wrong.

SIMON

It's hot, way too hot, and it stinks of chlorine and smoke and booze and bodies. Screams, shouts, and splashes echo against the tiles and the windows and the high ceiling, drowning out the music from the speakers. I recognize one of Tilda's playlists. It was her idea to have the party here. She still has the keys.

School was supposed to start today. That's why we're partying. We're pretending that it's something to celebrate. If things had been normal, I'd be a junior now.

I look at the large clock at the end of the swimming pool. Realize that I've spent an hour passed out in the bathroom. Wasted a huge chunk of time that's already getting shorter. The seconds relentlessly rush past.

Four weeks and five days left.

Our days are numbered. Today, our final, tiny bit of hope was taken from us. Goodbye, cruel world.

I take a sip of moonshine; it tastes awful, not matter what you mix it with, but it's the only thing available these days.

I search for Tilda among the heads bobbing in the turquoise water. This is her world, her place, her friends. I don't know where I fit in anymore. I only know that I don't want to stay. But I can't go home, either.

Everywhere around me, people are slipping across the wet floor. There's going to be an accident; it's in the air. Hampus flips into the water, and his neck grazes the concrete edge of the pool. When I dived in a little while ago, I had to struggle back to the surface.

There were arms and legs everywhere.

I empty the plastic bottle, and someone pounds me on the back. Ali. He laughs and says something I can't make out.

"Huh?"

"I said, *Where have you been?*"

"Have you seen Tilda?"

I can hear myself slurring: *Hseetllda?*

"Who gives a shit about Tilda?" Ali shouts, and runs toward the pool, gathering his legs up in the air to land in the water with an explosive splash.

I stumble on, past the bleachers where I've sat countless times to watch Tilda compete.

There are droves of bodies—some have fallen asleep, alone or curled up together. Others are having sex. A girl has wrapped a towel around herself and is riding a guy on the first row. I bump into his knee when I walk past them.

Johannes walks toward me from the short end of the pool. His curly hair is dripping, and his shoulders are up as if he's cold. He says hi to someone who passes him but doesn't take his eyes off me. My best friend. I can tell he's worried about me. His girlfriend, Amanda, is sitting with a group of people in front of the low, tiled wall. Elin says something that makes them all laugh, but Amanda sneaks a look at me as she gathers her hair and wrings it out.

Johannes puts his cold hands on my shoulder. His fingertips are wrinkled with water.

"What's up?" he says.

"Have you seen Tilda?"

This time, I manage not to slur. Johannes tries to smile. "I think she went home."

"Johannes," I say. "I love you, but you're a terrible liar."

He brushes aside the wet hair sticking to his forehead.

"Come on," he says. "You're wasted. Let's go somewhere and talk."

That would be a much better idea. I know that. But then I hear Tilda's laughter. Behind the low wall is the kids' pool with its red plastic slide. Johannes follows my gaze toward it. "Simon, come with me instead. We can get out of here if you want."

I don't say anything. It's too late. I have to know.

Johannes calls my name as I round the wall.

This side isn't as crowded. I spot her immediately. Tilda is on her belly on a float in the middle of the pool. Even from this distance, I can tell that she's high. Her pupils are wide and dark. She's in a swimsuit she used to wear during her competitions. The swim club's logo on the chest, *Tilda* in cursive on her ass.

Sait is on his knees next to her; the water only reaches halfway up his six-pack. He drags Tilda off the float. She shrieks with laughter. Their teeth glow in the underwater lights. *I still love you*, Tilda told me at the beginning of June. It was just days after we first heard about the comet.

She loves me, but it's not enough.

I just want to live life to the fullest in the time we have left, she'd said.

So do I. But I want to do it with her. To me, Tilda *is* life. She's the one I want to be with when the sky turns white.

Sait pulls her close in the water. I barely know him; he's a few years older than us. His hand is inside Tilda's swimsuit. His knuckles are clearly visible beneath the thin fabric. She closes her eyes when he kisses the side of her neck.

I should go, but I feel paralyzed.

I don't want to see more, but I can't look away, either.

Someone screams behind me. Tilda looks up. Our eyes

meet. Sait brushes drops of water from his eyes and spots me, too.

I can finally move. I walk as quickly as I can without slipping, vaguely aware that some girls lounging by the pool's edge are watching me. I jog past the dark café and into the locker room. When the door slides shut behind me, the music and the voices are muffled. I can hear my own breathing, heavy and panting.

It stinks in here. Someone vomited in one of the showers. Partly digested food is stuck in the drain grate. I continue between the rows of lockers, barely able to stay upright. It's as though all the strength has left my body. My skin is tingling, my head spinning.

I collapse on one of the benches. Think to myself that I should have gone with Johannes. I can't go back and look for him, but I just want to leave , and I don't think I can make it alone.

The door to the locker room opens and closes. Wet footsteps sound against the tile, then against the plastic carpet.

When I look up, she's standing there. Tilda has wrapped her arms around herself. Her dark hair is pushed back, dripping onto the floor by her feet. Her eyes are as glassy as a doll's. A few months ago, I would have laughed if anyone had told me Tilda would ever do drugs. A lot has changed since then.

"You weren't supposed to see that," she says. "I didn't think you were still here."

"Can't we leave?" I say. "Just go? I miss you so fucking much."

Tilda shakes her head. I should shut up, but what do I have to lose?

"I don't want to be alone," I say, and realize I'm slurring again.

"That's not a good reason to stay together."

"It's not the only reason."

I pull on the rubber band around my wrist. My locker key jangles against the numbered badge. I let go of the band, letting it snap against my skin over and over again, to clear my head. But I barely feel it.

"I love you," I say. "Why don't you want to be with me?"

"I don't want to be with anyone in the time we have left. You know that. I want to be able to do whatever I want."

"We can have an open relationship," I try.

A crooked smile. She doesn't believe me. I don't even believe myself.

"We can try it out," I insist. "We belong together."

Tilda sits down next to me. She looks sad, but I don't know in what way. Maybe she misses me, too. Maybe she just feels sorry for me.

"No," she says. "It's never going to be you and me again. The girl you were with ... she doesn't exist anymore. Maybe she never did."

I snort. "What does that even mean?"

"That you have to give up."

Now I'm sure it's pity I see in her eyes.

The room starts to spin. The taste of moonshine rises in my throat.

"You have to understand," Tilda says. "Is this really how you want to spend your final days?"

Suddenly, I just want her to leave. Having her so close when she's so far away hurts too much.

"You'll be sorry it when it comes," I say. "But you know what? Afterward, you can't take it back, because there won't be an afterward."

The doll's eyes blink.

Someone calls her name, and we both look up at the same time. Elin and Amanda. I don't know how long they've been standing there. Don't know how much they've heard.

"We have to get out of here," Amanda says.

The changing-room door opens again. Voices from the showers. Someone lets out a disgusted shriek. Boots against the floor. Two police officers approach between the rows of lockers: a man with a beard and a short-haired woman who looks vaguely familiar.

"Right, kids," the bearded one says. "Time to wrap it up."

I get to my feet too quickly. The floor comes rushing up to meet me. Tilda catches me before I fall.

"We'll have to give this one a ride home," the female officer says, and I try to protest.

"You can't walk all the way," Tilda says.

"It's fine."

The officers grab me by the arms. I try to pull free, but their grip tightens.

"Where are your clothes, Simon?" the woman asks.

"How do you know my name?"

"Let's discuss that later."

She looks at the badge on my wrist and marches me toward the locker.

I lose sight of Tilda as people pour into the changing room. Another police officer is ushering them in, shouting at them to hurry up. No one's paying attention to him. Not like they would have before.

And there won't be any consequences. There's no time for that. The world is ending. All the police can do is make sure we don't kill ourselves in the meantime.

SIMON

I wake up to panting in my ear. A wet nose is pressed against my cheek.

"Go away. I want to sleep," I say, and reach out a hand, trying to shove away the wall of warm fur.

Boomer licks his lips. I reluctantly look up into a pair of large brown eyes. Boomer's head obscures most of my field of vision. His tongue darts out, rough against my wrist.

Four weeks, four days left.

The panic comes crawling back. My thoughts spin in their endless circles.

I'm wide awake. I have to get up, have to move. It's the only way to stay sane.

When I sit up, it feels like my head's exploded. As if the comet has already smashed into my skull. Boomer barks excitedly and spins around on the spot. His tail sweeps my glass of water off the table; I manage to scoop my phone off the floor right before the water can hit it.

"Take it easy," I say and unlock the phone to read what I wrote to Tilda when I got home last night.

I apologized for being pathetic and, of course, only managed to sound even more pathetic. *It's ok*, she replied. But it doesn't feel all that fucking okay right now, and I can't help but wonder if she sent me that message from Sait's bed. I press the heels of my hands against my eyes until I see stars.

"Judette and I want to talk to you."

I lower my hands. Stina's in the doorway, dressed for work. Her strawberry-blonde hair is pulled back, and her priest's collar is around her neck.

"Hurry up," she says, and leaves.

I catch a whiff of smoke and chlorine from my jeans as I shove aside the covers. I fell asleep with my clothes on. Stars hover at the edge of my vision as I roll out of bed and push Boomer with my knee to get him to move.

They're sitting, waiting for me on one of the living room sofas. I can really tell that Stina's psyched herself up for this. We're about to have a serious talk. Judette only watches me coldly. She can communicate more with a look than Stina can in one of her lengthy lectures.

We were supposed to have a video call with Judette's friends in Dominica yesterday. I get that the moms are disappointed. But it's not as simple as me wanting to be out partying. I didn't want to stay home. I didn't want to sit here with them, thinking about the end of the world and about death. I didn't want to think at all.

"How are you feeling?" Stina asks.

"Like shit," I say.

"You've made your bed," Stina replies, turning to Judette for support.

Judette crosses one leg over the other. "Do you realize how humiliating it was for me to see Maria drive you home in a police car?"

Stina looks annoyed. "That was hardly the worst part."

My brain is still sluggish, but I'm starting to piece things together. The short-haired police officer—that's how I recognized her. I've met her a couple of times. She was on Judette's hockey team.

"I had a little too much to drink," I say. "I'm sorry."

Stina snorts loudly—gesturing exasperatedly at Judette—but I can tell that she's loving the chance to present a united front. I'm doing her a *favor* by being a difficult teen.

They've been divorced for six months now. Stina finally took off her wedding ring this past spring, but I know she still carries it around in her wallet. She's told me that I have to let Tilda go, but she's just as pathetic as I am.

"You can't keep staying out every night," Judette says.

"What does it even matter?"

"It matters a whole goddamn lot," Stina roars, slamming her palm down on the sofa's arm.

Dust whirls into the air, shimmering in the light coming through the window.

"Why?" I say. "It's not like I have a future to ruin."

"You know all about how dangerous the city is nowadays."

"I'm being careful."

Stina's face goes red. "You could try empathizing with us," she says. "You know we moved back in together because we wanted to see you as much as possible in the days we have left. Now we're seeing less of you than ever."

"I didn't ask you to move back in together for me."

I regret it as soon as the words cross my lips. Because I get them. But they don't get me.

They don't get that I really do miss them, but I can't stand it here, in this artificial atmosphere they've created. We can't have normal conversations anymore, because everything has to be so profound. We have to savor every memory, ask earnest questions, say important things before we die. Every word has to convey so much. Too much. What they're asking of me is impossible.

"Enough," Stina says in an unexpectedly calm voice. "Emma's coming in a few days."

Emma. My sister, who hasn't been thinking straight since she found out about the comet.

"Micke is visiting his parents in Överkalix," Stina continues. "She needs all the help she can get now. And she needs peace and quiet."

I nod, then look away. My eyes are drawn to the dark gray kitchen wall I helped paint. I remember just standing and looking at it one day. It was a few days after we'd heard about the comet. The wall still smelled faintly of paint, and I remember thinking, *How pointless that we painted it when it's going to disappear.* It was the first time I really grasped what was happening.

I started crying then, and I start crying now.

"It's going to be fine," Stina says gently.

"How?" I say, wiping at my eyes.

She looks disappointed. I always disappoint them these days.

"I only mean that Emma coming home for a while will be good for us. We have to cherish the time we have left."

"That means you, too, Simon," Judette adds.

NAME: LUCINDA
TELLUS # 0 392 811 002
POST 0002

There were riots in Gothenburg last night. It started out as a spontaneous demonstration against the rationing system—a few thousand people thought "real Swedes" ought to get more than "the others." The prime minister made a statement. Once again, she tried reminding us that Sweden is fortunate. It's summer, so we have plenty of fruit and vegetables, and we have enough cattle to last us for years. "But it's still unfair," one of the demonstrators complained in the television studio. "I've paid my taxes my whole life. I should get more than them." She means people who weren't born here. I want to scream at her that it's thanks to "the others" that our society is functioning as well as it is. Since we stopped using money, "the others" are over-represented among the volunteers. They transport people with trains and food with trucks, make sure we have water in the taps and electricity in the wires. Not because "the others" are saintlier, but because their loved ones aren't here. Of course they're trying to create some sense of community rather than just sitting around alone, waiting for the end.

If you were able to look at our planet from space right now, you wouldn't see any countries. The borders were never real; they're only lines we drew on a map. Yet some people have built their entire identity on which side of said line they ended up on. I thought it would matter less now, but it seems to have gone the other way for a lot of people. Not for everyone; the ones who care just happen to be the loudest of the bunch. (And complete idiots. A lot of the time, those things go hand in hand.)

Maybe this is a good time to point out that people can be wonderful. I'll probably forget to mention it often enough. If nothing else, I should get better at reminding myself of that. Catastrophes tend to bring out the best or the worst in us. And the vast majority are just trying to live their lives as best they can.

So what have I done with *my* life since you last heard from me? What have I done to grow as a person? What have

I done to help others? I've mostly slept. And looked at pictures of my old friends.

Apparently, they threw a party at the pool tonight. They look so much younger in the photos than how I feel. Their eyes shine in their sweaty, tanned faces. Plastic bottles and cigarette butts float in the water. People I thought would never smoke pose with cigarettes dangling from their mouths. And why not? It's not like anyone's going to have time to develop cancer.

Tilda is in all the pictures. She still has the same broad shoulders and strong arms. The lean muscles on her back are clearly visible beneath her skin. It's difficult to believe that I was ever as fit as she is. Body aside, though, Tilda's changed. The Tilda I knew had barely had a drink in her entire life, and certainly never smoked. We never went to parties because, even during the weekends, we were getting up early to swim. Dad told me Tilda's parents separated this summer. I wasn't surprised to hear it; they've been unhappy for a while. But I don't know how Tilda feels about it. I don't know anything about her life anymore, other than what I see in the photos.

She was my best friend. She's in all my most important memories. I can't tell you who I am without also telling you about Tilda.

We were in that pool so much that I can describe every little crack in the floor, every hole in the ceiling above our heads. The chlorine made our eyes burn. It ate away at our swimsuits and our skin. The scent of it was everywhere. Seven, eight, nine practices a week, plus at least one competition. It was usually mind-numbingly boring and monotonous. And yet, I loved it. I lived for the small moments of bliss. The adrenaline kicking in right before a race. The few moments during practice when my body's movements and my breathing were perfectly in sync. I felt more at home in the water than on land. Enveloped. Easy. Free. It was magical.

The pool was our place—Tilda's and mine. Without her, I would never have started swimming, and I definitely wouldn't have applied to a high school known for its champion swim team. She made me better. Our coach, Tommy, always said that we only compete against ourselves, but that didn't stop me from competing against Tilda. It didn't matter that I'd never be as good as her. No one could be. Elin, Amanda, and I fought for a decent second place. Tilda had what Tommy called a "winner's mentality." She had a whole plan laid out, from the Swedish Youth Swimming Championship to the national team to the Olympics. It was unrealistic. The chance of her succeeding was tiny. The chance of securing enough sponsorship to make a living was even smaller. And yet, I never doubted for a second that she'd pull it off.

Why am I even telling you this? Do you know what a competition is? A pool? I'm assuming you have water.

I can see the roof of Tilda's house from my window. We used to cut through our backyards when we were little and wanted to play.

I saw her in real life about a week ago. It was early in the morning, and I'd decided to head downtown for the first time in a long time. I thought I wouldn't bump into anyone I knew at that hour, but as I got closer, I heard a pounding bassline and shouting.

A group of girls stumbled along, arm in arm, singing "Save the World" by Swedish House Mafia.

Tilda was sitting in an open window, kissing some boy I'd

never seen before. Her hair, which I'd envied even when I still had my own, glowed almost red in the morning sun. Her makeup was perfect, and I wondered where she'd learned how to do it. We hardly ever wore makeup.

Elin and Amanda were there, too. I escaped before anyone could see me.

What does seventeen years mean to you? Is it young or old? Can you imagine being young and already feeling old? Kind of used up? Can you understand what I mean when I say that I've been hiding for so long, I don't know how to make my way back?

SIMON

The movie starts with an asteroid slamming into Earth and killing all the dinosaurs. A sea of fire engulfs the planet. The narrator informs us that it's going to happen again; it's just a matter of time.

No one says anything. Apart from the bombastic music, the only sound in the room is crunching from Hampus, who's lying on the floor in front of the television eating chips with his mouth open. His T-shirt has slipped up, revealing a stomach that's grown slightly pudgier this summer. Before, he and Sait went to the gym every day. All they talked about was protein shakes and shredding.

Sait, who still has his six-pack. Sait, who kissed Tilda's neck. Sait, who thankfully isn't here. But neither is Tilda. Maybe they're together right now.

We're at Hampus's house watching *Armageddon*, one of the movies they tried removing from the internet.

We see New York now. Sixty-five million years later. The first rocks fall from the sky like bombs, destroying skyscrapers. Hampus says it's the pre-cum. No one laughs. I do what I did when I was little and my sister Emma made me watch horror movies while she babysat me: I stare at the screen until I no longer see images, only shifting colors and shapes. The sounds are the worst. More difficult to shut out without people noticing.

But then the movie gets going, and we laugh as the main character shoots at his daughter's boyfriend, who's dodging around the explosives on the oil platform where they work.

"Nice incest vibe I'm getting from that guy," Johannes says.

"Yeah, he seems obsessed with her sex life," Amanda adds. "She's a grown fucking woman."

I breathe a little more easily. Sink deeper into the armchair. No one could possibly take this seriously.

It turns out the oil workers are going to be trained as astronauts in record time. Then they're being sent into space to drill a hole into the asteroid and blow it up. They only get one shot at it.

"Wouldn't it be a lot easier to just train real astronauts to drill holes?" I say.

The others laugh. Do they feel as relieved as I do? I think so.

I can't believe people talked about this movie as some blueprint to follow at the beginning of the summer. They said we should send up nukes. But Foxworth is too large and already too close. All the nuclear warheads in the world wouldn't have been enough.

"Did he just put crackers in her underwear?" Amanda says.

"I think so," Johannes says, and laughs.

He pulls her closer on the sofa. I feel a pang of envy. Johannes still has a girlfriend. He belongs here unquestionably. It was through Tilda and Amanda that everyone in this room got to know one another. Every time we hang out sober, I find myself wondering if they really want me there, now that Tilda and I are finished. I don't even hang out alone with Johannes anymore, even though he's my best friend. Sometimes, I get the feeling he's avoiding me.

Maybe I'm so unbearable nobody wants me around anymore.

"Has everyone forgotten about New York being utterly obliterated?" Ali asks, and I'm grateful for the distraction.

"Good thing they're getting drunk in a strip club before heading out to save the world," Elin says. "Great priorities. Kudos, heroes."

"Why did they bring machine guns into space?" asks Johannes.

"Does this girl do anything other than cry about her dad and her boyfriend?" says Amanda.

And then we start commenting on everything, laugh as the disgusting dad delivers a blubbering speech to his daughter before sacrificing himself. But we fall silent when the asteroid is destroyed. The people of Earth celebrate.

It's the happy ending we're never going to get.

"Good thing she got married so someone can take care of her," Amanda says as the credits roll across a montage of wedding pictures.

"Cool how every person who wasn't white was such a stereotype."

Elin looks at me when she says it. I don't respond. At the moment, I don't have it in me to affirm her wokeness or to care about racist shit in a movie older than me. I have other things to worry about.

"Has anyone talked to Tilda today?" Elin continues.

I glance at the others.

"She was going to have dinner with her dad and her uncle," Amanda says. "She wanted a quiet night in."

"That'd be a first," says Hampus, licking grease off his fingers.

Amanda starts braiding her hair. She goes slightly cross-eyed looking at it.

"I don't know what the hell Tilda's doing."

"Where does she even get that shit?" Ali says.

"I don't know."

"Wonder how she pays for it," Hampus says with a grin I would love to kick off his face.

The room goes quiet. Ali stares intently at his phone. Hampus starts eating chips with great concentration. Only Johannes meets my eyes. He shakes his head slightly.

It hits me that they probably talk about Tilda in a different way when I'm not around. "The question is how quiet it will be with Klas and his brother," Elin says.

She throws Amanda a meaningful look. Something I can't quite interpret passes between them. Johannes notices it, too.

"What?" he says, and I'm glad I don't have to ask them.

"Tilda didn't want us to say anything," Amanda says.

She and Elin exchange another look. It's obvious that they want to spill.

"Come on!" Hampus says.

Elin sighs. Crosses her legs and fingers the gold four-leaf clover in her earlobe.

"Klas has joined the Truthers," she says.

"That's why Caroline threw him out," Amanda says quickly, as though she's afraid someone else will get to share the nugget of gossip first.

"But . . . how did he end up there?" is all I can manage.

I try to imagine Klas in the True Church of Sweden. It's impossible. The closest I've seen him get to religion was his obsession with *Game of Thrones.*

"His brother recruited him," Elin says.

It still doesn't make sense. Tilda's uncle and his family moved here from Örebro this summer. I've only met them a handful of times. Klas's brother may be an idiot, but not the kind of idiot who'd join the Truthers.

On the other hand, who *is* the type?

Given how quickly the splinter group broke away from the Church of Sweden, Stina says it must have been a long time coming. A popular priest down in the south started preaching about the Christianity of old, based on a God who puts humanity through inhuman trials. A God who doesn't care for the Church of Sweden's "liberal, politically correct nonsense." The priest was fired, became a local martyr, and what started as a small group on social media has become a network of congregations all over the country. Some of the True Church's congregants made the mistake of knocking on our door to recruit members, but they're probably not coming back. They hadn't counted on being invited in for a cup of coffee by a lesbian priest from the Church of Sweden who never tires of spirited discussion. Has Klas been knocking on doors this summer, too?

Suddenly, it becomes clear how much the distance between Tilda and me has grown if I didn't even know about this.

"I find the True Church so creepy," Amanda says. "They

seem so . . ." She waves her hands around as if that'll help catch the word she's looking for.

"*Evangelical?*"Johannes suggests.

"Exactly!"

"What if they turn into one of those American sects that kill people for blood sacrifices?" Hampus says.

"Those weren't sects. They were just random psychos," Amanda replies.

"People always say that about Christians," Elin says, looking at Ali. "If they'd been Muslim . . ."

Ali shoots me a weary look.

"It makes sense that people believe God wants blood sacrifices," Johannes says. "He likes that kind of thing, doesn't he? Even his own son had to die on the cross for our sins."

"Well, look at you, all knowledgeable," Amanda says, glancing up at him.

"Simon's mom confirmed me." Johannes smirks at me. "But seriously, I bet some cults get up to things we never even get to hear about."

"Did you hear about the Bride of the True Church in Karlshamn?" Hampus says. "The Bible says you can't have tattoos, so she cut them off with a box cutter."

"Stop!" Amanda moans.

"She peeled off half her arm," Hampus goes on.

Amanda looks like she's about to throw up.

Elin says, "That was a hoax."

"Remember the Old Norse worshippers in Dalarna?" Ali starts. "On Midsummer's Eve, they sacrificed all those animals that—"

"Can we talk about something else?" Amanda says, cutting him off.

"I read about a Japanese cult." Hampus drags himself into

a sitting position. "They sacrificed their children. They used knives *this* size. They ripped them up from here to—"

"Please!" Amanda screams.

Hampus laughs so hard bits of chips spray across his shirt. "I'm just saying, people do crazy shit, and no one's as crazy as religious people. No offense, Simon."

I shrug.

"Christians are still the worst," Elin says. "Just look at all the people in the U.S. Congress who are just like the Truthers and claim that this is the punishment for abortions and gay sex."

"It'd be a bit of an overreaction if God wiped us all out just because some guys want to suck dick," Hampus says.

"Or think about the movie we just saw," Elin continues. "Talk about honor-based violence, with that dad and everyone he worked with . . ."

Hampus sighs loudly. Amanda throws a sofa cushion at him.

Elin ignores them, leaning closer to Ali. "What does Islam say about what's happening?"

"No idea," he says, and shoots me another look. "But my family will be out tomorrow. Party at my place before the soccer game?"

Without hesitating, we all say yes.

NAME: LUCINDA
TELLUS # 0 392 811 002
POST 0003

This is what the Swedes care about at the moment, at least if you believe the news: soccer and food.

Soccer has been an ongoing obsession all summer. There's not enough time left to finish the season, so this year's Swedish champions are going to be crowned at the end of a national tournament. Tonight is the first semifinal. Everyone wants their team to be the last winners in the history of humanity. Cities all over the country have decided to show the game on giant screens. On the news, all they're talking about is the "festivities."

Dad has been called in to do an extra shift at the hospital. They're expecting Hieronymus Bosch–type scenes as thousands of people—who all need to vent feelings of fear and anxiety and rage—gather in the center of town.

I'm the one who told him to go. I promised him that it was fine. I've kept him from work long enough.

Back to the news. People are bitter about the "bland food" now that we can't import anymore. A cheerful food blogger shares "inspiring tips" on how to spice up that chicken casserole with Swedish lemon balm to give it a hint of "the Thai kitchen." Cut to a thirty-second segment about the millions of people in refugee camps who have nowhere to go.

They're either starving to death or dying of diarrhea.

But how are those of us who miss our lemongrass going to survive?

I should stop watching the news so much. Observing the world at a distance isn't healthy. I lose all sense of perspective. But now that our days are numbered, it feels more important than ever to find out what's going on. To be brave enough to see how it ends, and to try to understand.

SIMON

I'm jostled between the bodies in Ali's cramped kitchen. The music from the living room is so loud that the floor is shaking under our feet. Any moment now, we're going to crash into the apartment below. No one lives there anymore. In this part of town, a lot of apartments stand empty.

Moa from my science class is dancing on the table. She's found Ali's grandmother's jewelry and wrapped it around her neck and arms. A pair of black bedazzled sunglasses hides half her face. Hampus slams into me, holding out his phone; I can see that the TellUs app is recording.

"Say something to the aliens!" he yells.

I push the phone away. Closing my eyes, I listen to the music, swaying with the movements of other bodies.

Everyone is here except Tilda. My only consolation is that Sait is in the living room, so he isn't with her, either. It shouldn't matter. Tilda still isn't with me. But it *is* a consolation.

I take a big gulp of moonshine mixed with blueberry juice. We weren't able to get any soda tonight. When I open my eyes again, I see Oscar on the other side of the table. He digs in his plastic cup, fishes out an ice cube, and pops it into his mouth, grinning as he looks around.

The ice game. I don't know when we started playing it, but it's become a must at every party. Oscar turns to a girl I've never seen before with a bleach-blonde pixie cut. They kiss and she accepts the ice cube, keeping it between her teeth while she looks up at Moa and tugs her hand. And Moa gets on her knees. I hear the necklaces jingle and clink against each other over the music. They make a show of it, laughing when people cheer. When their mouths finally separate, Moa turns to me. She crawls to my side of the table. Her lips form a soft O around the melting ice cube. She wraps a hand around my neck. Her mouth is cold against mine. Our tongues play with the ice cube from opposite directions. It's nearly hollow in the middle. Filled with saliva. Someone grabs my shoulder; when I turn around, Johannes is standing there.

My mouth is the cold one now. Johannes's lips feel hot against mine. He manages to get the ice cube, but we don't stop kissing. I try to take it back. He laughs, sucks on my tongue, holding it in his mouth for a second before pulling back. Then he laughs again as he chews on the ice cube.

Someone in the living room changes the music, turning the volume up even more. Johannes's sweaty cheek brushes against mine. He whispers something. I can't quite catch what. I'm just about to ask him to repeat it when something in his eyes makes me change my mind.

He's nervous about something. And suddenly, I know that I'm not capable of dealing with whatever he wants to say right now.

Amanda appears out of nowhere and tries to pull Johannes out of the kitchen.

"What's your problem?" I ask her.

"You're the problem," Amanda snaps. "Can you come here, Johannes?"

She storms out of the kitchen without waiting for a reply.

"Hey, what's going on?" I shout.

"I'll talk to her," Johannes says. "I'm the one she's mad at."

I have no idea what's going on. I don't have the energy to figure it out.

My phone vibrates in the pocket of my jeans. It's a message from my mom Stina: PROMISE ME YOU WON'T GO OUT AND WATCH THE GAME? THERE'S ALREADY FIGHTING.

I type out a promise. When I look up again, Johannes is gone.

I drink more. At least the quality of the moonshine is better than the stuff we had at the pool. Now and then, new ice cubes pass through my mouth. In the living room, "Save the World" comes on and everyone cheers.

It's so hot. I'm so drunk. Someone is watching me. The bleach-blonde girl. She's perched on the kitchen counter now, getting a glass of water, waving at me to come over. I move toward her, squeezing past a couple who seem to be having sex in the middle of the floor. The bleach-blonde girl hands me her glass and I drink it down. Water trickles down my chin, and she laughs. When I put the glass back down by the counter, she says something—I assume it's her name—and I put my hand next to her hip, say my name into her ear.

"I know," she says, and smiles.

The vibrations from the bassline travel up my legs. My body starts throbbing in time with the music.

I really only want Tilda. I only want Tilda to want me.

But Tilda isn't here. And I need the closeness of another human being. I want it so much my skin aches.

I should let go. Everyone else does.

My lips brush against the unknown girl's lips. They're thinner than Tilda's; they feel so different. She shifts so that one soft breast presses against my arm. One thigh ends up between my legs. And my body responds immediately.

She takes my hand. We push our way into the hallway, sneaking out to the stairway without turning the lights on. On the landing above Ali's apartment, she kisses me again. A red light glints next to us like a staring eye. I fumble to get her skirt up over her hips, touch her like I used to touch Tilda. She gasps in my ear.

It feels like Tilda is here with me in the darkness. As if she's the one I'm entering. The music from Ali's apartment booms through the stairwell, drowning out the sound of our bodies moving against each other. We should hurry up before someone catches us, but I don't want it to end. I know that the moment it's done, reality will come rushing back into my head.

She's breathing faster now.

Ali's door is thrown open with a bang. The music in the stairwell is even louder. Someone turns the light on, and we're suddenly bathed in light. The spell is broken. The girl giggles while we rush to put our clothes back on.

Voices and laughter drift out from the apartment, bodies falling over each other as they try to find their jackets in the hallway.

"Are you guys done?" Ali says, and grins at me from the doorway. "The game is about to start."

NAME: LUCINDA
TELLUS # 0 392 811 002
POST 0004

My little sister, Miranda, is sleeping in my bed. She's eleven years old, but this summer she started sucking her thumb again. Her speech has regressed. She's become afraid of the dark. Now, she's finally snoring in the tangled mess she's made of my sheets, but I can't sleep. I can barely breathe. It feels like I'm falling through a bottomless black pit.

I try to remind myself that the anxiety will pass. The body can't sustain it for too long. I know that, really.

The game has started. The roars from town can be heard all the way here. They rise and surge in waves that echo between the buildings. Echo inside my body. Multiply into new waves of panic. Right now, I just want to call the ER and ask Dad to come home. Miranda isn't the only one who needs to be comforted tonight.

She and I watched a documentary about the rainforest. (It was her choice—she loves anything to do with animals.) The camera tracked a frog, blue and gleaming and poisonous, and I stared at it and realized for the first time that it's going to be gone. It's not just us humans; it's the animals, too. Not even bacteria will survive. Nothing. Scientists say that the planet will be "sterilized."

Outside the windows, the sky is dark. The moon and the stars are hidden behind thick clouds. Foxworth is up there somewhere, incredibly far away, but on its way, closer with every second that passes.

Miranda asked me so many questions tonight; so much is going on inside her head. She wondered what was going to happen after the comet, and I said something cowardly and pointless about how we're going meet in heaven afterward. Miranda wondered how we'd find each other there, considering heaven must be a big place if we were all going to fit. My lovely sister, who's been so neglected this past year when everything's revolved around me—how long has she been wondering about these things?

She didn't want to sleep alone, and honestly, neither did I. Her heart pounded hard against my arm as she lay next to me in bed. And I thought about her heart, and mine, and the almost eight billion hearts that will cease beating at the same time.

And now my heart is pounding so hard it hurts, as if it's trying to make up for all the beats it's going to miss.

SIMON

I can barely see what's happening on the screens, but I roar when everyone else does. I scream like I've never screamed before. Let out all the darkness inside of me.

There must be thousands of us gathered in the square. Our voices become one voice; our bodies turn into one creature. It feels like I'm dissolving, and I find myself liking it. Together, we're strong. Invincible.

And then it's all over. Östersunds FK has won at home, and the screens shut down. We become individuals again, and we're all moving in different directions at the same time. I land in my own body. Only now, I'm aware of a cold drizzle falling from the dark sky. The droplets are so small they look like rippling mist in the glow from the spotlights. The smoke from the flares is heavy on one side of the square. I can smell the stench from here. I try to stay close to Ali and Hampus, but other people keep pushing between us. Someone screams—*in rage? Pain?*—and panic swells like a mushroom cloud in my chest when I realize I can't move. I'm trapped.

Someone slams into me. All of a sudden, blood is pouring from my right eyebrow. I've been headbutted, but can barely feel it. Ali shouts; I can't see him anywhere. I wipe the blood away as best I can, and spot a fight by the fountain in the middle of the square. Flushed faces, hateful glares. Everyone around them is trying to get away, shoving anyone who stands in their way. A few seconds later, the domino effect reaches me. I stumble backward, accidentally planting my elbow in someone's chest, but manage to stay upright. If I fall, there's no way I'll get up again.

I set a course for the H&M sign, trying to focus on getting there, but moving in a straight line is impossible. Bodies press against me from every direction. I have to walk around people who won't let go of one another's hands, swerve past glowing cigarettes, duck so I don't get my eye poked out by an umbrella that someone has, unbelievably, opened in this mess.

Screams are echoing across the square now. I don't know how long I can keep myself from just charging forward, not giving a shit about who I trample, and not giving a shit about getting trampled myself.

"Simon!"

Tilda's voice. I spot her a few feet away. She's high again, looking around confused.

"Tilda!" I shout, and try to move toward her. "Take my hand!"

She reaches for me. Just when we touch, she's pushed aside, but she doesn't fall. She reaches for me again, and I twine my fingers with hers. Squeeze her hand hard.

"You're bleeding," she says, her glassy eyes fascinated.

I put an arm around her, taking in the blood that's splashed across my jacket. We stick close together while we move through the crush. Tilda's laces have come undone, and people are stepping on them, but we finally reach the edge of the square.

Tilda crouches by a shop window and starts to clumsily tie her shoelaces while I make sure no one trips over her. Her shoelaces are black with dirt. They smudge her fingers.

The naked mannequins in the window stare out at the square, where the chaos is only growing. The pounding in my eyebrow makes me realize how quickly my heart is beating.

Cautiously, I touch the wound and watch the blood mix with rain on my fingertips.

Tilda gets up unsteadily, using the window to keep her balance.

"I met Amanda and Elin," she says, "but I don't know where they've gone."

"I lost Ali and Hampus. And I haven't even seen Johannes since we came."

My voice is hoarse and scratchy from all the shouting. A police van with its lights flashing drives into the square. People beat their palms against it, roaring excitedly. I take my phone out of my pocket, relieved when I see a message from Johannes.

WENT HOME EARLY. COULDN'T DEAL WITH AMANDA'S DRAMA. TALK TOMO.

At least he's okay. I look up at Tilda. She's tilted her head to one side, watching the police officers as they pour out of the van and attempt to break up one of the fights.

"Something terrible is going to happen tonight," she says in a singsong voice.

My skin crawls. I look at the officers. There are so few.

Tilda is right.

Suddenly, I feel completely sober.

"We have to get out of here," I say.

She just grins when I take her hand again. Her head droops oddly.

"Tilda, what did you take tonight?"

She giggles. It sounds creepy, like the echo of someone long gone. She's here, and yet she isn't.

"What's so fucking funny?" I ask.

She goes silent, seeming to ponder the question.

"I don't know."

I give up, and squeeze her hand tightly. "Hold on to me so we don't get separated."

At least she doesn't protest. We stick close to the walls until we reach Storgatan, and follow the crowd, stepping over glass shards and cigarette butts, broken umbrellas and plastic bags.

Somewhere nearby, a kid is crying. I look around. I can't spot the kid, but another fight has broken out behind us. I speed up, almost dragging Tilda behind me. We pass the broken shop windows of the florist where Judette used to work, the café where Tilda and I spent our first date. A different time, a different world, where everything frightening seemed so distant.

Tilda was someone else back then. So was I.

The girl you were with ... she doesn't exist anymore.

Maybe she never did.

"How are you doing?" I ask.

Tilda smiles sleepily, stumbling along behind me.

"One hundred percent."

"One hundred percent what?"

She tilts her head back, looking at me from under hooded eyes.

"One hundred percent fucked up."

Then she laughs and pulls herself free from my grasp.

"I'll be fine. You can go now," she says.

A part of me wishes I could. It hurts too much to see her like this.

"Go," she says again. "I can't stand it ... when you just look at me with those ... *puppy dog eyes.*"

I yank her back by the arm. She almost falls over.

"What are you doing?" she snaps.

My grip around her arm tightens. I want to shake her until the glassy film disappears from her eyes.

"I'm not going to leave you here. You can barely fucking stand."

"Let me go!"

I hear running footsteps, and when I turn to look, I see a few men in their thirties coming toward us. They're neat and tidy—sober—dressed in identical black windbreakers.

"Is everything okay?" one of them says.

Fear seeps into me like a poison.

"Yeah," Tilda says. "We're just talking."

"Are you sure? We can walk you home, if you want."

The others come closer. Glare at me. I know what they

see: the black guy with a bleeding eyebrow and the girl who's trying to escape him.

"It's fine," Tilda says.

"You can tell us. We'll protect you."

"I don't need your *protection*. Leave us alone, assholes!"

The men don't move. Someone shatters a window farther down the street, but the guys don't even turn to look. Their spokesperson seems disappointed. He wants something to do. He wants to be Tilda's savior. For that to work, he has to save her from something, whether she wants him to or not.

He takes a step toward me. The pounding in my eyebrow speeds up. I haven't been in a fight since I was a kid, and it's three against one.

"Come on," Tilda says, and now she's the one dragging me along behind her.

I stare straight ahead. Say nothing. The fear only drains away when I'm sure they're not following us, leaving behind space for the rage. And when that dies down, shame.

"Thank you," I say.

But Tilda doesn't respond. I'm not even sure she hears me.

Glass crunches under our shoes as we pass the smashed shop window. It's the place where my moms and I used to get candy every Saturday when I was a kid. The shelves are tipped over. Empty plexiglass bins lie strewn across the floor.

I hear running steps behind us again. Turning around, I'm sure I'll see the men in black jackets, but this time it's a topless guy with a balled-up polo shirt pressed against his bleeding nose. Our eyes meet before he rushes on.

I pull Tilda into a side street. There are fewer people here. Most of them are completely silent and seem as shaken as I am.

"I have to smoke," Tilda says, and stops abruptly.

She leans against a power box, taking out a packet of cigarettes with Russian health warnings. Her dirty hands tremble. I have to help her light her cigarette. It's already dotted with tiny pinpricks of rain. She pulls on the cigarette so hard it crackles as she sucks the smoke deep into her lungs. Tilda, who used to be so obsessed with her oxygen intake.

People shoot us suspicious looks as they pass by. Tilda doesn't even seem to notice. She's rocking back and forth.

"What have you taken tonight?" I ask her again.

"None of your fucking business."

"You have to stop."

"Shut up, Simon. You're not exactly a saint yourself nowadays."

"It's not the same thing. Do you even know what you're taking?"

Tilda smiles mockingly. "Are you *worried* about me, Simon?"

"Of course I am!"

"Everyone is. Everyone wants to tell me what I should be doing. *Little Tilda, who can be such a good girl when she wants to be.*" She gives me a disgusted look. "You're all such fucking hypocrites."

"We just want to help you."

v"Sure."

She stumbles, bracing herself against the power box, then takes another drag on her cigarette and squints against the smoke.

"I'm leaving now," she announces.

"Where are you going?"

"It doesn't matter."

"To Sait?"

"Stop it. Sait is *nothing*."

"Tilda ... If you're going to get more of that shit ... don't. Please."

She throws her cigarette aside; it hisses against the wet pavement. But she doesn't move, turning her gaze up to the sky, blinking against the rain. Tiny droplets sparkle in her hair.

"Do you know what I've realized?" she says. "Everyone who says they know what's best for me ... and think they're that much fucking better than me ... they're the worst ones. And I'm not putting up with it anymore."

"Tilda," I say. "I don't think I'm better than you."

She starts crying and shakes her head. I try to put my arm around her, but she pulls away.

"You don't get it. There's only one person who could, but she's ..." Tilda goes silent, angrily rubbing her cheeks dry.

"I'd get it if you *talked* to me," I say. "We used to talk about everything."

"No. We didn't."

Does she even know what she's saying? Is she deliberately trying to hurt me? I can't read this Tilda. I don't know who she is.

"You should go home," I say. "I'll come with you. I promise I won't try to stay. I just need to know that you're—"

"I can't go home. I can't stand it."

She wipes away fresh tears. I want to tell her that I know about Klas and the True Church. And I want to tell her that I can't stand being at home, either. That I don't feel at home anywhere since she left me.

But Tilda's spotted something behind my back. Her face changes, as if she's put on a mask. Her smile is huge. Fake. A poor imitation of her old self. I turn around just as Amanda and Elin throw their arms around us. Hampus and Ali are with them.

"Shit, it's so good to see you. That was super scary," Amanda says, kissing Tilda on the cheek before shooting me a look.

"What happened to your eyebrow?" Elin asks.

I raise my hand, touching the wound gently. "Someone accidentally brained me."

"Afteeer-paaarty," Hampus hollers, and does a pirouette that makes him stumble off the curb. "Come on. We're going back to Ali's."

"We'll be right there," I say.

"Simon will be right there," Tilda says quickly. "I have to go and talk to someone."

Elin and Amanda exchange a look.

"Come with us instead," Amanda says.

But Tilda shakes her head.

Hampus is getting antsy, and finally, Elin and Amanda give up. Tilda and I stay on the corner watching the others as they disappear toward the apartment complex on the other side of the tracks.

Tilda takes out a new cigarette. This time, she manages to light it herself. Her hands have stopped trembling.

"I'll walk with you, wherever you're going," I say. "You shouldn't be alone in the city when—"

"Leave me alone, Simon. I've got my own life now. It's got nothing to do with you." She starts to walk away. I follow her, and she whirls around.

"If you don't leave me alone, I'll scream."

I look up toward Storgatan, wondering if the men in windbreakers are still there, still eager to rush to her rescue.

I don't say anything. I stay where I am. I let her go.

SIMON

B oomer starts howling as soon as I get the key into the lock. The entire stairwell shakes when I open the door. I quickly pull the door shut behind me, shushing him until he stops barking, but a hundred and fifty pounds of dog running around in circles in the hall still makes a lot of noise.

"Take it easy, boy," I croak, and fall over as I try to pull my shoes off.

A wet tongue squelches at me before I manage to get back up again. I stagger into the bathroom and look at myself in the mirror. The Band-Aid I got from Ali at the after-party came off on the way home. There are spots of blood on my cheek. My eyebrow is swollen and tender.

I brush my teeth, nearly vomiting when my toothbrush slips toward the back of tongue. Afterward, I rinse my mouth with water straight from the tap, then stay slumped over the sink.

The mood was odd at Ali's place. I think we were all shocked by the chaos in the city—it was like walking through a war zone. I kept hoping Tilda would show up, and drank way too much while I waited for her.

Your ex is a fucking whore!

The bleach-blonde girl screamed it at me. I still don't know her name. We made out again, but I was too drunk to hide the fact that I was texting Tilda at the same time. I tried to explain that I was worried about her, that I wanted to know she'd arrived safely wherever she was going. But then I got moonshine poured over me. Everyone stared. And Tilda still hasn't replied to the message.

I'm so tired. More tired than I've ever been. If I turned the lights off, I could curl up on the bathroom rug and sleep until the comet hits and everything's over. Instead, I pull myself together and straighten up. Dry my mouth.

When I step out of the bathroom, Judette is waiting for me in the low light. She's wearing her robe. Her eyes are bloodshot.

"Sorry if I woke you," I say.

"You think I could sleep? You *promised* to get home early."

She practically pushes me into the kitchen. I cautiously take a seat. The window is ajar, and birds are chirping like crazy outside. It's stopped raining. The sky is brighter.

"What happened to your face?" Judette says, placing a glass of water in front of me. "Did you go down to the square?"

"We didn't plan to do it. It just happened."

Judette's eyes are burning with rage. I look away, toward the expensive and beautiful orchids that nestle together on the windowsill—Venus slipper, pink and yellow Paphiopedilum Pinocchio. Judette brought them with her from the flower shop when it closed down. When I was a kid, I knew the name of every flower in that place. Now it's just an abandoned building on Storgatan with its windows smashed in.

"Sorry," I say.

"Have you been in a fight?"

"Someone just bumped into me. It was an accident."

"And then what?"

"And then?"

"What did you do after the game?"

"We just sat and talked for a while at Ali's place."

Judette watches me in silence. I know that this is a trick. She waits until I start talking, letting me dig my own grave. And I still can't resist picking up the spade and starting to shovel.

"I thought that since you'd already gone to bed, it wouldn't matter when—"

"Bullshit," she interrupts. "You weren't thinking about us at all."

She's wrong. I did think about them. I just decided I didn't care.

A headache comes creeping up on me, a warm, throbbing glow inside my skull. "Do you realize how worried I've been?" Judette says. "Don't you think I've heard how crazy it was out there?"

"I just wanted to be with my friends. They're important to me, too."

"Simon." Judette sighs. "This is destructive."

"So? What does it matter? It's almost over, anyway."

"I get that it feels that way, but are you actually having fun? Because this doesn't look like fun."

Now the headache presses against the backs of my eyes. I carefully sip the water Judette gave me. It barely reaches my stomach before it threatens to come back up again.

"I'm having loads of fun," I say. "I'm having the time of my life."

"And how are you going to feel tomorrow?" she says, but cuts me off me before I can respond. "And don't say it doesn't matter."

I shut my mouth again.

"We have to do the best we can with the time we have left," Judette says.

I look at her dark eyes, her skin glowing in the light from the ceiling lamp. I miss her so much. I miss my old life. And all those things I don't want to think about are threatening to catch up with me.

"I don't know how to do that," I say quietly.

She leans across the table. "It isn't easy for any of us. But you can't figure it out like this."

Judette's voice is warm, so warm she could melt something inside me, make the feelings rush out. I don't want to cry right now. I'm so sick of crying.

I clear my throat to rid myself of the lump in there. "Where's Stina?"

"She's doing a home visit."

The way Judette says it tells me all I need to know. Another suicide. Stina takes care of the loved ones left behind by those who can't bear waiting around for the comet. Some people prefer to take matters into their own hands. Get it over with. I had a hard time understanding it at first. It seemed so contradictory, killing yourself because you were afraid to die. But sometimes, I feel like I understand it all too well—only occasionally and briefly. I could never really hurt myself.

At least, I don't think so.

"When did she leave?"

"Ten thirty. I haven't told her you didn't come home, if that's what you're asking."

"Thank you."

"It's for her sake, not yours. I didn't want her to worry. But I'm going to tell her tomorrow."

"Great."

Judette's eyes narrow.

"I'm going to get my shit together," I say. "I promise." My words hang in the air, sounding empty and false.

"I'm going to hit the shower before work," Judette finally says before stretching.

"Why shower *before* work?"

Judette has gone from working at the flower shop to volunteering with garbage disposal. The comet has pushed her to the other end of the olfactory spectrum.

"I have to wake myself up somehow," she says. "God, let it be Thursday soon so we can get new coffee rations."

She rubs her face and gets to her feet. Boomer raises his head expectantly, but she just pats him distractedly and heads out of the kitchen.

"Set the alarm," she yells. "You're taking him out for his morning walk."

NAME: LUCINDA
TELLUS # 0 392 811 002
POST 0005

The garbage truck woke me up around ten. Miranda's knees were shoved against my back, and her scrawny body emitted snores louder than seemed physically possible. When Dad came home a little later, I gave up on going back to sleep and joined him for breakfast.

He seemed so tired that I suddenly envisioned what he would have looked like if he had the chance to grow old. He looked more like grandpa than ever.

Dad asked me how I was feeling, and I replied, "All right. I just have a touch of cancer," and he said, "You'd do anything for attention, wouldn't you?" It's not a super normal way to talk, but we've been doing it since I got my diagnosis. It's how we deal with it.

I told him about Miranda's questions about the comet, but didn't mention my own anxiety. It wasn't the right time. And what was he supposed to do about it? He would've just worried about me, and he's already done enough of that. I made us oatmeal, noticing how happy he was when I went back for another half-serving.

We watched the morning news. The same inferno has been raging throughout the country, throughout every square and city park where the game was screened. Dad told me about his night in the ER. Lacerations were sutured. Skulls were x-rayed. Stomachs were pumped.

Fights. Rapes. Overdoses. Manslaughter. Vandalism. It was almost as bad as when we first heard about the comet and people lost their minds. If I have a hard time remembering the goodness in the world, it must be even harder for Dad. He has to see the results of humanity's worst instincts and impulses. (Then again, I think Dad is a better person than I am. He thinks the best of everyone until he's proven wrong. Sometimes, I'm afraid I'm the exact opposite.) Anyone who's ever had a secret urge is satisfying it now. *Seize the day.* The chance of being caught and held accountable is slim to none. There aren't enough police officers left, no time for investigations or trials, not to mention prison sentences.

There aren't enough people at the hospital, either. No time for long-term treatments. Dad keeps going in to work. He says he has to because so many people need doctors right now, but I think he does it for his own sake, too. It's his way of feeling like himself again, despite the world changing. I would do the same thing if I could.

I need to get out of the house. Maybe take a walk down to the lake. If I cut through the woods, I probably won't risk meeting anyone.

Write more later.

SIMON

The air is hot and humid. There's no breeze as I run along the rolling hills on the other side of the lake. I'm dripping with sweat. Boomer looks up at me with a huge doggy smile, thrilled to be off-leash. Now and then he stops, sniffing around a bush or at some interesting spot in the grass. His tail points straight up like a white plume.

When the forest starts to get thicker around the trail, I pull my phone out of my pocket. Still no response from Tilda to the message I sent last night. I promise myself not to check again before I get home.

Not that I want to go home. Stina was so angry at me for going into town last night she cried.

I speed up, even though the hangover pounds through my body, and it feels like my heart is going to burst inside my chest. Loud music pulses in my ears. I keep my arms tight against my sides, focusing on my feet hitting the ground, which is strewn with woodchips and bark.

Soon it'll all be gone, Tilda said the morning when we'd heard about the comet.

The ground beneath my feet. And the lake. And the birch trees. And Boomer.

A sudden feeling of vertigo almost trips me up, but I force

myself to keep going. Now I can glimpse the old waterslide between the trees, once turquoise, now bleached to some noncolor. A tarp covers the pool. The ice cream stand is shut. The mini golf courses haven't been used for a long time. I push myself harder for the final stretch, run to the beach, then stop and put my hands on my knees, breathing hard, the taste of blood in my mouth. New beads of sweat push through my skin.

Boomer splashes around the water's edge and gets hold of an old plastic bag.

"Let go of that!" I shout, and yank my headphones out.

He looks up at me. Laps some water. Snorts. Frolics clumsily. Comes back up on the beach and shakes himself off.

Someone is sitting at the edge of the swimming dock, her black hat pulled down low. When I look at her, she turns away, but not before I recognize her.

Lucinda. The girl who used to be Tilda's best friend. The girl who features in so many photos on Tilda's wall of inspiration—they're sleeping in a bus or hugging each other at the edge of a pool. In some pictures, they're surrounded by other people from the swim team, but there's always an invisible bubble around the two of them. It's like they belong together.

I only met Lucinda a couple of times at the hospital. By then, she'd already started pulling away from everyone. Even from Tilda. How many times did I console her after a call or a message went unanswered?

I look away, too, relieved that Lucinda clearly wants to ignore me. I have no idea what I'd even say to her.

Sweat drips from my head to the sand as I stretch the backs of my thighs.

When Tilda and I got together last fall, everyone was talking about Lucinda, "the cancer girl." She had just gotten her diagnosis. The entire swim team went to visit her in the hospital. Amanda and Elin posted photos of themselves at her bedside. They called her *strong* and *brave*. Tilda hated it. She said it was like Lucinda wasn't a real person to them, just some kind of character. The lovely, wonderful friend with the tragic destiny. Lucinda, whose mother had died of cancer. Lucinda, whose father the doctor couldn't save either his wife or his daughter. But the months passed, and the prognoses were unclear and contradictory. Everything was so complicated, not at all like in the movies.

It's been a long time since anyone talked about Lucinda.

I straighten slowly, shake the lactic acid out of my legs. Hear Boomer bark. When I look over, he's already halfway along the swimming dock.

"Boomer! *Come here!*"

He pretends not to hear me. His tail wags as he burrows his giant head in under Lucinda's arm. Panic rushes through me as I remember having to wear a mask when I visited her in the hospital. The slightest cold or infection could kill her.

I race to the dock, shouting for Boomer. He looks up at me happily before licking Lucinda's cheek. She tries to push him away. I thought dogs had some kind of sixth sense for when people were sick, but that's obviously not true with Boomer. The dock sways beneath my feet. I yank Boomer away as he playfully nips at my hand.

"Leave her alone!" I tell him sternly.

Lucinda wipes her cheek with her sleeve, and then reluctantly looks up at me.

There's something weird about her face. It takes me a moment to realize that she doesn't have any eyebrows. Her cheeks are hollow in the hard white daylight. Still, she looks healthier than before. More *alive*.

"Sorry," I say. "I didn't see him run."

"It's okay."

Her shoulder blades are clearly visible beneath her hoodie. And now I see that the hair poking out from the thin hat is short and downy.

I wish I could just leave. I know she wants me to. And still, I sit down next to her. I have to find out if what Boomer did is serious.

He's still trotting happily behind us. I turn around and shout at him to lie down. Incredibly, he obeys me, shooting me an affronted look while breathing so hard, the dock shakes. I lean out over the water, splashing my face and neck before looking back at Lucinda.

"Are you sure you're okay?" I say.

"It would have been worse if a human had licked my face."

"I'll try not to."

It's a bad attempt at a joke, but she smiles faintly.

"How are you doing?" I say, and hesitate. "You look better."

"I stopped taking CTX."

"What's that?"

"Chemo."

I wince instinctively at the word and can only hope she doesn't notice.

"Are you all right now?"

She glances at me.

"No. But the comet will probably kill me before the cancer does, so I might as well stop the treatments. So ... yay."

"Sorry," I say, feeling like an idiot. "I should've understood."

"No," she says quickly and looks out over the water. "I'm the one who should be sorry. I've forgotten how to talk to people."

I wonder how literally she means that. How lonely she's actually been. Maybe she doesn't know that Tilda and I broke up.

Tilda, who left me. Tilda, who Lucinda left.

She's the only thing we have in common, and I don't think either of us wants to talk about her.

A bird flies past us over the lake, so low it nearly dips its wings in the water.

"And how about you?" Lucinda says. "How are you doing? What happened to your eyebrow?"

"I went to watch the game last night."

"Then you were lucky. Dad worked in the ER last night, and..."

She falls silent when my pocket vibrates. I pull the phone out. See that Tilda has finally replied to my message. I wipe my fingers on my shorts so I can unlock the screen.

EVERYTHING IS OK. YOU DON'T NEED TO WORRY ABOUT ME.

I try to think of something to write back, but I don't know if there's anything to add after last night. In the end, I send her an emoji of a koala bear.

We used to do that when we wanted the other person to know we were thinking of them. It began when Tilda said I hugged her like a koala bear in my sleep. Then we found out koalas often have chlamydia. It only got funnier after that.

I put my phone back into my pocket. Lucinda's looking away politely. I try to think of something else to say before I leave. Something simple to make the situation less awkward.

"How are your moms?" Lucinda asks suddenly. "What are their names again?"

"Stina and Judette," I answer, surprised. "Have you met them?"

"Don't you remember? We were in the same class in first grade. It was only for a few months, before I moved."

I think back, suddenly recalling the feeling of someone disappearing. A vague image of a girl with long blonde hair and watchful eyes.

"We came to your house to learn about Dominica," Lucinda says.

I groan aloud, because I remember that day all too well.

It goes without saying that it was Stina who came up with the idea of inviting the entire class over to our place. They were going to see that we were a regular family, despite the fact that we seemed different on the surface. Judette had made food from the island. Yams and cassava, a variety of stews and homemade bread. But I didn't want to join in. I didn't understand other children, didn't know how to talk to them, and I definitely didn't want them to invade our home.

It turned out to be even worse than I'd imagined.

Lucinda must be able to imagine what I'm thinking, because she snickers.

"Stop it," she says. "It was so much fun."

"Not for me. Everyone kept asking how two moms could have kids together. And of course, Stina had to tell the class about it in detail. No one understood what she was talking about."

"I told my dad I wanted to be a lesbian when I got home," Lucinda says. "Your place seemed like way more fun."

"You'd find it less appealing now. They got a divorce. But they're living together again."

"Oh? How's that working out?"

"Surprisingly okay, actually. They agree on most things. Like they both want me to stay at home more."

"Why don't you?" She cuts herself off. "Sorry. It's none of my business."

"No, it's fine. I just don't know how to explain it."

In the water, I see murky shadows of fish swimming with jerky, nervous movements.

"I wish they hadn't moved back in with each other again for my sake," I say. "We had just settled into the new routine. I enjoyed spending time with each of them separately. Now it's like I'm the one who has to make this whole living-together-again thing seem worth it and ... and that'd be okay, if it wasn't for ... It's like everything we do has to be so meaningful. You know? It just feels unnatural."

"That's how my dad acted when I first got sick. Like some never-fucking-ending *seize the day* with no breathing space."

I laugh when she rolls her eyes.

"Exactly," I say. "But it might be getting better soon. My sister, Emma, is staying with us for a while, so they'll have someone else to focus on."

Boomer heaves a deep sigh, watching us with his head resting on his front paws. I look over at the waterslide. When I was little, Emma told me it was closed because someone had taped razor blades to it and anyone who went down was slashed up.

The parents would wait in the pool for their kids ... First the blood came pouring down ... Then the rest of them.

The image of the red water rushing down the slide is so clear in my mind that it feels like a real memory. I haven't thought about it since I was a kid. I wonder if it was an urban legend or something Emma came up with herself. She loved to scare me. And, oddly enough, I liked it, too. My sister epitomized everything exciting to me: sneaking cigarettes on the balcony when the moms weren't home; wearing dark clothes and pools of black makeup around her eyes; making secret phone calls at night; laughing at things I couldn't understand.

I turn to Lucinda to ask if she's heard about the razor blades, too.

"Emma is pregnant," I hear myself saying instead.

"How far along is she?"

"Six months," I say, and without warning start to cry.

Lucinda goes stiff beside me, but I can't stop the tears from streaming down my cheeks.

"Sorry," I say. "It's just ..."

"No, no. I get it. Of course."

But I can tell she's uncomfortable. Fortunately, Boomer shows up to soothe me. He whines, worried, and puts a paw on my shoulder, distracting us from the awkward mood.

"What breed is he?" Lucinda asks while I ruffle his fur.

"Landseer. They're in the same family as Newfoundlands."

"Are you sure he isn't a pony?"

I laugh.

"Why's he called Boomer?"

I sniffle as discreetly as I can before telling her that I named him Boomer when I was little and we'd just gotten him from the breeder. He overturned chairs, fell over his huge paws, and crashed into doorframes.

That makes Lucinda laugh, finally easing the tension between us.

After a while, she tells me that she's started posting to TellUs.

"I don't think anyone out there is going to read it," she says with a nod at the sky. "But it's sort of like therapy."

I wonder if it's her way of saying I should try it. I probably seem like I need therapy.

"I'm mostly trying not to think about what's going on at all," I say. "It's not going very well."

She smiles, and suddenly I have a vision of her younger self: gaps from lost teeth, a pink sweater. Her standing in front of the class.

"Now I remember," I say. "You always said you were going to become a writer."

"Did I?"

"The pooping giant made a powerful impression on me."

Lucinda laughs. "What pooping giant?"

"You wrote a fairy tale that you read aloud to us. The giant ate everything in the village, depriving the people of food. Then he pooped in the river so they couldn't drink the water anymore."

Lucinda's cheeks go pink.

"You were so pleased about the fact that your story was actually about destroying the environment," I continue. "You taught us that it was called a *metaphor*."

Now we're both laughing.

"I must have been unbearable," she says, and then gets up abruptly. "I have to go home now. But it was nice seeing you."

I find myself agreeing with her. But I also find myself staying put, rather than offering to join her, not wanting to risk our conversation turning awkward and uncertain again.

"See you around," I say.

It used to be a completely normal thing to say, but not anymore. Who knows if we'll ever see each other again?

"Maybe," she says, as if the same thing has just occurred to her.

NAME: LUCINDA
TELLUS # 0 392 811 002
POST 0006

Walking to the lake was more difficult than I thought it would be. I got tired and shaky halfway there. I tried to tell myself it was the humidity making me drip with sweat, but I knew better. A smarter person would have turned back and gone home. This person continued on.

I sat on the swimming dock to try get my strength back, but I was already considering calling Dad and asking him to pick me up. It was the worst possible moment for me to run into anyone from my old life, so naturally, that's exactly what happened. And naturally, it wasn't just anyone. It was Simon, Tilda's ex.

He was out for a brisk jog, and smelled like sweat and fresh air—smelled like *health*—and I wondered what I smelled like. I'd slept in the T-shirt I was wearing underneath my hoodie, and sometimes I think that I smell like chemicals, but I don't know if it's just in my head. I only know that I wanted him to leave. I could tell that he was trying not to stare at me. I tried to crack some jokes, but they kept coming out wrong. All I could think about was what Tilda must have said about me. She must hate me. I would hate me.

I asked Simon questions about anything and everything I could think of so I wouldn't have to talk about myself. I even asked him how his moms were doing. The whole class was invited to their house when I was little. I mostly remember being jealous of him. He had two moms, and I had none. Stina told us they'd chosen to let Judette get pregnant, since

Stina had already experienced pregnancy. They picked a white sperm donor, so that Simon would look like a combination of them both. I was so impressed by the idea that they could choose like that. And you could tell they had fun together. I also preferred playing with girls rather than boys. Then and there, I decided to become a lesbian when I grew up. That didn't end up happening. Unfortunately, it's not that simple.

Back then, Simon was a shy little boy who liked to draw and mostly played by himself. By the time Tilda and I started high school and I spotted him in the corridors, I'd forgotten all about him. Everyone talked about how hot he was, with his high cheekbones and thick lashes, the tiny gap between his front teeth, his kissable lips. We wondered if he even knew how attractive he was. Amanda said something about how his mouth looked like it would taste like a raindrop, and Tilda scoffed at it. But I saw something in her eyes I hadn't seen before. When I remembered that Simon and I had been in the same class for a few months in first grade, everyone wanted to hear all about what he'd been like. They thought it was so *adorable* that he'd been shy as a kid. Elin said it was *cool* that he had two moms. A girl from his class said she thought he was still pretty shy—he could be silent for long stretches, and seemed to think a lot. It was so *sweet*. Because this is how it goes: when someone is attractive, everything about that person seems glamorous and mysterious and thrilling.

Back to the dock. I made Simon cry. He told me his sister is pregnant, and I asked him how far along she was. In my defense, it's a question that popped out automatically, but I really should have known better. Nowadays, all possible answers are sad ones. Who wants to bring a baby into this world? And who, like his sister, wants to carry a child that will never be born?

I could tell that Simon was trying to stop crying, but I don't think he noticed that I was fighting back tears, too. It's just so tragic, but it wasn't for me to cry about. I know what it's like to be sad or terrified and, at the same time, forced to deal with everyone else's emotions. I didn't want Simon to have to go through that. But I could have done *something*. I'm so fucking worthless in situations like that one; I get so caught up thinking about what I should do, and then there's suddenly no time to do anything at all.

After I got back, I was completely exhausted. Dad was worried that I'd worn myself out on my walk, but that's not the reason I was so tired. Except for the staff at the hospital, this was the first time in a long time that I'd had a conversation with someone other than my dad or Miranda. In the end, it was like someone had flipped a switch. I had to cut our chat off so quickly, it must have seemed like I was fleeing.

I fell asleep the moment I came home.

P.S.: I made a big deal about telling Simon that I don't think anyone is going to read what I write here. That's not quite true. More and more, I've started to think of you as real. As if you really exist. And you're the only one I can be honest with.

Maybe I *need* to believe in you. So what if I and all the others who use TellUs are kidding ourselves? People have built their lives around believing in stranger things than you.

NAME: LUCINDA
TELLUS # 0 392 811 002
POST 0007

The big news is that the six people onboard the International Space Station are returning to Earth. Not even their orbit—over two hundred miles above us—is a safe distance from the comet. They'd rather die back home.

Cut to a woman who was beaten up during the "festivities." She was sitting at her kitchen table with a black eye, saying she's too afraid to leave her house. "It feels like I'm going to stay here until I die." Most towns (including ours) have canceled plans to screen the final two games. People will have to watch from their homes, instead. Experts in the studio discuss whether soccer should be canceled completely, but that would probably lead to even worse riots.

Cut to the news that several superstars are going to perform at a global charity gala that will be broadcast live from Buenos Aires, Johannesburg, New York, Paris, Tel Aviv, and Tokyo. The Red Cross will be collecting food and necessary supplies during the event. A lot of people need it. But, being a cynic, I can't help but wonder if the main attraction for the artists is the chance to enjoy their final moment in the spotlight. Recordings of the show are being preserved. You might come and dig them up in a few million years. I wonder what it'll sound like to your ears (if you have any).

Cut to me, who's still tired after yesterday. It terrifies me, because this is how it started when I first got sick. But I'm okay. I have to be.

SIMON

L oud music wakes me up—one of Stina's favorite songs from the '90s. I pick my phone up from the floor and realize that it's almost eleven.

Tomorrow, we'll have four weeks left.

I sit up in bed. Try to focus on recalling what I dreamed. The memories are as sheer as cobwebs, impossible to get ahold of without tearing them. Johannes was in one of the dreams. We were playing the ice game, but his mouth was full of shattered glass. Somehow, it was my fault.

I get up and almost crash into Stina in the hallway. Her arms are full of clothes.

"Hello, honey," she says. "You scared me."

"What are you doing?"

"I'm moving Judette's things so Emma can have her old room back tomorrow."

"Judette is sharing a room with you?"

Stina turns bright red.

"Yes," she says. "It'll be fine."

I watch her as she disappears into the bedroom.

Once, after Judette had had too much wine, she said that she and Stina brought out the best and the worst in each other. The year before the divorce was definitely the worst. Stina's self-conscious neediness made her more demanding than she realized. To everyone else, it was painfully obvious that Judette was pulling away. Stina begged, clung to her, tried to hold on—but Judette pulled away even more. And so it went.

But they had good times, too. I keep thinking about what Lucinda said yesterday. That our home seemed like fun.

I go into Emma's room, unscrew one of the gold bed knobs, and peer into the small hole. It's empty. My sister used to hide cigarettes and condoms in there. I would threaten to tell on her unless she got me candy.

A worn plaster statuette of the Virgin Mary, painted in bright colors, rests on the nightstand. I pick it up and inspect her mild smile. Rays of gold shoot out like feelers from her head. A heart ringed with flowers hovers in front of her chest. Judette never used to keep Catholic items around before. I wonder if this small statue has followed her all the way from Dominica. In that case, where has she been keeping it since then?

My moms have found their own relationship to God together. It's a loving God who wants the best for everyone. He doesn't meddle too much, but is there when you need Him. He forgives everything and judges no one. A perfect parent.

But finding Him took a long time. Their own parents believed in a different God. Stina's father was a priest of the old-school sort. He was against homosexuality, against female priests, against *Stina*. If he were alive today, he would probably be a Truther. Still, Stina tried "meeting him halfway." It was the joy he took in her divorce that finally prompted Stina to cut him off. And now he's gone. Judette's dad and brother still live in Dominica. I've never met them. Their God is sending Judette straight from the devastated Earth to the flames of hell, just for marrying a woman.

I'm glad my moms found their God, and that He's the one I grew up with. I liked listening to their stories about the

Bible, liked praying together before I fell asleep. When I was a kid, I believed in God in the same way I believed in Santa Claus. But now I'm not so sure. When I try to pray, it feels like no one is listening.

I think about Tilda's dad. I wonder if Klas is one of those hypocrites she was talking about.

Stina turns the volume down in the living room. I consider leaving Emma's room and asking her what she thinks of the True Church—how someone like Klas could join it. But I don't have the energy. I know she'd blow it out of proportion. She'd be overjoyed that I finally wanted to talk to her about something big and important. Her happiness would make me feel guilty for never giving her what she wants.

I walk to the bookshelf instead and feel a thrill when I see the titles, just like when I was a kid.

Pet Sematary. The Silence of the Lambs. American Psycho. Exquisite Corpse. The Night Eternal. Uzumaki. Locke & Key. Reading the descriptions on the back used to be enough to make me scared of the dark. But now my eyes are drawn to the shelf of children's books. One of them is called *Comet in Moominland.*

I pull it out. Unsurprisingly, it's a book about the Moomins. It's so old, it must have belonged to Stina or Emma's dad. The cover shows three characters walking on stilts in a mountain landscape. A burning orb is hurtling across the sky.

The smell of dusty paper hits me when I flip through the pages.

"I don't think we're particularly brave," Moomintroll mused. "It's just that we've grown used to this comet. Almost familiar with it. We were the first ones to find out about it and we've watched it grow and get bigger. Imagine how lonely it must be . . ."

"Yes," said Snufkin. "Imagine how lonely it must be if everyone is afraid of you."

I shut the book and put it back on the shelf.

"If we ever want to dance, we have to do it now," Stina says from the doorway. I turn around. Look at her inquiringly.

"Snork Maiden says it. In the book. You should read it."

"It's a kid's book."

"It's full of wisdom for adults, too," Stina says, and sits down on the bed. "A comet is heading straight for Moomin Valley. Everyone is very terrified, of course. But they also make sure to do everything they feel like doing while there's still time."

She looks at me expectantly. Her eyes are bright with longing. I can't stand it. It feels as if the walls are closing in.

"I was going to go to a party tonight," I say. "If that's all right?"

"I want you to stay home," Stina says.

"That isn't what I *feel like doing.*"

Why am I so fucking mean to her? She presses her lips together in a thin line. I brush some dust from my fingers and mumble that I'm taking a shower.

I rush out of the room. Lock the bathroom door and try to rinse the panic away with hot water. I turn up the heat until I can barely stand it, just to feel my own body again, where it begins and ends.

When I get back into my room, I look at the most recent picture Tilda has posted. It was taken during the soccer game. She and Elin are standing in the middle of the crowd. A black-and-white filter. Tilda is laughing at the camera. She looks happy.

One hundred percent fucked up.

I check the pictures Tilda has been tagged in, a total of four from the game. No photos from earlier that same night. No photos after it.

NAME: LUCINDA
TELLUS # 0 392 811 002
POST 0008

I wrote that you're the only one I can be honest with. That's not completely true. There are a lot of things I don't write about because they feel petty or pathetic. Like that I still think it sucks that I barely have any hair. What does it matter when we're all about to burn to death?

The algorithms that control my social media channels suggest that I join a group called "Those of Us Who Don't Want to Die as Virgins." I'm sad to say I almost fit the bill. The first and only time I had sex hardly counts. It was with a mind-numbingly boring German boy at a training camp in Rimini. It didn't really hurt; mostly, it was uncomfortable, and I really only did it to get it over and done with. (And to tell Tilda about it afterward. He had a pointy little tongue that darted in and out of my mouth, and I kept thinking about how I'd describe it to her, so I started laughing in the middle of it. He was so pissed. But that didn't stop him from sending me playlists for six months, half-demanding I admire him for his taste in music and infer from the lyrics what a wonderful guy he was.)

Another group's called "'Virginity' is a Social Construct," which I suppose I agree with, but it doesn't change the fact that I want to have sex. I want to have sex and enjoy it. I want to know what it's like. So fucking embarrassing that that's something that really makes me feel sad, out of all the things to feel sad about. There are people on this planet who'll never have full stomachs, and still, I feel sorry for myself.

I'm babysitting Miranda again tonight. I let her do pretty much whatever she wants. It isn't easy to get someone to brush their teeth when they're never going to get cavities, anyway. She's finally fallen asleep now, and I can't stop thinking about honesty.

I've been reading my old diaries. Almost everything is about swimming. I don't think I'd quite grasped how much Tilda and I sacrificed. We rarely went on vacations, because every time we had a break from school, we were sleeping on air mattresses in school gyms. At the camp in Rimini, we swam four hours a day in a freezing pool and didn't even go to the beach. We were cold all the time. We got up at five thirty in the morning in February, were cold all the way to the pool, and froze when we leapt into the water. We went to competitions even when we weren't swimming ourselves. We hardly hung out with anyone who wasn't on the team.

There's a lot about my body, too. I trained it, I slathered lotion on it since it was always dry, I was obsessed with what I put in it. I thought about food all the time. We burned so many calories that we were always famished. The others on the team bought fast food and candy from the swimming pool cafeteria, but I wanted to be like Tilda. We always stuffed our bags with bananas and protein bars and raw food snacks so we wouldn't be tempted. And I thought a lot about how other people viewed my body. I loved being in the water, but I hated standing by the pool's edge listening to Tommy's lengthy lectures while I shivered in swimsuits that revealed absolutely everything. Despite having turned my body into a perfect machine, I was unhappy with it.

It's there in my diary, but between the lines. Only I can read it.

I rewrote history. I didn't lie, exactly, but I made myself out to be a little braver, a little bit less interested in what other people thought of me. I've always been too trapped in my own head. I've never been able to let loose in a way that seems to come so naturally to everybody else. But in the diaries, I always tried to embellish things. Improve them. I don't even think I was aware that I was doing it.

I didn't even want to admit that I was sick.

If I'm going to write things here, I'm going to do it properly. Otherwise, there's no point.

I'll do what I can to be honest and truthful. And I know just where to start. Next time.

P.S.: Simon said that when I was little, I told everyone I wanted to be a writer. But in the diaries, which start a few years later, I couldn't even admit that to myself. I only mention my writing in passing. Short stories I'd begun, fan fiction I'd published anonymously online. I didn't even tell Tilda about it. If I'd had an entire lifetime to do it, would I ever have tried to write a book? Would I have dared to risk failing at it? I don't know. Failing would have been a greater defeat than placing last in any race.

NAME: LUCINDA
TELLUS # 0 392 811 002
POST 0009

It started out with a few bruises. It wasn't anything I thought about too much.

There were other signs, too. I was more tired than usual. Got easily winded. Sometimes when I woke up, my sheets would be soaked with sweat. I'd get a stubborn fever, but I assumed that it was just the effects of a cold I couldn't shake. I didn't tell anyone. I didn't want to be forced to skip practices.

It wasn't until my back started hurting that I spoke to my dad. He figured I'd overdone it in the pool. It made sense. I'd pushed myself too hard, that was all. I went for a massage. It got worse. I saw a physiotherapist. She noticed the bruises. And when Dad found out about them, I realized for the first time that he was worried.

He tried to hide it. That terrified me.

Then came the blood tests and the bone marrow biopsies. Then the diagnosis. And then time was of the essence.

I had drawn the short straw in the genetic lottery. AML. Acute myeloid leukemia. Blood cancer. The same thing that killed my mom when Miranda was barely a year old.

I had a central line surgically inserted in my throat. They pumped me full of cytotoxic agents and said that the treatment might make me infertile, so did I want to save some of my eggs for future use? They're probably still in some freezer. I had blood transfusions until my blood had been completely replaced several times over, and I lost my hair—the eyebrows, the eyelashes, the hair on my body, which I'd spent so much time shaving and waxing for swimming. I had hair on my pillows, on my clothes, in the drain in the shower. And then I didn't have any hair at all. It was all gone. My immune system gave up. I stopped going to school so I wouldn't catch something, and I got tons of antibiotics, but infections and inflammations erupted in my body anyway. Once, I got a septic fever and nearly died. Everything that had touched my body was disposed of in bags for hazardous waste. After each chemo session, I vomited until I felt like I was turning inside out. I felt so sick that I actually wanted to die. In between, my mouth hurt so much I could barely eat, and they had to feed me intravenously.

But the worst thing was the uncertainty. Always new tests, always waiting for results. Waiting for a stem cell donor. No one wanted to tell me what would happen if they couldn't find anyone in time. No one wanted to tell me *how* I'd die—if it would hurt, if it would be slow. And I didn't know how to ask. I was constantly afraid, but couldn't show it to anyone. Least of all Dad. I knew he was breaking. He'd already seen Mom die. He peppered the staff with questions, controlled every test result, followed every curve. I became a project. A failed one, at that.

I haven't been able to cry in front of Dad since I got my diagnosis. There's nothing noble or brave about it. I just can't. His grief and helplessness make me feel responsible. Or maybe not responsible, but guilty. Remember what I wrote about eating oatmeal with him a few days back? I took an extra helping even though I wasn't hungry, just because I know how happy it makes him when I eat. I do things like that all the time, like some kind of penance.

And Miranda. My wonderful sister. At the hospital, she mostly just sat and stared at her iPad. She seemed shy around me, as if I'd transformed into a stranger—something *strange*—a tangle of questions she didn't know how to ask, and that I didn't know how to answer.

There was nothing left of me. I was just the cancer. And my world kept shrinking. I let it happen; I just wanted to disappear. I pulled away from my friends. Pretended to be asleep when they came for visits. Closed my eyes and listened to their nervous whispers. Felt relieved when they left. They brought flowers I wasn't allowed to keep in my room, chocolate I couldn't eat. They took selfies with me when I couldn't stand looking at myself in the mirror.

I said that I wanted everyone to behave normally, but I couldn't bear listening to them talk about parties or plans for the future. I didn't want to hear them complain about bad hair days when I didn't have any hair. I didn't want them to act normally at all; I wanted *me* to be normal. My weeks spent in isolation were almost a relief, and when I wasn't in isolation, I made up excuses for why I couldn't have visitors. I knew my friends only wanted the best for me—I knew they were trying—but I also knew they couldn't understand what I was going through. I didn't want to hear that I was "strong" and "brave." I wasn't any of those things. I just didn't have a choice. They should have known how scared I was. How bitter I was. How unfair it all felt. I never thought *Why is this happening to me?* because that would be like saying someone else deserved it instead. But if I'd had the chance, I would have given my cancer to someone else in a heartbeat. That's the truth.

Our coach, Tommy, never once sat down during the few occasions he came to the hospital. He stood next to my bed, hovering over me, talking about how I should "see this as a competition" and "keep my eyes on the prize." For years, he'd been a demigod in my eyes. To keep hitting the pool every morning, to sacrifice so much, we needed someone like Tommy to believe that swimming was the most important thing in the world. That it was all worth it. He made us go a little farther, push a little harder, keep fighting. We vomited during the lactate tolerance training, struggled through the exhaustion that turned our bodies into concrete, while he measured our achievements—our worth—in tenths of a second. And during those brief moments when we reached the swimmers' nirvana, high on adrenaline and endorphins, it felt as if we had Tommy to thank as much as ourselves. It's no wonder we wanted to please him. Swimming made us feel immortal. Or at least invincible.

But he was a different person outside the pool. At the hospital, he suddenly looked *ordinary*, just a middle-aged man in a tracksuit. As far as my life was concerned, he wasn't convincing at all. He was just lost.

I stopped going out because I hated meeting other people's eyes and hearing conversations die around me. People think they're so good at being discreet, but they're really not. I even stopped using social media, where all the photos I'd been tagged in were from the hospital. I couldn't deal with all the virtual hugs, crying emojis, promises of prayers, and clichés about my "battle" against cancer. (I wasn't battling cancer—the chemo was. I was just the battlefield, and I couldn't do a thing.) And I couldn't bear to see their lives, which were so easy. I didn't want to be reminded of everything I was missing out on. I've only started checking in again recently, but always without leaving a trace of my presence.

Tilda was the last person to disappear from my life.

When I got sick, we'd just started high school at a school with a championship swim team. We loved it. Our schedules were built around our training. Before, no one outside the team had really cared about swimming. In fact, swimming was for nerds. But at this new school, we suddenly had higher status. For the first time, we were popular. Amanda was dating a guy named Johannes. After I was hospitalized, Tilda started going out with Johannes's best friend. Simon. She was in love. She was happy. She was going places. Tilda had decided to become a sports medicine doctor after her swimming career, and Dad loved all her questions. When she stopped by the hospital, it was always with a wet towel and a swimsuit in her bag, and she always smelled like chlorine. I was so jealous. People talk about bitterness as an emotion, but it was a physical feeling; it poisoned me until I couldn't distinguish it from all the other shit being pumped through my system. And the only thing worse than that was seeing how guilty Tilda felt about her life continuing according to plan, while mine had reached a dead end.

So I forced her away. I was relieved when she finally gave up. I felt awful, but I told myself I was doing her a favor.

I miss her. Maybe it would be easier seeing Tilda now that we're all going to die. I toy with the idea of getting in touch, but I'm afraid to. I don't know if she'll be able to forgive me.

I've quit chemo. No one knows how quickly the cancer will spread. My greatest fear isn't dying before the comet hits; it's spending the final weeks in the hospital. But I've decided to risk it.

Convincing Dad wasn't the easiest thing in the world, but I know he understands. He's seen up close what the treatments do to me. And he knows how the health care system works nowadays, or how it *doesn't* work.

So far, it's going well. I was tired yesterday and the day before, but on the whole, I'm starting to recognize myself again.

That's probably why I had panic attacks the other night.

I finally have something to lose again.

SIMON

At first glance, my sister looks the same, except her face is slightly rounder. She still laughs a lot. She has the same red hair, the same bright red lipstick. I try not to stare at her stomach. It's clearly visible under her black velvet shirt. I wonder what the baby looks like. If it's got hair and nails yet. If it ever opens its eyes in there.

A popping sound by the kitchen counter makes me jump. When I look over, Judette has opened a bottle of champagne.

"I've had this lying around for a while now," she says, and puts four glasses out on the table.

It glugs and fizzes as she pours each of us champagne. Emma declines, filling her glass with nonalcoholic cider, instead. I glance at her, then quickly look away when she meets my eyes, feeling vaguely guilty.

"I don't know how I feel about condoning..." Stina says as Judette tops up my glass.

"You don't think Simon's had alcohol before?" Emma smirks and looks at me. "You were still hungover when I got here."

Stina smiles back at her. Judette is standing behind Stina's chair. She puts a hand on her shoulder and raises her glass.

"I'd like to make a toast. I'm so happy you're here, Emma."

"I'm happy to be here. And Micke says hi, of course."

Stina pats Judette's hand and looks up at her. Then she turns to me and Emma. And I know how badly she wants this picture to be true. For us to be a family again.

The champagne flutes clink together.

"Let's eat!" Stina says after we've all had a sip.

We lift our cutlery. Blow on the food we've speared on our forks. The potatoes au gratin burn the roof of my mouth. I chew a slice of cucumber, and it helps a little. Judette says the food is lovely. Stina wonders if it needs more salt.

"But adding salt afterward is better," she says, just like I knew she would. "If the food's too salty to begin with, there's nothing you can do about it."

"That's so true," Emma says. "I've never thought about it like that before."

We exchange a look. When I was little, Emma was so good at impersonating Stina that I'd collapse on the floor laughing.

Stina, who would have been a grandmother. Who cried with joy in the kitchen when Emma called us and told us she was pregnant. Who went out the very next day to buy baby clothes and toys. *I couldn't help myself, they're adorable; look at these tiny shoes.*

"I was thinking we could have moose one of these days," Stina says. "One of my parishioners hunts, and he'd happily swap for some fish rations. Wouldn't it be nice with a proper Sunday steak?"

I drain my glass, then pour myself some more. Stina

looks at me but doesn't say anything. They start talking about Judette's job as a waste collector. Emma tells us about Micke's parents, who help out with home care in Överkalix. Both of them used to be unemployed.

"They're more energetic than they've been in years. I think it makes it easier for Micke to leave."

I think about Micke. Soon he'll have to stand on a train platform and say goodbye to his parents for the final time. What do you say in a situation like that? I barely know him. I'm not sure you can get to know him. He's like Teflon, with his even tan and blue shirts, his superficial talk about his job and sports. I've never understood what my sister sees in him. But now I can feel a lump growing in my throat. I take a gulp of champagne. Stina shoots me a glance before turning back to Emma.

"When will he be back?"

"Next week, as long as the trains from Luleå keep running."

"They wouldn't cancel them without warning."

Emma plays with the base of her glass.

"No," she says. "No, I guess not."

"And you know you're both very welcome here," says Stina.

"I know. We'll see what he says when he comes back."

"Yes, only if Micke wants to, of course," Stina says quickly. "It would just be so nice to have the two of you here."

Mom, stop. This is how you run people off. Can't you tell?

"How are you otherwise?" Judette asks.

"I haven't thrown up all day," Emma says with a jazz hands *ta-da.*

"I was the same when I was expecting you," Stina says. "I thought morning sickness sounded like a dream. I was sick constantly."

Emma laughs.

"I definitely don't feel like I'm *glowing*, that's for sure."

"Did you feel sick when you were pregnant with me?" I ask Judette.

She grins. "Not even once."

"I found it pretty aggravating." The champagne has made Stina's cheeks rosy.

"You made us all sick when you came out instead," Emma informs me.

We laugh. And everything almost feels normal.

"I think Tiny's kicking now," Emma says. "Or maybe it's just gas."

Stina places her hand on Emma's stomach, and her eyes immediately well up with tears. "Yes. It's kicking," she confirms, and smiles.

"God, I can't wait to meet him," Emma says. "Or her. But I think it's going to be a boy."

I swallow the potatoes in my mouth. Judette shoots me a warning look. *Don't argue with her.*

"Micke wanted us to find out," Emma continues. "He's always so practical, you know. He wants to know what color the baby's things should be. But I think it should be a surprise. And it's not like I want everything to be pink or pale blue, anyway."

"No, of course not," Stina says, hastily wiping her cheeks dry.

"Micke's so old-fashioned about things like that," Emma continues. "We still don't know what kind of child it will be, regardless of gender. I mean, if you know in advance, you might just end up with a lot of outdated expectations."

I can't listen to this. I stand up and start clearing the table. Let the tap run as I rinse the plates. They clatter loudly as I fill up the dishwasher and turn on the coffee maker. My pulse rushes in my ears, pounds dully in the wound by my eyebrow.

When I'm finished and rejoin them at the table, Stina's talking about the church. Her voice has steadied and grown more reassuring. Calmer. And I wonder if her voice reflects how she feels about it. In that case, I understand why she loves to work.

"It's really not that different from the conversations I've had with people who've received a fatal diagnosis or lost a loved one," she says. "It's the same questions and feelings. *What's the point of it all? Who do I want to be in the time that I have left? What happens afterward?*"

She looks at the bubbles rising in her glass.

"But there's one important difference. And that's the fact that no one is alone in this. We're all affected. I think there's a comfort in that, too, even though it's difficult for most people to admit."

I have a vision of Lucinda's downy hair under her hat. I wonder what it's like to have been "the cancer girl" for so long and suddenly just be a person again. Everyone has the same death sentence now.

Is she afraid of dying, or is she used to the idea of it? Can you ever get used to it?

"Hunger is easier to endure if you don't have to see people stuffing themselves," Stina goes on. "At least this is . . . fair."

She starts talking about the final night. Stina is holding a service from midnight to when Foxworth smashes into us at four in the morning on September 16. She has to find the right words—the words people want to hear—while the minutes pass.

"So, no pressure, huh?" Emma says.

And I wonder how my sister's brain works. How does she

go from talking about the baby like it's actually being born to talking about our imminent death?

I reach for my phone on the windowsill, looking at a new photo Tilda's posted today, a close-up of her face. She's smiling wearily at the camera.

HI, LOVELIES. TAKING A BREAK FROM EVERYTHING FOR A WHILE, SO DON'T WORRY IF YOU DON'T HEAR FROM ME. GOT A LOT TO THINK ABOUT. SEE YOU SOON.

"Simon," Judette says. "Put that away, will you?"

"Okay."

But I look at the picture for a few more seconds. Hope flutters stubbornly inside me. Tilda wasn't at the party last night. Neither was Johannes. Amanda barely spoke to me. I don't know what's going on. But maybe it doesn't matter.

There is a possibility that I'm one of those things Tilda has to think about. Maybe she's realized that she misses me.

NAME: LUCINDA
TELLUS # 0 392 811 002
ENTRY 0010

Another thing, if I'm going to be honest: in my first post, I wrote that I felt relief, or something like relief, over Foxworth. I meant it then, but right now, I hate the person who wrote that post. I want to take it back, but it's already in the system. Has already been beamed into space. I hope you don't judge me too harshly.

The most difficult thing about being sick hasn't been the fear of death. It's been knowing how much I would miss out on. The Earth would keep spinning, the seasons would come and go.

Without me.

I wouldn't know what Miranda was like when she grew up. I wouldn't be there when she and Dad did things together; I wouldn't fall in love or hear new music or find out how my favorite TV shows end. And a small part of me—a small and revolting part of me—thought, *Now I won't miss out on anything. I'll see how it ends.*

So, yes. I felt a relief of sorts.

I might as well make another confession while I'm at it: I don't know what to do with myself. When I was sick, everything revolved around survival. Now I suddenly have to choose how to spend my last few weeks, and I have no idea. People keep talking about *seizing the day*. What a sick fucking requirement that is. Nothing gives me more anxiety. When I got cancer, I didn't miss adventures, or traveling, or things like that. I missed staying in bed all day, binge-watching movies. I even missed being bored. You have to feel pretty good to be bored.

And you have to assume you're going to be bored in the future, too.

Predictably, that whole *seize the day* thing blew up this summer. There's a Bucket List app that people connect to their social media. You can't travel particularly far anymore, or treat yourself to expensive things, or take a class—things people would have put on the list before. But my social media is filling up with messages like: *Elin Bergmark has completed two items on her Bucket List today: Write a poem about someone she likes and read it aloud to him/her! Tell someone she's in love with him/her!* People are dancing naked in the rain. Saying yes to everything for a whole day. Smashing electric guitars like rock stars. Asking people to punch them, just to find out how it feels.

There's a page called the FuckIt List, too. It isn't connected to social media, so fortunately, I don't have to find out when my relatives or old teachers attend their first swingers party.

NAME: LUCINDA
TELLUS # 0 392 811 002
POST 0011

I had a fight with Dad. I'm so angry I'm shaking. And it all started with *flower bulbs*.

This morning, our neighbor, Gill, came by in a gardening hat and muddy clothes, asking if we wanted some bulbs from her garden. She talked about the flowers she was planting, how beautiful they'd look come next spring.

Gill used to babysit Miranda and me when Mom died and Dad started working again. She was kind, but so unpredictable I could never relax around her. One moment, she'd be spoiling us with candy and taking us for rides, the next she'd be weeping into her coffee at some roadside café, loudly asking herself what would become of us without our mother. Now Gill is one of the comet deniers. Whenever Foxworth comes up, she chuckles indulgently and says, "Well, well. We'll see what happens when the sun rises on September sixteenth and nothing's happened."

Dad accepted the bulbs, listened patiently to Gill's instructions about light and shade and north and south. When she'd left, he said that he envied her.

He said that it must be nice to shut your eyes sometimes. He talked about the comet deniers as though they were harmless ostriches that should be left alone to stick their heads in the sand. But I'm so sick of them. They're idiots who are taking up way too much space in the media because "both sides need to be heard." But there aren't two sides to this. We're going to die. The deniers pollute social media with their high-handedness and contempt, raging over how messy the world's become since we fell for the "hoax." Today, I saw that some of them wanted to stop TellUs, because the transmissions could attract hostile aliens.

And now the deniers caused a fight between me and my dad. He said that there wasn't anything wrong with wanting to retain a bit of hope. But the deniers aren't hopeful. They're a pain in the ass. They're arrogant, and they can't be ignored. And they're not harmless. They're people who lie to themselves, who think everything is going to be fine, who won't help out during the current crisis.

That was when I brought up what things had been like at the beginning of the summer. So many people needed help. In this town alone, there were homeless men and women who couldn't get back to their families, and we had so much more than most. If Dad had done something those few days, while currency still mattered, we could have made a difference.

"Back then, we weren't even sure we'd get hit," Dad said.

"What were we going to do without money if the comet just harmlessly passed us by?" I exploded. I never said that we should give away *everything*, and he *knows* it. And I realized that I'd been angry at him all summer without having admitted it to myself.

We've avoided real arguments since I got sick. Today, it was as if everything came out at once. All my frustrations over a thousand things, both big and small. And I even used the most forbidden tactic: "What do you think Mom would say if she knew how selfish you're being?"

It was so manipulative of me. I don't actually know what Mom would have said. I was so little when she died.

Dad stormed out of the house, and the sound of the front door slamming shut behind him was the most satisfying thing I'd ever heard.

That feeling lasted for about five seconds. Then I noticed that my hands were trembling and I heard Miranda crying in her room. I still feel bad about it. For her, not Dad.

SIMON

This morning, Tilda sent me a koala emoji. I'm trying not to get my hopes up; maybe the koala doesn't mean anything in particular to her anymore. But I couldn't help asking Johannes if she'd said anything to Amanda about me. He replied that he had no idea. From the briefness of his message, I could tell he's getting sick of me, of this. And I get it. I'm so fucking sick of myself.

I put my elbows on the handle of the shopping cart and push, rolling away across the speckled tiles of the supermarket floor. I gaze over Swedish apples and carrots, bundles of celery and onions, plums and bags of spinach. The absence of prices on the signs still strikes me as weird.

Our planet is doing better than it has in a long time. We're no longer shipping food and other resources back and forth across the globe. Factories that gulped down energy and spewed out waste, like hundreds of thousands of Lucinda's pooping giants, have shut down. We've stopped flying and rarely drive, and we waste only a fraction of the electricity we used to.

If we'd lived like this before, we might even have saved the environment.

All it took was a comet.

Tilda said I spent too much time stressing out over things I couldn't change. I used to start every morning reaching for my phone and reading the news. And every morning, I hated myself for it. It was like drowning. It all seemed connected. One piece of bad news led to another—the apocalypse in slow motion.

Judette comes up to me and throws a jar of pickles and lingonberry jam in the cart. My eyes go to one of the lids, marked with an expiration date that will never come.

"They're almost out of tomatoes," I say.

"We only need potatoes. Stina is making steak this weekend."

"You mean a real Sunday dinner?"

Judette raises an eyebrow. "So? What's wrong with that?"

"There's nothing wrong with it, but she made it sound like ... I don't know. We've never had that before, have we?"

Judette sighs. Suddenly, I can tell just how tired she is. Last night, I overheard her crying in the bathroom.

"You could cut Stina some slack, you know," she says. "She's really trying."

"I know."

I lean over the handle again and roll away. Why don't I cut Stina some slack? Why do her efforts make me so uncomfortable? The answer might be obvious. They say we're always bothered by people who remind us of the things we don't like about ourselves.

I wait until Judette catches up with me, carrying a bag of potatoes in her arms like a baby. We walk past the meat section, which looks unchanged. I wonder who spends their final weeks volunteering at a slaughterhouse. The dairy section is well stocked, too, even though the cartons look different, and there's less of a selection than there used to be.

We grab flour and oil off the shelves. There are hardly any brands I recognize left. The government-issue packages simply state what's inside. Dark green text, white background. No photos of billowing rapeseed fields, no drawings of ears of wheat stretching toward the sky.

"What's wrong with Emma?" I say, and jump onto the cart again. "I thought it would pass."

Judette grabs the handle. "I'm in charge of this now."

"But seriously. She's acting like the baby's really coming."

"So what?" Judette says, and takes hold of the shopping cart.

"She's sick."

"Or she's healthier than any of us."

"But she's lying to herself! And how can Micke stand it? It would have been his kid, too."

We stop by the canned goods. Judette turns toward me, appearing to consider something.

"Maybe he can't," she says.

"Can't what?"

"Stand it. It seems like he might be staying in Överkalix."

My shock must be written all over my face, because Judette's features soften.

"How do you know?" I ask her.

"We talked to him this morning. Emma doesn't know."

"But then ... maybe he'd come back if Emma didn't act so ..."

Judette puts a hand on my shoulder. "We think the best

we can do for Emma right now is to let her keep her fantasies. Do you think you can do that?"

I nod. If Micke isn't coming back, Emma has to stay with us until the end.

We walk to the registers in silence, joining the line for the self-service machines. When it's our turn, I scan and bag the food while Judette pays with the rationing app.

"I saw your Virgin Mary," I say as we walk out of the supermarket. "Did you bring it from Dominica?"

Judette gives me a surprised look.

"Yes. I found her in a box when I moved and, I don't know, it felt like a sign or something."

She opens the trunk of her Toyota. I put the bags in and think about the apartment she lived in for only a few months before moving back home again. It was nice, but impersonal. Most of the furniture had been bought somewhat hastily at Ikea. It's all there, including the TV where we saw the prime minister announce the inevitable at a press conference.

Back then, we'd had three and a half months left. Now it's less than four weeks.

I look at Judette and decide to ask her straight-out for the first time.

"Are you afraid?"

"At least it will be quick," she says, and shuts the trunk.

"Great."

Judette smiles sadly, then gives me a quick hug and kisses me on the cheek.

"Do you want to talk about it?" she asks.

"No."

"Me, neither."

We get in the car, and I think about how *at least it will be quick* has become a mantra people cling to. Suddenly, every-one's sharing links about the old asteroid, AJ129, bigger than a skyscraper but significantly smaller than Foxworth. In cosmic terms, it brushed past us in February 2018. Hardly any newspapers mentioned it. But for a few days this sum-mer, AJ129 became something of an obsession. If we'd been hit by that instead, a few billion people would have been killed instantly, but the rest of us would have died slowly, gradually, in a dystopia. Ash would have covered the planet and obscured the sun. Foxworth is better that way. *At least it will be quick.*

Our seat belts swoosh as we pull them on. Judette squints against the light and folds down the sun visor.

We drive out of the parking lot and she turns on the an-cient car radio, trying to find a news broadcast. I gaze out the window. The town has been calm since the soccer game, but there's still trash strewn across the streets. Over the speakers, voices break through the static and disappear again. Judette gives up and turns the radio off as we reach the highway. From the corner of my eye, I catch her looking at me.

"Tilda's mom is worried about her," she says. "You don't know where she is, do you?"

"You've met with Caroline?" I say, and turn to look at her.

"No. Maria told me about it."

"Which Maria?"

"The officer who drove you home from the pool," Judette says, her face blank.

I turn to face the road again.

"Oh."

"She asked me to ask you. Tilda hasn't been back home since the game."

"Caroline doesn't have to worry. Tilda's been texting."

"But you don't know where she is?"

"No, I have no idea."

"Just promise me you'll let me know if you hear anything," Judette says. "I know you want to be loyal to Tilda, but I'm thinking about her parents. I'd lose my mind if you disappeared."

"But I'm right here."

"You better be."

Judette starts humming something, tapping her fingers against the steering wheel. I look up Tilda's selfie, trying to shake the growing feeling that something is wrong, but I can't quite manage it. The selfie is still the most recently posted picture. Light falls across the right side of her face. The background is barely visible, just a blur. I zoom in, but the effect doesn't exactly make things clearer. And yet. That could be the pattern on the wallpaper in Tilda's room. And the light, slanting in like that, could be coming from her window. But if she's at home, Caroline ought to know. Right?

Stop it, I tell myself. *There's nothing weird about it. She just posted an old picture.*

I skim the comments. Spot one from Caroline: *Answer your phone, sweetie.* Klas has written, too. *Get in touch with me or your mom. We're worried.* I keep reading. See a comment from Amanda. *Where are you?*

I call Tilda, but it goes straight to voice mail. "You know who you've called and what to do."

I don't leave a message.

"What's up?" Judette asks as we turn onto our street.

"I'm just thinking."

If you don't leave me alone, I'll scream.

I shouldn't have let her go.

You don't get it. There's only one person who could.

I suddenly realize who Tilda might have been talking about. Is that where she was going that night?

NAME: LUCINDA
TELLUS # 0 392 811 002
POST 0012

Simon just called and asked me if I've met up with Tilda. I've seen her post about taking a break for a few days, but apparently no one knows where she is. I couldn't understand why Simon contacted *me* of all people.

Simon said that the last time he saw Tilda was after the game. She was on her way to talk to someone. She'd said there was only one person who could understand what she was going through.

Simon thought she meant me. He told me that the whole time they were together, she missed me.

It made me so happy.

I've written her a message for the first time since I cut her off. There's less than four weeks to go. I can't keep wondering if she'll forgive me. I simply have to find out.

It took me almost an hour to piece together two sentences. In that time, I can write an entire post to an unknown alien; it's harder to find the right words to say to my best friend. Are you curious about the amazing result? Here you go.

I miss you. Can we meet up?

And now I'm sitting here, staring at my phone.

P.S.: In other news, I'm still fighting with Dad.

SIMON

A heavy rain pounds against the window behind me. We're sitting in the kitchen, going through an old photo album Emma brought with her. Stina is overjoyed. This is exactly what she's spent all summer dreaming we would do. Personally, I'm grateful for the distraction from the fact that Tilda isn't the only one who's disappeared without a trace. Today, no one I know is replying to my messages.

The spiral-bound album creaks as Emma turns the page. Most of the photos are new to me. They're from Stina's previous life, when she was married to Emma's dad. Judette hadn't moved to Sweden yet. My arrival was still years away. Stina's hair is long and fluffy, her lips crimson, her outfits all neat little blouses and jackets. She's almost impossible to recognize.

"How can you look older twenty-five years ago?" I say, and start laughing at a picture from Emma's christening.

"That used to be in style," Stina says with a giggle.

"Looking like an old lady?"

"Just wait until you're the one seeing old pictures of yourself. One day, you'll—"

She cuts herself off. Her eyes dart around nervously. I smile to show her it's okay.

We look at the howling, bright red creature in Stina's arms. The christening gown almost reaches the floor. Emma's dad is wearing a suit several sizes too big. I've never met him.

A few years after the christening, he already had a new family. He moved to another city and vanished. Emma's always said it doesn't bother her. I don't know if I believe her. All I know is that if I ever had kids, I'd never throw them aside like that.

Emma turns the page again. The photographs are glued to stiff black paper. Here and there, Stina has written cheery rhymes in silver ink. There are a lot of exclamation points.

Noisy daughter in the water!

Cauliflower mess = success!

"I was really ugly," Emma says.

"There's no such thing as an ugly baby," Stina scolds automatically.

We look at her. She grins, then points to a picture where Emma is lying on her stomach on the changing table, looking like a tiny, cross-eyed old man.

"I was slightly worried for a few weeks, sure," Stina says. "But you turned out all right. You had character."

Emma rolls her eyes. "That's exactly what people say about ugly babies."

We continue flipping through the album to a photograph where Emma is in the arms of Grandpa. He looks kind, large, and fat, with a huge smile framed by a beard that reminds me of small yellow eggs in a bird's nest. But he wasn't kind. I hated him for how he treated the moms.

Grandpa rocks my socks!

"That onesie is nice, though," Emma says. "Do you still have that lying around somewhere?"

"I don't know. It might still be in the attic."

"Why don't we go through my old baby clothes while I'm here? You can't buy anything anymore."

I look up at Stina. For a moment, the kitchen is so quiet I can hear Boomer's soft snores from the living room.

"Sure," Stina says. "All the better if they're used."

The sound of the doorbell slices through the apartment. I hear Boomer's paws slide over the hardwood floor as he gets up, thundering toward the hallway, howling in that shrill, singing way that means he's excited.

"Is anyone expecting a visitor?" Stina asks as she gets to her feet.

Emma and I both say no. We stay seated, listening as the front door opens. I hear a voice I can't place. It's a woman, but I can't make out the words. They are drowned out by Boomer's howls and Stina's attempts to hush him.

"Do you think it's someone from the church?" Emma whispers. "I hope she puts her foot down if they start showing up here, too."

We hear the squeaking of hangers against steel as someone places a coat on the rack. When Stina returns to the kitchen, I look down at the album again.

A happy girl in Teletubby world!

It doesn't even rhyme.

"Simon?"

Stina's voice sounds stiff and strange. It takes me a few seconds to recognize the woman who's followed her into the kitchen. She's not wearing her uniform tonight, having replaced it with jeans and a thin jacket over a T-shirt.

Maria, the hockey-playing police officer.

"Hi, Simon," she says. "How are you doing?"

"Better than last time."

Maria smiles, but it doesn't reach her eyes.

"She's here to ask us a few questions about Tilda," Stina says. "Why don't you go into the living room while I make some coffee?"

"Okay," I say, and get up.

I try to ignore the pounding of my heart. I already know Caroline has spoken to Maria about Tilda. That's why Maria is here now. There's nothing to worry about. I know that Tilda's okay.

Don't I?

Emma starts following us into the living room, but Stina tells her to go to her room.

My fingertips prickle like pins and needles.

Maria and I sit facing each other on the sofas. She looks around.

"Judette is at a friend's house," I say.

Maria nods.

"You have a lovely home," she says.

"Thank you."

"It's hard to believe that this used to be a working-class neighborhood. And now it's one of the nicest parts of town."

A sharp undertone. Is she jealous? Judging?

"Stina's had the place for a long time," I say.

The coffee maker gurgles from the kitchen.

"Is plain filter coffee all right?" Stina calls.

"Of course. Plain old cop's coffee for me," Maria calls back.

Stina laughs dutifully. I rub my fingers together to bring them to life.

I picture Tilda's back in front of me. How she turns around before she leaves.

"Would you mind waiting for me?" Stina shouts.

"Not at all!"

Maria looks at me again. She puts her elbows on her knees and folds her hands together. Her nails are short and manicured. Time stretches as she studies me. She's trying to read me. I don't know if I should look away or return her stare. Suddenly, doing the right thing feels crucial.

But I don't know what the right thing to do is. She has the upper hand. She's the one who knows what this is all about.

Finally, I hear the clatter of cupboards, the clink of china.

"How did you you hurt yourself?" Maria says.

My hand automatically goes to my face, to the crusty scab.

"Someone headbutted me during the game."

Maria's face is neutral.

"Not on purpose," I add.

"I understand. It was a pretty wild night."

She takes out a small notepad and a pen from the inner pocket of her jacket and flips to a clean page.

"Were you there?"

"I picked a few people up in the van."

Maria writes something in the pad, and I think about the police officers pouring out of the car to stop the fighting.

Boomer shuffles into the living room and stops in front of Maria. She bends down and scratches him on the back, down toward the base of his tail. When she pulls away, he turns his head and looks demandingly at her, wanting more.

"That's exactly where he likes to be scratched," I say. "You must be used to dogs."

"I'm crazy about them."

This time, Maria's smile is genuine. Boomer gives in, collapsing at her feet with a huff.

Stina enters and puts a tray on the table. She hands out cups and pours coffee from the pot before sinking down next to me on the sofa.

"Nice coffee," Maria says after a quick sip.

"Thank you," Stina says, and looks down at Boomer, who lazily wags his tail. "This is about Tilda, right?"

"Yes, exactly," Maria says, and turns to me, tapping her pen against the pad. "When did you last see her?"

"After the game. In the square."

"Have you heard from her since?"

I nod. Maria takes another sip of her coffee. Stina and I still haven't touched our cups.

"In what way?"

I don't quite understand the question. My brain has gone strangely sluggish.

"What do you mean?"

"Well, have you spoken on the phone, for instance? Or have you texted, stuff like that?"

"Oh, I see. No, we haven't spoken."

Maria's pen moves across the pad. The paper rustles when she turns to a fresh page.

"Could I have a look at your messages?" she asks without looking up. Stina shifts in her seat.

"Is that really necessary?" she says. "I'm sure you wouldn't want people to read what you'd written to an ex." Her voice is calm and friendly. It's her priest voice.

"No, of course I wouldn't." Maria smiles. "But it would be helpful."

I glance at Stina, who gives me a brief nod. I lean back in the sofa so I can get my phone out of the pocket of my jeans. It's warm in my hand when I unlock it.

"Here," I say, and glance at the two koalas before I hand her the phone over the table.

The screen lights up Maria's face from below, tinting it blue and turning it shadowy. Her index finger moves quickly, and I realize she's scrolling backward, reading my pathetic, drunken rants, my pleas.

"Could I borrow this for a while?" she asks, again without looking up.

"I'd rather you didn't."

"I understand," Maria says, and smiles again. "I couldn't get by without my phone. When Stina and I were young, only yuppies had them."

"Why do you need his phone?" Stina says.

"I can take screenshots instead. Is that okay?"

It doesn't sound like a question. I nod reluctantly. If I refuse, she might change her mind and take the phone anyway.

"I just don't understand why," I say.

A click from the camera. Two. Three. Pause. Four. Then I hear a message being sent from my phone before Maria hands it back to me.

"Thanks," she says. "Now you've got my number, in case you need to get in touch."

She hits the pad with her pen again, looking thoughtful. I get the vague feeling she's acting—that she knows exactly what her next question is going to be.

"Simon, do you know where Tilda is?" she finally says.

"No."

"Are you sure?"

"*Maria*," Stina says, sounding almost amused. "If you want to have this conversation, you're going to have to trust him to tell the truth."

Maria looks apologetic. "I just want to emphasize that this is serious. If you know anything, you need to tell us."

"I don't know where she is," I say, trying to sound calm. "If anyone does, it'd be Amanda or Elin."

Maria watches me silently. She doesn't write their names down on the pad.

Does she already know who they are? Has she spoken to them?

"The last time you saw Tilda was after the game," Maria says. "How did she seem to you?"

I hesitate, searching for the right words.

"She was pretty angry and upset . . . She'd been partying," I say after a moment. "I guess we all had."

"You went to a party together?"

"No. We met there. In the center of town, I mean. I don't know where she'd spent the evening."

"So you met during the game?"

"It had just finished."

"And *that* had happened by then?" Maria says, pointing at my eyebrow with her pen.

"Yes."

"And who did you say headbutted you?"

"I didn't say. I mean, I don't know. I didn't see who it was. It was a mess."

Maria nods. The pen scratches loudly against the pad.

"Then what happened?"

"We helped each other get away from the square."

"You said she was angry and upset. Had something happened?"

"I don't really know. She said people were hypocrites."

Maria looks up from her notepad. "What do you think she meant by that?"

I glance at Stina. "Tilda was . . . she partied a lot and . . . there were rumors."

"About what?" Maria asks. "Drugs? Sex?"

I shrug.

"Was there any truth to those rumors?"

A vision of Tilda's glassy eyes.

One hundred percent fucked up.

I don't want to land her in trouble when she gets back.

But should I tell the truth? Maybe someone can help her.

"Simon?" Maria says.

Tilda would never forgive me.

"I don't know," I say.

"Did she think you were a hypocrite, too?"

Did she? Am I?

Shut up, Simon. You're not exactly a saint yourself nowadays.

"I don't know," I say again.

"Why are you asking him these questions?" Stina says. "It's their business, isn't it?"

"We've been told Simon and Tilda had a fight in the square. Some people tried to intervene."

Stina turns to me on the sofa. For the first time, I can tell that she's worried.

The prickling in my fingers spreads to my arms.

"Some guys came up to us," I say.

Is everything okay? You can tell us. We'll protect you.

"I don't know who they were," I continue. "They were wearing identical windbreakers. Black."

Anger gleams in Stina's eyes when she turns back to Maria.

"You know as well as I do that those pathetic citizen militias have an agenda."

"Yes," Maria says quickly. "I'm not a fan. I just have to follow up on what they've told us."

She looks at me. Brushes some dog hairs off her jacket.

"They claim you pulled her arm."

"I didn't want her to walk away alone. There was so much going on downtown and she was ... she was pretty wasted."

"I understand," Maria says. "Then what happened?"

"We walked into that side street, what's it called . . . toward the tracks?"

"Gamla kvarngatan?"

"Yeah. We met some friends there. Elin and Amanda, who I told you about. And Ali and Hampus. They wanted us to go to Ali's for an after-party."

"So did you?"

"I went there by myself later on."

"After you and Tilda had parted ways?"

I nod.

"Where was she going?"

"I don't know. She said she wanted to talk to someone, but she didn't say who."

"And you have no idea who she could have meant?"

"No."

Maria studies me, and I suddenly realize that she doesn't believe me.

She knows something I don't.

I'm afraid now. Really afraid.

"When did you arrive at the after-party?"

"I don't know what time it was. I walked around for a while. Just to clear my head."

"Did you meet anyone you knew on the way there?"

I shake my head.

I need to get hold of Tilda. She has to say that she's okay, that she was fine when she left me.

"What were you arguing about at the pool party?"

"Arguing?"

"Yes. You told her she'd be sorry. When you were talking to each other in the changing room. Remember?"

"Yeah. But I didn't mean it like that, that she'd be sorry. It was more . . . I meant that she . . ."

The skin on my back starts crawling when I realize that Maria and her colleague weren't in the changing room at that point.

But Elin and Amanda were.

Have they spoken to Maria already?

Is that why no one has responded to my messages all day?

My mind is racing, and I can't steady myself.

Stina puts an arm around my back. It feels too heavy. Makes it harder to breathe. I twist away.

"I was talking about the comet," I manage. "I meant that she'd be sorry if she didn't give us another chance before . . . before it was too late. No one wants to be alone when the world ends, do they?"

It feels like I'm making things worse. Something shifts in the room.

My palms are sticky with sweat. I feel a desperate urge to wash my hands.

"I was drunk," I say. "I didn't know what I was saying."

"Were you angry with her for leaving you?"

"No. I was sad. I missed her."

"Missed her? You don't miss her now?"

My mind is racing.

"Simon is talking about how he felt back then," Stina says coolly. "Since that's what you were asking about."

"She was seeing other guys," Maria continues without taking her eyes off me. "Didn't that upset you?"

I automatically shake my head.

"Not even when you caught her with another guy in the pool?"

"How do you know about that?" I say before I can stop myself.

Maria doesn't respond. But now I know that she's spoken to our friends. Who? And what have they said?

What do they think?

What do people think I'm capable of?

"It sounds like you've had a hard time accepting that it was over," Maria says.

"That's hardly unusual," Stina interjects. "We've all had our hearts broken, haven't we?"

"Of course."

"I think it would be better if you leave," Stina says, and gets to her feet. "You should be out looking for Tilda."

Maria's polite smile is tense. I can tell she's come to some decision.

And suddenly, I *know*. But it's impossible. It doesn't fit.

I want to run away before she says it out loud. As long as I don't hear the words, I can pretend that nothing's wrong.

Afterward, it's going to be too late.

Maria opens her mouth. My whole body tenses, ready to flee. But I stay seated.

NAME: LUCINDA
TELLUS # 0 392 811 002
POST 0013

D ad came home from the hospital and told me.
She's dead.

Tilda is dead.

I'm staring at the words, and still can't understand them.

SIMON

W e found Tilda's body this morning," Maria says.

"Oh my God." Stina sinks back down next to me on the sofa. "Oh my *God*."

I can't speak. I'm frozen. Even my chest is still. The seconds tick away. It's like my body has forgotten how to breathe.

"Where did you find her?" Stina asks.

I try to force air into my lungs. Every breath requires effort.

"Someone left Tilda's body behind the old glass factory over on North," Maria says. "We don't know if that's where she died."

North Gate—the old industrial park on the other side of the highway. The glass factory is a large box covered in blue corrugated metal. It's surrounded by stores selling kitchen tiles and cars, a printer's, a gas station that shut down long before this summer. No one lives there. Hardly anyone passes through it. It's the perfect place to hide a body.

I hear Stina ask Maria why we weren't told at once. I hear Maria reply that she wanted to hear what I had to say first. Their voices sound faint. My thoughts drown them out.

Someone left Tilda behind the glass factory.

Someone left her there.

Were her eyes open or closed?

Don't think about that. Don't think at all.

"Do you want to change any of your statement, Simon?"

"No," I say, but it comes out like a whisper.

Stina takes my hand. Squeezes it tightly.

"As I'm sure you understand, getting hold of a medical examiner isn't easy," Maria says. "An ordinary doctor has examined her and determined that she's been dead since the night of the game. She's still wearing the same clothes."

Relief pours through my body, releasing it from its paralysis.

"Then it can't be her," I say.

"What do you mean?" Maria asks, and I almost want to laugh.

"You saw it yourself. She wrote to me yesterday."

The koalas. Our koalas.

"You saw our messages," I continue eagerly. "She's been in touch with other people, too. It can't be her."

What kind of useless police officer doesn't get it? Why do I have to be the one to explain everything? Why is she subjecting us to this for *no reason* when—

"We know we've found Tilda." Maria's words slow and clear. "She didn't have her phone on her. Someone else has been using it to text you and her friends."

"But it has to be her. That koala at the end, that was our thing," I say, and hear how insignificant and silly it sounds.

How could Maria understand the history behind that emoji?

"I understand that it's difficult to take in," she says. "But it would be easy to go through her old messages and figure out how to imitate her."

I shake my head. Start to feel desperate. "Tilda always locks her phone," I explain. "She's really careful about it."

"She unlocked it with a thumbprint, is that right?"

Maria waits. After a beat, it begins to sink in.

Someone took Tilda's dead hand, pressed her thumb

against the screen, and then changed her password. So simple.

My thoughts start racing again. Way too quickly, now. My brain feels electric.

That image of Tilda's dead hand finally makes my brain process it.

She's gone.

The whooshing in my ears turns to a roar, then fades to little more than a whisper.

Pulse. I still have a pulse. Tilda doesn't.

"Then you know it wasn't Simon," Stina says. "He received messages from Tilda's phone."

Maria looks at me. Seeing if I understand why it doesn't exonerate me. And I do understand.

"If I'd been the murderer, I would have just sent messages to myself so I could show them to you later. Right?"

Maria's face is blank.

"That's what you're thinking?" Stina asks her.

"First of all, we don't know if it's a murder. Tilda was killed by a blow to the back of the head."

The back of the head.

I see Tilda's neck before me, her thick hair. It must have been soaked with blood.

It turns my stomach. My mouth fills with cold metallic saliva. I swallow hard.

"It could have been an accident," Maria continues. "Or manslaughter. There's nothing to suggest it was premeditated."

She watches me carefully. I realize that she's trying to make it easier for me to confess.

Murder or manslaughter, what does it even matter? And even if it was an accident, someone placed Tilda in North Gate. Someone didn't want her to be found.

"I shouldn't have let her go." My voice cracks like I'm going through puberty again.

"Is this an interrogation?" Stina asks.

"Not officially," Maria says.

"So what is it?"

I look at Stina. If this were an American television show, we would have demanded to speak to a lawyer by this point. But this is real life. And in this reality, there are no lawyers to call.

Maria sighs. "You know our situation. We won't be able to investigate this properly. I just wanted to find out more. For the family's sake. And Simon happens to be the last person seen with Tilda."

Stina glances at me. Is there a hint of uncertainty in her eyes?

Mom. You can't think it was me. It wasn't me.

"Simon," Maria says. "Could I take a look in your room?"

I nod, exhausted. I just want this to be over with.

"No, Maria," Stina says. "That's enough. I'd like you to leave now."

"Mom, it's okay."

"No, it isn't," she says firmly.

Maria gets to her feet. Boomer raises his head to look at her.

"I really am sorry," she says.

It's directed more at Stina than at me. But Stina doesn't respond. She just puts her arm around me again, and this time, I let her.

Boomer struggles to his feet and shuffles after Maria into the hallway.

I hear the coat being pulled from the hanger again. The door opens and closes. Then I hear the footsteps in the stairwell. Boomer remains standing in the hallway, panting.

Suddenly, I remember Tilda's eerie, singsong statement—*Something terrible is going to happen tonight*—and goose bumps spread across my arms.

NAME: LUCINDA
TELLUS # 0 392 811 002
POST 0014

Now that it's too late, I realize how much I've missed her. I've missed her all along. And somewhere, somehow, I've always thought we would find our way back to each other again.

I dreamed about her last night. She was waiting for me in the bleachers by the pool. We were the only people there. Everything was dark except the water. Outside the windows, night had fallen. Her face was still marked by her swimming goggles. In the dream, I knew she was dead, but it didn't matter. I was thrilled to see her.

Everything was quiet. The only sound was the water lapping at the pool's edge. Even the clock on the wall had stopped. Tilda hugged me. Her cold, wet body pressed against mine, and she held me so tightly the air was squeezed out of my lungs.

She exhaled with me. Nodded once. And then we fell into the water. She wrapped her legs around me when I landed on the pool's floor, keeping me close. I wasn't scared. Not until I woke up.

The day has felt unreal. All my movements have slowed down, as if I'm still underwater.

Was she heading to my house when she died? In that case, what did she want from me?

If we'd still been friends, she might not have been out that night. She might still be alive. I can't stop thinking about it.

Dad stayed home from work today. He knows the doctor who examined Tilda. She died of a fractured skull. She doesn't appear to have been raped. That should be a consolation. That she didn't have to endure that, too.

I tried to find out more, but in the end, Dad asked me to stop. That's when I noticed he was crying.

I haven't cried yet. I haven't quite grasped that by the time I'd sent her that message, Tilda was already dead.

SIMON

I lie perfectly still in my bed. I've only been up once to go to the bathroom. I haven't been hungry or thirsty. I just drift in and out of sleep.

I don't want to be in a world without Tilda. I just want to stay in this increasingly unreal state.

Occasionally, I take out my phone to read what people have written about her.

> Thinking of you and your family.
> Heaven has gotten a perfect angel.
> See you soon, sweetie.

Poems and song lyrics. Broken-heart emojis. And pictures. Loads of pictures. In the afternoon, new kinds of comments start making an appearance.

Sad, yeah, but not totally unexpected.
tilda wasn't doing well, she's been out of control for a while.

As if Tilda brought it on herself. And worse, they're trying to veil their judgment with concern.

I write to our friends. Johannes is the only one who replies. He promises to come by tomorrow. No one else bothers to get in touch. But I can still see all of them commenting on social media.

They must have seen my messages.

I fall asleep, but wake up when Judette knocks on the door and places a sandwich and a cup of tea on the bedside table. She lays her cool hand against my cheek.

"It feels like you have a fever," she says.

Roaring voices wake me up later. The room's dark. Through the window, I can see it's already evening. I fumble along the lamp's cord until I find the switch. New howls— an infernal chorus—and I remember: there's a game to-night. The second semifinal. The voices are coming from the apartment beneath ours. I turn the lights off, put my headphones on, and find a playlist on my phone, raising the volume until my ears hurt. It doesn't help. I can still hear the voices, real and imagined.

The light from the screen hurts my eyes when I read the new comments on Tilda's last selfie.

It must have been the ex, he was totally obsessed with her.

I feel cold. I click the unknown account, but it's locked, so I return to the picture and read the replies:

He always seemed weird.

This from a girl who just started the ninth grade the other week. She was also on the swim team.

Simon would never do something like that.

Johannes is defending me. The person who wrote the original comment replies.

Not like you're biased, he's just your best friend.

My heart is beating so hard, I don't think I'll be able to fall asleep again, but I startle awake when the music suddenly goes quiet. I check my phone again. The battery is dead. Light's coming in through the window, and the bed is way too hot. I take my headphones off and turn around, jumping when I see Stina lying next to me, one cheek pressed into the pillow, her glasses crooked.

The heat is making me claustrophobic. I tear the covers off, accidentally waking Stina up. She casts a confused look around the room.

"I must have fallen asleep," she says, rubbing her eyes.

"Aren't you supposed to be working tonight?"

"I took the evening off. I was hoping we could talk about what happened." She straightens her glasses.

What would I have done if she hadn't been there when Maria came knocking?

I suddenly want to talk to her. I *need* to talk to her.

"Do you think I did it?" I hear myself say.

Stina blinks. Props herself up on her elbow.

"Absolutely not," she says emphatically, and it's a relief to hear her sound so certain. "A lot of things were going on that night. Tilda was just in the wrong place at the wrong time."

"Maybe," I say.

But I know she was heading somewhere. She was going to talk to someone.

Who was it? I have no clue. I know so little of what Tilda's been up to this summer, who she's spent time with. And all our mutual friends were already at the after-party at Ali's place when I got there.

"Simon. You know you can talk to us about anything, right?"

"Sure."

Stina perches on the edge of the bed and takes my hand. I can tell that she's unsure about how to put whatever she's going to say next into words, but that she needs to get it off her chest.

Don't say anything, I think. *I* want *to talk about Tilda, but I don't know how to begin. Just give me some time. Please.*

Stina clears her throat and I know it's too late.

"You know we love you unconditionally," she says. "Even if you did this. We're going to solve this together."

I yank my hand back.

"I don't think you *did* do it," Stina adds quickly. "I just want you to know that *if* you had, we'd—"

"Go away," I say, and turn to face the wall.

always seemed weird

he was totally obsessed with her

"Go away!"

"We have to talk about this," Stina says.

"Tilda is dead. It doesn't matter if we talk. She's still not coming back."

The sound of our breathing fills the room.

"I'm so fucking sick of this," Stina says at last. "Half the town comes to my church for help, but my own son doesn't even want to . . ."

Her voice grows quiet. She's crying now. Part of me aches with guilt. Another part of me hates her for staying here and feeling sorry for herself. This isn't about her.

But both parts agree on one thing: I can't deal with this scene right now. I just want to lie here until it's all over. And I do mean *over*.

Let the fucking comet come.

"Mom," I say. "Can you leave? Please?"

She sniffles wetly and gets up, but stays standing on the floor next to the bed.

Leave. Leave. Leave.

The door shuts behind her quietly. I'm finally alone.

NAME: LUCINDA
TELLUS # 0 392 811 002
POST 0015

I read comments and posts all day and can't recognize the Tilda being described—someone out of control, someone wild, someone lost. The fact that she was taking drugs seems widely known, even though it's only there between the lines.

How is that possible? I know people do what they can to deal with the idea of Foxworth. But *Tilda*?

I scroll through her social media. Look at photographs from the summer. Am I imagining things, or can I see it in her eyes? I look at the people around her and wonder if one of them killed her.

More and more comments about Simon start popping up. Apparently, he was "obsessed with her." People saw them arguing in the square after the soccer game and at the pool party. I study photos taken there, but can't come up with any answers.

I keep returning to her profile picture. It was taken just as she turned toward the camera. Her hair fans across half her face, but you can tell by her eyes that she's smiling.

Tilda's death is exactly the sort of case the newspapers would have loved to write about before the comet: A beautiful teenage girl. Good grades. An ambitious athlete. Well-liked by everyone who knew her. But most importantly, young and lovely. With long hair. Neat, clean, from a good family. Found in a dirty and deserted industrial park.

And then the secrets would be exposed: The drugs. The parties. She'd be made to seem weak, be cast as a victim, even in life.

People would have loved it. We love beautiful dead girls. We get our kicks hearing the gory details. We make movies and television shows about them, write books and articles about them. We want to see them raped and brutally murdered. We let them be discovered naked, posed as if in a perfume ad. Cut to a medical examiner who nonchalantly eats his sandwich while leaning over a body that's become a cold slab of meat in a morgue. Cut to a flashback scene in which we see the victim alive, sexy, unaware of her imminent demise.

But nowadays, a case like Tilda's doesn't get attention outside the social media circuit. We have to get our kicks there instead. People try to make Tilda out to be either an innocent angel or a bad girl who was doomed from the start.

I hope Simon didn't do it. I don't want to believe that, in her last moments, Tilda knew her murderer was someone she loved, or had loved, once.

Thinking about that day on the swimming dock or about the times they visited me at the hospital, I find it hard to believe Simon is responsible. He loved Tilda. I know that. Not that that means anything. I know what the statistics look like: the attacker is rarely a random stranger jumping out from behind a bush. That's just what we like to think. Those are the stories we tell one another, again and again, to forget the fact that we're most at risk in our own homes. But the night Tilda died was the night of the game: people had let go of their inhibitions; they had nothing to lose. Tilda being killed might just have been a coincidence. Besides, if Simon had murdered her, would he have called me and asked me if Tilda had been in touch?

It occurs to me that Simon had a cut over his eyebrow when we met on the dock.

Had Tilda tried to fight him off?

I don't know anything. And I might never know.

I'm not sure how I'm supposed to live with that.

SIMON

I've spent all summer running away from thinking about death. Now, there's no place left to run. Not even sleep is a safe, because I keep dreaming about Tilda—her dead body, the eyes that were either open or closed. I dream about a sky roiling with fire. When I wake up, my heart beats so hard against the mattress that I have to roll onto my back to breathe.

More and more people are posting pictures of Tilda. More and more of the comments are about me. Elin writes that nine times out of ten, it's the boyfriend. Moa writes, *hmmm he arrived p late to the afterparty*, with an emoji scratching its chin. Amanda has liked both comments.

My moms come in with plates of food I can't bring myself to eat.

Emma stands in the doorway with her laptop in her arms and suggests watching a movie together. I pass. I only want to talk to Johannes. He's coming by at seven. Just a couple of hours left.

Boomer pushes past Emma, approaches the bed, and wags his tail. Whines softly.

"Do you want me to take him?" Emma asks.

"It's fine. Can you close the door behind you?"

I scooch closer to the wall and call Boomer to hop up onto the bed. He tilts his head, clearly wondering if this is some kind of trick. The bed is usually out of bounds. I pat the mattress next to me.

"Come on. Come here."

Boomer gathers himself for a leap, then climbs rather than jumps onto the bed. He's still energetic, but sometimes his age catches up with him. He spins around on the mattress, his large paws heavy on my chest, his tail brushing against my face, until he's comfortably curled up in the sheets.

In the street, someone screams. My panic goes from zero to a hundred before the scream turns into laughter. I hear glass breaking against the pavement and wonder if Tilda tried to scream for help.

Boomer isn't worried about whatever's happening outside the apartment. Soon, my body is vibrating with his snores. When I was little, I used to get up early and fall asleep next to him on the floor. Now, I try to match his breathing.

A cool breeze wakes me up. Boomer has abandoned me and the bed. It looks like someone's left the window slightly ajar. A silhouette is visible against the faint glow from the streetlights outside. For a second, I wonder if someone's climbed through the window.

"How are you?" the silhouette says.

Johannes.

"What time is it?" I ask.

My mouth is so dry that my tongue feels sticky.

"It's almost midnight. Sorry I'm late."

He sits down at the foot of the bed. I fumble for the bed-side lamp's cord.

"Don't turn it on," he says.

"Okay."

I drag myself into a sitting position. The cold wind caresses my arms. It's the end of August, but I've lost track of how many days we have left.

"Can you close the window?" I ask.

"I think this room could use some fresh air."

I can hear the smile in his voice. He fumbles along the covers. His fingers briefly brush against my hand as he takes my phone.

"You need to stop looking at that thing. It's self-harm."

"It's better than not knowing what they're writing about me."

Johannes hands me a glass that someone has left on my bedside table. The water is surprisingly cold, and my mind clears a little with each sip. "I don't know what to say, except I'm so fucking sorry. I can't believe she's gone," he says when I've put aside the empty glass.

Gone. It feels more real now that Johannes is here. He's a link to the best part of my life with Tilda. She and I, Johannes and Amanda, did almost everything together. Me, the guy who'd never really fit in anywhere, suddenly belonged.

I wasn't just in love with Tilda; I was in love with my life with her. I couldn't understand what she saw in me. I couldn't believe I'd been so lucky.

"Does everyone think I did it?" I say.

"No. *I* don't think you did it."

Johannes places a hand on my knee. I can feel the warmth of it through the covers. For some reason, that gentle touch is enough to make me cry.

"I shouldn't have let her walk away alone," I say.

"It wasn't your fault."

"I couldn't . . . She didn't want to stay with me," I go on, and I no longer know if I'm talking about that night or the entire summer. "If I hadn't begged, if I hadn't been so pathetic, she might have—"

"Of course you were pathetic," Johannes cuts in. "You loved her. Plus, the world is ending. You didn't exactly have time to play hard to get."

I laugh, snot spraying over half my face. I'm grateful it's so dark in here.

"They know me," I say. "How the hell can they think I'd kill Tilda?"

Johannes waits a long moment before answering me.

"It's got nothing to do with you," he says at last. "It's just easier to think that it's you."

"Easier how?"

"It's easier to move on if there aren't any question marks."

Move on? What a fucking joke.

I hate them. And yet, I know I would have reacted the same way. I can't stand not knowing what happened to Tilda. Just finding out the truth would be such a relief. Even if it turned out that someone I know is the murderer.

You know our situation, Maria said. *We won't be able to investigate this properly.*

If whoever killed Tilda isn't found, everyone is going to keep thinking I did it. In which case, I probably won't see any of my friends again.

"Can't you talk to Amanda?" I say. "Get her to understand?"

"I've tried. But I'll try again."

We sit silently in the dark. Johannes's hand is still on my knee.

"Amanda and I broke up."

"What?"

A part of me feels relieved, though it's tinged with guilt. Johannes will have more time for me. And I need him more than ever.

"What happened?" I ask.

Johannes hesitates. "Being with her didn't feel fair anymore. I have feelings for someone else." He clears his throat. "I've had them for a while now."

My eyes start adjusting to the darkness. I can tell that he's gazing up at the ceiling as if searching it for some way to continue.

"Is it someone we know?" I say. "It isn't Elin, is it?"

He laughs. "No. It isn't Elin."

Johannes shifts positions, but his hand is still on my knee. His fingers start tapping gently against the covers.

"There's something I have to tell you," he says.

I can tell by the tone of his voice that it's bad news. And I can't take any more bad news.

"I'm leaving town tomorrow," he says. "I'm staying in a commune in Stockholm."

I sit completely still while his words puncture me, a bullet that tears me apart.

"What are you going to do in Stockholm?"

"There are some things I need to try before it's too late."

"Like what?"

"I'm sorry. I know the timing sucks, but I have to do this."

"Why?"

His eyes gleam in the darkness as he turns to face me.

"Simon," he says. "Don't you get it?"

I open my mouth to say no, but close it again. Things start falling into place.

Our kiss during the latest ice game. The feeling that he wanted to tell me something.

Amanda's tantrum.

His voice just a second ago.

Yes. I get it.

I don't say anything. All I can think to say is too selfish. *Don't go. Stay here for my sake.*

"Will you be back?" I say instead.

"I don't know. I don't think so."

"What have your parents said? Your brothers?"

"They don't know yet. I've written them a letter."

In the darkness, it feels easy to take his hand. It's so much larger than the hands I'm used to holding: my moms', Emma's, Tilda's.

Johannes stiffens but doesn't pull away.

"You'll never feel the same way I do," he says in a low voice. "Will you?"

I squeeze his hand harder before I let it go. Everything would be so much simpler if I could say yes.

"No."

"I know. I just had to ask." He tries to laugh. "Considering there's no time to play hard to get."

"If I could ..."

"I know."

I try to think of something to say. How long has he felt this way about me? How could I not see it?

"I'll get going," Johannes says.

No. I need someone who believes in me. I need a friend. Don't leave me, too. We'll never see each other again if you do. You and Tilda were the most important people in my life, and if you leave, you'll both be gone forever.

"Take care," I say.

"You too."

"Text me when you make it to Stockholm."

NAME: LUCINDA
TELLUS # 0 392 811 002
POST 0016

W e told Miranda that Tilda is dead. And I've been making promises about heaven again.

I don't know if you have religion where you are. To summarize: some people are convinced they know all about those things you can't possibly know anything about. In our part of the world, a lot of people believe in a fantasy novel full of plot holes and contradictions that was written a few thousand years ago. The protagonist, God, acts like a spoiled brat whenever people don't behave according to his orders or don't love him deeply enough.

Did I tell you that one of Simon's moms is a priest? That's a person who teaches others about the contents of said fantasy novel. I wonder what she has to say about Foxworth. Does she shrug and go, "The Lord works in mysterious ways"? That's what Christians usually say when God acts like a douche. With the comet, though, he's probably beat some kind of personal record. (Christians also say that God doesn't give you more than you can handle. I've always hated that; the world consistently shows us that's not the case. Especially now.)

And still, I found myself promising Miranda that Tilda is one of the people we'll meet again in heaven—in God's eternal paradise. I even catch myself wishing I could believe it. I actually don't believe anything happens when you die. I think it just ends. The thought is less frightening to me than the idea of enduring eternity somewhere.

My little sister loved Tilda, who always listened patiently to her stories about the intricate workings of middle school life. They drew, they chased each other around the house, they recorded short movies on Miranda's phone and looked at adorable animals on YouTube. All those things I never took the time to do.

"Why would someone kill Tilda when she was going to die anyway?" Miranda asked.

How could I answer that? Now I can't stop thinking about it.

Tilda should have had the chance to make the most of the time we had left. And someone took that away from her.

NAME: LUCINDA
TELLUS # 0 392 811 002
POST 0017

They're talking about the American prison system on the news. Half the U.S. wants to let everyone except the worst offenders walk free. The other half wants to execute prisoners as quickly as possible, thereby depriving them of the privilege of dying with the rest of us and escaping their punishments. The broadcast showed images from a prison filmed with a hidden phone. It looked like hell on Earth. Most of the staff has just stopped going to work. Prisoners are starving to death in solitary confinement.

Cut to a debate in the studio. A celebrity lawyer and a celebrity cop talk about our Swedish solution: letting everyone sentenced to fewer than two years go. But what about those who commit violent crimes *now*? Who's going to find them, judge them, punish them? It makes me think of Tilda. What sort of sentence would her killer receive if we actually found them? The internet is full of "justice porn," page after page of people being hunted down by lone avengers and citizen militias. They're being shot, stabbed, stoned, and buried alive. Most of the videos are from Russia. I refuse to look at them.

Amanda wrote to me this morning. It was the first time in a long time that I responded to the outside world's attempts to get in touch with me. And it added some pieces to the puzzle that was Tilda's life. I've pasted the messages below.

AMANDA:

hi lucinda! been a while. wish the circumstances were different but I just wanted to make sure you knew what had happened to tilda.

don't know if you still use this chat. haven't got ur number.

LUCINDA:

Hi.

I've heard. Thanks for thinking about me.

AMANDA:

hi <3 it's awful. i can't stop crying.

we were so worried something like this would happen & it still feels totally unreal.

LUCINDA:

How was Tilda doing? I've seen people hint at stuff, but I don't know what to believe.

AMANDA:

most of it is true tbh, esp the drugs. she wasn't doing well at all, we didn't know what to do.

LUCINDA:

But it's so unlike her, it doesn't make any sense.

AMANDA:

i thought so too. but now I think it does make sense, in a way.

u know what she was like in the water, always pushing herself. so fucking stubborn.

it's like she did the same thing with this bad-girl trip she was on, pushing pushing and pushing, more & faster, etc.

a lot of people lost control this summer but I think it was worse for tilda cause she'd only had one goal her whole life & then it was taken from her.

she was so out of it during the final weeks u could hardly talk to her.

LUCINDA:

Sorry I'm so slow at replying. A lot to take in.

AMANDA:

it must be a bit of a shock.

LUCINDA:

What did she take?

AMANDA:

i think amphetamines mostly. & weed when she wanted to chill out.

i know she tried molly & shrooms too, like everything she could get her hands on.

elin & i were gonna tell her parents but we chickened out. don't feel great about that now but maybe it wouldn't have made a difference

it seems like simon did it & he wasn't doing
drugs

> LUCINDA:
> Saw your comments. Do you really think he did it?

AMANDA:
not sure but the last time I saw tilda they
were fighting. it was the night she died

> LUCINDA:
> Wasn't he at the afterparty? Saw some pics from it.

AMANDA:
only later. could have done it before he came

> LUCINDA:
> Did she seem afraid of him?

AMANDA:
no don't think so but he stuck to her like a
band aid. made her panic.
wonder how caroline's doing

> LUCINDA:
> I think about her, too.

AMANDA:
klas will be doing some jesus thing I guess

> LUCINDA:
> Sorry, I don't understand.

AMANDA:

he's a truther!

LUCINDA:

Whaaaat?!?!?

AMANDA:

yeah that was my reaction too.
klas brother started it. they're back in town.
the true church is SO CREEPY
felt so bad for tilda. klas was her only normal
parent

LUCINDA:

Sorry, I don't get it. Again. What about Caroline?

AMANDA:

ok she's normal but so difficult. hated when
she'd join us at practice
didn't you?

LUCINDA:

No.

AMANDA:

she was always questioning tommy's
strategy & thinking he should focus more
on tilda
it really stressed me out when she came to
the competitions.
maybe it's just me.
we missed you on the team

LUCINDA:
Thanks.

AMANDA:
i've started writing in tellus. it's kinda like
summarizing your life & we were never super
close but i always liked you & hope/believe
it was mutual. we've done so much together
these past few years.

LUCINDA:
Thanks. I'm also writing in TellUs and get what you
mean. Am slightly addicted.

AMANDA:
how r u doing?

LUCINDA:
I've stopped with the treatments so I feel better. You?

AMANDA:
honestly?

LUCINDA:
Of course.

AMANDA:

feel like shit

johannes broke up with me & it feels like he's
been lying to me this whole time. great timing when you've just lost your best friend &
the world is ending

maybe I should follow tilda's example and do
drugs

jk. sorry inappropriate

LUCINDA:

I've become an expert at inappropriate jokes this year.

AMANDA:

we're having a small memorial thing tmrw at
ali's. wanna come?

LUCINDA:

I don't think I can.

AMANDA:

u coming to the funeral?

LUCINDA:

Maybe. I don't know. Crowds are difficult for me, in
case someone has a cold or something, you know?

AMANDA:

yeah god totally

but let's hang out someday? we can talk
about tilda

or something else

LUCINDA:

I'd love to.

AMANDA:

great

feels good to have talked

LUCINDA:

I think so, too.

AMANDA:

cool let's keep in touch HUGS

LUCINDA:

<3

See how easily I use the cancer card? No one questions me when I tell them I'm sick.

It's not quite a lie. My immune system *is* bad. But that's not why I won't go to the funeral or their memorial thing. The thought of seeing everyone I've avoided for so long gives me intense anxiety. And I don't even know if I'd be welcome at the funeral. Tilda and I weren't friends in the end, and her parents haven't invited me.

I got goose bumps when Amanda wrote that Tilda was always pushing herself. I can picture her determined face, her eyes focused on the finish line. Her body, which could always work a little harder.

Suddenly, it makes perfect sense. Whenever Tilda settled on something, she went full-out. It was her greatest strength, but this summer, it might have turned into her greatest weakness. She fainted while holding her breath underwater trying to beat her personal best. I had to get her out of the pool when she started sinking. I was in panic mode, but she wasn't even fazed. Just angry with herself for not pulling it off.

We quizzed each other on Spanish verbs and the fall of the Roman Empire during rest periods in interval training. Her brain was as quick as her body. I couldn't keep up with that, either.

She comforted me when she made the Swedish Youth Swimming Championship and I couldn't hide my jealousy. "You're next, I swear," she said. But we both knew that if the choice was between me and her, I'd never make it. When you swim, you always know exactly how far away you are from your dream, how much better someone else is; you can measure it down to the tenth of a second. It can break you. And I wasn't nearly as committed as Tilda was.

Amanda is right. Swimming mattered more than anything to Tilda. She was addicted to it.

Competing was her whole life. And suddenly, it was all over. What was she going to focus on instead? What was she going to do with all that energy? She needed to get her kicks somewhere else.

Foxworth has changed people in ways no one could have anticipated just a few months ago.

I was shocked to hear that Klas has joined the True Church. I told you about religion yesterday, and they're a pretty extreme version of it. They came knocking on our door once and almost wet themselves with excitement when they saw that I was sick. They assured me that Foxworth was a sign of the rapture. They talked about labor pains that had to be endured before a new and glorious world could be born. My suffering wasn't in vain—as long as I joined them, the ones who truly know the answers to life's greatest mysteries. The ones who truly love God.

I would never have guessed that Klas would join them. He never seemed particularly interested in anything but his construction company and buying new and exciting gadgets. He let Caroline decide everything else. I don't think I ever heard him express an opinion on anything. Klas was happy to lie on the sofa and watch TV until it was time for bed. I used to wonder how Caroline could stand it. It's hard to imagine that Tilda inherited half her genetic makeup from him, but she loved her dad. How did she feel about him becoming a Truther?

I'm less surprised about Tilda's uncle joining them. I hated it when Anders and his family visited Tilda. He scared me when we were kids, and he upset me as I got older. I've never heard Anders refer to himself as an "alpha male," but he's definitely the type to consider himself one. (So-called So alpha males think they're better and smarter and stronger than everyone else, especially women. They're actually just obnoxious and full of BS. I don't know who told them that those qualities made them the pinnacle of creation. You can probably guess from this description that I don't love them. Historically, they're the cause of most of our problems here on Earth.) Someone like Anders would never admit that he was afraid of anything, not even the apocalypse, but he needs something to believe in, too. A religion that provides simple, straightforward answers, that doesn't complicate things by encouraging independent thinking, would suit him. Like every other alpha male, he just wants to follow a strong leader. Which, ironically, is the opposite of being an alpha. Anders is married to a woman named Erika, who laughs at his terrible jokes. She dresses herself and their daughter, Molly, in matching dresses on Christmas, and introduces herself as "Anders's wife." I don't think Erika even gave it a thought before becoming a Truther. She doesn't follow their God; she follows Anders, her personal deity.

I've looked at their profiles on social media. They were at church the night Tilda died. Klas is smiling piously in a way I don't recognize. Maybe the True Church suits him. It's yet another place where he doesn't have to make his own decisions; he can just cede control to someone else again.

But what do I know? Maybe they're happy.

I feel sorry for Molly, though. Tilda's cousin is the same age as my little sister, and they would play with each other occasionally as kids. It's difficult to believe now. Miranda is still a kid. Her body is all long legs and long arms; she's thin and coltish. She still secretly plays with her Barbies. She's stopped sleeping in her own room. Molly appears to have gone the other way. Judging from the photos, she's hit puberty. She's always been precocious, but now she looks like a smaller version of her mom—a child-sized adult. Long, neatly coiffed hair; clothes that never look wrinkled; concealer carefully covering the zits around her nose and forehead. Her eyes, gazing into the camera, are nervous, her smile fake.

If Amanda finds the Truthers "creepy," what must it be like for Molly? Her world has been turned upside down. She's just moved here, to a town she's visited but never lived in. Her parents and her uncle Klas have changed completely. Her cousin's been found dead. And the world is ending. She knows she's going to die.

I don't like to think about it. I have to go and hug Miranda now.

P.S.: I should get in touch with Caroline. I just have no clue what to say to her.

SIMON

Judette is the one who forces me back into the world. She tells Boomer to jump onto my bed, and this time, he doesn't hesitate.

"Boomer! Wanna go for a *walk*?" Judette says in the enthusiastic way that always gets him fired up.

He yelps excitedly, trampling the bed until I have to choose between getting up or getting squashed. Judette throws me the leash and tells me to take him out, then drive Stina to work, since Emma needs to borrow her car this afternoon.

I take Boomer for a short walk through the park. My body is stiff from having been still for so long. When we get back, I shower for the first time in days. Let the warm jets massage my shoulders. It doesn't do anything to change the fact that none of this feels real. When I drive off with Stina, it's as though the world outside the car window is just scenery. I've pulled my hat down—I don't want to accidentally meet anyone's eye—but from time to time, the surrounding cars seem to slow down. Can they see me? Are they saying *Isn't that the guy who killed his ex*?

We pass the entrance to North Gate. I stare straight ahead, but it's impossible not to see the glass factory's turquoise façade from the corner of my eye.

"Simon," Stina says. "Won't you talk to me?"

"About what?"

"You know what."

She straightens her glasses. They're still sort of bent from when she fell asleep in my bed. I take the old bridge across the tracks, and we drive along the edge of a lush green neighborhood. The forest grows thicker on the other side of the houses. The old church tower peeks out above the treetops.

"Are you going to church or to the fellowship hall?" I ask.

"The fellowship hall."

The silence that follows is heavy with everything Stina wants to say and that I don't want to talk about. I drive past the entrance to the small chapel where Tilda's funeral will be held. I'm not invited. I've reached out to both Klas and Caroline but haven't received a response. Maybe they think I killed Tilda, too.

It shouldn't matter. We'll all be gone soon anyway.

My grip tightens on the steering wheel. If I start to cry, Stina will never leave me alone.

The car feels like it's shrinking. Sealing us in like a tin can.

The forest ends abruptly, and I glance up at the white stucco church that's been there since the nineteenth century. Grass has grown around the gravestones, but the gravel path leading up to the church stairs looks freshly raked. I continue on toward the fellowship hall. We're nearly there. In just a moment, I can go home and back to bed again.

More and more cars line the drive to the low brick building. When we get closer, I see that every parking spot is taken. It's actually startling.

"I've never seen it this busy before," I say, slowing down.

"Right?" Stina says, her smile ironic. "This was my dream when I was studying to become a priest."

An old man in a denim shirt steps out of the car in front of us, gesturing wildly A few senior citizens down by the parking lot laugh and wave back. I see families with children and middle-aged ladies who've dressed up. Mr. Andersson, my old math teacher who told us about the comet, is smoking at the entrance.

"Do they believe in God?" I ask.

"A lot of people want to be baptized now, just to make sure," Stina says, and smiles again. "But they don't have to believe in order to come. The church should be open to everyone."

"But what are they even doing here if they don't believe?"

"People need a community. Togetherness. I think our group discussions are really helpful. So many people come here alone, but I get to see these amazing connections being made between complete strangers."

"It almost sounds like you think the comet is a good thing."

"No. Of course not. But . . . I wish we'd dared to be more like this before."

In the rearview mirror, I spot a group of moms with strollers walking past the car. I wonder if they knew each other before they started attending church.

"People are opening up in a way I've never seen before," Stina continues. "And a lot of them are burying the hatchet right now. People want to forgive and be forgiven. They want to ease their consciences."

I wonder if the person who killed Tilda wants to ease their conscience. Could I get them to confess if I only knew who it was?

"Doesn't it drive you crazy to sit and talk about death all the time?" I say.

"We don't actually spend that much time talking about death. We mostly talk about life, and how to make the final weeks matter."

Tears burn behind my eyelids. I blink hard a few times.

"What do you tell them then? What *is* the meaning of life?"

Stina smiles faintly. "I mostly try to listen. That's what people need right now."

"But you have to say something. Isn't that your job?"

"I can't tell anyone what the meaning of their life is. But I can help them figure it out for themselves. And the answer is usually ... people need their loved ones. Just think of the people who try to call their families from crashing planes, or the calls that went out from the twin towers in New York."

I wonder if she's actually talking about us now. About our family. That we have to stick together. But all I can think about is Tilda. Our planet is a crashing plane, and Tilda didn't need me like I needed her.

"Okay. Call me when you want me to pick you up," I say.

Stina undoes her seat belt and pulls the strap of her handbag over her shoulder. But she stays. She reaches out a hand, carefully, like she's afraid I'm going to pull away. And I have to suppress the urge to do just that.

She hastily brushes her fingers across my cheek.

"I miss Tilda, too. I liked her a lot. And she loved you."

"Not enough," I manage to say. "Otherwise, she wouldn't have broken up with me."

"You were important to her. I know that."

"Stop. You don't know anything about how Tilda felt. You don't know who she became."

Stina looks away. Straightens her glasses again.

"No. You're right, of course." She opens the car door. "Maybe you should talk to her. She might hear you."

Stina steps out of the car and I shake my head. Tilda didn't want to talk to me when she was alive. Why would she answer now, even if she could?

"You don't want to come in?" Stina says, leaning in.

I shake my head again, and she sighs before slamming the car door. But when I see her pass the hood of the car, she's donned a welcoming smile and is waving happily to someone who greets her.

SIMON

Emma and I are lying in her bed watching a movie on her laptop, but I'm struggling to focus on the action hero's thrilling chase through a crowded railroad station. All I can think about is that the actors and every extra in the background will soon be dead; the station, the desert landscape, the city streets the car chase goes through will soon be gone.

Judette has gone with Stina to the church. Besides Boomer, we're home alone. We've made popcorn, and Emma has sprinkled butter, pepper, and shredded Parmesan over hers. Her hand moves between the bowl and her mouth in time with the upbeat music.

"God, it's really kicking!" she says between mouthfuls. "I think it likes popcorn."

"Does it hurt?"

"No." She laughs. "Can you believe I have tiny feet in my stomach? How weird is that?"

"Extremely weird."

"Do you want to feel it?"

I shake my head. She turns back to the computer as another explosion turns the room a flaming orange.

"I just wish Micke was here," she says.

I hesitate. "When did you last talk to him?"

"Today. You've got to see the pictures he sent me."

She wipes her fingers on a paper towel and gets out her

phone, pulls up a photo and shows it to me. Micke is wearing something that resembles a windbreaker made of mosquito netting. The thin mesh covers his face, too, but when I zoom in, I can tell that he's smiling.

"His brother basically lives in a mosquito-filled marsh outside Överkalix."

"Cozy. No wonder he likes it up there."

"Right? Look at this one."

The next picture shows the inside of the house. Micke and his family are sitting by the kitchen window. With their backs to the light, they're dark silhouettes. Through the window I can glimpse a smoking grill on the lawn.

"They can't sit outside because of the mosquitoes, so they rush out to turn the meat."

"Gross."

I suddenly get the feeling that tiny insects are crawling up my legs and across my face. My nose and ears start itching.

"I'm not heartbroken about not being there," Emma says. "I like his parents. I actually do. His brother, on the other hand . . . a world of *eww*."

She lowers her phone. I notice that the photos were sent this morning. At least Micke is still in touch. She's not imagining that, too.

I scratch the phantom feeling of mosquitoes from my calves.

"Your popcorn stinks. I can't believe you're eating that stuff."

"It isn't me, it's the baby."

"Yeah, right."

Emma scrapes the final kernels out of the bowl and pours them into her mouth. They crunch between her teeth as she chews.

"I hope Micke comes home soon," she says. "But there are so many people to say goodbye to. His whole family is up there. And you know how much he loves nature."

Machine-gun fire throws pulsing lights across the room. Emma wipes her mouth with her paper towel.

"He can't wait too long, can he?" she says, placing a hand on her stomach. "We haven't even childproofed the apartment."

She turns back to the computer. Again, I struggle to understand how she can make sense of this whole mess. I have the sneaking suspicion that trying to understand her will make my head hurt, too.

And I can't ask her about it. I promised Judette.

I take out my phone, checking to see if I've missed a message from Johannes. He still hasn't contacted me.

"Who was that guy again?" Emma asks, pointing at the computer screen.

"No idea."

My attention's been caught by the image on my phone screen. It's from Ali's apartment. Hampus and Amanda are on the living room sofa, curled up between two girls I've never seen before. Candles glow on the low table. There are pink and violet dahlias that must've come from someone's garden. They've printed out Tilda's profile picture and framed it.

I took that picture of her. We were on a walk in the forest with Boomer. She'd gotten ahead of me on the broad path, and I'd called her name, snapping the photo just as she turned around.

I scroll down. More pictures. Hampus calls it a memorial service. When I try to click on Amanda's and Elin's profiles, I notice that they've both blocked me.

Emma reaches toward my popcorn bowl, then stops herself. From the corner of my eye, I spot her looking at my phone.

When I get out of bed, it's not actually a conscious decision. My body just walks itself into the hallway. I take my old Adidas out of the closet, the ones I can just step into.

"Where are you going?" Emma asks, following me into the hall.

"There's something I have to do."

Boomer comes barreling out of the living room, wagging his tail hopefully.

"You're staying here," I inform him.

He yawns and stretches his back, then looks up at me and starts wagging his tail again.

"Don't go," Emma says.

I don't respond. I lift my red track jacket off the hook.

"Simon. It's late."

"I'll be back before the moms are."

"It's not that. I'm just worried that . . ." She falls silent.

"What?"

"People want someone to blame. It sucks that they chose you. But . . . I'm just worried."

I shake my head.

"I'm sick of hiding."

NAME: LUCINDA
TELLUS # 0 392 811 002
POST 0018

I look at the pictures from the "memorial thing" Amanda invited me to. There's no sign of Simon. Some of the guys from his class are there, a few people from the swim team, but most of them are strangers to me.

They upload clips of themselves raising their glasses to Tilda's memory; they photograph themselves crying and holding each other; they call her the loveliest, the best—the same soppy things people said about me. I picture them posing for photos before wiping away mascara tears.

They haven't earned their tears, but they probably don't understand that.

People often thought they were closer to Tilda than they actually were. She talked so openly about herself, said things that could seem intimate, but she'd never tell you how she really *felt*. The stories were only ever superficial, and it fascinated me how rarely people realized that. Not that Tilda was fake or shallow. I understand if it sounds that way. It's just that she was always *on*. If you were sad, she could comfort you; if you were angry, she wouldn't hesitate to take your side; if you needed to laugh, she'd crack jokes until you did. She could be anything you wanted her to be, as long as you didn't want her to be weak.

She barely even exposed that side of herself to me. I've known her since I was seven years old, and she could still be an enigma.

I miss her so much.

SIMON

S imon," Ali says when he opens the door. "Shit."
He glances over his shoulder. Muted music is playing inside. I hear sobs and low murmurs.

"Can I come in?"

My voice echoes through the stairwell. I notice the shoes
strewn behind Ali and across the hallway floor.

"Bro," he says. "I wanted to invite you. I just don't know if
this is the time."

I stare at him. Apart from Johannes, he was the one I liked
the most. I had no idea he was such a coward.

"So you're not going to let me in?"

Elin peeks into the hallway and then vanishes when she
sees that it's me.

"Hi, Elin!" I shout. "Nice to see you!"

"This was a spontaneous thing," Ali insists.

A few jackets fall to the floor as I push past him into the
apartment.

Everyone is gathered in the living room. Everyone I chose
over my moms this summer.

Their eyes are red rimmed. Their cheeks are flushed. I can
almost smell the tears. There's a sense of hysteria in the air.

And I realize how wrecked we all are—how much pressure we're under. A little while ago, we had our whole lives
ahead of us. Now we're all going to die, and no one will ar-
range memorial services for us. This is bigger than Tilda.
They're mourning themselves and the loss of a future.

Elin begins sobbing loudly. Sait laughs nervously at something Moa whispers. She glares at me.

Not one of them wants me here. Johannes was right: It's easier for them to imagine I did it.

The balcony door is open. Amanda is standing there smoking, her back to the room.

"Hey, man." Hampus's words are slurred. "You're really fucking sweaty. Did you run all the way here?"

I take him in. The hooded eyes. The slack mouth.

"What are you even doing here?" Moa asks.

"What are *you* doing here?" I shoot back, lightning-fast. "You barely knew her."

Moa's eyes narrow, but she doesn't respond. Sait puts his hand on her knee.

The room is perfectly quiet except for Elin's soft whimpers and the cheesy song coming from the speakers. I've never heard it before, but I know Tilda would have hated it.

I walk up to the low table and pick up the photo of Tilda.

Why did you leave me here and let everyone think I murdered you? Who were you going to talk to? What was so fucking important that it couldn't wait?

I can feel everyone's eyes on me. The room is sweltering. My breaths seem too loud. The more aware of them I become, the more difficult I find it to breathe.

When I finally look up, black dots dance before my eyes. How does someone who isn't a murderer act, and how do I mimic that accurately? I'm so afraid to seem guilty that I'm sure I must look it.

"You'd better leave."

Amanda's come in from the balcony.

"Can everyone just relax?" Hampus says.

Amanda silences him with a glare. He looks at the floor.

"We saw you," she says, coming toward me, bringing with her the scents of cool night air and cigarette smoke.

Up close, I can tell she's fighting back tears.

Don't you get it, Amanda? We both miss her. And we miss Johannes. We need each other.

"Why would I have done it?" I say.

"Because she didn't want you," Elin sneers from the sofa. "And you didn't want anyone else to have her either."

I try to laugh, but it comes out as a gasp. A drop of sweat rolls down my back and into my underwear.

"You've watched too much bad television."

"You know it happens in real life, too," Amanda says. "Especially nowadays."

"I loved her."

"Maybe that's why," Elin says.

totally obsessed with her

My rage comes back full force when I spot Ali. "What about you? Do you think I did it?"

His eyes dart away. "Honestly, I don't know."

"You have to believe *something*."

Ali slides a look at Hampus, who is still staring at the floor.

I put the photograph of Tilda back on the table. It falls over, face-first.

I've had enough.

"If I killed her, we all did," I say.

"Simon, leave," Amanda snaps.

"We knew what she was doing. You all knew she needed help. But we were too fucking scared."

Elin shakes her head. "We tried."

"Not hard enough. Not you, not me, no one in here did enough."

"Get out!" Moa yells.

"You just talked about her behind her back. You spread rumors about her. Fucking *hypocrites*."

Tilda's word. It seems to sink in. I can feel the room shift. And now I can't stop myself. Being angry is so gratifying.

"How can you be so sure it's me?" I ask to Amanda. "Are you? Or is this to get back at me for Johannes?"

Amanda gives me a disgusted look.

"This is about *Tilda*. And she wouldn't want you here, either." She opens something on her phone and holds it up to my face. "Look what she wrote about you," she says. "This is how she felt."

I don't want to see it, but Tilda's message glows up at me: WOULD LOVE TO CHILL BUT DON'T WANT TO COME IF SIMON IS THERE. HE'S MAKING ME PANIC RIGHT NOW. CAN'T HE GET THAT IT'S OVER? GOING TO DAD'S INSTEAD.

It was sent on the night we watched *Armageddon* together.

Every sentence is like a punch to the gut. I wonder if Tilda wrote similar messages to the others in this room. Some of them probably showed them to the police.

"It's probably for the best if you leave," Ali says.

"Yeah," I say. "It's probably for the best."

I'm going to show them. I don't know how, but I'm going to find out who killed Tilda.

NAME: LUCINDA
TELLUS # 0 392 811 002
POST 0019

I went to see Tilda's mom, Caroline, today. I walked along the neighborhood streets rather than cutting through the yards. In the past, I wouldn't even knock before entering the house. Now, I wasn't even sure I was welcome.

I rang the bell and hoped that no one would come to the door. Then at least I'd be able to tell myself (and you) that I'd tried. But I heard steps, quick and light, so similar to Tilda's. Caroline opened the door, and I don't know which one of us was more shocked.

It was like seeing a ghost. As if whoever killed Tilda had killed Caroline, too.

The Caroline I knew was gone. Caroline, with her clear eyes and shiny hair, who glowed from daily exercise, and chia pudding for breakfast, and freshly pressed vegetable juices. Whose bright smile was a living advertisement for the clinic where she worked as a dental hygienist, whose posture was still straight and supple after a short career as a figure skater when she was my age. Caroline, who had more energy than anyone I knew. Now, her eyes were dead. Her lips were peeling. A vein in her forehead pounded like it was trying to burst through the skin.

I thought I caught the scent of chlorine and wet towels when I stepped into the hallway—the scent of Tilda and my

old life. Everything was as it used to be, and yet nothing was
the same. How can I make you understand how unnerving it
felt? It was as if the house, itself, were in mourning, as if the
sunlight couldn't penetrate the windows. It felt *dead*. We sat
in the living room, on the sofa where Tilda and I used to lie
watching shows after school, where we'd quizzed each other,
fantasized about the future together. An entire family lived
here back then. Caroline is alone in the house now.

She asked me how I was, and I answered her briefly. She
was looking at me like she couldn't quite believe I was there.
Maybe she also felt as if she were seeing a ghost. I had put
on my wig and tried to draw my eyebrows on with a pen I'd
never used, but I know what I look like, how my clothes hang
off my body. Caroline suddenly looked ashamed. I think she
thought something like *You were supposed to die, not Tilda.*

Caroline asked me if I thought Simon had done it, and I
said I didn't know.

She talked about which flowers she was going to pick
from the garden to decorate the coffin. We looked at the
picture she'd chosen of Tilda. It had been in the local paper
a few years ago, taken at the pool—Tilda is wearing her
swimming cap. It was from that moment I've told you about,
when Tilda qualified for the Swedish Youth Swimming
Championship and had to comfort me afterward.

"I was always so proud of Tilda," Caroline said. "But now I
can't help but wonder if I pushed her too hard."

I promised her she hadn't. That no one pushed Tilda as
hard as she pushed herself.

"But maybe I made her that way," Caroline said. "Maybe
she thought she had to keep performing for my sake."

I've thought a lot about what Amanda wrote in the chat.
Where did Tilda's winner mentality come from?

"I just wanted the best for her," Caroline said.

Was there something to her fears? Caroline was, without a doubt, the parent who'd come to the most competitions and training camps. She'd screamed herself hoarse in the bleachers. Followed us into the changing rooms to talk strategy. Questioned Tommy's plans in front of everyone with statements like "You know Amanda can't take the pressure of the final stretch." Once, Tilda was disqualified for making a mistake in a turn. Caroline had yelled at the judge until Tommy forced her to leave. Other parents complained about her sometimes.

It looks harsh when I write it down like this. I hardly even considered it at the time. It was just the way it was. Caroline *cared*. It was good and bad. She'd cheer us on, help us out, organize carpools, make hotel reservations, and raise money. Sometimes, I'd be jealous that Tilda had so much support from home. Dad supported me, too, of course; he came to meets when he could. But it didn't come close to Caroline.

Tilda found it hard at times. But more than anything, she was proud of her mom.

She loved her.

I said everything I could think of to comfort Caroline, but no words would ever really be enough. If there were more time, she might learn to live with the grief, but we only have three weeks to go. And Klas isn't any help. On the contrary, they disagree on everything about the funeral. He wants a Truther priest to lead the service. And he doesn't want Tilda to be cremated. But the morgues are overcrowded. There is no guarantee that any of the the bodies will be buried before September 16.

"I refuse to let her lie in some freezer," Caroline said.

She's gotten her way. The body Tilda pushed so hard is going to be burned.

Caroline took my hand as I was leaving. She said that she didn't know what had happened between Tilda and me but that it didn't matter anymore, because what we'd had was special.

And then she said: "You're coming to the funcral, aren't you?"

And then she said: "Tilda would have wanted you to."

I couldn't say no.

I've only been able to think about one thing since I got home. Tilda could have been killed by a complete stranger, but if it was someone who knew her, they'll probably be at the funeral.

I've been watching the news: almost a hundred dead and thousands left homeless after an earthquake in Istanbul; an understaffed nuclear power plant in Rajasthan has gone into meltdown; new skirmishes in Syria, where people have been living for a long time in something like an apocalypse.

The world keeps going until it doesn't. There's nothing I can do about that. I can't even do anything about my own body. But I might be able to find the person responsible for Tilda's death. I'd like to write to you and tell you that I accomplished something. That I actually did something good, something important with my life, before it's over.

You might wonder if this really *is* important. Does it matter that a seventeen-year-old girl died a few weeks before the rest of humanity did?

It doesn't matter to the world at all. But it matters in *my* world.

I wasn't there for her when she lived. I want to be there for her now.

And I have to know who killed her.

SIMON

The *Mona Lisa* is being wrapped in silk by a woman clad in black wearing white gloves. The world's most famous painting (though I've never understood why) is much smaller than I thought it would be. The woman informs us that it's going to be sealed into a stainless steel case and then sterilized with radiation and argon gas so mold can't grow inside the capsule. She shows us more works of art that they're attempting to preserve at the Louvre, looking up affectionately at the armless statue of Venus de Milo. She was chipped out of the marble as if she'd been there all along and the artist had just helped her into the light of day. That statue had been in Greece over two thousand years ago. Now she's going back into the rock, into a diamond mine in East Siberia. A narrator tells us about the terrible conditions in the mine when it was opened in the 1950s. During the winters, it got so cold that metal burst and oil froze.

"It's unbelievable, the things we did to get hold of gold and diamonds," Judette says. "Just because we'd assigned them some arbitrary value, despite the fact that you can't use them for anything. And now they're worthless." She laughs and downs her glass. She's already had a little too much to drink and is slurring her words slightly, but she's right. It hadn't occurred to me before that gold and jewels aren't valuable by nature.

On the TV, lasers engrave the history of man. Factual texts, poetry, our greatest literary works. Music from Bach and Beethoven to the Beatles and Beyoncé. Two hundred and fifty movies are also being preserved. A reviewer proudly reveals that there are two Ingmar Bergman movies in the collection.

"Have you noticed how they're only talking about Western art?" Judette says.

"Mm," I say. "But they're gathering things from all—"

"I know," Judette interrupts. "But that's not what they're *talking* about."

She gets to her feet and goes into the kitchen, humming tunelessly as she fills a pitcher with water.

An animated graphic shows us how the satellites that send coordinates into space work. Next is an interview with one of the project managers. He's excited, as though we're hiding everything underground like a Christmas present. Judette occasionally glances over at the screen, muttering to herself while watering the flowers.

My hip vibrates, and I dig around for my phone, which had fallen out of the pocket of my shorts. Finally, I sit up, lift one of the sofa cushions, and find it among breads crumbs, dog hair, dusty breath mints, and no fewer than three ballpoint pens.

It's a message from Johannes. And it's long.

I replace the cushion and tell Judette I'll be right back, then go to my room and close the door behind me.

Sorry I haven't been in touch until just now. Spent my first night in Stockholm sleeping in the station because I missed the last subway train. Second night in the commune. Weirdly enough, I feel at home. Hundreds of people live here. It's like a small town.

Been thinking a lot about what happened this summer

and how everything turned out. I'm glad I finally told you, even though you don't feel the same way about me. It's as if I can see everything a little more clearly from a distance. I should have trusted you sooner. You're my best friend, but I realize now that it's hard to get to know someone who's hiding so much of themself. Apparently, a real Armageddon was all I needed to be honest, even with myself. I don't know why I was so afraid; I knew all of you would be okay with it. (Except maybe Hampus, but would that really be such a loss?) Just didn't want to hurt Amanda, or at least, that's what I told myself. (Think I hurt her even more by waiting so long.) It was easier to put it off, I guess. Can't do that anymore. I'd better hurry up if I want to find myself, or whatever. I've sent a message to everyone we know, so nothing's secret anymore. I'm shutting down my social media, but keeping my number. You know you're more than welcome to visit me if you can or want to, but I don't think it's going to happen, is it? It's okay. Just know that you're the only one I miss.

I've seen people write about you re: Tilda. Fuck them. You know you didn't do it, and that's all that matters now, right? You're a good person, Simon. Tilda knew it, too, regardless of how she changed toward the end. Remember that.

I have to wipe my eyes while reading. I try to picture Johannes sending me this message, but I can't place him anywhere. I have no idea what his new surroundings look like.

Johannes knew where he was going. He had a goal, and he's reached it now.

I'm happy for his sake. But I also feel lonelier than ever.

I'm trying to think how to answer him when my phone vibrates in my hand. It's a new message. Significantly shorter.

WE KNOW YOU DID IT.

I get out of bed, heart pounding, and call the unknown number. I can hear the rings coming through one after the other, but no one picks up. I write, asking who they are. Pace the room. The phone remains silent. I Google the number, but there are no hits.

NAME: LUCINDA
TELLUS # 0 392 811 002
POST 0020

Another thing happened at Caroline's just as we were talking about the funeral. I hadn't planned on mentioning it here. We heard a loud bang on the ceiling above us. Something falling flat onto the floor, maybe a book.

I'd been so tense that the bang felt like a gunshot. And I saw Caroline twitch, despite trying to pretend it didn't bother her.

Above the living room are the upstairs hallway and Tilda's room.

I don't believe in ghosts, but that can be hard to remember now that it's nearly midnight.

From my window, I can see that the lights on the upper floor of Caroline's house are on.

Is Tilda still in that house? Was she trying to tell us something?

P.S.: I want to reiterate that I don't actually believe in ghosts. But what if they *are* real? What happens after September 16? Now I can't stop thinking about eight billion souls trapped on a dead planet with no one left to haunt.

NAME: LUCINDA
TELLUS # 0 392 811 002
POST 0021

First things first: I'm slightly embarrassed by my previous post. The night does strange things to us. Forget what I wrote.

I've barely slept since I last wrote. I looked at old pictures of Tilda, ones she'd uploaded or been tagged in. I traveled back in time through August, July, June. From May backward, she spent all her time with Simon. The further back I go, the more in love they seem. Winter came with Valentine's Day dinners, New Year's parties, Christmas with the parents, sledding with Amanda and her boyfriend. The whole gang dressed up as characters from Harry Potter for Halloween. I paused at a photo from September. They had just gotten together. Tilda is looking straight into the camera and holding the phone. Simon's in profile, his skin dark against her pale face, their lips pressed gently together. His eyes are closed. I've seen the picture before. Tilda showed it to me during one of her final visits to the hospital.

They seemed so happy together. But online we only share success stories.

I read every RIP message, checked the profile of every person who'd written one, scanned the posts for rumors. I even trawled the anonymous comments in one of the internet's more fetid swamps. There wasn't a lot, but the stuff that was there was vile. Someone claims Simon is Muslim and writes that he should be sent "back to his own country." Someone who knows he's grown up with two moms writes that it's turned him into a misogynist.

Unsurprisingly, the idiots are the most confident ones. But the fact that disgusting false rumors are floating around doesn't mean he *didn't* kill her.

If I'm going to find out who did it, I have to start with him. I wrote him a message saying I wanted to see him and talk about Tilda. It's naïve to think that searching his face will reveal the truth; I don't even know him. But I have to try.

Do you have any tactics for figuring out if someone's lying? Maybe you can read minds. Or use one of your tentacles to root around in someone's brain. Sadly, I have no such skills.

Simon replied almost immediately. He suggested we meet on the dock by the lake again.

I'm going to record the conversation. Just in case.

SIMON

I ran a lap around the lake, and now I'm sweating in the college sweatshirt I put on. Mosquitoes buzz hungrily around me when I sit at the dock. Twilight is coming. As I look across the lake, the automatic lights along the trail switch on. They look like hovering orbs between the trees, their glow forming a yellow band around the water. But there are no other joggers out tonight. I'm alone by the lake. Apart from the water lapping against the dock, it's perfectly quiet, perfectly still.

I've searched social media for information about what Tilda did that night, but I can't find anything useful.

The funeral is tomorrow, and I won't be there.

She's dead. Gone forever. They say we live on through the memories of those who have known us, but in less than three weeks, there won't be anybody left to remember her. Death is more final than ever. No one will remember me, either. Or my moms, or Emma.

I empty my water bottle. I've received two more anonymous messages from different numbers. I left my phone at home. I didn't want to see more. But Lucinda is late, and now she won't be able to contact me if she's been held up.

She wrote that she needs to talk about Tilda. I need to talk about her, too. Remember her with someone. I can't bear being alone with my thoughts anymore.

I turn around. Someone is walking down the slope toward the beach. In the darkness, I can only make out a shadowy figure.

Fear grips me.

What if someone's followed me here to avenge Tilda?

I suggested that Lucinda and I meet here because I wanted us to be able to talk without being interrupted. Now, I'm suddenly very aware of the fact that I'm alone in a place without witnesses and without my phone.

The shadowy figure steps into the circle of light from one of the lamps by the beach, and I see that it's Lucinda.

"I'd forgotten night comes so quickly" is the first thing she says when she steps onto the dock.

Does she sound nervous? I don't know her well enough to tell.

Has she heard the rumors about me? If she had, she wouldn't have agreed to meet me here, right?

I wonder if I should get up so we can hug, but I don't think Lucinda is the type. Sure enough, she sits down so far away from me that at least a couple of people could fit between us.

"Thanks for agreeing to meet me," she says, adjusting her hat.

"I was happy you got in touch. We're the ones who were the closest to Tilda."

"I hardly knew her toward the end."

"But you knew her for way longer than me."

There's so much I want to know about Tilda—so much I want to ask Lucinda—but I don't really know where to start.

"It's weird that we've barely met," I say.

I regret it immediately, because it isn't weird at all. We both know why it turned out that way. I feel stiff and awkward, like I always did before high school, back when I could barely talk to people. Instead, I would kind of float above my body, analyzing everything. And now I'm doing it again.

"I dreamed about her last night," I continue. "She was in my room and was just like ... *What are you doing? Did you really think I was the one they found? You're so stupid. I told you I was just taking a break.*"

Lucinda nods.

"I dream about her all the time. When I can sleep."

A mosquito lands on my neck, and I slap a hand over it. Lucinda jerks back. Tries to smile. But now I know she's scared.

She's scared of *me.*

"There are people out there who say I killed her," I say. "Have you heard?"

She doesn't respond. And that's really the only response I need.

"Do you think so, too?" I press.

"I don't know what to think."

The disappointment is so overwhelming that blood rushes to my head.

"I didn't do it. But whatever I say can't help my case, can it? It's just what a killer would say."

Lucinda looks away. Her angular face is full of shadows.

Suddenly, I recall one of the first times Caroline and Klas let me stay the night. Tilda's room was dark. We had spread a blanket across the floor. She lay on my arm, her voice so low I had to strain to hear her. *I'm so fucking scared she's going to die, but we can't talk about it. We can't talk about anything anymore. I can't tell her about the bad things, because my problems are nothing compared to hers, and I can't tell her about the good things, because it ... it feels like I'm reminding her of everything she'll never have.* It was the first time Tilda cried in front of me. *You can talk to me instead*, I'd said. She lightly stroked my forearm with her fingers. *I know. But she's my best friend. And you're one of those really good things I wish I could tell her about.*

"I'm sorry," Lucinda says, and gets up. "I shouldn't have—"

Her phone falls out of her pocket, and I automatically reach out to catch it before it drops into the water.

A microphone icon fills the screen. Large numbers count out the seconds.

She's been recording us.

I don't even want to look at her when I give her phone back.

"Are you happy?" I say. "Or should I add something more?"

Lucinda doesn't reply.

"If you think I killed Tilda, it's pretty stupid of you to meet me here alone."

"My dad is coming to pick me up soon," she says quickly.

Her voice trembles; her mouth sounds dry. I'm sure she's lying, and I think about the Moomin book in Emma's room.

Imagine how lonely it must be if everyone is afraid of you.

"You'd better hurry up, then," I say, still not looking at her.

Her hurried steps make the wood vibrate and the water splash against the underside of the dock. Then, abruptly, she stops.

"How was Tilda actually doing?"

I turn around. Lucinda has shoved her hands into the pockets of her hoodie. She's looking at me from the other end of the dock.

"How was she *doing*?" I ask.

"Yes."

You're all such fucking hypocrites

"Maybe you should have showed her you cared while she was still alive," I say.

Watching Lucinda stiffen is satisfying. She deserves it. She may be "the cancer girl," but she's not a saint.

"You don't know what it was like," she says softly. "I was sick. I couldn't do it."

"It wasn't easy for Tilda, either. Her best friend was dying of cancer and didn't even want to see her."

We stare at each other. A car drives past, far away, on the highway.

"Why did you think she was going to my place that night?" Lucinda asks. "What did she say?"

"Fuck it. I was wrong. She was probably going to get more of that shit she was taking."

Lucinda looks down at her shoes. "Didn't anyone try to get her to stop?" she asks.

"Of course I tried!" A lump is growing in my throat. I won't cry. I refuse to give her that satisfaction. "She didn't want my help," I manage to squeeze out. "I tried, but I should have done more. I should have said something to Klas and Caroline. I was just afraid she wouldn't forgive me if I did. I thought that if we got back together, I could help her stop. She'd become herself again. I would *heal her with my love*, and then we'd live happily ever after until the end of time."

Lucinda stands frozen while all the things I haven't even wanted to admit to myself come pouring out. It's like the words are clawing their way out of my body.

"I wanted to be her fucking knight in shining armor," I say, "but I was just being selfish." I get to my feet. Walk toward Lucinda. I wait for her to shrink back, but she stands firm. As I get closer, I can see that she's crying.

"You can believe whatever you want. It doesn't matter," I say when we're facing each other. "I let her down, and so did you, and everyone else."

"You think I don't know that?" she whispers. "That I don't think about it all the time?"

I shake my head. Run across the stretch of beach. Speed up on the grassy rise. Follow the beat of my blood rushing through my body.

NAME: LUCINDA
TELLUS # 0 392 811 002
POST 0022

Simon realized what I was up to right away. If he didn't kill Tilda, he must hate me now.

I'm having such a hard time believing he did it. But if he did, he might be a psychopath, and psychopaths can be very convincing. I'm only sure of one thing: he was right— I *was* stupid to meet him alone by the lake.

Dad was waiting for me when I got home. It was later than I thought, and he was upset. "Don't you understand that I get worried when I can't reach you?" he said. It struck me that it was the first time he'd sounded like a stereotypical parent of a teenager. Not because he tends to be original, but because it's the first time I behaved like a stereotypical teenager and stayed out past my curfew.

Tilda's funeral is tomorrow. I'm going to see everyone again. I've picked out a pair of black jeans and a long dark gray cardigan, the only items in my wardrobe that even remotely fit the occasion. Do I even have to tell you I'm petrified? Dad seriously suggested I try one of the mindfulness exercises the government released on YouTube this summer. Sometimes it's like he doesn't know me at all.

While I'm writing this, Miranda is slamming doors and screaming that she hates him. She wants to come to the funeral, and I have a feeling she'll win this particular battle of wills. Maybe this is a taste of what she would have been like as a teen.

P.S.: One of the mindfulness exercises they tried to get me to do at the hospital: visualize putting all my anxiety on a tiny leaf, then lay that leaf in a bubbling brook and watch it sail away.

NAME: LUCINDA
TELLUS # 0 392 811 002
POST 0023

During the drive to the woodland chapel, I kept thinking: *This is really happening, this is really happening. I'm about to see everyone again.* Dad asked me a bunch of times if I had the energy to go through with it, only managing to make me even more nervous. *Thanks, Dad.* I nearly asked him to turn the car around, and might have done it if Miranda hadn't been with us. I couldn't break down or back out in front of her. (I was right. She did win the fight.)

When we arrived at the chapel, I noticed that everyone was more elegantly dressed than me, the women wearing black dresses and nice shoes, their hair carefully styled. People milled around the parking lot, talking to each other as if they were mingling at a party. I realized they weren't here to say goodbye just to Tilda, but also to each other. We sat in the car, waiting until the crowd thinned out. At exactly one o'clock, the little bell tower started ringing and we couldn't put it off any longer.

Tilda's entire family stood in the lobby to receive the attendees. The priest was there, too, and I was shocked when I realized why he looked familiar: he had officiated at my mother's funeral.

Caroline hugged us, thanking us for coming. Tilda's grandmother and grandfather were also there, sticking close by Caroline's side, ready to catch her if she fell apart. Klas stood a bit farther away, with Anders and his family. When I hugged Klas, I spotted the silver cross he wore on a chain around his neck. Other than that, he seemed almost normal. At least at that point.

Naturally, Tilda's cousin, Molly, was wearing a copy of her mother Erika's black, white-collared dress. (I wondered how they'd gotten their hands on matching funeral clothes, but Molly proudly shared that Erika had made them.) In an earlier post, I wrote that I had seen pictures of Molly and that she seemed so mature, but now I understand that she's as awkward as ever. I feel awful admitting this—especially considering what happened later—but I was reminded of how Molly could make my skin crawl. It's not her fault, but she's too anxious, too earnest, and she laughs too much and too eagerly. She worshiped Tilda—followed her around like a puppy when her family came to visit. We did everything we could to avoid her.

Dad, Miranda, and I walked into the chapel. The sun shone through the greenery outside the windows and threw patterns across the walls. An old lady was playing the pipe organ. Tilda's coffin had been draped with the cloth I remember from Mom's funeral. Flowers from Caroline's garden covered it: roses and asters, more kinds I couldn't name. The picture of Tilda was front and center, her triumphant smile frozen in time.

I immediately picked up Tommy's voice in the din. My body is still trained to obey him after all those times he'd stood at the pool's edge and yelled out instructions. He looked handsome, but clearly uncomfortable, in his suit. Amanda and Elin and the rest of the team were there, too, and others from the swimming world who I'd only met during competitions. I hardly recognized them, especially not the guys, who I'd mostly seen in bathing suits and swim caps. Chairs squeaked as people turned to look at me. I heard scattered whispers. We sat down at the very back, and I focused on Miranda so I wouldn't look up and accidentally make eye contact with someone, pretending my little sister needed my help when it was actually the other way around.

It was a relief when the priest finally took his place at the front of the room, drawing everyone's attention.

I concentrated on the picture of Tilda, trying to grasp the fact that she was lying in that coffin. I wondered what she looked like. Had someone crossed her arms over her chest? And what state was the body in? She had been outside for days. Sporadically, there'd been rain, followed by baking sun. Were there animals in North Gate that had gnawed on the corpse? Did she smell?

I hated my brain so much.

The priest talked about Tilda like he'd known her well. The beloved daughter, the popular, promising girl, excellent in school and ambitious in sports. Caroline must have told him what to say. Her sobs echoed through the chapel. I studied her bent neck as her hair glittered like gold in the light from the windows, and I wanted to cry, too. I wanted that release. But my thoughts were so loud, there didn't seem to be room for anything else.

The priest told us about the time Tilda's parents brought her to swimming class when she was little. "She wasn't a natural, but she was stubborn, even then. She wanted all the badges." I heard Molly's affected laughter. It sounded like a cooing dove. The priest finished by saying that Tilda knew that the most important thing in life was doing the best you could. "It should be an example to us during this difficult time."

He talked about a perfect Tilda.

I remembered something she'd told me once, after a competition. She'd clocked a time that to most of us was excellent, but not to her. She was driving herself (and to be honest, me) insane by brooding over what had gone wrong. Hours later, when I thought she'd finally let it go, she looked at me and said: "People always tell you to do the best you can, but how do you *know* you've done your best?" I didn't have an answer. I just felt bad for her at the time.

I haven't thought about that conversation in years.

During the psalms, I took the time to look around the room, searching the faces surrounding me. What was I hoping for? Someone looking guilty? Tormented by remorse? If only it could be that simple.

One of the psalms had lyrics that were directed at the dead person, with lines like, *He waits for you tonight*; *From eternity, he has chosen to meet you here;* and *There is a dark haven, you can't see it now, but you're traveling there.* All I could think of was someone waiting for Tilda in the dark. Who had been there to meet her?

Afterward, they served coffee in the fellowship hall. Dad asked me if I wanted to go home instead. "Everyone would understand," he said. He sounded like he was the one who wanted to leave.

It was only the thought of my personal mission that made me walk into the congregation's main hall. I did it for Tilda. And it wasn't awful. It was the opposite, in fact. I met Elin and Amanda again. We shared stories about the living Tilda, the Tilda before this summer. It was unexpectedly nice to remember her. And to remember ourselves—who we used to be. The girls who giggled quietly at our classmates and their awkward, clumsy movements in the school pool during gym class. The four of us had become something else: creatures adapted to life in the water.

I briefly met some of their friends, too. I recognized most of them from social media and confirmed my assumptions about most of them. Elin is clearly in love with this guy, Ali, who only has eyes for Moa. And their friend Hampus is just as irritating as I'd guessed. He cracked jokes almost compulsively. He'd just dyed his hair blue and painted his nails black, radiating, *Look at me! Look at me! I'm such a rebel now that the world is ending!*

Surprisingly, Tommy kept to the background. I noticed that Caroline barely glanced at him, and wondered why. I'd been planning on talking to him later, but that didn't happen. I didn't get the chance.

When all the new impressions finally tired me out, I went to sit next to Dad. We didn't get any peace, though. Every person in the room wanted to discuss their maladies with the town doctor. I pretended not to notice the ones who peered at me curiously. Miranda had joined Molly out back, so I couldn't distract myself with her. I felt grateful for the priest when he started reading aloud messages from family and friends who hadn't been able to make it to the funeral. It took a while. Hardly anyone who lives outside of town was there. (There's only one train a day, and if you have to change trains along the way, it can take you several days to get to your final destination. Very few people have saved enough gas rations to get far in a car.)

It was when the final message had been put aside that Klas rose from his seat, tapping his spoon against his cup to get everyone's attention. Thank God Miranda wasn't there.

I need a quick break. It usually helps to write things down, but right now, it feels more like I'm reliving the ordeal.

SIMON

My moms are arguing in their bedroom. No actual words penetrate the wall into my room, but I can hear Stina's upset voice, and pauses when Judette's either saying something quietly or not speaking at all. I lie on my back as anxiety washes over me like a tidal wave. I don't know exactly what the argument is about, but I do know it has to do with me. The apartment's felt like a pressure cooker all day. Maria called Judette earlier to say that I should stay home, considering Tilda's funeral is being held today. Someone who thinks I killed her might get the idea that I need to be punished.

Stina's voice goes shrill on the other side of the wall. I climb out of bed without turning on the lamp, and go to the window. The sky is pitch-black above the city lights. Not even the moon is visible. A soft rain whispers against the window. The droplets are so small they cling to the glass, glittering in the glow from the streetlights. It reminds me of the rain that fell the night of Tilda's disappearance.

The glass factory where her body was found is there in the darkness, beyond the highway. It's been a week since I found out she was dead. It feels so long ago and so recent at the same time. Time is behaving strangely. I know it's because of the shock, but it feels as if the comet is affecting time along with everything else.

Will time even exist afterward, when we're not left to measure it?

Condensation forms on the glass in front of my mouth. I wipe it away with the sleeve of my sweatshirt, then look down at the street's gleaming asphalt. A white car's parked across the street. In the driver's seat, a woman is fiddling with her phone.

Klas uploaded a photo of Tilda and me this morning. I've never seen it before, but I remember when he took it on Christmas Eve. We were happy. Klas's caption seemed lifted from the Bible, one of the parts Stina never uses in her sermons: *The Lord is slow to anger, and great in power, and will not at all acquit the wicked.* Klas's brother, Anders, shared the post. The comments piled on. Messages poured in. Finally, I turned my phone off and asked Emma to hide it. I couldn't bear to torture myself anymore, couldn't stop myself from doing it. Unfortunately, it's not as easy to turn off my thoughts and ask someone to hide them from me.

How did we get here? I remember hugging Klas awkwardly in the doorway when we first heard about the comet. I remember him calling me his "son-in-law" on Christmas Eve.

Hypocrites.

I used to prefer him to Caroline. Now, I almost wish Klas and his brother had something to do with Tilda's death— but according to their profiles, they were both in the True Church until late that night.

The door of the white car opens. A red umbrella with white spots unfolds. I see a pair of legs in dark tights.

I wipe away mist from the window again. My hand freezes on the glass when a face peeks out from underneath the umbrella.

Erika. Anders's wife.

The chill from the window spreads up my arm, traveling through my body.

Erika looks up at the windows on our floor; her phone glows in her hand. I step back, even though I doubt she can see me in my darkened room.

Claustrophobia makes the walls close in. There is no one else in the car, not as far as I can see.

But maybe she's waiting for Anders and Klas, maybe they've gathered a crowd and they're planning on breaking into the apartment, what are they going to do to me, what are they going to do with the moms, the Truthers hate gay people, Emma could get hurt, and the baby—

My thoughts race so fast my synapses feel like they're crackling in my skull.

They can't come up. If they want something from me, they're going to have to get me alone.

I go into the hallway. I can hear Stina crying through the closed bedroom door. I open one of the closets and find a box cutter in the toolbox on the lowest shelf, and tuck it into the pocket of my jeans.

Just in case.

Self-defense.

I take the leash from the hook and hear Boomer's claws scrape against the floor of the living room. The tall plume of his tail sticks out from behind the sofa like a periscope. He whines eagerly when he lumbers into the hall, bumping his head against the leash while I try to fasten it.

The bedroom has gone quiet.

"Hush," I snap at Boomer.

He turns around in circles on the spot. I consider leaving without him, but he's the one I'm intending to blame if my moms catch me sneaking out. *He needs to pee.* Besides, there's a small chance Boomer would protect me if someone tries to hurt me. Does he have any of those instincts at all? Maybe he could lovingly lick the attackers to death.

I force him to sit and finally get the leash around his neck. Cautiously, I open the apartment door, closing it quietly behind us, then listen, tense, as we hurry down the stairs. But all I can hear is Boomer's panting breaths. No one seems to have noticed us leaving.

Through the front door's window, I see that Erika is still staring up at our floor. She startles and almost drops the umbrella when I push the door open. I cross the street in the light rain, Boomer leaping joyfully behind me.

Erika throws me a nervous glance. She puts her phone into the pocket of her coat.

"Hello," she says, brushing the hair from her forehead.

She looks tired and worn out, as if she hasn't slept all summer. Two deep creases have appeared in her forehead, and there are dark circles under her eyes.

Boomer pulls at the leash to sniff her shoes, wags his tail, yips.

"What are you doing here?" I ask.

"I wanted to talk to you, but you weren't answering your phone, so I ..."

"I turned it off. You can tell Klas and Anders thank you for that post."

Erika looks unhappy. Boomer licks her hand, and she pats him on the head.

"I think he remembers me," she says. "We had so much fun together when you brought him along to Klas and Caroline's last Christmas."

I wait quietly, like Judette tends to do. Listen to the soft, almost inaudible patter of rain against the umbrella. Erika hastily looks up at me before glancing away again.

"My family doesn't know I'm here," she says. "I drove some friends home and decided to take this route back."

"Why?"

"I don't think you … did it. I just wanted you to know."

I stare at her. If Erika is telling the truth, this is a huge step for her. Tilda used to say she hadn't had an independent thought in her life.

Boomer follows a trail along the pavement, pulling on the leash. He already smells like wet fur.

"If it had been up to me, you'd obviously have been invited to the funeral," Erika continues. "You must understand that they don't mean anything by it. Everything is just so strange. Maybe you've heard what happened at the fellowship hall?"

"No."

Erika looks around, as if searching for support from someone who isn't here. Maybe it's become an automatic impulse. I've never met her alone before. Every time I saw her, she was running after Molly, warning her not to get her clothes dirty, to be careful, to wash her hands. Or she'd be devoting all her attention to Anders, hardly saying a thing, just reacting to him. I don't know who Erika is without them. Neither does she, apparently.

"Klas isn't doing well," she says. "I mean, of course he isn't, after all that's happened."

Boomer's finished sniffing everything in the vicinity of the leash. He looks up at me impatiently.

"Why don't you think it was me?" I ask.

"We don't know anything right now, do we? It could have been a stranger." She hesitates. "And you had something special. I could tell that you loved her."

I can see that Erika means it. There is a naïve childishness in her weary face.

She should know better. My love isn't a sign that I didn't kill Tilda. But it's so nice to meet someone who doesn't think I did the unthinkable. I'll take what I can get, even if it's just Erika.

"Will you walk with me through the park?" I ask.

"I'd love to."

Erika offers to cover us both with her umbrella, but I wave her off. Her heels click against the pavement as we walk. I throw a glance at the library as we pass by it. Before they shut down permanently, they gave away all the books people wanted to keep. The rest were abandoned in heaps on the floor and on the shelves.

"Like I said, Klas isn't doing so well right now," Erika says. "Did you know he's staying at our house now?"

"Yes."

"He and my husband have become very religious recently."

"And what about you?"

We reach the park, which smells like wet grass, bark, and asphalt. A hare races past, terrified by Boomer's sudden appearance.

"I can't," Erika says. "I've tried; I mostly go with them to the True Church to be with my husband and ... because I don't know what else to do."

That statement would have had Tilda rolling her eyes behind Erika's back.

"I hope they'll be over it soon," Erika continues. "Honestly, I've never been very interested in asking the big questions. We're never getting any answers anyway, so what's the point? We'll find out in a few weeks. Until then, I'm busy making sure *this* life is going as well as it can."

Now she's speaking so quickly, she nearly stumbles over her words. She must have been dying to tell someone the truth. And I understand what she means.

"Do they know you don't believe?" I ask.

Erika glances at me. Shakes her head.

We stop when Boomer finds a spot on the grass that requires his full attention. Erika's face glows red as a streetlight's beam filters through the umbrella.

"They say you were the last person to see Tilda alive," she says.

"Not the last person."

Erika looks at me, curious.

"Who was?"

"Whoever killed her."

Erika flinches, and I immediately regret my words.

"But I did see Tilda that night," I say. "In the square."

We start walking again. I tug the leash and Boomer reluctantly follows us.

"What were you talking about?" Erika asks.

"She was going to meet someone."

"And you don't know who?"

"No."

"Are you sure?"

"Of course I'm sure," I say. "I haven't been able to think about anything else."

"No. . . . No, of course not."

There's a whiff of something rotten in the air. We're getting closer to the fountain in the middle of the park. It's dry. Garbage and plastic bags are piled around the trash cans; birds are picking at scraps of food. Boomer pulls at his leash to go sniff around. I keep him away.

"I wonder who it was," Erika says. "Like I said, she could

have met anyone on the way. That night was terrifying. We were in the True Church, but we could hear the sirens loud and clear. I'd forgotten they were showing the game in town that night."

"How could you forget? It was all over the news."

Erika's smile is stiff. "We don't watch the news anymore."

We've almost crossed the entire park. I look back at my street, search the windows of our apartment.

"I've wondered if her coach didn't have something to do with it," Erika says. "She was so angry with him the last time I was with her."

"Tommy? Why?"

Erika shakes her head.

"I don't know. She wouldn't say."

Another thing I'll never know about Tilda.

"Or it could be the drugs," Erika goes on. "It took a long time for Klas to believe the rumors, but I could tell she was high sometimes."

I don't know what to say to that. I gaze at our windows again, and spot Judette. She waves at me to come in. Even from this distance, I can tell that she's angry.

"What happened to Tilda is so incredibly tragic," Erika says.

"I have to go."

"Of course," Erika says, following my gaze. "I should get going, too, before anyone wonders where I've disappeared to."

We say goodbye at her car. Even though both moms are waiting in the window now, I stay on the street and watch the red lights of the car until they round the corner.

I feel bad for Erika. She's sacrificing so much of her final days to keep her family functioning.

But who am I to question that? I was ready to put up with just about anything to stay with Tilda.

NAME: LUCINDA
TELLUS # 0 392 811 002
POST 0024

We often say that someone has gone "crazy," when all we really mean is that they're angry or confused. We can even refer to someone who's kind of spontaneous or oh-so-wonderfully upbeat as "wild and crazy," and mean it in a positive way (if you like that kind of thing).

But actually seeing someone go *crazy* is something else entirely. It's a reminder that there's something inside all of us that can break at any time.

So Klas tapped his spoon against his cup and thanked everyone for coming. Then he informed us that we were going to pray for Tilda's soul, even though she hadn't turned to God in time. We were supposed to praise God for the coming rapture.

"God is casting a net over our souls," he said. "Only the chosen ones will be caught in it and get pulled into heaven."

Those who were rotting and ruined would be left behind in the devastation. And unlike Tilda, we could still be saved.

You can tell by the eyes when someone's cracked under pressure. It's in the smile, the way it widens until it hardly looks human anymore.

Caroline got to her feet so quickly the chair fell over. She begged him to stop, saying that this wasn't the right time to convert anyone. He replied with quotes from the Bible. I found some of them online:

> *The stars shall fall from heaven, and the powers of the heavens will be shaken. And then shall appear the sign of the Son of man in heaven: and then shall all the tribes of the earth mourn, and they shall see the Son of man coming in the clouds of heaven with power and great glory.*

When Caroline tried to put an arm around him to get him to sit down, he pushed her. I glimpsed the panic behind the frenzied smile. He shouted that Caroline had just confirmed that the truth was in the scripture.

> *There shall come in the last days scoffers, walking after their own lusts. And saying, "Where is the promise of his coming?"*

He said it was Caroline's fault that Tilda hadn't come to God in her last days.

When Tilda's grandpa and a few others tried to drag him out, Klas broke free and fell across one of the tables. Coffee cups and plates shattered on the stone floor. Caroline screamed that he was ruining everything.

I got the feeling something had been started that couldn't be stopped. It vibrated around the room. Klas had reminded us that we were all going to die soon. Everyone was so afraid. And fear easily turns into hatred.

Klas's brother, Anders, finally got him out of the room. Unsurprisingly, Erika followed them. Those of us who were left behind heard Klas's shouts until the front doors shut.

Caroline was comforted by her parents and the priest. And I ran out to look for Miranda. She was sitting with

Molly on a bench behind the fellowship hall. I felt so proud of my sister when I spotted her; she was comforting Molly in the same way Tilda would comfort me sometimes when we were younger, stroking Molly's back in that easy way I'd never been good at.

They had heard the screams and the porcelain breaking.

"Do I have to leave now?" Molly asked.

"I think so," I said, though my heart nearly broke when I thought about what her life had become.

Molly looked at me, her shoulders pulled up to her ears, and said she hated the True Church and hated Klas. "They spend every night at the service, and they sit and read the Bible for hours every morning. Mom is the only normal one, and she pretends to be like them so there won't be any fights." I asked Molly if she also has to pretend. And she looked at me defiantly, in a way that gave me some hope. She said that though she'd been baptized in the True Church, "They know I don't believe in God, so I don't have to go anymore. They said God can tell that I'm false, so they pray for me instead."

A moment later, Anders came running, his face bright red. "Come here, Molly," he said. "We have to go now. Klas isn't feeling well." Molly's shoulders went up a little more before she rose from her seat.

Afterward, Miranda said she'd asked Molly if she wanted to come and visit us sometime, but that Molly isn't allowed to fraternize with non-believers. They'd exchanged numbers, though, so they can talk in secret.

Molly needs a friend like my sister.

Dad came and got us. Miranda had so many questions, and Dad got more and more upset the longer we talked. He's a classic scientist, despising anything to do with religion.

All of a sudden, I found myself defending it, explaining to Miranda that all Christians aren't like the Truthers.

We took the road past the cemetery where Mom's ashes are interred, where Tilda's going to be soon. In less than three weeks, Dad, Miranda, and I will be ashes, too. "Good thing the comet is coming so I don't have to plan your funeral," Dad said when Miranda wasn't listening. He said it as one of our too-real jokes, and I laughed. But I think there was more to what he said than we pretended. He must have been fearing what Caroline has just gone through: having to bury your child.

SIMON

I didn't know we had a test today, I say, and stare down at a paper covered in numbers and letters I've never seen before. I look around the classroom. The sun shines through the windows; the branches of the birch trees stir slowly in the air. Their leaves are fresh. It's spring. Johannes looks up and shoots me a pitying look before turning back to his test. Pens rasp against paper. Hampus is already done. He grins at me before leaning over his desk and pulling his cap down over his eyes to take a nap. Next to him, Ali is entering something into his calculator. I jump when someone slams a hand onto my desk. I turn in my chair. Our math teacher, Mr. Andersson, looks at me inquiringly. *Did you need some help?* he says. *I haven't studied,* I admit. *I didn't think we still had school.* Someone giggles. Mr. Andersson bends down toward me. *You realize I have to fail you if you can't pass the test?* And I realize it's all been a dream. There is no comet. The world has kept going without me; I've thrown away my entire future. The feeling of failure is a cold, heavy stone in my chest when I look down at the test. Now the pages are empty. But if the comet isn't real . . . and everything is as it's always been . . . that must mean Tilda is alive. I jump to my feet. Run out of the classroom and into her bedroom. She's standing by the window. The sun makes her dark hair shimmer like copper. *Hi,* I say. Tilda doesn't respond, just turns to look at me. A fly is crawling over one eye. She tries to blink it away, but it stays there. *We shouldn't be here*, she says. *Something terrible is going to happen tonight.* We're behind the glass factory now. More flies crawl out from between her lips. I'm too late.

When I wake up, my heart is pounding so hard it feels like it's trying to burst through my chest.

Judette's standing in the doorway with her laptop in her hands. Did she knock? I search for my phone on the floor, then remember that I gave it to Emma yesterday.

"What time is it?" I ask.

"Almost one thirty."

I've slept half the day away. Slept my way closer to the end.

"Simon," Judette says, and now I can tell that there's something strange in her expression. "Maria just called me. There's a video about you on YouTube."

My skin suddenly feels too tight.

"What video?" I say.

Judette steps into the room and sits on the edge of my bed. Hesitates.

"It's a girl saying she slept with you. The night Tilda died."

The bleach-blonde girl. The girl whose name I never found out. I stare at the laptop.

"Show me," I say.

Judette opens the laptop. The window is already open on YouTube. Large eyes gaze straight into the camera. Her face is stripped of makeup, evenly illuminated, as if she's in front of a window. The video's called, "I had sex with a killer." It has 238 views so far.

I shake my head. Judette closes the laptop again.

"What does she say?" I ask.

"She doesn't claim that it wasn't consensual," Judette says quickly. "Nothing like that. There's just a lot of talk about how she could have been the one to die, that you seemed distracted . . . that you must have been planning the murder already."

I laugh.

"We've reported it," Judette continues. "But, well, you know . . ."

She doesn't have to finish the sentence. Neither of us believes that the video will be taken down, that anyone is even reading the reports anymore.

"If you decide to watch it later, don't read the comments," Judette insists.

I nod. Then rage crashes through me like a wave. I hate Tilda, passionately and irrationally, for landing me in this mess.

"I'm so sorry this shit keeps happening to you," Judette says.

"So am I," I say, and get out of bed.

Emma's left my phone on the kitchen table. Judette turns the TV on, and I listen while I make myself a cup of tea. Numerous European countries have opened suicide clinics—dead bodies, sometimes entire families, have become a public health issue in crowded areas.

I pour water into my cup. Make myself a sandwich.

Stina was called away last night. Someone had found their wife in the bathtub. Was it pills? A razor blade?

Could I do that?

I try to imagine it, and my heart beats faster. *Could* I do it? No. But what if I someday I come up with another answer? What if I can't take it anymore?

Suddenly, two and a half weeks feel too long to endure. I sit down at the table. Icy needles prick my forehead and temples. I look at my phone. Grab it. Turn it on.

It connects to the internet and the messages start pouring in. Twelve, total. Almost all of them from numbers I don't recognize.

I get up from the table. I want to leave, but there's nowhere to go. The phone vibrates against the table. Lucinda's name flashes on the screen. As I lift it, the vibrations shake my entire body. I answer it just to get them to stop.

"What do you want?" I demand.

"Sorry. I really mean it. I'm so sorry about what happened before." Her voice is breathless. Maybe nervous. "Can you meet me?"

"Why should I?"

Emma looks at me when she enters the kitchen.

"I understand why you wouldn't want to," Lucinda says. "But we need to talk."

I look out the window. Thick white clouds rush across a white sky like a sped-up video.

"It's about Tilda," Lucinda says. "She's written me a letter."

NAME: LUCINDA
TELLUS # 0 392 811 002
POST 0025

Caroline's phone call woke me up this morning. She said that she had something she needed to show me and asked me to come over.

I couldn't smell any ghostly chlorine in the house this time. I heard no sounds coming from upstairs. But Tilda felt more present than ever.

The police had returned her laptop that morning, and on it, Caroline had found a letter to me. She left me alone in the living room with the computer so that I could take my time to read it privately. She trusted me, and I had already decided to betray that trust. But first, I opened the document. It was written the day before Tilda died. While reading it, I kept having to remind myself that it wasn't meant as a farewell. Tilda couldn't have possibly known that she would be dead by the time I read it.

I emailed the letter to myself. I've pasted it below. What I write here in TellUs is so often about Tilda; it's only fair that she gets to tell her version of the events, in her own words.

I just wish you could hear her voice while reading this. I can, as clearly as if she's sitting right next to me. It's rambling and incoherent, faster than usual, but it's still *her*.

Lucinda. I don't even know where to start. There is so much I want to tell you that my mind just goes completely blank. I miss you so fucking much, but I'm too much of a coward to get in touch with you in any other way than this. I'm so afraid you'd be disappointed in me if you saw me now, but I want to try to reach out. I've thought about it for ages (have you been thinking of me, too? I hope so). Mom met your dad in town, and he said you've stopped your chemo treatment and that THE OLD LUCINDA IS BACK. She told me when we had dinner the other night and I decided to write you this letter. I don't know if I'll ever send it. I can't really think clearly nowadays. I don't want to waste the nights (or days) when we have so few left and they just get fewer and fewer. I want to experience as much as possible; there's so much I want to try, and we always put things off, because we were such good little girls who always did what was expected of us and exercised and studied and did our best and got home in time. Our entire lives were based around planning for the future, and now there is no future. You have to BE ABLE TO LAUGH IN THE FACE OF MISERY, they say. I miss laughing at things with you. If we ever meet again, I'm going to tell you that I wasn't a good girl like everyone thought, including you and Simon, even though you knew me better than anyone. I cheated and lied and there is a reason why I'm like this now. I know what people are saying about me behind my back and you might hear it, too, if you haven't already, but I want to tell you about it in my way. Not to lay the blame on anyone else, but because I know you'd understand. YOU ARE THE ONLY ONE WHO WOULD. We had a party at the pool the other night and it was my idea, like a "fuck you" to Tommy because he's ruined everything, and now I'll never be free of him, I don't have the energy to write about it, but I'll explain it to you when we see each other again. I thought it would feel like revenge, having everyone drink and fuck and messing with the place, but Lucinda Lucinda Lucinda, I regret it because it was YOURS AND MINE before it was ever his, the only place where I've known who I am, and I ruined it.

Simon was there, too. He thinks he still loves me, and I have to force myself to be mean to him to get him to stop. He shouldn't waste more of his time on me. It would have ended between us sooner or later, but he only remembers the good things because he's scared to be alone and he thinks I'm the solution to everything. He deserves someone who can give him what he wants, but that person isn't me. I don't want to belong to anyone but myself. But it hurts because I still like him and he's one of the best people I know, but now I have to cut him away with surgical precision, snip snip, *so he doesn't think there's a chance we'll get together again, it's better for the both of us if he gets it. I wish it could be different.*

Now I don't have you or Simon. And I don't recognize my-

self anymore. I don't know who I am in this world, the way everything is now.

Writing this makes me feel a little bit better, as if I'm already talking to you. The problem is you can't answer me, and I need your help I think.

I'm so scared all the time, that's why I can't stand still. I talked to Stina, Simon's mom. She's a priest, did you know that? I needed to know what she thought would happen when we're all dead. Dad's become a Truther and is convinced I'll go to hell if I don't get baptized at their church. Unbelievable, right? My lovably dorky dad has started acting like a crazy priest in some horror movie. But I had a good talk with Stina. I like her. She managed to calm me down about a few things. Then she said she wished I believed in God, and I asked her if she wished it because that way I'd get into heaven, and she just laughed and said I'd go to heaven anyway, but that it would easier for me to have someone to turn to in this life. I thought that was nice. I would like to turn to someone I believe in. But, honestly, heaven feels like as much of a threat as hell, because I can't think of ETERNITY without wanting to throw up with panic. I hope that everything just ends and that afterward you don't have to know anything and never have to think again.

I think I get it now, why you didn't want to see me when you got sick. I didn't get it then. I was sad and hurt and tried to hate you, but now that I know what it's like to be told that you're dying, I don't want anyone to look at me and try to save me.

But I think I need to be saved. I think I've been running from myself for so long, that I won't find my way back until it's too late. I just don't know what's going to happen if I stop. It's been going on for way longer than everyone thinks. If I don't stop to think about it, it's not that bad and I try not to let people get too close. I pretend to be friends with Elin and Amanda and the rest, but it's never real or deep. Not like with you.

There's only one other person I can really be myself with. He makes me laugh, sometimes without meaning to. Other people would say he's A BAD INFLUENCE, but he listens without judging, and I know he'd never tell anyone else. I'm writing this at his place and IF HE'S TRYING TO READ THIS OVER MY SHOULDER, HE CAN STOP RIGHT NOW. He's a little (okay, A LOT) obsessed with space, and was long before we knew about the comet—he has a telescope and says that soon we'll be able to see it coming. He told me that a few years ago, they found a solar system around a dwarf star called Trappist-1 and there should be habitable planets there. It's forty light-years away, which is inconceivably far away, but still pretty close considering space is INFINITE (nearly threw up again, it's as bad as ETERNITY). NASA looked at it through their telescopes and tried to figure out what it was like over there. And it occurred to me that if someone out there is LOOKING BACK AT US???!!!? they'd see the Earth like it was forty years ago. That's the light that reaches them now. Maybe they're seeing our parents, but they'd still be kids, and we wouldn't even be born yet. We are in the FUTURE. It's such a wild thought, but nice, I think. It's like we get a second chance.

I've got to stop now. Maybe sleep if I can. Will reread this letter before I send it because I'm like 100% fucked up at the moment. I probably sound disturbed. But you always got me when I was acting like a weirdo. TAKES ONE TO KNOW ONE. Haha.

Hugs. Love. All that jazz.
Tilda

I didn't cry when I was reading the letter at Caroline's house. My brain took charge. I knew this was my only chance to find out more, and I didn't have time to wonder if what I was doing was wrong. So I waited until Caroline busied herself with something in the kitchen. Tilda hadn't logged out from her social media, and her laptop was connected to her phone, so I could read her messages. The police had probably done the same thing, hunting for the same things I was: clear threats to her life; plans to meet someone in North Gate. There wasn't anything like that. But there were other messages. Both before and after her death. Someone had stolen her phone and pretended to be her so that no one would come looking for her. They stopped the day after Tilda's body was found; at that point, there was no use pretending anymore.

I took pictures of the things I needed more time to think about, maybe look up. Then I said goodbye to Caroline and thanked her for letting me read the letter. I held her while she cried, and still didn't feel anything. I couldn't even comfort her about what happened at the fellowship hall yesterday. My own tears only came when I got back home.

I can't remember the last time I cried like that. I didn't even know I could do it.

Afterward, I was utterly exhausted, like I'd run a marathon.

Can you cry? Or do you have some other way of venting?

I've spoken to Simon. He'll be here soon. He deserves to know what Tilda has to say about him, how much he meant to her.

Maybe we end up helping each other. I need him. And he needs me.

He didn't kill Tilda. I know that now.

The doorbell's ringing. Write more later.

SIMON

A middle-school-aged girl opens the door. She looks just like the Lucinda in Tilda's old photos.

"Hi. I'm here to see Lucinda," I say, and try not to use that fake-sounding grown-up voice I hated at that age.

"Who are you?" She looks at me skeptically. "Are you a Truther?"

"No. I'm her friend."

The girl doesn't seem convinced. And it hits me that not a lot of people have visited Lucinda in the past year.

"I'm Simon," I add, and that seems to pique her interest.

"Were you dating Tilda?"

Impatience starts to creep up on me.

"Lucinda told me to come," I say. "Maybe you could get her."

"Wait here."

The door slams, and I hear the girl screaming Lucinda's name inside. In the meantime, I gaze out at the garden, where the apple trees are heavy with unripe fruit. The sunset washes the air in golden colors. Cress in red, yellow, and other fiery tones spills over the edges of a flower bed, almost like it's trying to make the most of the final time it has to bloom.

I try to spot Tilda's house, but it's hidden behind the tree canopies.

And soon it'll all be gone.

Tilda understood it before I did. She didn't close her eyes to what was happening. What did she think about when we lay on the floor of her room? She was so quiet that I thought she must have been asleep, but she was watching the news—she couldn't tear her eyes from the broadcast. Had she decided to break up with me then and there, as I was holding her? When I told her I loved her?

The door opens behind me.

"Come in," Lucinda says.

She's wrapped a cardigan around herself and is wearing her knit hat indoors. She seems tired; it looks like she's been crying. I follow her into the hallway and step out of my shoes. The house smells nice. Clean. Cool. Freshly aired out. On the wall opposite the hat rack, framed photographs of family members from different eras hang so close together they're touching. In the middle is a picture of a bride and groom on the beach. The man is blond and a little sunburned. He's wearing a pair of glasses with wire frames so thin they're hardly visible. The woman is taller than him and enormously pregnant, dressed in a simple white gown. In the background, I can see a handful of dressed-up guests and someone who looks like he officiated the ceremony.

Lucinda's parents seem happy in their wedding photos. It must have been a day full of hope for the future. They had no idea what was coming. And that beach, wherever it is, will soon be gone forever.

I push the thought away. Lucinda asks if I'd like anything to drink, but I decline. I don't want to wait a second longer than necessary to see what's in that letter.

We step into a kitchen, where the floorboards squeak and move almost imperceptibly beneath our feet. There's white-painted wooden paneling halfway up the wall, and paned windows. Lucinda walks ahead of me into a corridor, and we pass a dining room, continuing past built-in cabinets and sideboards. This house has a palpable sense of history. In the past, staff probably rushed around here in neat little uniforms. Girls probably curtsied and put up with getting pinched on the ass. This has always been the nice part of town, where those who profited off the woods and the mines settled. It strikes me that back then, no one in this house would have had anything to do with a person from my neighborhood.

"I thought we could go to my room," Lucinda says.

We walk up a staircase, and on the next floor, I catch a glimpse of a large room. The furniture and lampshades look expensive, and only someone who knew their shit would dare mix the patterns. Lucinda walks up the staircase, stopping on a landing with two white-painted doors. She opens one of them, sounding out of breath as we step inside.

I look around her room. Against one wall is a desk strewn with paper and pens, and a heap of something that looks like old diaries. A small sofa and two small armchairs are in the center of the room. The bed is messily made. A closed laptop lies on top of her blanket, and I hear its fan whirring softly. I wonder if she was writing on TellUs when I arrived.

Tilda must have spent so much time in here. Stayed the night. I walk up to one of the small windows. From between the branches, I think I can see the roof of her house. I wonder how Caroline is feeling. If she's in there right now.

I turn around. Bookshelves cover the entire wall around the doorway we just walked through. Books are tightly pressed together or stacked on top of one another. Has Lucinda read them all?

She grabs her laptop and settles down in one of the armchairs. I sink onto the sofa opposite her. It's surprisingly soft.

"I hope Tilda would be okay with me showing you this," Lucinda says, and places the laptop on the round table between us.

I want to grab it. Instead, I sit completely still while Lucinda turns the screen to face me.

My eyes automatically search for my name in the wall of text.

Simon was there, too. He thinks he still loves me.

I spoke to Stina, Simon's mom.

I take a deep breath. Start over. Read the text again and again, until the lines start to blur together.

I have to cut him away with surgical precision, snip snip.

He's one of the best people I know.

When I lean back into the sofa, Lucinda is watching me, trying to gauge my reaction.

"Are you okay?"

"I don't know," I answer.

How could I be okay? How could I ever be okay again, even if I had a lifetime left?

I choke, and it feels like a sob until I realize I'm laughing. It's like putting your finger in cold water and, for a second, thinking that you've burned it. I have no idea what or how to feel.

Am I happy about what Tilda's written about me? Or does it make everything worse?

I keep laughing. I laugh so hard I'm crying, and I can't stop. I start to feel afraid. This laughter isn't my own. It's a creature that has crept inside me, *taken me over.*

Then all of a sudden, it's gone, leaving behind only a roaring emptiness.

"I don't think I can handle this anymore," I say.

"You're not the only one."

It stings when I wipe my eyes, as if the salt's eating away at my skin.

"Tilda said something terrible was going to happen. It's like she knew," I hear myself say.

Lucinda's gaze is determined.

"We can't think like that. She didn't know. You couldn't have known."

"I knew she needed help."

Lucinda digs her phone out of the pocket of her cardigan.

"I want to help her now," she says. "I want to find out what happened. And I need your help."

I slowly shake my head. "The other night, you thought I killed her. Why have you changed your mind?"

"Because I read Tilda's messages on her laptop."

Lucinda waits a beat for me to react; I wait for her to keep going.

"She'd connected her phone messages to it," she says.

I look out the window. Remember again how I held Tilda on the floor of her room. The notifications on the computer screen. Messages from people who wanted to know if she'd heard what was happening.

"Remember when we met on the dock that first time?" Lucinda continues. "You got a message from Tilda's phone, remember?"

"Yeah."

Everything is ok. You don't need to worry about me.

"But she was already dead at that point," Lucinda says. "And whoever had her phone must have killed her. Since I was with you when you got the message . . . I know you didn't send it."

It takes a moment for the words to sink in and make sense. Then relief floods my body. Makes my eyes water again. I had almost given up hope, but now there's something approaching real evidence that I didn't do it.

"Thank you," I whisper.

Lucinda keeps fiddling with her phone.

"I took photos of some of her messages," she says. "If we help each other out, we could find something the police missed."

I look at her. I want nothing more than to say yes. But first, there's a question I need to ask.

"Why do you want to do this?"

"What do you mean?"

"Everyone is going to die. What does it matter?"

"It matters. It has to." Lucinda looks away. "If nothing matters, then everything is meaningless." She clears her throat, tries to swallow down tears. "You were right," she says. "I know that now that I've read the letter. Tilda needed me when she was alive. I owe her this."

"And then what? What do we do if we find out what really happened?"

Lucinda looks back at me. It takes me a second to read her face—the tense lines around her mouth are suppressed rage.

"I want to look whoever did it in the eye and say: 'I know it was you. And everyone you care about will know it, too.' That's the only punishment left, isn't it? No one wants to be alone and out in the cold now."

I, of all people, know that's true. I wonder if Lucinda's saying it to manipulate me. If that's the case, she doesn't need to.

"And besides, what's the alternative?" she adds. "Just sit around and think about doomsday?"

I study Lucinda. Look at her phone.

Finding the person responsible for Tilda's death would at least give the final two weeks and four days meaning.

"Show me, then," I say.

NAME: LUCINDA
TELLUS # 0 392 811 002
POST 0026

D ad came home from work a moment ago, and Miranda happily informed him that Simon had been here. I forgot to tell her to keep it secret.

Naturally, he'd heard the rumors about Simon. We had another fight. When I told Dad about the message that exonerated Simon, I could hear how *vague* it all sounded. It's the kind of explanation that *invites* you to undermine it. Dad said Simon could have had an accomplice who'd sent him the message from Tilda's phone. I told him there was no way for Simon to know we'd bump into each other. We wouldn't even have spoken if his dog hadn't aggressively licked me. But Dad made me promise not to see Simon again.

I haven't exactly had the opportunity to practice lying to him. Now, I'm going to have to get good at it fast. Simon and I are meeting at North Gate tomorrow to check out the place where Tilda was found. I've seen online that people have been leaving flowers and cards there. They say murderers like to return to the scene of the crime. Maybe Simon and I will find something.

And we've gone through all of Tilda's messages. I'll tell you more about them once I sort out my thoughts. Right now, I'm trying to convince people that Simon is innocent. His mom Judette is going to ask her friend, who's a police officer, to call me tonight. I've posted online for the first time since I got sick, and wrote a text to Caroline and Klas. I just hope it helps.

I know Tilda wouldn't want people to think Simon had killed her.

P.S.: I wonder if Dad is worried about me getting strong enough to do things by myself again. I don't necessarily mean he preferred it when I was sick, but at least he always knew what I was up to.

He would never admit it. Not even to himself. But I think there might be some truth to it.

SIMON

I sit at the kitchen table looking at Lucinda's post. She made it public, and more and more people are sharing it. The comments are rolling in. A lot of people are still unconvinced. *No smoke without fire*, one of Tilda's old teachers has written. I know he still goes to the school every workday, preparing lessons no one will attend. But what really pisses me off are the ones who thank Lucinda, writing that they knew I was innocent all along. Where were they when I needed them the most? Ali has written, too, asking for forgiveness, but when I asked him if we could meet up, he told me it wasn't a good idea. That cowardly fuck.

I try to hold on to the fact that I'm not alone anymore. Lucinda is on my side now. We have a plan.

Judette's in the bedroom talking on the phone with Maria.

Emma's gone to bed. Only Stina and I are still in the kitchen. She's stuffing empty cans into the trash. She smiles when our eyes meet.

"Yuck," she says. "It still feels wrong not to recycle."

I nod. A few weeks ago, I threw away a pair of batteries for the first time in my life. I always used to be careful about things like that. I used to think I had to do what was necessary to save the earth.

I look at Stina. See how relieved she is by what she's just found out. Was she worried in her heart of hearts that I'd done it?

She's a priest, did you know that?

There's so much in Tilda's letter I haven't taken in yet.

"Why didn't you tell me you spoke to Tilda?"

Stina stiffens. Pulls out the trash bag and ties it.

"What do you mean?"

"You know what I mean. This summer."

Stina's still standing with the trash bag in her hand. It's dripping, but she doesn't seem to notice.

"Tilda wanted to meet me as a priest, not as your mother," she says. "You know I can't—"

"Why the hell does confidentiality matter now?"

"It mattered to Tilda," Stina says, and something firm comes into her voice. "How do you know we spoke?"

"Did she say anything that could explain what happened?"

"No."

"Can you think about it for more than a second before answering me?"

Stina's cheeks flush red. Garbage juice keeps dripping from the bag, forming small puddles on the floor.

"Did you talk about me?" I continue.

Stina's eyes narrow. She's almost purple now.

"The world is ending, Simon. Tilda had other things on her mind. And maybe it's about time you did, too."

"It might be easier to think about something else if everyone didn't think I murdered her. But you care more about confidentiality than me."

"Don't you think I'd help you if I could?" Stina shouts. "Do you think I *enjoy* being worried about you?"

Boomer shuffles into the kitchen, watching us with large eyes. He sniffs the air.

"Why do you think I'm staying home tonight?" Stina asks, her voice shaking slightly.

"You said it's your night off."

"Yes, it is! Because one of the discussion groups asked for another priest! They said they didn't want pastoral care from someone who'd *raised a murderer!*"

I literally lose my breath. Boomer's eyes travel between us; he whines anxiously.

"So this doesn't just affect you!" Stina continues. "But I'd gladly stay home from work if you'd at least talk to me *once* without fucking sighing or acting like it's a massive sacrifice, or like I'm a complete moron! But that's too much to ask, isn't it?"

She waves her arms around, making the juice from the bottom of the bag splash across the floor.

"What are you doing out here?" asks Judette as she comes out of the bedroom.

Stina shakes her head. "Did you get ahold of Maria?" she says with strained patience.

"She's going to call Lucinda now."

"And then what? What is Maria going to do to make the people of this fucking town understand that our son is innocent?"

"I don't know," Judette says. "One thing at a time."

"I don't want to take one thing at a time! I want to know that someone is doing something!"

Boomer carefully sniffs at the pools on the floor. It's only when he starts licking them that Stina notices what's happened, and she shouts again, wordlessly this time.

I get up, take the trash bag from her hand, and place it on the floor. Stina sucks in a deep breath, then slowly exhales through her mouth.

"I'm sorry," she says. "I just feel so goddamn powerless."

"I know," I say, and put my arms around her.

NAME: LUCINDA
TELLUS # 0 392 811 002
POST 0027

The police officer sounded friendly and attentive. I could tell that she believed me. It must have been a relief for her as well, since she knows Judette. She promised me she'd think about the best way to use my information to exonerate Simon publicly. She said it's hard to know what the best course of action would be. Most people outside the inner circle have already forgotten about Tilda. Reminding everyone of Simon could make things worse for him.

I don't think the police know what to do about *anything* anymore. None of the old rules apply, and too much is going on. Earlier tonight, a few girls around Miranda's age let out all the horses from a stable, wanting them to run free before the world ends. At this moment, panicked horses are galloping through the streets in the heart of town, and there have been car accidents up and down the highway.

Finding the person responsible for Tilda's death is up to Simon and me now. And the comments on my post only confirm that this is the only way to clear his name.

I can't write any more tonight. I'm exhausted.

SIMON

I wake up before the alarm goes off and immediately feel like something's changed. My body's light in a way I'd almost forgotten it could be. I pick up my phone from the floor. In about an hour, I'm meeting Lucinda by the glass factory. She sent me a message during the night.

GOT A REPLY FROM CAROLINE. SHE DOESN'T THINK YOU DID IT ANYMORE.

I smile, and write back that I'll see her soon. Thank her again.

Johannes replied to the message I sent him yesterday.

SHIT, THAT'S AMAZING! COME TO STOCKHOLM AND CELE-BRATE!!!

I write back that I wish I could. Then I get out of bed and pull on a pair of jeans and a T-shirt hanging over the desk chair. That's when I realize what's so different.

I have more energy than I've had all summer. And not that nervous energy that just messes with your body. This energy can be directed at something. This is what it feels like to have a goal again. And it's all thanks to Lucinda.

When I step into the kitchen, Emma is at the table, stirring a cup of tea.

"Shit, I've slept for forever," I say. "I passed out at eleven."

"Maybe you needed it."

"I think I did."

My sister lifts her spoon. It's covered in cheese that's

melted into the hot tea. She sticks it into her mouth. She doesn't even swallow before cutting herself another slice of cheese, folding it into a square and pressing it into the cup. I lean over the table. The milky tea smells flowery and sweet. Greasy pools have spread across the surface.

"That looks disgusting."

"Try it."

"No, thanks."

"It's melted cheese," Emma says, like that's the only argument she needs.

I make a cup of tea and some sandwiches, and settle down at the table.

"I heard you and Stina cleared the air yesterday," Emma says.

"Are they at home?" I ask, nodding at the bedroom door.

"Mom's just left for work. I think Judette's gone back to sleep." Emma leans forward in the chair. "You missed the Third World War this morning."

I blow into my cup to cool the tea.

"What were they fighting about this time?"

Emma sticks her cheesy spoon into her mouth, then taps it against her front teeth. "Have you seen what Maria posted about you on the police department's official Facebook page this morning?"

"No," I say, and haul out my phone.

"Stina thinks Maria should have done more," Emma says in a low voice while I search for the post.

The police would like to remind the public
that in the case regarding the seventeen-year-old girl
found dead in North Gate, there are at present
no suspects, and no circumstantial evidence has been

corroborated. Rumors can cause serious harm
to the victim's family and the innocent person(s)
accused of the crime, as well as impede
the investigation.

I study the impersonal words. The post has received more than forty comments.

"Are you okay, Simon? Have you got anyone to talk to about all this?"

The tea burns my tongue when I try to drink it, and I curse under my breath.

"You know you can always talk to me, right?" Emma presses on.

"Absolutely."

"You'll go insane if you don't talk to someone."

I blow into my tea again. My sister, who has somehow managed to repress the fact that the end of the world will affect the baby in her belly, is worried *I'll* go insane.

I take a gulp of tea and start reading the comments. Some of them are actually on my side.

"It isn't easy for Mom, being so dependent on Maria," Emma whispers. "I think she still feels betrayed."

I'm about to ask her what she's talking about when my eye goes to one of the latest comments.

Of course that's what the police say. Must be nice having
your mother's lesbian girlfriend on the force.

There's a comment under that one, too.

Wouldn't mind if those two cuffed me 😊

I look up from the phone.

"I'm not saying Judette did anything wrong," Emma hisses, glancing at the bedroom door. "They were divorced. But . . ."

"Judette and Maria were dating?"

Emma puts her head in her hands, rubbing her eyes. "Fuuuuck. I thought you knew."

"Now the whole town knows about it," I say, placing my phone on the table in front of her.

Emma lowers her hands. Her eyes have gone bloodshot.

While she's reading the comments, I remember small, seemingly inconsequential things I noticed last spring. The weeks I stayed at Judette's place were full of signs.

Shampoo for a white person's hair. A tube of pale concealer. Traces of an unknown perfume in the room when I returned after a week at Stina's. When I asked, Judette said a friend of hers had stayed over. There were other signs, too. Like Judette always checking her phone, smiling at all the wrong moments when we were watching movies together. And she'd been listening to music again.

It's so obvious now that I honestly can't believe I missed it.

Emma pushes the phone away with a look of deep disgust.

"When did it end?" I ask, and think of Judette's secret smiles again.

She must have had feelings for Maria. They must have been good together.

"In June," Emma says quietly. "It was Mom's condition for letting Judette move back in."

So Judette had broken up with her girlfriend to be able to live with me full-time again.

And I did everything but stay at home.

My guilt makes my throat close up.

"How could Stina do something like that?" I say.

"Like what?" Emma asks.

We look at each other. Sometimes, I forget that Judette is just an extra mom to my sister. Laughing at Stina together is one thing, but when our moms are fighting, she almost always takes Stina's side. Which means I have to defend Judette.

"Mom is at least trying to make it work," Emma says.

"Blackmail is so romantic."

"It's not blackmail! She just couldn't live with Judette while Judette was dating someone else. How is that weird?"

We could end up arguing like we used to. When Stina and Judette had issues, they didn't just bring out the worst in each other, but in us, too.

I don't want to fight. I don't know what I might let slip. So I get to my feet, put my teacup in the sink, and leave the sandwiches, untouched, on the kitchen table.

NAME: LUCINDA
TELLUS # 0 392 811 002
POST 0028

I didn't have time to check all the messages on Tilda's laptop. I focused on the people who'd been in touch with her during the last month.

Elin and Amanda, of course, and the rest of their loose friend group. Reading their messages felt wrong. Tons of tiny dramas, but nothing that had anything to do with Tilda's death. And they had all been at the after-party. They couldn't have done it.

I saw messages from Molly, who mostly sent emojis. Tilda's grandmother seemed to use an ancient phone, since she only wrote in capital letters. There were goodbye-before-the-comet-comes messages sent from other relatives around the country.

Reading Caroline's texts was almost unbearable, especially during the final days when she desperately begged Tilda to call her back and tell her where she was. And the person pretending to be Tilda—the person who knew she was rotting behind an abandoned factory—kept answering that she was coming home. *I love you, too. You're the best mom in the world.*

Tilda wasn't exaggerating when she wrote that Klas was trying to convert her. On an almost daily basis, he sent her links to signs of the Second Coming. Lists of events said to be predicted by the Bible (three super moons in a row, the Zika virus, the Second World War). I shiver when I read them. I'm almost swept away by the feeling that our doom was predestined. Klas sent quotes from the Bible, too. I recognize some of them from his breakdown (or explosion) at the fellowship hall. Other examples:

And there shall be signs in the sun, and in the moon, and in the stars; and upon the earth distress of nations, with perplexity; the sea and the waves roaring.

Men's hearts failing them for fear, and for looking after those things which are coming on the earth: for the powers of heaven shall be shaken.

And then they shall see the Son of man coming in a cloud with power and great glory. And when these things begin to come to pass, then look up, and lift up your heads; for your redemption draweth nigh.

Klas begged her, again and again, to come with him to the True Church. To be redeemed before it was too late. Maybe him acting "crazy" at the funeral isn't strange at all; I mean, he does believe that his daughter is burning in hell. That she will do so for all eternity, while he's in heaven, a safe distance from the flames. Forever apart. That must be a horrible thing to imagine.

But Tilda resisted Klas's attempts to "save" her. She rarely replied to his messages. He kept sending them until the day Tilda's body was found. He couldn't have done it, even though Tilda compared him to a priest in a horror movie. There are pictures of him, Anders, and Erika in the True Church on the night Tilda died.

Then there were messages exchanged with boys Tilda had had sex with this summer. I didn't show them to Simon. Seeing them was difficult, even for me. I know Tilda's body so well. We've seen each other in changing rooms thousands of times; we've massaged each other in the sauna when our legs and arms cramped. When we stayed over at each other's houses, we never hid behind towels when we showered. Our naked bodies were completely ordinary. But seeing the pictures Tilda had sent to these guys is something completely different. I've looked at their public profiles. Some of them watched the game with a bunch of friends in their own homes; others weren't even in town that night. A couple of them *were* in the square—and checking them out could possibly be worth it—but I don't think any of them did it. When Simon told me what he and Tilda had talked about, it became clear that she was going to see someone she knew well—either to talk to me or to confront one of the "hypocrites." Regardless, it was someone who meant a lot to her. In the messages to these guys, there are no feelings involved. They hardly seem to know each other.

There are really only two, maybe three, people we know we should talk to:

TOMMY: Tilda's final message to him was sent a few days before her disappearance. It looks like she's commenting on something they've discussed. She wanted to add one last thing: *If what I'm doing is wrong it's YOUR FAULT.* Before that, the messages are from the end of May, and there's only the usual info about schedules and competitions. So what happened during the summer? It was something that made Tilda write in her letter that she wanted to say "fuck you" to what Tommy represented. Erika said something had happened between them, but didn't know what. For fuck's sake, Tilda, why were you so secretive?

Does Caroline know something? I noticed her avoiding Tommy at the funeral.

Tommy hasn't posted anything on social media all summer. We don't know what he was doing on the night of the game.

THE NEW FRIEND: Neither Simon nor I know whose home she was at when she wrote me the letter. Amanda didn't know about anyone who was obsessed with space. I couldn't find any messages to him either, unless he's the same person who was selling her drugs.

TILDA'S DEALER: We don't know who this is, but at least we now have a phone number. I found messages to someone who wasn't in her list of contacts. It started in the beginning of June. The messages are short. Often Tilda would just suggest a time, and get an *okay* or *can't* in response. They never had to decide on a place, which means they always met at the same spot.

The messages were rarely longer. The person was worried Tilda would expose them. She promised never to do that. *It's not like I want to risk not seeing you again.* They were going to meet in the afternoon the same day she died. It can hardly get more suspicious than that.

We'll get in touch with them. But what do you say to a criminally inclined and clearly paranoid person? "Sorry, but did you happen to murder my best friend in a drug deal gone wrong?"

I'll admit: Simon and I don't have much to go on. Fantasizing about our important mission was easier last night. I have to hurry if I'm going to meet up with him, but part of me wants to call the whole thing off. What the fuck do we know about catching a killer?

SIMON

It's the first time I've ever seen the glass factory up close. I park Judette's car in front of the turquoise box made of corrugated metal. Five signs, one letter on each, spell out the word GLASS, no more nor less. Lucinda isn't around, but I'm early.

I pull out the key, lean forward in the driver's seat, and see lanterns made of plastic, flowers in different stages of decomposition, notes and trash that have been scattered by the wind across the asphalt; some of them stick to the net fencing behind the factory. I squeeze the steering wheel with one hand, listening to my breathing and the sound of the wind finding its way through the gap between the car door and the frame.

It would have ended between us sooner or later, but he only remembers the good things, Tilda wrote in that letter.

Is that true?

When Tilda and I were together, I sometimes felt that there were things she wasn't telling me. Something in her eyes. A sentence left unfinished.

She was the person who knew me better than anyone else in the world. But she wrote that she'd kept secrets from Lucinda and me long before Foxworth.

I'm afraid of what we'll find once we start looking. Will I discover things that force me to reevaluate our whole relationship, something that will ruin even the good memories?

The girl you were with ... she doesn't exist anymore. Maybe she never did.

Why didn't I take her seriously? I was willing to do anything to get back together with Tilda. Anything except listen to what she was actually saying.

It feels like Foxworth is a spotlight that illuminates everything we do to try to hold on to the people we love the most. Judette sacrificed a relationship with Maria. And I have no right to be angry with Stina for giving Judette an ultimatum. It was what she needed.

A gust of wind whispers through the crack in the door. Bits of paper tumble across the asphalt.

There are no streetlights around. Did Tilda come here to meet someone? Or was she already dead when her body was left here?

No one would have heard her if she'd screamed for help. That night was full of screams.

Would I hear her now? If I really listened?

When I drove Stina to work, she suggested I try talking to Tilda.

The idea makes my heart beat faster.

"Tilda," I say.

Her name feels strange in my mouth, like her death has transformed it into something else.

I shiver. Close my eyes.

"Tilda, if you can hear me, I want you to know that I'm thinking about you. And I miss you. A lot."

There's no reply. I feel ridiculous, but force myself to continue.

"Lucinda and I are trying to find out who left you here. She misses you, too. If you can help us in any way, please try."

I jump in my seat when someone knocks on the side window. Lucinda is standing outside the car. She mimes *sorry*. Her hair is blonde, with bangs, just like in the photos in Tilda's room. It takes me half a second to realize it's a wig.

Has she seen me talking to myself?

I step out of the car and pull my hood up against the wind.

"Sorry I scared you," Lucinda says.

In her black sunglasses, I'm reflected against the sky. This time, I'd like to hug her if she makes the first move. She doesn't.

"Thanks for talking to Maria yesterday," I say.

"You don't have to thank me again. It's nothing."

"No, it's something."

She smiles, but I can tell that something's wrong.

"Is everything okay?" I ask her.

"I don't know. Is it ridiculous to think we can do this? I mean, even if we find the person who did it, why would they confess?"

I swallow the desperate impulse to try to persuade her. I don't want Lucinda to agree to this if she doesn't actually want to.

But I want her to want to.

"I don't know if it's ridiculous," I say. "All I know is that I have to try. And the person who did it might want to confess."

Lucinda brushes a strand of hair from her face. She looks doubtful, but is still listening.

"Stina says that the people who come to church nowadays want to unburden themselves," I continue. "She says people who know they're dying tend to share their secrets with someone."

"I never did. I didn't want to talk to anyone."

I don't know how to reply to that. For a long moment, Lucinda's quiet.

"We'll have to hope that whoever we're looking for isn't like me," she says after a while, and then looks at the piles of flowers and cards. "Did you bring anything?"

"I didn't even think of that. Should we have?"

She shakes her head firmly. "Tilda lay dead here for days. It's the last place I'd like to leave her flowers."

I follow her gaze. Consider how cold and wet the asphalt must have been that night. Lucinda is right.

"Okay." She sighs. "Let's do this."

We cross the parking lot side by side. I pick up a discarded note. The text is unreadable—the ink's dissolved in the rain, blossomed into storm-colored clouds, and dried again. I let the paper go, and the wind catches it while we keep walking. The sun shimmers in shattered glass, gleams in empty bottles. Cigarette butts are everywhere, as if there's been a party here. There's a faint rustle when the wind moves through drying bouquets.

Lucinda removes her sunglasses. The circles under her eyes are as dark as bruises. Together, we look at the teddy bears and stuffed animals. Some of them have fallen on their sides, like passed-out drunks. Their eyes gaze emptily at us. Two furry bears each hold out a heart-shaped pillow with factory-made greetings in cursive. *I miss you!* and *You rock!* I squat down, inspecting them more closely.

"They used to sell those at the hospital," Lucinda says, face unmoving. "I got five of them while I stayed there."

I take photos of the bears with my phone. Lucinda picks up a bouquet. The leaves are so dry they crumble when she pulls out the card that's been taped to the stems.

"'From Elin and Amanda,'" she says. "'We love you. Rest in peace.'"

She puts the flowers back without photographing them, then lifts a white plush rabbit that dirt and rain has turned a speckled gray. Her phone clicks. I lift a candle that weighs down a checkered piece of paper. The handwriting looks like it belongs to an older person who, with hands that trembled slightly, tried to write as beautifully as they could.

Do not say that nothing is left
Of the loveliest butterfly life has blessed.
Don't say the colorful wings are lashed
By winds that turn them to ash, to ash.

If the butterfly's body
Is buried of late,
Yet still the dizzying flight awaits!

The poem is signed by someone named Gill. I look up at Lucinda, who's been reading over my shoulder. She's donned the sunglasses again, and pushes them up her nose.

"What a bunch of bullshit," she says, and takes a photo.

There are more poems. Song lyrics. Collages made up of photos of Tilda.

"Look at this," Lucinda says, holding out a laminated piece of paper.

I immediately recognize the text, which is printed in a font meant to suggest calligraphy. It's the start of a poem that was everywhere at the beginning of the summer. The poet, Lord Byron, was one of Emma's favorites when she was our age.

I had a dream, which was not all a dream.
The bright sun was extinguish'd, and the stars
Did wander darkling in the eternal space,
Rayless, and pathless, and the icy earth
Swung blind and blackening in the moonless air.

"Whoever left this probably didn't even know who Tilda was," Lucinda says.

I dutifully take a picture of it, but I suspect she's right. The poem has nothing whatsoever to do with Tilda. It's about all of us. An attempt to elevate our own deaths, to make them something darkly romantic and haunting.

We find a few greetings from old classmates I've never met, and one from the teacher who wrote "no smoke without fire." Metal gleams under a bouquet with uneven, torn stems. Someone has picked woodland sage and red valerian from a flower bed. The purple and pink blossoms have turned brown and faded. There's a pile of medals with different-colored ribbons underneath them.

"They're from relays the team won with Tilda," Lucinda says, handing them to me.

The metal is cold against my fingers. I trace the names, trying to recall if I watched any of these competitions, but it's difficult to separate all those different pools in my mind.

The relays were the only times the swimmers worked together, were a real team, and I see Tilda in my mind's eye. How she flowed through the water. Her open mouth sucking in air before her head disappeared back under the surface.

"No note," I say.

"There doesn't need to be. Tommy had them. But it's only right that he give them to Tilda. It's because of her we won so many."

The medals clink together when I place them back on the asphalt.

"Did you like it?" I ask.

"What?"

"Swimming?"

A couple of seconds of silence pass.

"Yes. I loved it more than anything."

She gets to her feet.

"Can I ask you something?" I ask.

"Sure."

I follow her to the fence. Now I see that what I took to be trash are paper flowers, attached to the fence with pipe cleaners. The thin, silky paper has been ruined by the rain and the wind.

"When you were sick … did you get used to the idea of dying?" I ask.

"Yes."

Lucinda plucks a pale-yellow flower from the fence, takes a picture, and then reattaches it.

"So you can get used to it," I say.

"There's a difference. I was so sick I didn't care anymore."

"But do you think you had a head start? Compared to the rest of us."

Lucinda turns to me.

"I've missed out on so much, I don't know which of us really has a *head start*."

"Sorry. I didn't mean to—"

"I know. But it's just like Tilda wrote. She and I were good girls who always did what we were supposed to do. We thought we were going to live life *later*. And look at us now." Lucinda wipes away tears from under her sunglasses; her breathing is heavy.

"Sorry," I say again.

"You don't have to apologize. But I don't have any fucking cancer wisdom to share to make things easier for you."

She starts picking at a pile of stuffed animals. I pick up the stump of a candle. A note with a heart on it. Sait has scrawled his name on it. But he was also at the after-party when I got there.

"I recognize this," Lucinda says.

She holds out a tiger cub with large paws, long whiskers, and oversized blue glass eyes. I've never seen it before. When Lucinda photographs it, it looks like its half-open mouth is smiling at the camera.

We're finishing up, and I shiver when a breeze creeps into and under my hoodie. Lucinda gets up. Looks at me.

"Shit," she says, and touches a hand to her forehead.

I reach her just as she collapses.

NAME: LUCINDA
TELLUS # 0 392 811 002
POST 0029

I fainted in North Gate. It was a head rush; I got up too quickly. And I haven't been sleeping enough.

Simon drove me home. He stopped a block away so Dad wouldn't see us together. At that point, I felt fine, albeit somewhat embarrassed.

When I stepped into the house, I could hear Christmas carols echoing through the halls; it was the kind they play in shops throughout December, prompting you to wonder how the employees can stand it. Someone had placed the ugly knitted Santas I'd made ages ago in school on the chest of drawers in the hall. I went into the kitchen, where Dad and Miranda were enjoying non-alcoholic mulled wine. There were Santas everywhere. The Christmas lights were on. I don't know how to convey how bizarre it was to see a Christmas star in the window while the garden was blooming outside.

Miranda had been down in the cellar and brought up boxes of Christmas things. She'd found the wine and spices in the cupboard. I wondered how long she'd been planning it. "I wanted to celebrate Christmas one last time," she explained, and I didn't dare look at Dad. I knew that if I did, one of us was going to cry, and it would probably be me. My little sister loves Christmas. Most kids do, but I do mean *loves*. Not just the presents, but the food and the gaudy decorations and the cheery carols.

Dad found a tin of anchovies in the fridge and made Christmas casserole, while Miranda and I decorated the tree. And I actually got into the holiday spirit, especially when the sky got dark. While we ate, we watched Donald Duck's Christmas on YouTube, and as usual, Dad went on about the show being the most important thing about Christmas when he was a kid, "because they never showed cartoons on TV back then, and we only had two channels, and no internet. You wouldn't have lasted a day." This speech is pretty much a Christmas tradition of its own. And now we got to experience it one final time. Then we watched a movie called *Home Alone*. I grinned and suffered through it for Miranda's sake. She laughed herself sick when the thieves got all beat up.

I don't write enough about my sister. I don't want you to think she isn't important to me. I'd love it if she wrote in TellUs, too, so you could get to know her properly. Maybe she's already doing it. It would be typical of Miranda not to tell me or Dad about it. Have a look and see if you can find her stories on here.

The two of us are so different. Miranda has always been a thinker, but it hasn't stopped her from having lots of friends. I wonder what she would have been like in junior high, when so much can happen so unbelievably quickly. We ended up in new classes, in new and unpredictable roles. Pacts and loyalties could change on a daily basis, friends becoming enemies overnight. Nothing was reliable. Not even your own body was the same from one day to the next. I was glad I had swimming, just so I had something else to focus on. We were outsiders to the invisible wars raging through the corridors. We were in a bubble not many people were interested in penetrating. But Miranda didn't have a refuge.

Simon and I didn't find anything in North Gate, but we're going to keep looking. My hesitation went away as soon as I met him. Strange how much braver you get when there are two of you.

I wonder what so much time spent alone has done to me? Have I become a coward? Difficult for you to respond, I know. You haven't known me for long, and can only get a part of me through these posts. And you can never really know me, not even if I wrote down every single thought I've ever had. Not even if we met. Not even if you were human, too.

Tomorrow at noon, Simon is meeting Caroline. He might find out something new about Tilda, about why she was so angry with Tommy.

In the afternoon, after we've found out what Caroline knows, I'm meeting Tommy in town. I promised Simon I'd suggest a public place. Just to be safe. Ironic, isn't it? I've been avoiding town so I wouldn't be seen, but now I have to go there to *be* seen.

If Tommy doesn't give us any leads, we're going to contact Tilda's dealer. I've figured out what to say to him or her. I just hope I don't need to.

I'm going to try to sleep now. I dozed off after the movie, for half an hour or so, but when I woke up, my sheets were soaked with sweat. It can happen to anyone; it doesn't have to mean anything. It really doesn't. But that's exactly what I told myself when I first got sick and refused to consider that something was seriously wrong.

P.S.: Simon's mom Stina said people want to share their secrets before they die. I didn't think I was like that. But isn't this my way of doing just that? Even if I'm writing to someone who might not be real?

P.P.S.: Our "Christmas" really made me miss winter. And I normally hate the darkness and the cold. Now I find myself longing for the cover of snow, the way it makes everything shiny and luminous. I keep thinking about the way snow creaks beneath your boots.

NAME: LUCINDA
TELLUS # 0 392 811 002
POST 0030

S o, the plan was to (a) meet Tommy in a public place, and (b) do it *after* Simon had spoken to Caroline. But Tommy called me this morning and said that something had come up. If I wanted, he was "in the area" and could pick me up in his car.

I imagine I seem somewhat intelligent and eloquent on TellUs, but when faced with something unexpected, it's like my brain starts lagging. And that's the best possible outcome. Other times, I completely shut down. Like when Tommy called and wanted to come pick me up. I couldn't think of a single excuse. So I said yes. *Sure. That's fine. How nice. Please don't kill me.*

I decided to record the conversation with Tommy, even though it didn't go particularly well the last time I tried that, with Simon on the dock. (I never told you this, but I dropped my phone right in front of him. Had he been the murderer, I might not be writing this.)

Since I am, you can probably guess that I wasn't horrifically murdered. But I was scared stiff when Tommy's car stopped on my street. I had visions of nightmare scenarios: I ask the wrong question, Tommy panics and hits me over the head so hard I pass out, the car drives to North Gate and stops outside the glass factory.

What actually happened was that I sat down in the passenger seat while Tommy unfastened his seat belt so that he
could hug me tightly. He said, "I'm so glad you got in touch,"
and "I was hoping we'd have the chance to speak at the funeral, but well, it got kind of messy." While driving us toward
town, he told me he'd started group therapy this summer to
deal with comet-related anxiety (his expression, not mine).
And he's met someone who means a lot to him. He's never
felt like this before.

He never used to talk about himself much, especially
not about things that could be seen as weaknesses. I guess
it would have undermined his authority. I was grateful to
Foxworth for transforming him into such an open, talka-
tive person, because I didn't really have to contribute to the
conversation. Now and then, I caught him glancing at me,
sneaking looks. As if it was forbidden to notice how thin I've
gotten, the fact that I was wearing a wig. It's usually exhaust-
ing to know that you make other people uncomfortable
simply by existing, but at that moment, it felt like a kind of
protection. Tommy didn't dare eye me so carefully that he'd
notice how nervous I was; and even if he did, he'd think it
was because of my illness.

He started crying when he parked the car in the square.
"I'm so sorry, Lucinda. I'm so sorry about what's happened."
It took me a while to realize he hadn't just confessed to
murder, but meant everything else: the cancer, Tilda's death,
doomsday.

The square was still full of litter after the soccer game.
I looked at the ads on the bus stop and in the windows of
abandoned shops. There was something macabre about
them. They were reminders of a future that would never
come. We have no use for driving lessons, diet pills, year-long

subscriptions, anti-aging creams, or pension plans anymore. There won't be any vacations abroad during Christmas. The movies on the posters will never be screened.

We walked past the square and sat next to each other in the park. People were sprawled all over the grass. They had connected speakers to their phones and kept trying to drown each other out with music. A lonely old man must have spent his entire bread ration on feeding pigeons and gulls. They were everywhere with their flapping wings, their eager beaks. An old woman handed out leaflets about the Foxworth fraud. "It's the communists," she said. "They've been preparing this since the wall came down."

The more Tommy and I talked, the more I realized that I like him. It was like I was meeting the actual *person* Tommy for the first time, despite him having been a huge part of my life for so many years.

He said he swims every day, far more frequently than he did as a coach. And he mentioned the party at the pool. I saw my chance to bring up the subject of Tilda. But I fucked up.

I've run the final part of the recording through the TellUs app. You can read it in my next post. I keep rereading it (because I definitely don't want to hear it again), but I can't get any answers.

Goddamn it. This would have been easier if I hadn't liked him so much.

NAME: LUCINDA
TELLUS # 0 392 811 002
POST 0031

TOMMY: Took me days to clean up the shit they left behind.

LUCINDA: I can imagine.

(pause)

LUCINDA: I really miss swimming.

TOMMY: You were one of the best.

LUCINDA: Mmm. But I wasn't close to Tilda's level.

TOMMY: No. No one was.

(laughs)

LUCINDA: No.

TOMMY: I think she's the one who threw that party.

(pause)

TOMMY: I can't believe she's gone. I just can't.

LUCINDA: I know.

(pause)

LUCINDA: How did you find out?

TOMMY: I think it was the morning after they found her. Word got around quickly. How about you?

LUCINDA: Dad told me. He was at the hospital when they brought her in.

TOMMY: Oh my God. Did he have to see her?

LUCINDA: Yes. But he wasn't the one who examined her.

TOMMY: No. . . . Oh my God. No, of course not. He's known her since she was a kid.

LUCINDA: Mmm.

TOMMY: At least you got to hear it from your dad. It's better than seeing it online or something.

LUCINDA: Yeah, it was.

TOMMY: I hope they find the person who did it. Though I don't know if they can investigate it nowadays.

(pause)

TOMMY: How are you? Are you okay?

LUCINDA: Huh? Yes.

TOMMY: You just looked tired. I wondered if you . . .

LUCINDA: No. I mean, I . . . It's just difficult to talk about.

TOMMY: I get it. It's probably for the best if we change the subject.

LUCINDA: No. I'd like to talk about Tilda. I saw you left the medals at North Gate.

TOMMY: Yes. It felt like they belonged to her.

LUCINDA: Mmm.

(pause)

LUCINDA: When did you last see her?

TOMMY: I don't remember.

LUCINDA: You don't?

(pause)

TOMMY: No.

LUCINDA: But you did see her after the team broke up?

TOMMY: Yes. A few times.

LUCINDA: I heard you weren't really seeing eye to eye on something.

TOMMY: (inaudible)

LUCINDA: That she was mad at you.

TOMMY: Who told you that?

LUCINDA: It doesn't matter.

TOMMY: It matters to me.

LUCINDA: I heard it from Erika. Tilda's aunt.

(pause)

LUCINDA: Is it true? Were you fighting?

TOMMY: I really don't want to talk to you about this. I really don't.

LUCINDA: But ...

TOMMY: Whatever was going on was between me and her. What if I asked you a bunch of questions about why you two weren't friends anymore?

LUCINDA: I'd tell you if you asked.

(pause)

TOMMY: I know I could be tough sometimes. Especially on those of you who were good.

LUCINDA: And Tilda was the best. So you were the toughest on her.

TOMMY: Yeah, you could say that.

LUCINDA: Mmm.

TOMMY: Tilda was kind of lost when ... when she didn't have swimming anymore. I think she ... (inaudible)

LUCINDA: What did you say?

TOMMY: I think she was angry about having sacrificed so much for swimming. And blaming me was easier. I became ... the symbol of everything she'd missed out on.

(pause)

LUCINDA: Was that it?

(pause)

LUCINDA: Does Caroline feel the same way?

TOMMY: Caroline?

LUCINDA: You didn't talk to each other after the funeral. Have you fallen out, too?

(pause)

TOMMY: No. I haven't fallen out with Caroline.

(pause)

LUCINDA: Can you believe how much trash there was in the square?

(pause)

LUCINDA: Did you come here to watch the game?

TOMMY: No, I ... Why?

LUCINDA: I stayed at home. But I usually do.

TOMMY: What are you actually asking me?

(pause)

TOMMY: Why are you acting so strange?

LUCINDA: Strange?

TOMMY: You seem nervous.

LUCINDA: I'm just not used to crowds.

(pause)

TOMMY: You think I did it?

(pause)

TOMMY: That you could even imagine—

LUCINDA: Tell me what you did the night of the game, then.

TOMMY: I'm sorry, but that's none of your business.

(pause)

TOMMY: Is that why you wanted to see me? Is that why we're sitting here?

LUCINDA: It's not the only reason.

TOMMY. Isn't it?

(pause)

TOMMY: Lucinda, I understand you're upset about what happened. We all are. But you can't dig around like this.

LUCINDA: I just want to know what happened.

TOMMY: What you're doing right now is dangerous.

LUCINDA: I know.

TOMMY: Not to mention the fact that you're hurting other people.

LUCINDA: I know!

TOMMY: Do you?

(pause)

TOMMY: I think it's time we get going. Can I drive you home?

LUCINDA: I can walk.

(pause)

TOMMY: Damn it, Lucinda. This is probably the last time we'll ever see each other. And it had to turn out like this.

NAME: LUCINDA
TELLUS # 0 392 811 002
POST 0032

Having read my conversation with Tommy several times now, I'm not as embarrassed. Doesn't it feel like he's hiding something from me? Something must have happened between him and Tilda. Doesn't his explanation sound rehearsed? And he got cagey when I asked him about when they'd last met.

Tommy is almost fifty. He looks good in an entirely nondescript way, like an aging soap star, and he's obviously fit. Amanda called him a DILF once.

Could Tilda have fallen for him? What if they were in a relationship?

Or did he do something to Tilda against her will?

As you know, I have a tendency to think the worst of people. Now that the idea's stuck in my head, I can't get it out.

Simon will be at Caroline's now. He's coming over afterward. (Dad's at work and Miranda's at a friend's house.) I'm looking at Caroline's house as I'm writing this. They're so close, but naturally, I have no clue what they're talking about over there. I'll have to wait.

Will she tell him why she kept away from Tommy during

the funeral? If not, what should I do? Should I bring my idea up with Simon? Do I really want it to get stuck in his head, too?

SIMON

I was so angry with Tilda for not coming home," Caroline says. "I called and called her, but she'd only ever text back."

We're sitting on the porch around the back of the house. Caroline is watching me, and yet not. She's a million miles away. A vein throbs in her forehead, and her hand trembles slightly as she adjusts the collar of her blue-and-white striped blouse.

"I was worried about her, but I never doubted that Tilda wrote those texts." She blinks. Focuses on me. "How couldn't I see that it wasn't my daughter? Can you explain that to me?"

"No," I say. "I didn't know, either."

A late-summer wasp crawls across the table. I watch the gleaming body, following its slow, heavy movements.

"I keep waiting for her to come home," Caroline says. "Sometimes, I think I can hear her in the house."

I shiver, despite the sun's warmth on my back.

The wasp has found a spot of what looks like spilled red wine. Its lower body sways up and down, and I remember from biology that that's where a wasp's heart beats.

Caroline brushes the wasp off the table. "I was so happy when Lucinda told me," she says. "I really didn't want it to have been you."

My vision goes cloudy, and I quickly blink away the tears.

I have to get myself together. Have to focus on what I'm here to do.

"Tilda told me that night that she was going to meet someone," I say.

Caroline nods. She doesn't look surprised. The police must have already told her.

"You don't know who it could have been?" I ask her.

Caroline laughs. It comes out as a bitter snort. "No. I clearly had no idea what Tilda was up to."

The wasp buzzes half-heartedly around my head. I bat it away, and it zooms off across the garden.

"Did you know she was doing drugs?" Caroline demands.

Even now, admitting it to her is difficult.

"I should have said something," I say.

"Yes, maybe you should have." She leans forward, and takes my hand. "There are things we all wish we'd done differently."

The phone rings inside the house, an inappropriately cheery tune for the occasion. But Caroline doesn't react.

"Sometimes, I wonder if it was my fault." She lets go of my hand, crosses her arms over her chest. The phone finally stops ringing. "I pushed her too hard, just like my mom pushed me too hard with figure skating. She's the one who taught me that you don't waste talent."

Caroline gazes out over the garden. Most of the flowers have bloomed already, but the flower beds still carry colorful globe thistles and orpines, something that looks like daisies, and clusters of red valerian.

"I told myself that Tilda wanted it," Caroline continues. "You couldn't keep her away from the pool. She always wanted to stay and train for a little while longer, didn't she?"

"Yeah," I say, but Caroline barely seems to register my presence. "She had fun doing it." I look at the red valerian again and spot torn stems. Someone's been picking flowers.

"Was it my fault that it happened like it did? What do you think?" Caroline asks. She's watching me again, wide-eyed and hungry.

"No," I say. "It wasn't your fault." I do my best to sound convinced. Convincing. But I don't know what to think. I just want to leave.

"Are you sure? Did she think I was a good mom?"

"Yeah, she did."

Caroline's smile is exhausted. She shakes her head.

"I'm sorry. I shouldn't put this on you. I've just been having all these doubts since she died. . . ."

Caroline takes out a balled-up tissue and wipes her cheeks, then scrubs at her nose.

I look away, toward where Lucinda's roof sticks up above the tree line, and see the upper half of a window that must be hers. She's waiting there for me. Tommy didn't give her any answers. It's up to me.

"If anyone pushed Tilda, it was Tommy," I say. "I mean, it was his job as a coach, but . . ."

Caroline sniffles a little and tucks the tissue back into her pocket. "What do you mean?" she asks.

"He was sort of over-the-top sometimes, wasn't he? He was never satisfied, no matter what she did."

Caroline studies me silently. Her eyes suddenly look clearer. In an instant, something's changed between us, but I don't know what.

"Do you know why he and Tilda were fighting?" I ask.

"Who said they were fighting?"

I realize that she has her guard up; I just don't know why.

"Everyone says so."

Caroline laughs. My uneasiness grows.

"You think Tommy did it? Is that why you're asking me about this?"

I can't get a word out. And Caroline's eyes are still fixed on mine.

"Is that what the rumor mill is saying?"

I shake my head. Try to smile. "Not that I know of. Everyone seems pretty convinced it was me."

Caroline doesn't return my smile. I look away, go back to the red valerian, and remember the dry bouquet on top of the tangled medals. I search for the woodland sage and spot it by the fence.

Out of the corner of my eye, something stirs. When I look over, the door to the porch closes with a sucking sound. There's a draft coming from inside the house. The front door slams shut, and Caroline abruptly gets to her feet.

"Stay here," she says.

Her feet move swiftly across the wooden deck. She's almost reached the door when it's pushed open again.

"Honey? Are you there?"

I recognize his voice. I just can't get it to make sense.

"Wait!" Caroline shouts.

But he's already stepped out onto the porch. We've already made eye contact.

Tommy is wearing his tracksuit. His hair is still wet. I can smell the chlorine from his bag, the scent of *Tilda*. Even diffused through the fresh air, it's so strong it almost feels like she's here.

"Simon," he says, and stops to collect himself. "How nice to see you. I hope I'm not disturbing you. I just came to run some things by Caroline..."

But Caroline doesn't make any attempt to play along with the scene Tommy is preparing for them. She remains standing between us.

"I was just going," I say, and get up.

"No. Stop," Caroline says.

She walks up to Tommy and gives him a slight nod. "It doesn't matter anymore. We have nothing to hide."

NAME: LUCINDA
TELLUS # 0 392 811 002
POST 0033

Now I know why Tommy wouldn't tell me what he was doing the night Tilda died. And why I smelled chlorine at Caroline's house the first time I visited, why I heard a thud from the upper floor.

I know why Tommy was "in the area" this morning.

He was at Caroline's place. And he was with her when Tilda died.

He couldn't have done it.

Now I also know why they avoided each other at the funeral. They were so worried people would be suspicious that they went too far in the other direction. They've kept their relationship secret all summer so they wouldn't have to deal with Klas's reaction.

Caroline's the person Tommy was talking about in the car when he said he'd never felt like this before.

It feels weird to picture them together, but maybe it's actually weirder that it didn't happen sooner. Now I keep thinking of all the camps Caroline came along to, all the hotel restaurants where we celebrated after competitions, the long bus rides when Caroline sat up front with Tommy.

And they shared so many interests: Tilda's successes, her future career, her tenths of a second.

They told Simon that Tilda had found out about their relationship and didn't like it. That it was the reason why she was angry with Tommy.

It sounds logical. But it doesn't sound like Tilda. Would she really care that much? I can't help but wonder if there was something else lurking beneath the surface. Something even Caroline didn't know about.

While I've been writing this, Tommy's texted me: YOU AND SIMON HAVE TO STOP PLAYING NANCY DREW. THIS ISN'T A GAME. I'M WORRIED ABOUT YOU. I'M SERIOUSLY CONSIDERING TELLING YOUR DAD WHAT YOU'RE DOING.

Maybe he's right to worry about me. I am obsessed. This morning, a cult committed mass suicide by holding one another's hands and jumping into the Grand Canyon. Armed comet deniers have taken over a sizeable area of Australia and founded their own republic. But I've barely been following the news. All I can think about is Tilda.

NAME: LUCINDA
TELLUS # 0 392 811 002
POST 0034

It's been a while since Dad woke Miranda and me up with any sense of urgency. We haven't had any place we had to be in a long time. No school, no visits to the doctor. But this morning, he stormed into my room and shook me awake. "We've got to go to Dad's," he said.

My sister had wrapped herself in my covers, pushed me against the wall, and trapped me there with a leg over my waist. By the time I got her out of bed, Dad had made breakfast. The star from our fake Christmas shone in the kitchen window. The world outside was gray and rainy, the kind of morning where it's impossible to tell the time.

Grandpa had called to say he was picking up Grandma from the retirement home. She's lived there for almost fifteen years. I don't remember anything about the person I see in our old photo albums. The Grandma who always seems happy. It's not only because she's smiling at the camera—you can tell by her wrinkles that she laughed a lot. But Grandma doesn't laugh anymore. She doesn't cry, either. I don't know what her voice sounds like. She can't talk. She can't even go to the bathroom on her own.

Dad told us not to shower unless we really needed to. We had to hurry if he was going to make it back to town in time for his night shift. He'd used the entire week's gas ration to fill up the car. It's almost two hundred miles to Grandpa's house.

There were hardly any cars on the highway—just a few trucks. An ambulance passed us, its flashing sirens silent. When we drove along the smaller roads, we went for miles without seeing anything other than a couple of cars and a bus. We spotted a few horses and carriages, too.

We went shopping for food, mostly canned and freeze-dried items, at a large supermarket. People seemed quiet and focused. No one dawdles anymore. There isn't exactly much to see. It was almost haunting to walk through such a large store with so many empty shelves, where toys and gadgets used to be.

By the time we arrived at Grandpa's, it was early afternoon. Grandpa hugged us more tightly than usual. Grandma was in her wheelchair by the kitchen table, watching us all silently. Dad cooked us lunch. I took care of the stacks of dishes and discreetly washed the ones in the drying rack again. Grandpa can hardly see, and the cups were marked by coffee stains, the glasses greasy.

Miranda sat and played something loud on her phone, but I caught her sneaking peeks at Grandma. "Does she know the comet's coming?" she said, and Grandpa patted her on the head and said, "No, sweetie. She's the lucky one." Then Grandma farted, a rumbling, wet noise that traveled through her inflatable seat cushion, and Miranda and I started giggling. We couldn't help it.

We told Grandpa we'd seen horses along the road, which led us to a conversation about what the world had been like when he was growing up. Telling you what things used to be like is old people's main interest, and it usually isn't particularly riveting; this time, however, I wanted to listen. The way the world has changed during Grandpa's lifetime is, frankly, unbelievable. He's a little over eighty. He never learned to use an online bank, or book train tickets on the computer, or even how to find his way around a phone.

Even Dad grew up in a different world. He likes to say that, nowadays, we're surrounded by things that used to be sci-fi when he was our age—like being able to see the person you're on the phone with, and GPS devices, and 3D printers, and Google Translate. I wonder what the world would look like if it kept existing until Miranda was old. Which sci-fi adventures would be considered everyday then? Maybe we would colonize Mars, having rendered Earth inhabitable. And having been upgraded with surgically inserted microchips.

While we were eating, Dad tried to convince Grandpa to move in with us, but he refused.

When Dad asked if he could really take care of Grandma, Grandpa said, "I think I can manage for a few weeks." There's barely any staff left at the retirement home anyway. People are sitting around in dirty diapers all day long, and no one checks to see if they're eating or drinking. "She's already better since she came home again," Grandpa said. Then he looked at Grandma, and I could tell he still loves her. I think he can see past the empty gaze, the helpless body, and find the woman he met more than sixty years ago.

While drinking coffee behind the house, I saw Grandma turn her face toward the sun. She looked peaceful. And I thought, then, that Grandpa was right. She was supposed to be there.

Dad had brought an old phone and tried to show Grandpa how to do a video call. I have no idea if he had any luck.

We said our goodbyes by the car. I hugged Grandpa, but not long enough. How do you say goodbye forever to someone? The moment was too big. Looking back, I regret it. I should have told him I love him. I'm not sure I do—I don't know him well enough—but I should have said it.

Dad was completely silent the whole way home. Miranda got anxious and started behaving like some perky kid on the Disney channel. She wanted to lighten the mood. It's exactly how she behaved when I got sick.

SIMON

It's almost midnight when I finally give up on trying to fall asleep. I've drawn a bath so hot I almost can't stand it as I sink into the water. I was supposed to meet Lucinda today, but she texted me when I'd just woken up. She can't meet until tomorrow. My whole day has felt like a waste of time. And there are so few days left.

Two weeks tomorrow.

I sink into the water until only my face is above the surface. The heat makes my skin throb, makes my thoughts sluggish. It numbs my restlessness.

I can hear a crowd cheering in the living room. Emma is watching the live broadcast of the twenty-four-hour charity concert. It's reached Paris now. Stina's started writing her sermon for the final Mass. Judette is at Hortense's salon getting her hair done one final time. It usually takes several hours. As for me, I haven't bothered to use the trimmer, even though it would only take a few minutes.

When the water starts to cool, I empty the bath, lying at

the bottom of the tub until I stop sweating. I still feel dizzy when I stand up to shower. But at least I also feel tired.

Emma is sitting in front of the TV when I enter the living room. I stand by the sofa. The camera sweeps across a human sea stretching all the way toward the horizon. It zooms in on an aging singer who looks like a Hollywood actor from the black-and-white era. He holds the microphone out to the audience. The screen's filled with close-ups on faces screaming along to the chorus about loving angels instead.

"Who's that?" I ask.

"No idea," Emma says, and yawns. "They have to take what they can get to fill an entire day."

"I had a secret crush on him when that song came out," Stina calls from the kitchen.

The singer cups the microphone in his hands, gathering strength for what seems like the final line. He lingers over it.

When he looks out at the audience, he bursts into tears. They cry, too.

"Wonder what it's like to stand on that stage knowing it's the last time," Emma says.

Drumsticks beat against each other in Paris. Flames roll across the stage. More cheers. A close-up on a few women Stina's age with their arms around one another's waists. A close-up on a screaming drag queen. A drone films the audience from above; in the flickering lights from the stage, I catch a glimpse of its round shadow.

"Isn't it weird to think that they're all right there, right now?" I say. "And they're experiencing the same thing at the same time, but they experience it differently, because they *are* different people."

"Are you okay, Simon?" Emma says, smirking.

I grin back. This is the kind of thing that would have had Tilda rolling her eyes at me. But I continue watching the crowd. The singer. The drummer. They all have their own experiences, memories, hopes, fears, associations. Stina would probably call it *souls*. I would say they each have a world inside them. When the comet hits us, it won't just destroy our world; it will destroy nearly eight billion worlds.

Tilda was a whole world, too.

Soon it'll all be gone.

I avert my eyes and walk into the kitchen.

"Watch out for Boomer!" Stina says, and I stop myself just before tripping over him.

He's sleeping in the middle of the kitchen floor, and whines softly, waving his paws. I wonder what's going on in his huge dog head. Is he being chased, or is he chasing something? Do I ever appear in his dreams?

I sit on the floor next to him. Scratch him behind his ear. He turns red-rimmed eyes toward me and lets out a huge yawn. I find myself envying his ignorance.

"How is it coming along?" I ask, looking up at Stina.

"I want psalms everyone can sing along to," she says without lifting her eyes from the laptop. "What do you think of 'Children of the Heavenly Father'? The lyrics seem appropriate."

"Too appropriate," I say. "I think it could feel a bit ironic."

"You're probably right."

Stina smiles tiredly and closes her computer. She goes to the cabinet and grabs a bottle of red wine, holding it up to the light to see how much is left, before pulling the cork out and sniffing it cautiously.

"Would you like a glass? If it hasn't turned into vinegar, that is."

I give her a surprised look.

"I could have some."

Stina pours us each some wine. She sticks her nose deep into the glass to sniff it, then sips it carefully before swilling the wine around in her mouth.

"It's better than I expected," she says, handing me the second glass.

She sinks down across from me, leaning back against the cabinet doors under the sink, patting Boomer's hind legs a bit distractedly.

"Mom," I say. "What did you and Tilda talk about this summer?"

Her hand goes still.

"I don't want to fight about this again, Simon. Please."

"I don't want to fight, either. But did she say anything that could have been a clue? Maybe something that you haven't even considered?"

Stina takes a drink of her wine, and tilts her head back.

"We mostly talked about faith. Tilda wanted my perspective on the Truthers. She brought a list of questions she'd prepared."

That definitely sounds like Tilda. I imagine her in front of me, lying on her stomach in bed, her notebook by her hand. She used to bite the middle of her pen when she was thinking deeply about something.

"What do you think of them?" I ask.

"I think," Stina says slowly, glancing at her computer, "that the Truthers are very good at exploiting the fact that people are looking for simple answers right now. I almost catch myself being jealous of them, you know, as I'm sitting here and searching for the right words. But easy answers are the opposite of faith. We can't comprehend everything."

She takes another gulp of wine.

"Whoever's the most convinced is the one I would trust the least," she says. "That's what I think of the Truthers."

"But the Bible is pretty convinced."

"The Bible was written by humans."

She drains her glass, and massages the back of her neck. I think of Tilda's letter. Hesitate.

"Tilda appreciated your talk. She thought it really helped."

Stina glows. "Did she really say that?"

I nod. And it hits me that it's thanks to Tilda that we're talking about God and faith right now, things Stina's tried to get me to talk about all summer. Maybe even longer than that. We've hardly discussed these things since I was little.

"What do you think is going to happen?" I ask. "After the comet?" I swallow quickly. I've never learned to enjoy red wine.

"I think the good in this world will remain," Stina says. "In some form. And I think we will, too. We'll continue on."

"In heaven? Do you really believe in it?"

Stina rolls her empty glass between her palms. I push my glass over to her, and she picks it up with a grateful smile.

"Today, we'd probably talk about it like a different dimension, but I think it's something beyond what we can imagine. I don't even have to try. I trust God, because I know He loves us."

Boomer barks, his tail hitting the floor a couple of times. And then I hear the key in the front door.

Stina and I look up when Judette steps into the kitchen, her cornrows freshly done. She smells vaguely of coconut—a smell I associate with being a child and reading cartoons and eavesdropping on Judette and Hortense's gossip, surrounded by people who look like me.

"Hi," Stina says. "You look nice."

"Thanks," Judette says, and swears when she nearly falls over Boomer. "Why is he always in the way?"

"Because he's such a *good doggy*," I say, and get a few lazy movements of the tail in response.

"We might as well have bought a bear rug."

Now I notice that Judette's been drinking.

"She doesn't mean it," I say, and kiss Boomer on the forehead.

"How are you?" Stina asks.

"It is what it is," Judette says, and opens the fridge, making bottles and cans clink against each other on the door.

Stina looks at her longingly.

"How was Hortense? I can't believe she's still keeping the salon running."

"What else would she do?" Judette snaps.

"No, you're right," Stina says quickly.

And my heart breaks a little.

Judette closes the fridge again and turns toward us. Her eyes are gleaming. "I'm sorry. I didn't mean to sound cranky. It was a bit hard to say goodbye to everyone."

"I understand," Stina says.

"I think I'm going to bed."

Judette takes a careful step over Boomer this time, petting him on the head. I hear her choke down a sob as she leaves the kitchen. In the living room, there are more cheers from the crowd in Paris.

NAME: LUCINDA
TELLUS # 0 392 811 002
POST 0035

What do you think about when you see yourself in the mirror? Do you even care? I do. Despite everything that's happened, and everything that's going to happen, I still find myself caring.

I hated the way I looked before I got sick. It's something the world teaches us to do—and I was nothing if not an excellent student. I found faults in everything. In retrospect, I can admit that I actually looked pretty okay. I was just really average. I should have been a bank robber, because no one would have remembered my face well enough to describe it to the police.

Tilda was beautiful. She was someone you couldn't forget. And her death has forced me to participate in life online in a way I haven't done for over a year.

I'm looking for a space fanatic with a telescope. I've sent friend requests to people I've never met. Friends of Tilda's friends. When they accept, I scan their profiles for information. Now and then, Tilda will make an appearance. I know exactly which pictures she hated, even before I check and see that she's untagged herself. I can readjust my gaze and look through her eyes at the shoulders she thought were too broad, the hair she found too frizzy, the nose that looked a little crooked from certain angles or in certain lighting.

There's only two weeks left now. People are desperately trying to make plans for September 16. It's the anxiety before every Christmas and New Year's and Midsummer's Eve combined, multiplied by a thousand. Everyone wants to be surrounded by their loved ones while simultaneously *avoiding* their loved ones. A lot of people are planning on going to church.

Simon's mom is in charge of the last sermon.

I read the status updates, spot groups forming, see people accepting invitations to several events so they can choose at the last second. But I also notice that some people aren't being invited to anything at all. The strained cheer in their posts is the saddest thing of all.

Hey, friends! Any room for me on the final night?
Haven't got any preferences—chilling at home or a wild party both have their upsides ☺

Everyone needs intimacy, but finding it isn't always easy. I read that the consumption of porn has increased by a thousand percent since the news about the comet broke. Porn is what we call it when we watch strangers having sex, and yes, it's just as strange as it sounds.

How do you procreate? How much of your life revolves around it? Sometimes it feels like everything, at the end of the day, is about sex.

I'd love to know what your equivalent to porn is. I have a feeling it would tell me a lot about who you are as a species.

Fortunately, I have to go before I lose complete control of this post.

I'm going to Simon's apartment. We're going to contact the person who sold Tilda drugs, her dealer who might also be the space-fanatic friend. Simon has gotten his hands on a phone we can use to text them anonymously.

SIMON

I look at the kitchen clock—almost a quarter past twelve. Lucinda will be here any minute.

"I can't believe this used to fit you," Judette says, holding out a tiny leather jacket in front of me.

"God, I'd almost forgotten about this," Emma says, snatching it from Judette.

When I woke up, I was given the task of fetching the box of baby clothes from the attic. Naturally, it was at the very back of the storage room. It took me almost an hour to clear the junk that was in the way. Now, the kitchen table is covered in piles of small sweaters, hats, and onesies.

The leather jacket creaks in Emma's hands when she turns it over. Little metal buttons on the shoulders gleam in the light from the window.

"How old was Simon when he wore this?"

"He'd just learned how to walk, so maybe a year?" Judette smiles at me. "You were so unbelievably cute. And very bowlegged."

Emma laughs while testing the zipper.

"You really were," she says, folding the jacket in half. "One year is perfect. Tiny can wear it next fall."

Why do we play along with this? Is it really helping Emma? I glance at Judette. She seems to guess what I'm thinking, because she shakes her head almost imperceptibly.

"Good thing you saved so much stuff," Emma says.

"Most of it went to charity, but there are some things you just can't get rid of."

Judette laughs, pulling a tiny Hawaiian shirt from the box. And I realize she's enjoying this almost as much as Emma is. Last night, I woke up to the sound of crying from the bedroom, but there isn't a trace of grief on Judette's face now.

The doorbell finally rings, and Boomer storms howling into the hall.

I block him while I open the door. Lucinda's wearing her wig today, too. She looks down at Boomer, who presses his head against my knees, trying to push past me.

"Stop that," I snap, dragging him away so Lucinda can come in. "I'm sorry. He can be such a fucking pain."

"No problem," Lucinda says, stepping out of her shoes. "He looks even bigger indoors."

She walks into the kitchen before I can stop her. Her eyes are drawn to the baby clothes, and then to Emma's stomach.

"This is Lucinda," I say.

"I understand if you don't remember me," Lucinda says to Judette, reaching out a hand. "I was here with our class once when Simon and I were small."

But Judette ignores the outstretched hand, giving Lucinda a warm hug instead. "Lucinda! I'm so pleased to meet you!"

Lucinda doesn't hug Judette back, but allows herself to be embraced.

"Thanks for talking to the police about the message," Judette says.

"I don't know how helpful that was."

"At least you tried. I wish you knew how much it means to us, and to Simon."

"That's enough, Mom," I say.

When Judette lets her go, Lucinda's hand goes straight to

her forehead, checking to make sure that the wig hasn't gone crooked. She looks embarrassed and turns to Emma, who takes her hand and introduces herself, then waves around a onesie with a pattern of small leaping lambs.

"What do you think?"

Lucinda looks completely at a loss. "Nice," she says, and I curse myself for not warning her about this.

"So, what are you up to today?" Emma asks, and smiles.

"Nothing," I say.

Emma's smile broadens.

When I ask Lucinda to follow me to my room, she looks relieved. Boomer trails at our heels, panting. He looks deeply disappointed when I close the door in his face.

Lucinda sits on my bed. All of a sudden, I'm very aware that I smell slightly of sweat and that my T-shirt is smudged with dust from the attic. Sitting on the desk with my feet on the chair, I wonder if I should bring up the topic of Emma. But what is there to say?

"I think I recognize this room," Lucinda says, looking around. "Didn't you have loads of Star Wars Legos?"

"Yeah."

I don't want to talk about that day. It makes me feel like that awkward seven-year-old again, as if he's been here all along, just waiting for an opportunity to pop out.

"Stina says hi," I say, to change the subject. "She wanted to meet you, but she's at work."

Lucinda nods. "Are you going to church together? For the final night?"

"Yeah. What are you going to do?"

"I don't know. We'll probably just stay at home."

She smiles suddenly. I wonder if she had the same thought I did: that it sounds like we're talking about weekend plans instead of this planet's—and all of humanity's—final night, the last night of our lives.

"Why not go to church, then?" I say.

"I don't think so. Dad is a staunch atheist. Doctor, you know."

"How about you?"

Lucinda pulls her legs up onto the bed, lost in thought.

"I don't like it when people claim that they have all the answers," she finally says.

"Me neither. But Stina isn't like that."

"My dad is. He thinks science can explain everything. I think it's a mistake to be that sure of yourself, regardless of what you believe." She pats her wig. "I don't feel at home in either alternative, frankly. But I think I'd have a hard time liking a God who sends a comet the moment we piss him off."

I laugh. "Have you heard of theodicy? The problem of evil?"

Lucinda shakes her head, but she looks interested.

"Let's see if I can remember it," I say. "If God is good and almighty, then how can he allow evil? Does that mean God isn't good? Or is he not actually almighty?"

Lucinda sits there quietly. I realize that she wants me to continue.

"There isn't an answer," I say. "They've been pondering this for millennia."

"Great."

We smile at each other. It's almost like we know each other well, even though we really don't.

Maybe it's because Tilda talked about her so frequently.

If Lucinda hadn't gotten sick, would the three of us have hung out? What would we have done? I don't know a lot about Lucinda. What music does she listen to? Is there a place she's always wanted to visit? What was her passion, apart from swimming? Did she still want to be a writer? Is that why she writes in TellUs?

I realize I'm staring at her. I lean forward, open the drawer of the desk, and take out Judette's old work phone. "It's pre-paid."

"And you're sure the number isn't registered?"

"I've tested it."

Lucinda reaches for the phone.

"What do we say?" I ask, and hand it to her.

She fiddles with the phone and looks up at me.

"I've been thinking about something. They seem pretty paranoid, so it's probably better if I do this alone."

"No way," I say. "If anyone's doing this alone, it should be me."

"Why? Because you're a guy?"

"No. Of course not."

It's because she's sick. But I don't say that out loud. Sitting together in my room, it's easy to forget, but Lucinda fainted at the glass factory. She gets tired and breathless easily.

Lucinda's right, though. The person in question seems paranoid. And paranoid people can become dangerous. I don't know how good I am at defending myself if anything happens, but I know at least I'm good at running.

"It's my turn to take a risk," I say instead. "You met Tommy by yourself."

Lucinda stubbornly shakes her head. "It's better if I do it. Whoever's dealing drugs doesn't do it for money anymore, right? There has to be a reason for them to help me. And I can play the cancer card."

"The cancer card?"

"I can say I need weed because I can't get hold of pain-killers anymore."

I'm caught off guard. "Is that true?"

"No. Dad can get everything I need from the hospital."

"Okay. Good." I try to get us back on track. "So what are you saying? Are we hoping for a dealer with a heart of gold?"

Lucinda looks at me impatiently. "Do you have a better idea?"

"Yes. That we do it together. At least there will be two of us. We'll pretend I'm your worried boyfriend or something."

She opens her mouth to say something, then changes her mind. Instead, she looks down at Judette's phone and starts typing out a text.

NAME: LUCINDA
TELLUS # 0 392 811 002
POST 0036

I found Miranda's bucket list today. She didn't write it in the Bucket List app. It was on paper, in carefully printed capital letters.

I didn't mean to be nosy. I was just getting dirty laundry from her room. The list was on the desk. *Celebrate Christmas one more time* was on the list. She'd made a neat little checkmark in the margin with a different-colored pen. Other things on the list: *Stay up all night. Sleep in a pillow fort (indoors). Ride a horse. Spend a night in the bathtub. Solve a Rubik's Cube. Write a short song. Fall in love. Draw a poster. See a hedgehog. Volunteer (doggie day care?). Change my hair. Cook a three-course meal.* It was heartbreaking to see a list of small, simple, ordinary things, knowing she wouldn't have the time to do most of them. There was only one other thing on the list that was marked as done: *Invent a new dance with Molly.*

I had no idea Miranda had seen Tilda's cousin since the funeral. When I asked her (without mentioning that I'd seen the list), it turned out the friend Miranda had visited the other day was Molly. They'd hung out in town while Molly's family was in the True Church, but Erika had found out, and now Molly isn't even allowed to use her phone anymore.

Miranda was so upset. I tried promising her I'd go to their house sometime to see how Molly is doing. But Miranda told me not to. She said Molly would get in trouble if I did.

How the hell can Erika isolate her daughter like this? She doesn't even believe in the True Church herself. Or has she started to?

(People believe so many things nowadays; the latest mass movement is about *ancient aliens*. Aliens supposedly came to Earth a long time ago, helping us build pyramids and sporadically spiriting us away to modify our genetic code, trying to make us smarter. But now, they've realized it's an impossible task and want to conclude the experiment. Foxworth is their weapon in disguise. When I heard this theory, I couldn't exactly blame the aliens.)

Yesterday, we got in touch with Tilda's dealer. I wrote a short message: GOT YOUR NUMBER FROM A MUTUAL FRIEND. NEED YOUR HELP. I took the phone we used to send the message home and hid it under the windowsill. Now I'm waiting for a text from a potential murderer. Feels great.

Simon is going to play my "worried boyfriend." I was about to say something bitter about how it would be nice to have one of those at some point. Maybe it's because I wrote to you about sex right before going over to Simon's, but sitting on his bed, I was hyperaware of the fact that Tilda and he must have had sex in it all the time. And I know it was good. Tilda had told me about it, and naturally, I remembered all the details right then. I could barely look him in the eye.

Simon's sister, Emma, was going through old baby clothes in the kitchen with Judette, one of his moms. Emma held out a onesie and asked me what I thought of it. And I don't know, but I think I saw a spark of defiance in her eyes. *Just try to tell me I won't be a mom.* I had the feeling she was testing me. I didn't contradict her. I was too busy trying not to cry.

I've been checking social media all morning. No news about Tilda. No news about Simon, either. Maybe that post from the police actually made a difference. Or maybe people have things other than Tilda to think about. Simon and I are the only ones who can't let her go.

SIMON

A reporter is walking along the main road that runs through Las Vegas. The neon signs are turned off, the casinos closed, but America's couples are traveling there to get hitched quick. It's mostly young couples who want to have sex without living in sin.

I turn the video off just as the news on the TV turns to a story about people watching more porn than ever. "Escapism" is the most common reason for it, according to an online poll. I've only tried watching it once since Tilda died. It didn't help me escape. Actually, it was the total opposite. All I saw were girls in pain while they asked for more, close-ups on faces streaked with mascara, exaggerated screams and whimpers, hands closing around throats. It just made me think of Tilda at the glass factory.

I keep scrolling. There are more and more photos from a party at Hampus's place. Amanda is laughing in the grass. Moa and Ali are dancing. Sait stares straight into the camera, an ice cube in his mouth.

I don't want to look, but I can't help myself. Everyone is there. No one's reached out to me.

I miss them, but I don't know if I can forgive them.

Do they still think I killed Tilda? Or am I now just an embarrassing memory? Something they'd rather forget?

The apartment is quiet. My moms have gone to bed. They were giggling in the kitchen for a long time. And I couldn't help it—listening to them, I felt jealous. They got to live for so much longer than I will. They got to experience so much more.

Emma is staying at an old friend's house. I tried to reach Johannes. He's almost three hundred miles away, but everything would feel so much better if I could hear his voice.

My world has shrunk to this apartment. I barely even want to go out anymore. How did Lucinda stand being so isolated? Did it break her, like I worry it will do to me? All I can do is wait for her to call me and say we got a reply to our text. And I'm not entirely sure that I hope we get one.

I scroll faster and faster. Notice a blonde girl in a hammock talking to Amanda. I flinch when I see who it is.

Lucinda.

She's wearing her wig. Amanda seems to be laughing at something she's saying. Neither of them seem aware of the camera. Ali posted the picture.

What is she doing there?

I look at the picture. Ridiculously enough, I feel betrayed, as if she chose the others over me. As if she owed it to me to stay as lonely as I am.

But I realize that actually I'm scared. Scared that they'll get her to doubt me.

The phone vibrates in my hand. Lucinda's name flashes on the screen.

I clear my throat before answering.

Music and laughter rise and fall in the background—the sound of my old life. Her breaths sound close to my ear.

"Did you know that your friend Hampus is an idiot?"

I hear myself laugh. Can she tell I'm relieved?

"Yes," I say.

"Good."

The music fades. I hear shoes against the asphalt. She's leaving.

"He called me," Lucinda says. "Tilda's dealer."

I sit up on the sofa. My heart starts racing in my chest.

"He's agreed to meet me tomorrow," she continues. "But, Simon . . . he says I have to come alone. Or he won't see me."

I look around to make sure no one is nearby. "It's not worth it," I whisper. "It really isn't. No matter how badly we want to catch whoever did it."

She doesn't respond. I listen to her breathing until I can't wait any longer.

"We either do this together or not at all."

Lucinda sighs. "Okay. I'll call you at twelve tomorrow, and we'll come up with a place to meet."

A shiver runs up my spine.

Lucinda says goodbye before I can reply. I stay sitting in the dark with the phone in my hand.

NAME: LUCINDA
TELLUS # 0 392 811 002
POST 0037

I had just finished writing my last post yesterday at noon when Amanda asked if I wanted to meet up and go to a party. My instinct was, of course, to say no. But at that point, I didn't know if I was going to get a response from Tilda's dealer, and I'd given up searching online for Tilda's new friend, the space fanatic. My only way of finding out more was by heading into the real world.

Dad drove me to Amanda's house. He was glad that I was "meeting an old friend from the swim team." He thought we were going to drink tea and have a nice chat, or something like that. Luckily, he didn't follow me up to the house to say hi, because Amanda was already drunk and weepy when I got there. Her mom was staying over at her new boyfriend's house, so Amanda had taken some of her Xanax and washed them down with moonshine and apple juice.

In her letter, Tilda wrote that her friendship with Amanda and Elin wasn't real. But it was to Amanda. I saw that in all the messages she'd sent Tilda. I heard it tonight when Amanda talked about her.

She's lonelier than I thought. Her ex moved, and she tried to pretend she didn't care. Elin's left town, too. She and her mother have moved back to their old hometown. Moa has started dating Ali. ("The only thing they do except partying is play *Skyrim* all day. They refuse to live in the real world.") I realized I was at a casting session. Amanda was trying me out for the role of her new friend. A final best friend. But it isn't going to be me. The more she drank, the more she turned into a live version of the soppiest comments she wrote while I was in the hospital. I was *strong* and *brave* again. Not a person, but an accessory. At first, I felt sorry for her.

Amanda didn't want to tell me why things had ended with Johannes. I know anyway. The same day as the game night, she'd texted Tilda that Johannes had confessed to having feelings for Simon. *Please can we meet and talk?!?!?*

They fell for each other like dominoes. Amanda wanted Johannes, who wanted Simon, who wanted Tilda, who wanted no one at all.

Despite the fact that I was nervous about the party, it was a relief to get out of Amanda's house.

We were going to Hampus's place, just a few blocks away from Amanda's. I can honestly say that my second impression of him wasn't exactly better than the one I got at the funeral. He still doesn't seem to understand what's happening. He's a guy from a rich family who's been told his whole life that the world belongs to people like him. This entire thing with Foxworth must feel like a betrayal.

I've felt alone for a long time, but never as alone as I did tonight, surrounded by people. It was like I wasn't really there. Like I was still watching it all on a screen.

Now that you can't buy clothes anymore, more and more people have started to raid their parents' closets, the older and uglier the items, the better.

The party started with something they called "the ice game." An ice cube traveled from mouth to mouth through kissing. Saliva and meltwater dripped from it. I've never been happier about the cancer card. "But cancer isn't contagious," Moa said. I thought she was joking, because I know she's interested in biology, but it turned out she's just dumb. I had to explain that "No, you're dangerous to me."

I met Sait and couldn't repress the memory of the photos he'd sent Tilda this summer. I couldn't even talk to him without stuttering. It felt so wrong that I'd seen them.

Hanging out at the party sober was strange. Before I got there, I'd entertained the idea of letting loose, too. The first and final time. I'd be a little like Tilda. But when I was actually there, I wasn't even tempted. There was a weariness in the air. An emptiness. The party was somehow strained. I don't think anyone else noticed. They thought they were the only ones who weren't enjoying themselves, so they drank more, shouted more, psyched each other up for the night of the final soccer game.

Amanda said it was typical that no one cared about a women's soccer tournament, and Hampus disdainfully said that she sounded like Elin.

I tried to talk about Tilda, but no one had anything new to say. Finally, Hampus took me aside and said, "What does it matter who killed Tilda? She was dying anyway." And I asked him if that's what we should have done in the past, let people with deadly illnesses like mine be murdered because they were dying anyway. Hampus told me to shut up because this was a party and no one wanted to talk about Tilda or cancer patients, "because you're not that fucking special anymore."

When I was leaving the party, someone called Judette's phone (which I'd brought with me in case we finally got an answer to our message). It was a blocked number, but I knew who it was.

I spoke to the guy who'd supplied Tilda with drugs. I said my name was Sara. My middle name. My mother's name. I said I was sick and needed help.

The guy never mentioned his name. He was as paranoid as I thought. When he asked who'd given me his number, I said it had been Tilda.

It was a gamble. The connection to Tilda could have scared him away, but I knew he wouldn't agree to meet me if I was just anyone.

He told me come alone. I promised I'd stop by tomorrow.

I'm so nervous my whole body feels electrified. I won't be able to fall asleep.

But what Hampus said only made me more determined. I *am* going to find out what happened to Tilda.

SIMON

I look blankly at the message Lucinda sent me.

4 RINGVÄGEN. MAGNUSSON ON THE DOOR.

Something is wrong. Very wrong.

It's almost twelve o'clock. I've waited all morning for Lucinda to call me. Now the phone starts vibrating in my hand, and I close the door to my room.

"Don't be mad," she says. "Or be mad if you want, but listen to me first. I'm outside his house now."

I stand at the window. Ringvägen is only a few miles away, at the edge of my neighborhood.

"Why?" I ask.

"You know why. He won't agree to see me unless I'm alone."

The blood drains from my face. She must have decided on this plan while we were talking yesterday. I hadn't convinced her at all. She just didn't want to discuss it with me.

"You can't do it on your own," I say, and hear my voice go shrill.

"This way it's safer for us both. You can listen in the whole time. I have better pockets this time around, so I won't drop my phone." She tries to laugh, like this is some fucking joke. "If anything happens, you'll hear it. You've got the address. And you know a cop."

"How will that help you if he's got a gun or something?"

"How would you being here help me if he does?"

I don't have a good answer to that, but I can't just sit here twiddling my thumbs while she's with the person who could have killed Tilda.

"Wait for me," I plead.

"No."

"I'm on my way."

I walk into the hall and squeeze my feet into my old pair of Adidas. I hear my moms debating about something in the kitchen. Sizzling from a frying pan.

"All right. You can wait outside his building. But don't draw attention to yourself. It could put us both in danger."

Lucinda's right, and I hate it. She's planned this out well, even though the plan itself happens to be the worst idea possible.

"Lucinda," I whisper while digging around in Stina's purse for her car keys. "You said yourself that he's paranoid. Don't you think he'll notice what you're doing? What if he wants to look at your phone?"

"He won't."

"How can you be sure?"

Boomer comes running, panting excitedly. He looks up hopefully at the leash.

"I have to go in now," Lucinda says. "I don't want him to see me standing around talking to someone."

I hear the sound of a door opening. A rustling in the phone when she puts it into her pocket. A zipper is pulled up. Echoing steps in a stairwell.

My fingers brush Stina's car keys just as Emma walks past me. The look she throws me is a curious one.

"Are you going somewhere?"

"I've just got to do this thing."

She glances at the car keys. I give her a pleading look. She doesn't say a thing as she continues into the kitchen.

I shove at Boomer. He spins around in a circle on the hall floor, playfully snapping at my hand.

On the phone, I hear Lucinda introduce herself as Sara.

"Lars," a man's deep voice says.

Boomer tilts his head to one side, looking up at me so I can see the white under his pupils.

"Simon?" Judette calls from the kitchen. "Are you going somewhere?"

"What was that?" the man on the other end of the phone says.

Fuck. My sweaty fingers slip over the screen.

"Oh," I hear Lucinda say. "I was listening to a podcast on the way over."

"Simon?" Judette calls again.

I press the crossed-out microphone symbol so the sound from my side of the conversation is turned off.

"Be right back," I say, trying to sound normal. "I'm just helping a friend with something."

"Who?" Stina shouts.

"Lucinda! I'll be right back!"

I run out of the apartment. My footsteps pounding down the stairs make it difficult to hear what's going on in 4 Ringvägen. I press my phone against my ear so hard, it's like I'm trying to shove it into my skull. The man called Lars says something I can't make out while I push open the building's door.

And then I realize I did hear something. He just called her Lucinda.

He knows who she is.

Lucinda is quiet. I hold my breath while I run, pressing the button on the car keys. The lights on Stina's car blink once.

"I didn't think you were still friends," Lars says.

I throw myself into the driver's seat. Lucinda replies, but I can't hear what she says.

"... what happened," Lars is saying.

I start the car, connect the phone to the car stereo.

"Maybe we could have been again," Lucinda mumbles.

While pulling out onto the street, I hear Lars say something else. I turn the volume up. The sound of an unknown room in Ringvägen fills the car.

"But I didn't lie about why I needed your help," Lucinda says. "I mean, look at me."

"I thought your dad worked at the hospital."

My heart somersaults in my chest. *What the hell have you done, Lucinda? How could you be stupid enough to go alone?*

"How did you know?" Lucinda asks.

"Tilda told me a lot about you," Lars replies.

"She did?"

"How do you think I knew you the moment I saw you?"

I swear loudly when the traffic light in front of me switches to red. A man and his daughter cross the street in front of the hood. I immediately recognize her hunched posture. Molly turns toward me, and I gasp.

They don't look alike. Not really. But for a moment, it's as if I'm looking at a younger version of Tilda.

"They're really strict at the hospital," Lucinda says.

Molly looks away again, quickly, but I can tell she's scared. She still thinks I killed her cousin.

Anders squints at the sun. He hasn't seen me yet. The traffic light switches back to green and I slam on the accelerator as soon as they reach the sidewalk. Molly turns and watches the car as I pass.

"Sure," the man in Ringvägen says, and I realize that I've missed something. "How much do you want?"

Was that what he used to say to Tilda?

Didn't he ever feel guilty when he saw how badly she was doing?

Did he feel guilty when she died?

Does he feel guilty because he killed her?

There's silence as Lucinda hesitates. I hold my breath again.

"I don't know," she confesses after a beat. "I don't know anything about this. What can you give me?"

Someone gets up. Footsteps. A door opens.

"Do you know how to do this?"

"It's cool, I can look it up on YouTube."

"No, no. I'll show you."

Another red light. I decide to ignore it. There are hardly any other cars on the road.

I watched Tilda roll joints this summer. Now I can hear the man who taught her how to do it. While I race past another intersection, I hear the soft rustle of paper as he licks along the glue.

"Want to share it? Seeing as we're friends now?"

"Sure," Lucinda says.

Lars laughs. There's more rustling.

"Sweetheart," he says. "I'm just shitting you. I can tell you're not here to do business. You want to know if I did it, don't you?"

I turn into Ringvägen with a sinking feeling in my stomach.

The speakers are perfectly quiet.

Say something, Lucinda. Say anything so I know you're okay.

"Some woman cop came by a few days ago," Lars says while I frantically scan the numbers above the building's doors. "She'd seen Tilda's messages."

Brick buildings throw shadows across the asphalt. Some kids are playing with a jump rope on the sidewalk.

I drive past number 20. Hear the sound of a lighter.

18 ... 16 ...

A deep drag on the joint.

12 ... 10 ... 8.

"What did you tell her?" Lucinda asks, sounding surprisingly steady. "What did you do that night?"

There. Number four. The sound of the car's engine can be heard through the speakers. I stop by the sidewalk, look up at the façade, and spot an open window.

"It's pretty funny, actually," Lars says. "I have the world's best alibi."

"Which is?"

The faceless voice pauses dramatically.

"The woman cop picked me up after the game herself. I got into a fight in the square and spent the night down at the station."

He takes a pull on his joint and laughs. And despite the bright, sunny day I'm back in the soft rain and darkness of the square, watching the police van driving into town. People slam against it and roar hungrily. *Something terrible is going to happen tonight.* Not many officers had come out of the van, but Maria had been one of them. Is she the "woman cop"?

But Lars not killing Tilda doesn't mean he's not dangerous. I stare at the window.

Get out of there, Lucinda. That's enough. You've gotten all we need to know.

"Tilda was going to see someone," she says. "Do you know who it was?"

"No. But she was freaking out when she came here earlier that night. I could tell that she was upset about something."

His voice cracks. I realize that he's crying.

"We partied a little here, then headed into town together," he continues. "It was the first time we hung out outside of this apartment, actually. But she went to see her friends, and I met up with mine."

He sucks down smoke.

"We used to joke about being the unlikeliest of friends, she and I."

So that's how it was: Tilda's dealer was also her new friend. *Other people would say he's a bad influence, but he listens without judging.* Tilda had been sitting in that very apartment when she wrote her letter.

"We didn't exactly have a lot in common," Lars says.

"*We* did," Lucinda says slowly. "We did everything together. We were so close. And then we weren't anymore, and it was my fault. I was supposed to die, but she did, and I ... I ..." New sobs. Lucinda's this time.

"I don't know how to bear it," she whispers. "You've got to help me."

Silence.

"I don't know who killed her," Lars says.

"But you know who she was last summer. I have no clue. You have to tell me."

I'm crying now, too. We're all crying for Tilda.

"What do you want to know?" he says, his voice thick with emotion.

There's a pause as Lucinda considers this.

Two of the kids who were jumping rope race past the car.

"How did you meet?" she finally asks.

Lars laughs, more gently this time.

"It was just a coincidence. She'd been coming on to a friend of mine in town, but the two of us ended up talking all night. My friend was pretty angry about it, actually."

I remove my seat belt. It's too tight. There isn't enough space for my lungs to expand.

"Did you get her into it?" Lucinda asks.

"Into what?"

"Drugs."

There's a moment's silence.

"She'd been taking that stuff for a while before we even met."

I swallow hard, knowing that soon we'll have passed the point of no return.

If we ever meet again, I'm going to tell you that I wasn't a good girl like everyone thought, including you and Simon,

"I'm not the one to blame for that," Lars says.

Silence.

Lucinda asks, "Then who is?"

NAME: LUCINDA
TELLUS # 0 392 811 002
POST 0038

I'm writing this on my phone. My hands are shaking; my body's trembling. It's the final rush of adrenaline leaving my system.

I went to see Tilda's dealer. Alone.

The moment I stepped through his door, I knew that he was her new friend. A telescope stood by the living room window. A poster of the moon hung over the sofa.

Before I went over there, I was afraid of him. And I hated

him for the drugs he'd supplied Tilda with. But now I think I see why Tilda liked him. I also see why she confided in him, because who's more reliable than a paranoid person? There were rumors that Tilda paid for the drugs with sex, but I think they were just friends. And he's mourning her, too.

When she started getting to know him at the beginning of the summer, she was already addicted.

Back in junior high, Tilda had started worrying that swimming was hurting her grades. Her dream of becoming a doctor was slowly eclipsing the dream of becoming an athlete.

She didn't tell me straight out. I have a vague memory of her complaining about how difficult it was to keep up with her schoolwork; I remember thinking that Tilda, who had never seriously had to study, was spoiled.

But she'd told Tommy about her plans to lower her absurdly ambitious expectations about swimming, and he must have panicked. Tilda was his star. His creation. If she became a famous swimmer, he'd become a famous coach. She was his ticket to a successful career. And it was slipping out of his hands.

So Tommy offered to "help."

I know how easy it must have been to convince Tilda that she could have everything, that she could accomplish *all* her goals if she just trusted him. He was going to help her to focus and boost her energy levels.

Some people say that the addict is responsible for their addiction. But Tommy was the one who put Tilda on amphetamines, even if it was in the form of medication for ADHD. He knew a doctor who could make sure she'd get the right results when tested, and then write her a prescription. The problem was that the "medicine" would be caught in drug tests. But that could be resolved through a special dispensation from the swimming federation. And since Tilda was still a minor, he got Caroline to sign it.

She knew.

Caroline, who always said that you shouldn't waste your talent, that you should do the best you can. She must have thought she was doing Tilda a favor. And she made Tilda promise to only take the pills before important exams and other "emergencies."

But Tilda discovered that she liked them, especially when the pressure ratcheted up in high school. The pills made everything so much easier—they helped her be the perfect student, the perfect girlfriend, the perfect daughter, the perfect friend. But on the inside, she broke.

Tommy knew exactly how much Tilda was using. He made sure the prescriptions were renewed. But did Caroline know? Was that why she wanted Simon and me to assure her that she was a good mom, a cherished mom?

Or did she really not understand that Tilda was becoming addicted to the pills she'd helped supply? Did she make the connection when she found out Tilda had been doing drugs all summer? We humans can be incredibly good at closing our eyes to things we don't want to see. Just look at me. I closed my eyes to how Caroline was pushing Tilda because I was clinging to childish fantasies about having a mother like that. *So involved and interested.*

No wonder Tilda hated that Tommy and Caroline got together. No wonder she wrote what she did in that message to Tommy: *If what I'm doing is wrong, it's YOUR FAULT.* No wonder she didn't want to quit. There was nowhere to escape the end of the world, but the drugs at least helped her escape the fear.

A part of me wants to tell Caroline everything, just in case she's still living in denial. I want to tell her just how far the man she's dating was willing to go to use her daughter. But Simon and I talked about it for a long time, and we decided that we won't. Caroline's already a shadow of her former self.

There are only twelve days left until the end, and she'd be utterly alone.

Or she wouldn't be able to bring herself to break up with Tommy, and would hate herself even more for it.

Caroline's life is simply fucked up enough as it is. So we won't say anything.

That doesn't mean we forgive either of them. The fact is I had no idea I have such depths of hatred inside me. Tilda's dealer couldn't have killed her. The police took him in after a fight in the square that night. I'm waiting in the parking lot of the police station now. Simon's inside corroborating the story, but I already know Tilda's friend was telling the truth. I wouldn't say he's "a dealer with a heart of gold," but he is, ironically, one of the few people who didn't selfishly use Tilda.

I don't know if I'm going to keep writing here. At all, I mean. There's nothing left to add.

SIMON

Maria and I are alone at the station. It's empty and dark behind the service desks where people used to line up. No one's applying for new passports now. No one is going to read the pamphlets about community cooperation against crime.

We're on a bench just inside the lobby. She is wearing her uniform, sipping black coffee. *Plain old cop's coffee.* This close, I can catch the faint scent of her perfume, the same scent I used to catch in Judette's apartment.

"I don't want to know why you're asking," she says. "But yes, he was one of the people we brought in."

"And he was here all night?" I just need it confirmed.

"Yes," Maria says. "We let them sleep it off and released them the next day." She leans forward with her elbows on her knees, shaking her head slightly. "This is all I'm doing nowadays. Babysitting." She looks as dejected as I feel.

We've hit a dead end. I'll never know how Tilda died or why. But somehow, it feels even worse to know that I misunderstood everything while she was alive. I thought she started taking drugs when she heard about Foxworth—that it was a way of "living life to the fullest in the time we have left"—but Foxworth just made her stop hiding it.

Tilda was on drugs the entire time I knew her. And I didn't even notice.

All those nights she couldn't sleep. All those times I felt her heart beat hard against my chest. I just thought she was stressed.

Hypocrites.

Maybe she'd been talking about Caroline and Tommy. But they were with each other that night. So yes, they're hypocrites, but they didn't kill her.

I can't go home. I can't stand it.

Now I know what she meant.

I need your help, I think, she wrote in the letter to Lucinda.

Lucinda was the only one who could understand. She knew what it was like to sacrifice everything for swimming. She knew Tommy. She practically grew up with Caroline.

If they had talked to each other, would it have helped? Would things have been different?

No point dwelling on that now.

Tilda walked alone through the chaos, high and angry and sad. Maybe she saw something she shouldn't have, said the wrong thing to the wrong person, gave someone the wrong look. Anybody could have killed her. And we're never going to find out who it was. Trying to figure it out was ridiculous to begin with.

"How are you feeling?" Maria asks.

I look at her and feel like I've just woken up.

"I don't know," I answer honestly.

I study the short hair at the nape of Maria's neck, her short nails, her polished boots. Her uniform is perfectly ironed.

"Why do you do it?" I say. "Babysit, I mean. Why do you come here?"

She smiles. "That's a good question."

I wonder if she would have kept going to work if Judette had chosen her instead.

I wonder if it was a difficult choice for Judette.

"Thanks for trying to help me," I say. "With that Facebook post."

"Thank your friend. She's the one who convinced me."

"You really thought I did it, didn't you?"

Maria sips her coffee. "I was hoping you hadn't."

"For Judette's sake?"

Maria glances at me. "Yes," she says.

Her straight-to-the-point approach reminds me of Judette. They're more alike than Stina and Judette.

"You haven't got any other clues to follow up on?" I ask.

"No. Neither do you, I hope."

I shake my head.

"Good," Maria says, and it occurs to me that I like her.

"What would have happened if you'd found who did it?"

She appears to contemplate this. "I don't know. Whoever did it … that person has loved ones, too. Their lives would be ruined." She sighs deeply. "Let's hope the guilty party feels really fucking bad about it. I suppose that's the only punishment left for us."

We get to our feet at the same time. She holds out her hand, and I shake it. It feels oddly formal, considering how much we have in common.

If it hadn't been for Foxworth, she might have been a part of my life now, a part of dinners and vacations and walks with Boomer.

"Take care of yourself, Simon," she says.

"You too."

"Say hi to Judette from me."

I promise her I will.

When I reach the car, I see that Lucinda has fallen asleep in the passenger seat. I carefully close the door behind me. Start up the engine. Lucinda frowns, but doesn't wake up.

Her phone is in her hand. I wonder if she's been writing on TellUs.

Lucinda looks so much younger when I can't see her eyes; the golden evening sunlight softens her features. I drive as gently as I can until we reach her block, taking a detour past Tilda's house, where I see Tommy's car parked in the driveway. I turn onto Lucinda's street, stopping a little way down the road, where her father won't be able to see us if he's at home. Then I put a hand on Lucinda's shoulder. She looks up, perplexed. Blinks.

"Oops. I must have fallen asleep," she says.

Our eyes meet.

"What did she say? Was Lars there?"

"Yeah."

She leans back against the headrest. "So what do we do now?" she says.

But she's not expecting an answer. We both know there's nothing we can do.

Will she also disappear from my life when she steps out of the car?

Maybe Tilda was the only thing keeping us together. And now it's over.

Lucinda opens the car door.

"Hey—"

"Sorry," Lucinda interrupts. "I can't talk anymore right now."

SIMON

It's the final soccer game. Fifty thousand people are crowded into the arena in Stockholm. The prime minister is giving a speech; the audience is full of famous faces. The queen waves from the stands. Now and then, the commentators choke on their words. So far, three people have run naked across the field.

Judette's next to me, and Emma's sprawled on the other sofa. Despite that, I'm alone. I feel like a prisoner in my own head. Numb, just like that morning in May. My family can tell that something's wrong, but I can't share that we were looking for Tilda's murderer, and now we've given up.

Someone scores a goal and there are roars from the TV, from the apartments around ours, from open windows on the other side of the street. Boomer lifts his head, whining.

"This, if anything, is opium for the people," Stina says from the doorway of the kitchen.

"Huh?" I ask.

"Nothing."

She returns to her laptop. I catch a frustrated groan before her fingers start hitting the keys again.

Sirens wail outside the window. I wonder if Lucinda hears them, too. If her body's as tense as mine. Even if they're not showing the game on big screens, the streets will be chaotic tonight. How many people are going to get hurt? How many new Tildas are out there?

I get to my feet. Boomer looks up from the floor. His gaze tracks me as I walk to my room, where I sit down on my bed. Close my eyes.

"Tilda?" I say, listening hard.

I should have asked Stina *how* to talk to Tilda, and how I'd be able to tell if she responded.

"Tilda?" I say again. "We really tried to find the person who did it, but we failed."

Drunken laughter echoes from the apartment downstairs.

I force myself to focus on Tilda, trying to see her in front of me. I think about our first date at the café on Storgatan. Waking up together in this bed. Picnics in the park with Johannes and Amanda. But Tilda's features are blurred and vague, as if I've already forgotten what she looked like.

"People thought I killed you. I tried to make them understand ... so I could spend more time with them. I was so afraid of being alone. You know all about that, don't you? But I don't care anymore. I don't need them."

The words connect as I speak them out loud. This is the first time I've fully accepted the thought.

I don't need them.

I haven't for a while.

"You said the person I was with maybe never existed. But, Tilda, it wasn't like that. You were wrong. There were things I didn't know about you, but I knew who you *were*. And I loved you. I really did."

More shouting through the walls. It goes straight into me. Makes me feel like I'm dissolving. I take a deep breath.

"But you were right about one thing.... No matter how much I loved you, it was also ... I couldn't think of anything other than getting back together with you. I think that was easier than thinking about the end of the world. At least it was something I could *hope* for. . . . Just like I hoped I'd find who killed you."

For a moment, I see her clearly. She's at the window in her room. The sun makes her hair shimmer like copper.

"There's only a week and a half left. I still don't know how to handle this."

She turns around, looks at me with those eyes that could shift color to match their surroundings. Like water.

"So we were pretty alike this summer," I say. "You were *my* drug, Tilda."

SIMON

I walk down the grassy slope. Fog hangs heavy over the lake. The hills on the other side are swallowed up by a white nothingness. The waterslides look like tentacles against the pale sky, making me think of alien creatures.

I couldn't breathe when I woke up. My skin felt hot and tight, like it had shrunk overnight. It squeezed my flesh. My own body was making me claustrophobic. It had been Emma's idea to go for a walk. It was my idea that we come here.

No Lucinda on the swimming dock. I wonder how she's doing. What she's doing.

She hasn't replied to any of my messages.

Boomer impatiently pulls at his leash, and I let him loose as we approach the beach.

"Do you feel better?" Emma asks.

"I think so."

"Good."

She picks up a stick and throws it. Boomer rushes away, his wide bottom swinging wildly from side to side. Emma laughs.

I don't know if it's actually possible, but her stomach seems to have grown visibly in the last couple of days.

Boomer skids to a halt in the sand when he reaches the stick. He takes it in his mouth and turns around to receive praise.

"Fetch!" Emma calls.

Boomer spits the stick out and sniffs it, discovering another scent in the sand, which he starts to follow. The stick is left behind, already forgotten.

"Well, at least he found it," Emma says.

We start walking along the trail. Now and then, Emma stops, puts a hand on her hip.

"How do you feel?" I ask.

"Like I'm eighty years old."

Emma is experiencing SPD, a term I learned today. Her body is preparing for the baby. Cartilage is softening. Parts of her pelvis are slowly detaching from each other.

"But I guess this is nothing compared to squeezing out a whole human being," she says.

A few crows caw at one another from the trees. The streets on the way here were full of trash, smashed bottles, and shattered windows. Groups of people who were still drunk after the game yesterday were roaming around. But down by the lake, everything seems normal.

I wonder if Lucinda's dad worked at the ER last night. They've been talking about alcohol poisoning, extensive damage, murders, rapes, and fights on the news. The pictures from Stockholm's streets looked like scenes from a zombie movie. At least soccer is finally over for good.

"Imagining myself as a parent is so weird," Emma says. "I have no idea what I can teach another human being about the world."

A new wave of panic makes me feel like the ground is going to swallow me up. I stumble, but Emma doesn't notice it.

"I asked Mom if she felt ready when she was expecting me," Emma says, "because I sure as hell don't."

I look down at my feet, concentrating on trying to keep my balance.

"She said she still doesn't feel like a grown-up. Sometimes, it's like she's just pretending."

I unzip my track jacket and look out across the lake, trying to focus on the mist drifting across the water.

"It felt good to hear her say that," Emma goes on.

The air around the lake is unnaturally warm and damp; it feels oxygen-deficient. Is the comet affecting it?

No. Foxworth is still far away. It won't be until after it's entered the atmosphere that the air will heat up. And then we'll only have minutes left. But not yet. We have more than a week until the end.

Breathe.

"I'm so scared, honestly. But Micke doesn't want to listen when I try to bring it up. He says it'll be fine, but that's easy for him to say. He isn't giving birth."

It feels like I'm sucking down the same air over and over again, like it's already been used.

"I know I sound like I'm complaining. I'm looking forward to being a mom. It'd just be so much easier if he came home soon, so the two of us could deal with it together."

"I get that," I mumble.

I trip again. I have to focus on not falling off the world's edge.

Emma stops and turns toward me. I stop, too.

I have to leave. I have to get out of my own head. But I have nowhere to go.

Boomer comes running and stops at my side; he leans against my legs, wanting to be scratched. His fur is too hot.

"Simon, I know you'll always be in Tiny's life. You're

going to be an amazing uncle. Which is why I was wondering..."

Emma looks at me, and I don't understand how she can't see that I'm dying. Black spots gather at the edge of my vision.

"Would you like to be the baby's godfather?"

I stagger. Move away from Boomer's body. Breathe faster, hoping to scatter the black spots.

"Are you okay?" Emma asks me.

I can't deal with this anymore. I don't give a fuck what my moms say.

"Am I okay?" I say. "You know the comet is hitting us in ten days, right?"

Emma shoots me a questioning look. "Of course."

"You're not going to be a mom. You understand that, don't you? I'm not going to become a godfather. Micke is never becoming a dad."

Emma just stares at me, like *I'm* the crazy one.

"You don't have to worry about giving birth," I continue. "It doesn't matter what your body's telling you, it's never going to happen. If you stopped pretending, maybe Micke would come home. I wouldn't have been able to bear it if I were him, either."

I breathe more easily.

My sister had to pay the price, but something's been shaken loose inside of me now. "I'm sorry," I say. "I'm sorry, I didn't mean it."

Boomer licks my hand.

Emma walks up to me, and throws her arms around me.

"I can't stop planning just because the comet's coming," she says. "You get that, don't you?"

"No. I don't get it."

"We can't just stop living," Emma says. "We're not dead yet."

We remain where we are. Above our heads, the crows start screaming again.

SIMON

The lights switch on with a *click* when I step into the fabric softener-scented laundry room. I throw the rustling blue Ikea bag onto one of the benches, start sorting items of clothing in the sterile light, think about what to say when I call. *If* I call.

The ceiling is low, and I can feel the weight of the building above me. The floors that will soon be burning ash.

I've decided: I need perspective on everything that's happened. I need to leave. Not just the building, but town. And I have to see Johannes one more time. I refuse to let that evening when he sat on the edge of my bed be the last time I see my best friend.

There's a train to Stockholm the day after tomorrow, and I can be back the next day. I just need one single day of freedom. I'm not going to ask my moms for their blessing. They would never let me go. But I don't want them to worry for no reason. I feel bad enough for what I said to Emma yesterday.

As I fill two machines and pour in detergent, I'm struck by the thought that this is probably the last time I'll wash my clothes. I'll have enough clean underwear to last me until the end.

I start the machines, sit down on the bench, and take out my phone. I don't want my sister to be as lonely as I am. But do I even have the right to make this call?

I get his number out and call anyway. He picks up after the first ring.

"Hello? Is Emma okay?" Micke asks.

"Yeah, she's fine. But I am calling about her." My voice echoes back to me in the bare laundry room. "You have to come home. I've checked. There's a train from Luleå."

The phone is perfectly silent. I lower it and watch the seconds tick away on the screen.

"Hello?" I say.

The washing machines start spinning almost simultaneously.

"I don't think you understand," Micke says.

"What don't I understand?"

"You're young, Simon. You don't know what it's like."

One of the machines starts humming as it fills with water. I turn up the volume on my phone.

"Sure," I say. "I'm younger than you. But we've got the same amount of time left to live."

"That's not what I mean. When I was your age, I thought everything was simple, too. But it's not all black or white."

"Maybe it is sometimes."

"It's too difficult. You don't know how long I've fought for everything we had. We had it all figured out.... We had a *plan*. And then it just disappeared."

"That happened to everyone."

"But Emma ... When she talks like everything's like it used to be ... I can't. I can't fucking take it." His accent has become more pronounced after his weeks up north. "I can't do it, Simon. I understand that it upsets you, but I can't. I love Emma, but it's too hard."

"Too hard? Tilda was killed, and people thought I did it. That's also pretty *hard*."

Micke clears his throat.

"The world is one hundred percent fucked up," I go on. "And I know I'd do anything to be with someone who loved me until the end. Someone who needed me and who I—"

"I can't do it, okay?"

He sounds pathetic—angry—as if it's unfair of me not to let him wallow in self-pity. He disgusts me.

I stare through the washing machine's transparent window, watching our clothes spin in the foam behind the glass.

"Emma deserves better. I thought you both did. I was wrong," I say, and end the call.

NAME: LUCINDA
TELLUS # 0 392 811 002
POST 0039

My body crashed. I got a fever; my bones ached. I was so afraid I'd be hospitalized again. I wasn't just scared for my own sake; I didn't want Dad and Miranda to have to come and visit me at the hospital.

But it passed. I feel better. And my body only needs to last for one more week.

I haven't had the energy to write to you. I haven't even responded to Simon's messages. What is there to talk about? Our shared failure?

He writes that he's going to Stockholm the day after tomorrow to see his best friend, Johannes. At least he's doing something.

I know I should accept that we won't find out who killed Tilda—that it's all been for nothing—but I don't think I could, even if I wanted to. My brain won't let it go. It keeps circling in the same loop, desperately trying to find new angles and ideas.

SIMON

I walk past the train station, up Gamla kvarngatan, spotting the power box Tilda leaned against the final time we spoke to each other.

I stop and place my hand against the cool metal.

Everyone wants to tell me what I should be doing. Little Tilda, who can be such a good girl when she wants to be.

We were standing here when the others invited us to Ali's place for the after-party.

I've just been at his apartment. He and Moa were playing *Skyrim* with the curtains closed. The room was a cocoon full of trash and dirty plates. Both of them were pale and hollow-eyed, subterranean creatures made for a life in the dark. Ali's dad met me at the door. He asked me to try to convince them to go outside for a moment. I couldn't. But that wasn't why I was there anyway.

I said goodbye to Ali. I told him that I understand why he wasn't there for me. He didn't want to risk losing our friends so close to the end. He was a coward, but if I'd been in his place, I would probably have done the same thing.

I asked him for a final favor.

I'm telling my moms that I'm going to his house tomorrow— a small sleepover party to say goodbye to the gang. I don't think they'll have a problem with it. And after I get back home, I'm going to stay there.

I'm going to wait for the end with my family.

I cross Storgatan. Not a single shop window is still intact. Someone has spray-painted IT'S BETTER TO BURN OUT THAN TO FADE AWAY in flaming letters across the sidewalk, and the square is disconcertingly empty. I haven't seen a single person out and about since I left Ali's apartment. It supposedly looks like this all over the country. People have pulled back after venting during the soccer final.

I continue home in the twilight while more and more lamps turn on in the windows around me.

My phone vibrates when I reach the park near our house. Something flutters in my stomach when I see Lucinda's name on the screen. The feeling surprises me; I knew I'd missed her, but I only just realized how much.

"Sorry I haven't replied to your messages," she says.

"How are you feeling?"

"Like crap. But I'm better now."

"Really?"

"Really."

I look around the park where I walked with Erika less than two weeks ago. I was so relieved that someone believed me, even if it was just Tilda's aunt. Johannes had just left for Stockholm, and I didn't think we'd ever see each other again. Lucinda and I had just had our first argument by the lake. I wasn't allowed to go to Tilda's funeral. I felt so isolated. And even though we're closer to the end now, my life has improved significantly since then.

There's even more trash in the park now. The grass has grown wild. Someone has tossed a couple of bikes into the fountain. I sit down on its concrete edge, poke a balled-up pack of cigarettes with my foot.

"Do you know what I was thinking?" Lucinda says.

"No idea."

"Can you see the moon?"

I look up, searching the purple-violet sky between the houses. "Yes," I say.

The moon is full. Still pale and translucent. A ghostly image of itself.

I look up at the white disc, the dark bruises people used to think were oceans. *Sea of Tranquillity. Ocean of Storms.* The moon is full of craters from meteorites, a silent witness to the violence of outer space. They say it formed out of the wreckage when Earth collided with another, larger planet.

"If the moon makes it, there will still be human footsteps left up there," Lucinda says.

A shiver runs up my neck.

"Yeah," I say. "The only human footsteps in the universe."

"That's what I'm thinking about."

"Before Foxworth, I only ever thought about the sky as the sky," I say. "But space is actually up there. We are *in space*."

Lucinda laughs. "I have vertigo now," she says.

"Me too."

We sit in silence.

I notice that a few yellowed leaves have drifted to the ground: signs of a fall that won't come.

"Hey," Lucinda says.

"Yeah?"

"I was going to ask you something, but promise me you'll say no if you want to. It's fine. Promise."

"I promise."

She takes a deep breath, like she's preparing to dive into deep water.

"Can I come with you to Stockholm?"

My stomach flutters again.

"Do you have the energy?"

"I wouldn't ask if I didn't."

"Yes," I say. "Of course you're coming."

"Are you sure? Do you think it's okay with Johannes? I haven't even met him."

"You're going to like each other," I say.

"I really need to get away."

It sounds like she's trying to convince herself now.

"Come with me," I say, not caring that I sound too excited.

"I checked. There are seats left on the train."

"Then book one. What are you going to tell your dad?"

"I was going to ask Amanda to be my alibi. It feels wrong, seeing as I can't tell her I'm going to see Johannes. But I don't have anyone else I can ask."

"I get it."

"Don't tell anyone I'm coming with you. I really don't want her to find out."

I smile. "Who would I tell?"

Lucinda laughs again.

"We're *so* popular."

NAME: LUCINDA
TELLUS # 0 392 811 002
POST 0040

I'm going to Stockholm with Simon tomorrow. Dad has no clue.

I don't know what I'm doing. Why can't I just stay at home with him and Miranda instead? We only have one week left tomorrow.

But something occurred to me, and I can't let it go. If there's even a small chance that I'll find an answer, I have to take it.

I've lied to so many people now. Even to Simon. (*Especially* to Simon.)

I feel better today. No fever or anything. It should be fine.

SIMON

It's an unusually hot day for September. The sun shines down on the world rushing past the train window. Woods, houses, woods again, the shimmering surface of a lake in the distance.

Maybe the gardens aren't as well tended as usual, but they rush past so quickly, I can't tell. The driver stops the train now and then to go out and manually shift the tracks, but by now we've traveled uninterrupted for over an hour.

The train stinks. Trash bags are spilling over. All the toilets are clogged. Spilled soda sticks to the bottom of my shoe when I shift in my seat. Someone's smoked in here very recently.

We haven't passed a single train during the whole journey, and the car is surprisingly empty. An infant on the other side is screaming loudly; it doesn't even seem to breathe between each wail. Both parents meet my eyes at the same time when I look over. Their smiles are tired and apologetic.

Lucinda's sitting opposite me, writing in TellUs on her phone.

I promised to tell her if her real hair pokes out from under the wig, but now and then she touches her forehead anyway. I study her transparent reflection in the window.

The baby screams and screams.

"Just looking at the world like this, you'd think nothing's changed," I say.

In the window, I see Lucinda looking up.

"That's what messes with my head," she says. "It's impossible to process what's going to happen when everything appears the same."

We look out through the window together. Now the firs grow so close to the tracks that they're just blurred lines. After a moment, I catch her secretly watching me in the glass. She runs her fingers through her wig, laying the hair over one shoulder.

"But it was like this before, too," I say, turning to face her.

"Before?"

"With what happened to the environment. We couldn't really see that, either. Not here, anyway. I mean, we read about desertification and saw pictures of polar bears on tiny ice floes, but you couldn't really process it."

"People didn't want to process it," Lucinda says. "It was too difficult to think about."

We sit in silence for a while.

"I used to be so angry all the time," she says.

"Me too."

"I could never understand how people could be so incredibly intelligent and so fucking stupid and short-sighted at the same time. We knew what we were doing."

"I know. Sometimes I feel like the older generation ... get away with it now. They'll never have to take responsibility for how much they fucked us over."

"Right? I thought the worst thing was climate refugees. Where were they going to go? The same people who destroyed the world built the highest walls."

"I thought a lot about the permafrost," I say. "That it would thaw and release greenhouse gasses."

"Nuclear war could have ended us before that happened," Lucinda says, smirking.

"At least that would have solved the problem of over-population."

"Did you know that every four days, the world's population increases by a million inhabitants?"

"Shit. So we're going to be . . . at least a couple million more before we all die."

We look at each other and laugh. I don't know why.

"I wonder how it would have ended," Lucinda says. "If we'd just kept going."

"AI, maybe?" Lucinda says. "The machines strike back. They couldn't make a worse mess of taking care of this planet than we have."

"Or some super virus," I say. "Combined with antibiotic resistance."

"Super-volcanoes."

"The seas dying."

"The air becoming poisonous."

"Right-wing extremism."

"Multiple refugee crises, which lead to more right-wing extremism."

"No more clean water."

"The Gulf Stream changing directions."

"Heavy metals in the food."

"The last bee dying."

Lucinda's eyes sparkle as I try to come up with the next catastrophe we've evaded.

"Geoengineering," I say finally.

"What's that?"

I confess that I have no idea.

"Maybe it's got something to do with those researchers

who tried to create a black hole," Lucinda suggests. "Remember that? That seemed like a great idea."

I laugh again. While we've been talking, nature has disappeared, and I now see shopping malls decorated with signs that will never be lit again. Small clusters of buildings that seem scattered, almost at random. A car that's been abandoned in the middle of the highway.

I try to imagine what the landscape looked like when the first people arrived here. Before we blew up mountains, built roads, chopped down forests. It's impossible.

"In retrospect, I don't know why we didn't do everything we could to save the Earth," Lucinda says. "Why were we arguing about all kinds of petty shit instead? Maybe we could have done it if we'd really decided to. We should have rebelled against everyone who destroyed the planet just to make money. Put them in jail."

I notice that the baby has stopped crying.

"Do you want me to tell you something weird?" I say.

"Has anyone ever said no to that?" Her eyes glitter expectantly again, but what I've just caught myself thinking is something I haven't wanted to admit even to myself.

"I think there's something kind of beautiful about it ending this way," I say. "Not that I'm happy about it ... but if everything's going to hell anyway, at least it isn't our fault. And we can't do anything about it."

Lucinda's gaze is thoughtful.

"Do you know what I thought when I first heard about Foxworth?" she asks. "That I wouldn't have to miss out on everything by dying. I'd get to see how it ended. I was almost ... happy. Maybe not happy. But ... less sad. For a while. Sometimes."

"I can understand that."

The world suddenly tilts as the train goes around a curve. Lucinda's water bottle slides across the table and we both reach out to catch it. Our fingers touch. She looks away. Twists the lid on tighter, and throws the bottle into the tote bag on the seat next to her.

I want to touch her again.

The thought seems to come from nowhere, but I'm not surprised by it. It feels as if it's been there for a while, and only just surfaced. Maybe it's because we're so far from the places we know, in this no-man's-land between two cities.

Or maybe it's because talking about the apocalypse is so fucking sexy.

Lucinda goes back to writing in TellUs. I glimpse over-sized cranes, long since abandoned, outside the window. We pass a train station, then another one, pass the center of a suburb and cross another highway. And finally, the beautiful, old-fashioned houses in muted colors appear. Oxblood. Moss green. Mustard yellow.

"Ladies and gentlemen, we're entering Stockholm Central. Next, Stockholm Central. The final destination."

The voice coming through the speakers is unnaturally cheery. As the parents stand in the aisle and pull their bags from the shelf, the baby starts screaming again.

Lucinda sends her TellUs text into space and tucks her phone into her pocket.

The train slows down with a painful screech. I look out at the platform. Upturned faces look back at me; everyone's looking for someone. The car stops with a jolt that causes the baby's parents to stumble against each other. Then the train grinds to a halt, and I see him.

Johannes waves wildly outside the window.

He looks the same. Just happier than he has in a long time.

NAME: LUCINDA
TELLUS # 0 392 811 002
POST 0041

This is what I know:

Johannes was in love with Simon.

Simon was still in love with Tilda, talked about her all the time. It couldn't have been easy for Johannes.

Johannes was in town and watched the soccer game, but he disappeared early, and was the only one in the gang who wasn't at the after-party.

That same night, Tilda dies.

A few days later, Johannes leaves town. Deletes all his social media accounts.

Everything above is fact. Here are the speculations:

What if Johannes killed Tilda?

Tilda knew how Johannes felt about Simon. Maybe she tried to talk to him about it?

Or did he come to her?

Or maybe they just ran into each other in the chaos. Started fighting, things got out of hand.

Or it was planned. Maybe Johannes hoped Simon would forget Tilda if she vanished. Maybe he wanted to be the one to comfort Simon.

But Simon didn't forget Tilda. In fact, the exact opposite happened. And Johannes ran the risk of being discovered, so he fled to Stockholm.

* * *

Have you noticed how many *or*s I'm using here?

I don't know what to think. I don't know what to do.

Johannes is Simon's best friend, the only person who stood by him when Tilda's body was found.

What if I'm wrong?

But what if I'm right?

SIMON

S ome pigeons take off below the domed ceiling of Stockholm Central Station. All of the shops and cafés are closed. Only a few people are actually moving. Most of them are sleeping on benches, or sitting and looking at their phones.

We take the escalators to the underground entrance to the subway. More closed-down shops and cafés. Trash and old newspapers lie discarded in heaps along the walls. An ad for an apartment complex that was going to be built in Mälardalen still hangs on a wall: laughing men and women eating dinner on a dock in the sunset, glimmering water in the background.

A couple of women from Jehovah's Witnesses try to hand us garish flyers of Jesus and Mary, Jesus petting lambs, Jesus surrounded by children. We wave them off. I find myself thinking that all the religions were wrong in their predictions about when the world would end. Now, they finally have a date that won't disappoint them.

The ticket barriers stand open at the subway entrance. We walk past empty booths where guards once sat, take the escalator deeper underground, and eventually reach the platform for the red line going south.

"The trains come kind of sporadically," Johannes says, and nods to the turned-off signs. "They usually show up every hour or so."

"It's so quiet," Lucinda says, looking around.

"Most people don't go into the city anymore, unless they have to. There isn't much to do around here."

The tracks whistle and sing below us. Light approaches at the end of the tunnel.

"Shit, that's lucky," Johannes says, and leads us to the edge of the platform.

More newspapers and trash whirl up onto the tracks. The oncoming train is an older model. I glimpse the driver, a woman who looks like Judette, and wonder how she can stand spending her final days like a mole in these dark tunnels. Or is work the only thing that gets her out of bed?

What would I have done if Tilda hadn't died? Kept partying like before, doing anything to not to have to think?

The doors open in front us. I recognize a politician among the people leaving the car. He's shiny with sweat in his suit, possibly on his way to the Parliament House.

We sit by an open window in the middle of the car. As we leave Central Station, Johannes asks us if we know how Amanda's doing, and Lucinda tells him she's met up with her a few times.

"Maybe you could say hi from me?" Johannes says. "She doesn't want to talk to me anymore."

"I don't think I can," Lucinda says. "She doesn't know I'm here."

"No. Of course not."

We come out of the tunnel, passing Gamla Stan station and farther along the bridge. Fresh air blows through an open window.

"The subway doesn't stop here anymore," Johannes says. "The hall downstairs is flooded. The pumps have broken so many times, they finally decided to just shut it down."

I gaze out at the beautiful old houses lining the water. They seem to glow in the sunset. People are sitting in sparse groups along the quay.

"Lucky you were there when Simon got that message," Johannes says to Lucinda.

I sit quietly, watching them without really listening, enjoying seeing two people I care about so much getting to know each other.

The train stops at Slussen. A long-haired man in a leather coat is playing the guitar on the platform outside our window. I know the song. Emma used to listen to The Doors. This is the one about the end of the world.

People step on and off the train before it continues on. No one looks at me, wondering if I am a killer.

"I hope no one we know did it," Johannes says.

"So do I," Lucinda replies. "Because in that case, they knew Simon and still just let people think he did it."

I glance at her. That's an angle I hadn't even thought of. But I push the idea away. I've come here to let all of that go.

By Hornstull, Johannes tells me that lots of people in his commune have converted to Buddhism. He thinks that a lot of what they say makes sense. Lucinda wonders how it's all going to work after Foxworth, when there won't be any more bodies to be reborn into. Johannes looks at me, and I can tell he likes her. He says that the people he's talked to are open to the idea of other dimensions and timelines, even other civilizations in other solar systems.

The driver calls through the speakers that we've arrived at

Liljeholmen, the final destination. We get to our feet, grab-
bing the same rail so we won't lose our balance.

My hand touches Lucinda's again. I don't move it.

When we step out of the car, we're outdoors for the first
time since we came to Stockholm. The air's hot and dry,
smelling sweet and musty thanks to long-since-abandoned
garbage cans. We take the escalator up and reach a deso-
late plaza with a large mall. All that remains of the building's
vast windows is broken glass. A few local drunks have gathered around a couple of benches.

We walk in the opposite direction, past a streetcar station,
continuing along a road with tracks embedded in the pavement, passing buildings made of straight lines of glass and
metal. On poles supporting overhead lines hang ads for a
ballet at the Royal Opera. One shop window is filled with
sun-bleached posters offering great deals on graduation
caps. The road bends in a gentle curve. We turn left at the
intersection and reach an old industrial area.

"Here it is," Johannes says, and points to a worn brick
building in front of us.

For years, the house—on its way to being demolished—
has offered low rents to artists, writers, designers, activists,
small presses, comic book artists, spoken word poets, and
a couple of eccentric IT millionaires who skipped out way
before we found out about the comet. Now, more and more
of them have decided to move in permanently, and have invited others to join them.

A large rainbow flag hangs over the façade, and desks
and office chairs line the street. An old computer lies with
its screen flat against the pavement. It looks like it's been
thrown out a window.

The front door is decorated with two ornate old-fashioned

lamps that don't seem to fit with the rest of the building. WILH BECKER CORP is carved into the stone above a door covered in stickers and glued-on notes.

"Welcome to my place," Johannes says, and punches in the door's code.

NAME: LUCINDA
TELLUS # 0 392 811 002
POST 0042

We're here now. I'm writing this in Johannes's cramped room. He shares it with two other guys, but tonight, they're letting Simon and me borrow their beds. There's a factory chimney outside the window, and the lake is visible beyond the industrial park. A lone, red light bulb glows from the ceiling.

I think two hundred people or so are staying on this floor alone. Everyone seems to have lived on at least one other continent at some point. And I don't dare to comment on anything I see, because I'm not sure if it's an art exhibit or just garbage. In one room, sponges hang from the ceiling. But there's also a beautiful mural that some comic book artists have made, depicting blue giants and robots and a girl in a spacesuit. I wish I could send you pictures.

I love the vibe in this place, despite the fact that it makes me feel like the least remarkable person in the history of the world. Then again, that also has its upside: no one's staring at me. Lots of people here are wearing wigs, even without cancer.

I'm drinking dandelion wine straight out of a plastic bot-

tle as I'm writing this. It's so sweet, it makes my throat burn.
I didn't realize how potent it was until a girl convinced me to
let her do my makeup—when I closed my eyes so she could
add eye shadow, everything started spinning. She and her
girlfriend have a queer feminist theater company that is
livestreaming a show to a warehouse in Berlin tomorrow. I
didn't really get what it was about, but they told me about it
very solemnly.

Maybe drinking alcohol isn't the best idea in the world,
but it feels so good that it can't be entirely unhealthy. Somehow, it feels like everything's going to be okay.

I have to take the opportunity to confess something now,
or I never will (and I said I was going to be honest with you).
I think I have feelings for Simon. I've had them for a while,
but haven't admitted it to myself even. It's so embarrassing.
I think I felt it the first time we met on the dock. Or maybe
it was when Tilda and I spotted him in the halls during the
first weeks in high school.

Falling in love while waiting for the world to end is insane.
So many feelings, and they're all so big and incompatible,
and there's not enough room inside my body for all of them.
I feel like I'm going to explode. Sometimes, I dare to think
that he has feelings for me, too, but I'm pretty sure that I'm
imagining it. Simon's still in love with Tilda. I've become one
of those dominoes, remember?

Is it weird that I don't feel bad about him having been
Tilda's boyfriend? She wanted him to be with someone who
could give him what he needed. Am I that person?

It doesn't matter. Nothing is going to happen between us.

I have to go before they start wondering what I'm doing.
Plus, keeping one eye closed to see what I'm writing is starting to be a pain.

I like Johannes. And he seems to like me, too. That's the worst part.

The best thing would be if I could find out what he was doing that night without asking him point-blank. Simon would hate me if he knew what I was doing.

P.S.: Apparently, Buddhists believe in aliens. I may be reborn as your son or your pet. Keep an eye out.

NAME: LUCINDA
TELLUS # 0 392 811 002
POST 0043

LUCINDA: Hello, my dear friend! Now you're finally going to meet Simon.
SIMON: Hello!
LUCINDA: And Johannes.
JOHANNES: Hi.
LUCINDA: Tell them where we are.
JOHANNES: We're in Vinterviken.
LUCINDA: And I'm drunk for the first time in my life.
JOHANNES: Is this the first time?
LUCINDA: Yes!
SIMON: Cheers!
LUCINDA: Cheers!
JOHANNES: Cheers!
(pause)
JOHANNES: What do we say now?
LUCINDA: Just say something.
JOHANNES: Do you think someone's listening?

LUCINDA: I don't know.

SIMON: We're listening, aren't we?

JOHANNES: Okay. Seriously, then. I love that you're here.

SIMON: Me too. I needed this.

LUCINDA: Me too. This place is so fucking nice, Johannes.

(pause)

LUCINDA: Do you think you would've moved to Stockholm if it hadn't been for Foxworth?

JOHANNES: I would have waited until after high school. That was the plan.

(pause)

JOHANNES: And it wouldn't have been like this. I probably would have rented a tiny apartment with five roommates or sublet a place so far outside the city that the commute was three hours each way. And I would have been different, because everyone around me would have been different. It does something to people, doesn't it? That we all know?

SIMON: Mm.

JOHANNES: We're not spending half our time worrying about the future.

SIMON: There are still things I'm worried about, though.

LUCINDA: Me too.

JOHANNES: Not me. You know what? If I'd known before that everything was ending, I would have stopped caring about what people thought a lot sooner.

LUCINDA: But we've always known that. That everything is going to end at some point.

(pause)

LUCINDA: Everyone says you only live once, but we only die once, too.

JOHANNES. True. (laughs) So, in a way, the comet doesn't make much of a difference.

(pause)

JOHANNES: But I would have liked to live a little longer.

LUCINDA: Are you going to be here on the sixteenth?

JOHANNES: Yes. I think so. These people have become my family.

LUCINDA: Are you dating one of them?

JOHANNES: I don't know what to call it. We are ... We're all ...

LUCINDA: You're like one big happy incestuous family? (laughs)

JOHANNES: Something like that. (laughs)

SIMON: I once told Tilda we should have an open relationship. But I don't think I could have done it.

JOHANNES: I don't know if I could do it, either, not in a relationship. This is something else. I don't know. Things are different now. This is just how we live.

(pause)

JOHANNES: I can't believe it's only been a couple of weeks since I moved. I never thought I'd get over some things. But it's like time is behaving differently somehow, isn't it? Feelings, too. Everything is more condensed because it's almost over.

SIMON: I think I get what you mean.

JOHANNES: Good. (laughs) You're usually pretty slow on the uptake.

LUCINDA: I'm going for a swim.

SIMON

t's amazing!" Lucinda shouts. "You have to get in!"
Just like Tilda, Lucinda is a different creature in the water.
She laughs out loud a couple times. Dives and resurfaces.

I laugh, too.

Johannes and I are on the blanket we've spread over the grass at the edge of the bluff. He's smoking a cigarette. Every time he takes a drag, his face emerges out of the surrounding darkness. Vinterviken was a short walk from the commune, but on the way I paid attention to so many aspects of the world that's about to disappear: tall buildings stretching toward the sky, from the forested peak on the other side of a lake; beautiful, old wooden houses hidden under highways supported by pillars; an old dynamite factory converted into an idyllic café that now stands empty and undisturbed; tennis courts next to community gardens.

The final full moon ever is shining overhead, glittering in the water. We left the others by the first beach and continued on alone. I can still hear the music from a distance.

I'm so happy to be here, right here and right now, with Johannes and Lucinda.

"Have you thought about the fact that there will still be footsteps on the moon when we're gone?" I say.

Johannes turns his face toward the sky. "No, but now I'm going to think about that every time I see it."

"Lucinda was the one who told me."

Johannes nods, flicking ash onto the grass.

"You know," he says. "I like her. But having her here is kind of weird."

"Why?"

He takes another drag on his cigarette. Glances at me. "Forget it."

"No," I say. "What do you mean?"

"I know I said I was fine with her coming, but I didn't know you were in love with her."

I stare at him in shock. "What?"

"It's okay," Johannes adds quickly. "I just mean . . . you know how I felt about you. And I meant what I said. I'm over it. It just feels sort of weird to see you together like this."

"We're not together," I say. "I mean, I'm not in love."

Johannes laughs. "I've seen the way you look at each other."

I shake my head. Control the urge to ask him, *How? Does she look at me, too?*

"We're just friends," I say.

"So were we." Johannes grins. "You really had no idea how I felt about you, did you?"

"No. I thought you were avoiding me because you were sick of me."

"And here I thought I was being obvious."

Johannes flashes me a wide grin. He takes a final drag on his cigarette before putting it out. I watch as Lucinda swims through the mirror-blank water.

Why *has* she actually come with me?

What does she feel?

What do *I* feel?

Something. I know that. But am I just trying to fill a space left behind by Tilda? Is it just my usual fear of being alone?

"Lucinda's done so much for me," I say. "She was the only one who believed in me, other than you. I don't want to ruin anything."

"We only have one week left." Johannes lights another ciga-rette. "Maybe you'll ruin things more by not doing anything."

People on the other beach start singing along with the music. It's an old Britney Spears song. The one about danc-ing till the world ends.

I take a gulp of dandelion wine and hand the bottle to Johannes.

"I spoke to Tilda in the square that night," he says. "In the middle of the game. It was after you and I lost each other."

I swallow the last of the wine in my mouth. It's like drink-ing liquid sugar.

"Amanda had told her how I felt about you," he continues. "But Tilda already knew. She got it way before I did."

When he lifts the cigarette to his mouth, I see that he has tears in his eyes.

"I thought she'd be mad at me for Amanda's sake. But she said that she, if anyone, knew why a person would fall in love with you. And then she said"—he clears his throat—"she said she knew what it was like to feel like you couldn't be yourself. She said she'd always tried to be perfect and please everyone and . . . If you're too good at it, you end up not even knowing who you are."

In the darkness, I can picture it clearly. I can hear her voice.

Johannes looks at me. Releases smoke on a long sigh. It spills over the edges of his lips, rising into the sky, and van-ishes.

"That's why I gave up on the game and went home. That was the night I decided to come here. I'd already started messaging a few people."

He laughs, lifting his phone from the blanket.

"Look at this."

He swipes across the screen, again and again. Message after message after message appears. They wrote to each other all night.

"I packed while I was doing it," he says. "I would have stayed if you had asked me to, but I'm glad I'm here. And Tilda is a big part of that. I wish I could have told her I'm grateful."

"Are you coming, or what?" Lucinda shouts from the water.

Johannes smiles, throws an arm around me, and kisses me on the cheek. "I'll join the others. Stay for as long as you want."

I take his hand. Squeeze it hard, once, before we let go. Then I stay where I am, listening to his footsteps fade away in the night, trying to digest what he's said. About me and him, about Tilda and Lucinda.

I can't do it.

So instead, I get up, take off my shoes and socks. The grass is so cold against the soles of my feet that I nearly change my mind, but then I remove all my clothes except my underwear.

"Are you coming?" Lucinda shouts.

"I'm going to try!"

I reach the slippery rocks, carefully dipping a foot into the water. It's freezing. But I put my other foot in, too. Gather my courage. I lunge forward.

The cold leaves me breathless, washing the buzz out of my system. I try a few strokes. Snort.

Lucinda's treading water, waiting for me. She looks happy. This is a glimpse of a Lucinda in a different timeline, without cancer or comets.

Our knees knock together when I reach her. The water is as black as oil, moving as smoothly as silk between us.

"Thanks," I say.

"For what?"

"For everything."

She wipes water out of her eyes.

"We still don't know who did it," she says.

"At least we tried."

"Yes. We tried. With no results."

"With some results."

If she asks me what I mean, I intend to answer her honestly.

Her eyes glow in the darkness. Her short, soft hair is slicked to her skull.

Our bodies touch, smooth and invisible under the surface.

"I'm glad you came," I say.

"So am I."

Her lips are so close to mine. I can't stop looking at them.

"I have to tell you something," she says.

Something's has changed in her expression. And I understand that I've gone too far. Too quickly.

Johannes was wrong. She doesn't feel the same way about me.

I shiver in the water.

"Don't get mad at me," she says.

I get a sinking feeling in my stomach, and tread harder to stay above the surface.

"What is it?" I say, although I don't want to know.

"I like Johannes."

"He likes you, too."

Lucinda looks at me unhappily. And suddenly, I know exactly what this is about.

"He wasn't at the after-party," she says. "And he was in love with you. Did you know that?"

I swim backward. Don't even want to be near her.

"That's why you wanted to come with me?" I say.

"It's not the only reason."

I turn around and start to swim toward the beach. But moving is heavy, slow now, as if my body has been filled with rocks.

Naturally, she catches up with me easily. I feel as clumsy as Boomer as she glides through the water.

"Is it more far-fetched than when we talked to Tommy? Or Lars? Johannes has a motive."

I refuse to ask her what she means. My feet brush against the sandy floor, and I manage another few strokes before I start climbing the rocks.

"Maybe he was hoping it would be the two of you if Tilda disappeared," Lucinda presses on. "But when he realized his feelings were unrequited . . ."

"How do you know they were unrequited?" I say, and turn to face her.

Lucinda's eyes widen.

"I . . . I just assumed, because—"

"You don't know anything about me. We don't even know each other." My voice is satisfyingly cold. I grab a low-hanging branch and pull myself back onto the grass.

"I'm sorry," she says. "I didn't say anything because I didn't think you'd let me come with you if I did."

I walk over to the blanket and pull my jeans on over my wet boxers. "Just so you know, Johannes just told me what he was doing that night," I say. "And I saw the *evidence*. His *alibi*."

I yank my sweatshirt over my head. Hear her teeth chatter as she emerges from the water.

"I was just thinking—"

"I know what you were thinking," I cut in. "You shouldn't have come."

Our eyes meet. I'm the first to look away.

"You're right," she says. "We don't know each other."

NAME: LUCINDA
TELLUS # 0 392 811 002
POST 0044

W e're on the train home, and Simon isn't talking to me. He refuses to even look in my direction.

Now you know how I feel about him. Thank you, alcohol. Thanks for making my head hurt so badly it feels like it's splitting apart. We nearly missed the train because I couldn't run. I don't know what we would have done if we hadn't made it.

It's possible that I'll pee myself while writing this, but the bathroom onboard is the most disgusting place that's ever existed, and I'm going to vomit if I go near it. Everything is already swaying as it is.

Last night, everything was perfect. I swam. I felt like myself again, while also being *free from* myself. I was a different Lucinda. Just a normal girl. And Simon was with me in the water. We could have kissed in the moonlight. It would have been perfect. Almost ridiculously perfect. I knew he wanted it, too. And then Simon said that he was glad I'd come, and I had to tell him why I did.

It was some idiotic sense of honor that made me say it. I didn't want to kiss him without being honest. I hate that I'm such a prude.

Johannes can't have killed Tilda. He spent the night messaging some of the guys from the commune. If I had

only waited a little longer, I would have found out anyway.

Fortunately, Simon didn't tell Johannes what our fight
was about.

Right now, I just want to die. Luckily, my wish will be
granted in six days. (If I don't get sick from having worn
down my body with dandelion wine and swimming in freezing water. If the evening hadn't ended the way it did, it might
have been worth it. Now, I just feel awful.)

P.S.: Dad's called me twice. I can't bring myself to pick up. He
might hear that I'm on a train.

P.P.S.: Dad knows. He just sent me a text. He's waiting for me
at the station.

SIMON

B oomer barks as soon as I put my key into the lock. When
I open the door, he hurtles toward me as if he hasn't seen
me in years. I crouch down and ruffle his fur. He puts his
paws on my shoulders and licks me on the cheek.

"It's all right, boy. It's all right now."

*These are symptoms typical of stress and anxiety, and a lot
of people are stressed these days*, someone on the television
in the living room says.

I already know I've been busted. Lucinda's dad talked to
my moms. I have no idea how he found out we'd gone to
Stockholm.

This is just like being allergic to electricity. A different voice from the TV. *Just because we don't have a clear explanation for it doesn't mean we're imagining it.*

I struggle out of my backpack as Emma comes into the hall and gives me a hug. She bends forward to stop her stomach from pressing against mine.

"You're dead meat," she whispers before letting go. "Good luck."

I nod. Kick off my shoes. The door to Emma's room closes behind her. The hangover tingles like electricity under my skin. Stina calls from the living room. I might as well get this over with so I can spend some time alone.

Judette reaches for the remote and turns the sound off the moment I walk into the room.

COMET SICKNESS: TRUTH OR MYTH? the screen behind the two male hosts declares. Symptoms are listed along the bottom of the screen: ITCHING, TENSION HEADACHES, TREMBLING, HOT FLASHES, NUMBNESS.

"Come and have a seat," Stina says.

I obey. I almost fall onto the sofa opposite the moms.

Stina shakes her head. "You smell like a brewery."

"Please. I don't want to hear it right now."

"You don't have much of a choice." Judette snorts. "What were you doing in Stockholm?"

"I was visiting Johannes."

"But what were you thinking?" Stina says. "Don't you realize how risky that was? What if something had happened to you over there? Or if the trains stopped running? How would we get you home?"

I wonder how she even has the time to breathe. Her face is turning red.

From the corner of my eye, the two male hosts continue their debate.

"There's only six days left, Simon." Judette's bottom lip trembles. *"Six days."*

"I needed to see him one final time. He was the only one who believed me. Him and Lucinda."

"Yes, Lucinda. How could you go with her to Stockholm? She's sick!"

That's what Lucinda's dad told me at the station, too. But last night, I didn't think about Lucinda's cancer. She was just Lucinda.

I don't want to think about Lucinda at all right now. I refuse to be unlucky in love during the final week of my life. I've been unlucky in love all summer.

And I'm so tired. So terribly tired.

"You're right. Can I go to bed?"

"No," Stina says. "Not until we've finished talking about this."

"What is there to talk about?"

She sighs and looks at Judette. But Judette's eyes are fixed on me.

"This isn't the right time for that particular tone."

"Then stop talking to me like I'm a child."

"I would if you'd stop acting like a child."

"I thought we'd come further than this!" Stina says. "I thought we were doing really well. And then you go and do something like this. It's so incredibly disrespectful!"

"I can't just sit at home and think about the end."

"So what would you prefer to do? Pretend it's not happening?" Judette says.

"No." I stop myself. "Or, yes. That's exactly what I wanted. I didn't want to be ... dying. I wanted to feel like I had friends, like I'm *young*, like I'm *alive.*"

"I'm sorry we're not entertaining enough for you, Simon!"

Stina says. "But we *are* trying. We're doing everything we can!"

I've had it with them. They always insist I listen to them, but they're not listening to me.

"That's the problem with you," I say. "Maybe you should stop trying so goddamn hard." I get to my feet, and look at Judette. "And you don't have to stay here for my sake. I know Stina's blackmailed you into playing happy family, but it was better for everyone before. You must think so, too."

I walk toward the hall and accidentally step on Boomer's tail. He whines loudly, giving me a reproachful look like it's my fault he's always in the way. *Stupid dog.*

"Is that what you think?" Judette shouts.

I turn around. She's on her feet.

"This is my family!" she says. "I need you. I need *you*, Simon. And Stina. And Emma. Don't you get that? You want us to talk to you like an adult. Fine. I will."

Stina stays on the sofa, and takes Judette's hand when she starts to cry.

"I'm afraid, too," Judette says. "I wake up every day and count the hours we have left. I don't want to die. And I don't want you to die. I don't want any of this to happen."

Stina gazes up at her with so much love in her eyes that I can't stand it.

"I want to see Dominica again. I want to see my family and my old friends. I want Stina and me to grow old together, and I want to see Emma's kid grow up." Judette's whole body is shaking; Stina's hand seems to be the only thing keeping her upright. "And most of all, I want you and Emma to live long and happy lives. You're my son, Simon. I'm your mother. My most important job is protecting my children and ... I can't do it. I don't know how to bear it."

"Neither do I," I say.

This hurts too much. And all of a sudden, I understand why I've kept the moms at such a distance. It's not just because they want more than I can give them; it's because I love them. The more I let them in, the more I'm reminded that I'm going to lose them soon. That I'm going to lose everything soon. That nothing matters.

But if *nothing* matters, then *everything* is meaningless.

Lucinda said that.

I throw my arms around Judette. She cries against the side of my neck, and I hold her until she relaxes in my embrace.

Stina puts her arms around both of us. "We're together now," she whispers. "That's all that matters."

NAME: LUCINDA
TELLUS # 0 392 811 002
POST 0045

I wonder what Simon's going through right now. If he's thinking about me, and if so, what he's thinking. Maybe I don't want to know. If he ever felt the same about me, he's definitely over it now.

Our neighbor Gill is the one who spotted us boarding the train yesterday. Dad found out this morning. He still hasn't calmed down. But he will.

It feels like I'm waking up from some strange dream. I see the past few weeks so clearly now.

I've been obsessed with Tilda's death. I felt so bad for not being there for her when she was alive. I tried to make up for it by walking in her footsteps, looking for answers to the riddles she left behind. But no answer could've brought Tilda back. And my obsession made me repeat my mistake. Once again, I've forgotten about the living. The ones who are here now. I need to focus on them while there's still time. Tomorrow, there's five days left. A school week in the old world.

I once saw a documentary about a war photographer. He said he was never afraid in the field because as long as he looked through his camera, it felt like he wasn't really there. I understand him now. On the one hand, I see reality more clearly by attempting to describe it to you. On the other hand, I make it just unreal enough, turning it into something that isn't about me. When I write, I'm the god of this story. But the difference between this story and a fictional one is that the ending is already set in stone. No matter how much I write, I can't change it.

It's just as well that we never found the murderer. The police officer who spoke to Simon was right: whoever killed Tilda has loved ones, too—people whose lives would be ruined if they found out someone they care about had killed a teenage girl, hidden her body, stolen her phone, and pretended to be her.

I give up now.

I've been with Miranda all night. It's the only thing that makes me feel better. We built a pillow fort in the living room that she's going to sleep in. We've been talking about Tilda and looking at pictures of her. Dad doesn't let Miranda use social media—she didn't even own a phone until the news about Foxworth broke—so she hasn't seen most of the photos. We've laughed a lot and cried a lot. That's the only way to bring Tilda back, at least for a little while: making her live through our memories while we're still here.

SIMON

Judette's just come home from her final shift with the garbage truck when I get up. She's watering the plants in the living room as I step out of my room. I stay standing in the doorway, watching as she plucks dry leaves off the hibiscus while the watering can clugs.

"Why are you doing that?" I ask. "There's only five days left."

"Because it's depressing enough as it is without wilting flowers in the windows."

"Fair enough."

Judette smiles at me when she walks to the next window.

Something feels different. The air is easier to breathe.

"Are we the only ones here?"

Judette nods, and tells me Emma has gone with Stina to church today.

I step over Boomer and walk into the bathroom, drag the trimmer over my head for the last time, wipe the short hairs out of the sink and flush them away. Afterward, I take a shower, washing away the hair sticking to my face and shoulders, watching it disappear down the drain.

When I return to the living room, Judette's draped across the sofa, and the television's on. She's eating mandarin oranges straight out of the can.

"Want some?" she asks.

I take a piece. It's wet with sugar and dissolves in my mouth. The syrupy flavor makes me miss fresh citrus fruit. I can't even remember the last time I ate them. I should have cherished the memory.

But I remember when Judette bought the can. It was the same day we got the news about Foxworth. When I came home from Tilda's, we went to the supermarket and stuffed an entire cart full of cans and dry goods. The store was nearly empty, and the people who were there moved like sleepwalkers. We paid for the food with a regular credit card. Money was still being used back then. When we came back to Judette's apartment, she filled up plastic containers with water that she refilled every three days. *I've done this before*, she said. Dominica's always had hurricanes, erupting volcanoes, earthquakes.

This can was the last of its kind in the cupboard. And in the next few days, everything we do and say and eat will be for the last time.

I sit down next to Judette, leaning back against the armrest. On the television, people are walking toward the mine in Kiruna to move in underground. They're going to boil to death down there.

"Can you turn it off?" I say. "I can't watch this."

Judette picks up the remote from the table and aims it over her shoulder. The screen turns black.

"Have you spoken to Lucinda today?" she asks.

"No."

"Will you?"

"I don't know."

"Did something happen?"

I think about what to tell her, swiping another piece of fruit to play for time.

Lucinda in the water, her luminescent eyes. The glittering moonlight.

"I misunderstood why she wanted to come," I finally say.

"Did she only want to be friends?"

"I don't even know if she wanted that."

Judette makes a contemplative noise, but she doesn't ask again. And that's why I want to tell her about it all. I just don't know how.

"She won't want to see me again anyway," I say. "I was a fucking idiot yesterday."

"Was it that bad?"

"Yup."

I didn't even try to understand. Lucinda lied about why she came, but she couldn't know what I'd been hoping for. I didn't even know until me and Johannes talked in Vinterviken. Right? Or have I known for longer than that?

"It's complicated," I say.

"Does it need to be?"

"She was Tilda's best friend, for starters."

Judette raises an eyebrow. "So? You said it yourself. We have five days left."

Judette makes it sound so simple. *Is* it that simple?

"Were you in love with Maria?" I hear myself say.

Judette stiffens on the sofa.

"I thought we were talking about you," she says.

"Did you love her?"

She takes another mandarin piece, chews slowly. I have to smile when I realize how similar we are. She's also giving herself time to think.

"Yes," she says.

"Would you have stayed together if it hadn't been for the comet?"

"I don't think there's any point in thinking about that now."

"I just don't want you to give up on anything for my sake."

Judette's eyes are serious; they hold my gaze.

"I didn't give up anything. I made a choice. And it wasn't even difficult."

She holds the can out to me. A lone piece is left inside. I shake my head.

"You always seem so sure," I say. "Do you never hesitate?"

Judette bursts out laughing so suddenly that Boomer lifts his head in the hall. "Of course I do," she says.

"Then how do you know?"

"Stina and you have this way of always trying to *think* your way to what you feel about things, but you can't. . . . At least, it's an unnecessary detour."

She gives me an amused smile. And I realize I know the answer. I get to my feet.

I can't let the world end without telling her how I feel.

There's no time to lose. Not a single second.

NAME: LUCINDA
TELLUS # 0 392 811 002
POST 0046

Simon called me a moment ago, saying he needed to talk to me about something. I think I know what he wants, but I don't know if I can get my hopes up. What do I do if I've misunderstood him? What do I do if I haven't?

People who say they enjoy being in love must be insane. This is so much more stressful than looking for a murderer.

I wish he'd known me before I got sick. If he had, he might have caught a glimpse of the old me through the person I am now, just like Grandpa does with Grandma.

Dad's at work. At least this time I remembered to tell Miranda that Simon's visit is a secret. I could tell by her face that she thought it was exciting.

Shit. He's already here.

SIMON

We're sitting on an old-fashioned bench in the garden behind the house. Somewhere in the neighborhood, someone is rhythmically cleaning a rug. Lucinda catches me looking in that direction.

"It's the woman who saw us at the station," she says. "She's a comet denier."

"Still?"

"I guess so. Unless she wants her house to be presentable for the apocalypse."

This part of the garden is hidden from the wind. The sun is hot, but the day is cool. The fruit has ripened on the boughs of the apple tree.

What did Stina say about that Moomin book?

If we ever want to dance, we have to do it now.

"I'm sorry I overreacted," I say.

"I'm sorry I lied about why I tagged along. I didn't really think it was Johannes. Not once I'd met him."

A few birds chirp around the garden. Our hands rest between us on the bench. So close to each other.

"I was just so . . . ," I begin.

But I lose track of the sentence. I was in such a rush to get here that I didn't think of what to say when I did.

"I thought you came because you wanted to be with me," I press on. "That's why I was so fucking childish. Because the thing is . . . I like being with you."

"Me too," she says. "With you, I mean."

My little finger touches hers.

Lucinda smiles at me. And I know that Johannes was right. All your feelings are condensed now; you can't waste time anymore, but you *can* waste all the feelings you'd have otherwise spread out across an entire lifetime.

We hook our little fingers together.

"I hate the reason we met," I say, "but I'm glad we have each other."

She moves closer to me on the bench, leans against me. Our mouths are so close together I inhale her breath. In the trees, the birds chirp like crazy.

Her lips brush against mine.

I reluctantly pull away.

"What is it?" she says.

"Is this okay? I mean, what if I have a cold I don't know about, or something?"

"I'll take the risk," she says. "Shut up, will you?"

We kiss again, carefully, softly. Our tongues meet and I close my eyes.

The sun warms my neck. The wind caresses my arms. Lucinda strokes my leg lightly.

"Do you want to go up to my room?" she says, and I can only nod.

My lips are already missing hers as we stand up. We walk hand in hand down the paved path. Dark clouds have gathered above the trees. Any minute now, it's going to rain.

Miranda is sitting on the stairs in front of the door. She's wearing a denim jacket over her thin summer dress. Her fingers, busy with a Rubik's Cube, are long and thin. She glances up at us curiously.

"Hello," I say.

"Hello."

Lucinda opens the door and goes in. I'm about to follow her indoors when I notice that Miranda is staring at me.

I meet her gaze, getting the sense that she's gathering her courage somehow.

"Is everything okay?" I ask.

Miranda shrugs. "Do you know Molly? Tilda's cousin, I mean."

I don't know what I'd expected, but it wasn't this.

"Yes," I say. "A little."

"She's not like them."

"What do you mean?"

Miranda looks away. Large raindrops have started falling on the lawn. They patter against the small awning over the front steps.

"She knows you didn't do it. The thing with Tilda."

"Are you sure?" I ask before I have the time to think.

I see Molly before me: her terrified eyes at the crossing, how she turned to watch the car as I passed.

"Have you been talking to Molly again?" Lucinda says, coming back out onto the steps.

Miranda looks down at the cube. She pretends to be engrossed by it.

"Not since the day we celebrated Christmas."

Christmas? I look at Lucinda, who shakes her head.

I'll tell you later.

"She doesn't like her mom anymore," Miranda says, glancing at me again. "She says they're hypocrites."

Hypocrites. Tilda's word out of Molly's mouth. And now, out of Miranda's. Lucinda and I exchange a look.

"Has something happened in Molly's family?" Lucinda says, and crouches in front of her sister.

"I don't want to say anything. I promised."

The rain is pouring down now, splattering on Lucinda's back. The scent of damp grass and earth rises from the ground.

"This is important," Lucinda says. "Please tell me."

Miranda presses her mouth shut, but I can see that she wants to tell us something. This is something she's been thinking about a lot.

"Were Molly's parents the hypocrites?" I ask.

Miranda looks up at me.

"No. Her mom and Klas. They're together."

NAME: LUCINDA
TELLUS # 0 392 811 002
POST 0047

I knew I recognized the stuffed animal we found behind the glass factory—that tiger cub with the oversized eyes. Now I remember once when Molly and Miranda were younger. They were playing on the swings in the yard, and Tilda and I had been doing something in the kitchen, when we heard a scream. They'd been testing to see who could jump the farthest from the swings, and Molly had landed badly and sprained her ankle. She didn't want us to comfort her. She only wanted the tiger cub.

She chose to leave it where Tilda's body had lain. I wonder if it means something.

I have to sort through my thoughts.

Molly knows that Simon didn't do it.

She's said that Erika and Klas are hypocrites. That they're together. Tilda's father is having an affair with his brother's wife, something that goes against the Truthers' rules. Still, Klas made himself out to be all holier-than-thou in all his messages to Tilda.

Tilda said she was sick of hypocrites.

It can't be a coincidence that Molly used the exact same word. She adored Tilda.

Copied everything she did.

Is that where Tilda was going after the game? Were Klas and Erika the hypocrites she wanted to confront?

They weren't at home. They were in the True Church with Anders. But Molly was at home. She already told me she didn't have to go to church. In the post after the funeral, I even quote her: "They said God can tell that I'm false, so they pray for me instead."

Did she and Tilda see each other?

Molly couldn't have left Tilda behind the glass factory, but she may know how Tilda ended up there.

It feels like we're close to an answer, but we've felt like this before. Maybe this is another dead end.

I've been looking at the Truther website. They have a

massive service tomorrow night. Hopefully, Molly will be home alone.

I've got to stop writing now. Simon is still here. We have a few hours left until Dad comes home.

NAME: LUCINDA
TELLUS # 0 392 811 002
POST 0048

L ast night, Simon and I stayed in my room and hid from the world.

We kissed. His mouth was just as soft as I'd imagined. Easy to say now, maybe, but I don't think I will ever tire of kissing him.

I won't write a detailed report about what happened afterward. I'll just tell you that I was nervous. I wondered what Simon actually thought about my body. If he compared it to Tilda's. But he got me to stop thinking. And my body, which has been my enemy for so long, was finally on my side.

We're meeting again in a little. We're going to try to talk to Molly.

SIMON

R ain hammers against the roof of the car, large drops the windshield wipers barely manage to swipe away. I exit the highway and turn into a block of identical houses made of sand-lime brick. These streets are named after the town's old industries. We look for 9 Cylindervägen, where Tilda's uncle and his family moved this summer.

"The nearest parking lot should be up there," Lucinda says.

She looks up from the map on her phone and indicates a row of garage doors. On the strip of pavement out front is the van marked FIRST KLAS, INC.

I park by an abandoned bus stop, remove the key, and when the sound of the engine quiets, the pattering of the rain grows louder. It sounds as if the drops are trying to punch a hole through the roof.

We look toward the van. The service in the True Church starts in half an hour, and it takes at least that long to get there. If they're not attending the service, we have no chance of talking to Molly tonight.

"They should be gone by now," Lucinda says.

"Maybe they've taken Anders and Erika's car. Let's wait here for a while and see if they show up."

Lucinda nods. The cold light throws harsh shadows across her face.

I watch the drops explode against the windshield, flow together, and pour down the glass. The world outside gradually disappears; it's like someone has pulled a gray veil over the car.

"What a romantic date this is," Lucinda says.

I laugh, then lean toward her for a kiss.

"Wait," she says, looking through the windshield. "There they are."

Erika is carrying the same red umbrella with white polka dots that she had the night we walked through the park. She's holding it over herself and Anders. Klas runs ahead, throwing himself into the van's driver's seat.

Through the rain, I can make out Tilda's aunt closing her umbrella and getting into the backseat by herself. I wonder

why she wanted to meet me that night, what she was thinking when she asked me all those questions.

Does she know who did it? Did she want to find out if I
knew? Was she trying to lead me away from anything that
indicted her own family?

*I've wondered if her coach didn't have something to do with
it. She was so angry with him the last time I was with her.*

She could have met anyone on the way.

Or it could be the drugs.

The van's headlights turn on, and Klas pulls out of his
parking spot.

"Should we go?" Lucinda asks when they've disappeared
down the road.

"Let's wait a while, in case they realize they've forgotten
something."

We sit in silence. Listen to the sound of the rain.

"Do you still want to do this?" Lucinda asks.

I look at her. For a moment, I consider saying no. Molly's
just a kid. Regardless of what she knows, we're going to scare
her.

"Yes," I say. "We have to."

Lucinda nods. She presses record on her phone and puts
it in her pocket. Then she leans in and gives me a kiss.

We step out of the car. I pull the hood of my rain jacket
over my head and am surrounded by the pattering sound.
It's windier than I thought. Lucinda's umbrella turns inside
out, becoming a parabolic antenna.

We hurry across the street, continuing along a path and
into a short tunnel. The front of my jeans is already soaked.
We reach Cylindervägen, walk along the even row of hedges,
past the identical doors with neat, identical lawns, until we
reach number nine.

Through the window next to the door, I can see an illuminated sink. Coffee cups and plates have been left on the kitchen table. We walk up the steps to the front porch. I reach for the doorbell. Look at Lucinda. She nods decisively, so I press it.

The rain picks up again while we wait, blowing against us. Lucinda shivers just as I hear light footsteps approaching.

The door opens. Molly gives us a shocked look.

"I'm not allowed to see you," she says.

"Molly," Lucinda says. "You know us."

"I'm not allowed to talk to anyone anymore."

She starts to close the door, but I put my foot in the gap and immediately feel bad.

"Just for a little while," I say. "We want to know how you're doing."

"Miranda was worried about you," Lucinda says.

Molly hesitates. She glances at me.

"Please," I beg her.

She lets go of the door and backs into the hallway. Lucinda leaves her umbrella on the porch and we step inside. A wall of sweet scents wafts toward us.

"Are you baking?" Lucinda asks, and manages to sound completely normal.

Molly smiles nervously, but I can see a hint of pride in her eyes.

"Would you like cinnamon buns? You can take a seat in the living room while you wait."

Lucinda says yes for both of us, but I have no idea how I'm going to eat anything now. We hang our jackets on hooks. Remove our shoes. My rain jacket drips onto the beige tiles. We walk past a tall staircase with wooden paneling, reaching a living room in which everything is oversized: a large sofa in the corner, a large dining room table, a huge television. My cold, wet jeans stick to my thighs as I take a seat on the sofa. I throw a glance at the table's shelf and spot three Bibles on top of the piled newspapers.

"Here you go," Molly says, coming in carrying a round tray. Three large glasses filled to the brim with milk clink against one another beside a plate of buns. The glasses slide across the tray when she lowers it toward the table. They almost tip over, but Molly catches them at the last second.

"Help yourselves," Molly says in her strange grown-up voice.

She takes a seat, focusing on Lucinda and hardly looking at me. I force myself to take a bite of the cinnamon bun. It's still hot from the oven, dripping with butter and sugar.

"This is really good," Lucinda says.

"Really good," I agree.

Molly flushes, giggling from somewhere far back in her throat. "I used to want to be a chef. I love baking and cooking."

Lucinda smiles stiffly. She seems to be considering how to move the conversation forward. We have to be careful, but neither one of us wants to stay here a second longer than necessary.

"Doesn't it get lonely, not being allowed to meet anyone?" Lucinda asks.

"Not really. We spend time together as a family, and I try to help out at home while they're at church. Baking, for instance." More giggles.

"Don't you miss your friends?" I ask.

Molly throws me a quick look. "I've never had a lot of friends," she says.

I try not to look pitying. I know how humiliating it can be at that age.

When I saw Molly from the car, I thought she bore an uncanny resemblance to Tilda; now, there's no trace of her. Instead, I recognize myself in Molly. But while my shyness and insecurity made me silent and withdrawn, Molly tries to win everyone over. Her efforts are so heartbreakingly transparent.

"I didn't have a lot of friends at your age, either."

"*You* didn't?"

She dares to look at me a little longer this time.

"No. But it wasn't that bad. I preferred reading and watching movies and thinking by myself."

"Exactly," Molly says, and laughs affectedly. "People my age are so childish."

She sounds more like a child than ever.

"Miranda misses you, though," Lucinda says.

"Tell her hi from me."

"I will."

Lucinda and I exchange a glance.

"But staying at home by yourself must be scary sometimes," she says. "Like that night they showed the soccer game in town."

Molly's posture immediately changes, her shoulders going up to her ears.

Lucinda pretends not to notice.

"I was at home alone with Miranda because Dad was working," she continues. "It really scared me when people started roaring and yelling."

"Yeah," Molly says and attempts to giggle again. "At first, I didn't understand what was going on. It sounded like a war had started."

"But then Tilda came," Lucinda says.

Molly's eyes grow large. She shakes her head.

"No."

"Yes," Lucinda says calmly.

Molly sneaks a look at me. A sudden gust of wind makes the rain hammer harder against the window.

"Oh, right," she says. "Yeah, she was here for a while. I was confused."

"Why did she come here?" I ask carefully.

Molly's eyes move between the two of us. Her face changes as her thoughts race. I can tell she's scrambling.

"I wrote and asked her to come," she says. "I was scared."

"Molly," Lucinda says softly. "You and Tilda didn't write to each other that night."

"Yes, we did," Molly says, and starts to cry.

"No. I've seen Tilda's messages. There were none from you that night."

Molly shakes her head.

"You're just trying to trick me," she sobs. "You can't have read her messages."

"Because you've had her phone?"

"No," Molly says. "Mom had it."

NAME: LUCINDA
TELLUS # 0 392 811 002
POST 0049

LUCINDA: You didn't know Tilda was coming over, did you?

MOLLY: No.

LUCINDA: What did she want?

MOLLY: I don't know.

LUCINDA: Yes, Molly. I can tell that you know. And I think you want to tell us.

SIMON: It's okay, Molly. We won't be mad.

(pause)

MOLLY: She wanted to see Klas.

SIMON: But he was at the True Church.

MOLLY: Yeah. She was going to wait here until he came back.

SIMON: Why did she want to see him?

(pause)

SIMON: She thought he was a hypocrite, didn't she?

(pause)

MOLLY: Yes. They fought a lot during dinner the day before.

LUCINDA: What were they fighting about?

MOLLY: She was on drugs. And Klas had heard that she was with a bunch of different guys. He said she would go to hell if she wasn't baptized.

(pause)

MOLLY: At first, Klas didn't believe the rumors that she was doing drugs. He said Tilda was too smart for that, but I don't think it has anything to do with whether you're smart or not, you know?

LUCINDA: No, I get what you're saying.

MOLLY: But when we were having that dinner, you could really tell. And when she came over after the game, she took drugs even though I was there. She didn't care.

SIMON: Why did she think Klas was a hypocrite?

LUCINDA: Was it because he was seeing your mom?

MOLLY: How do you know that?

(pause)

MOLLY: Did Miranda tell you?

(pause)

MOLLY: You can't tell anyone.

LUCINDA: We promise.

MOLLY: I'm the one who told Tilda. No one else knew.

(pause)

MOLLY: It's really unfair that Klas said Tilda would go to hell, because it even says in the Commandmcnts that you're not supposed to be with someone else's wife. And he knows it.

(pause)

MOLLY: When I told Tilda, she felt sorry for me. She said kids shouldn't have to get mixed up with adults' secrets.

LUCINDA: She was right about that.

MOLLY: She was nice.

LUCINDA: I know.

MOLLY: But the night of the game, she was totally different.

(pause)

MOLLY: She was so mad. She was going to talk to Klas, even though she'd promised not to tell anyone.

(pause)

MOLLY: I just wanted her to leave so my dad wouldn't find out. Tilda would have ruined everything, and we only had a month left.

LUCINDA: I can understand that.

(pause)

MOLLY: I didn't mean to.

SIMON: Of course you didn't.

(pause)

MOLLY: We only argued because I wanted her to leave. And then she fell. Over there.

(pause)

MOLLY: You can't tell anyone. I didn't mean to.

(pause)

MOLLY: Do you think I'm going to hell?

SIMON: No. You won't. There is no hell.

MOLLY: That's what Tilda always said. She said everything would be fine.

NAME: LUCINDA
TELLUS # 0 392 811 002
POST 0050

'm back home again. Now we finally know the truth.

Tilda's death was an accident. But that doesn't mean no one was responsible.

Tilda was going to confront her dad. She could have destroyed Molly's family. From Molly's perspective, that would have been the biggest disaster imaginable. An apocalypse within an apocalypse.

Family is all Molly has, despite how twisted it's become this summer.

Molly and Tilda got in a fight. Tilda fell down the steep stairs. She hit her head on the cold tiles of the lower floor.

Molly called her mom and told her what had happened. And Erika must have panicked. I'm trying to understand what she was thinking. Maybe she wasn't thinking at all. It all happened so quickly. She told Anders and Klas that she was going home to check on Molly because there was so much mayhem after the game.

Writing about this is difficult. It all happened because of a stupid affair. I can't stop thinking about how pathetic that is.

If Erika had called the police, they probably wouldn't have questioned that it was an accident.

But Erika was afraid of what would happen if the police started asking Molly questions about what had happened. She was afraid that Molly would let slip why Tilda was so angry with her dad.

Molly, the anxious girl who never fit in, no matter how hard she tried. How has she lived with this for almost a month?

It takes at least half an hour to drive from the True Church to their house. And that's under normal circumstances. That night, the streets were full of wasted revelers. I wonder how long Molly was alone with Tilda's dead body while the world outside seemed to have collectively lost its mind.

Erika was just as afraid as Molly that their small family would fall apart.

Erika was the one who wiped up the blood. She took the car around back, and Molly had to help her drag the body over there. When Erika went back to the True Church, she took the road past North Gate. She laid Tilda behind the abandoned glass factory.

"Mom said I couldn't tell anyone," Molly said. "I'm not even allowed to talk to her about it."

Simon and I stayed for a long time and just listened. Once Molly started talking, she found it hard to stop. She needed it so badly. Now I understand why Erika wouldn't let her see my sister.

If anyone's guilty, it's Erika. She's kept the truth about what happened to Klas's own daughter from him. She let Caroline worry for days before Tilda's body was found.

She let Molly carry the secret and the fear and all the guilt alone. She let suspicion land on Simon, but pretended to care about him. She stayed a hypocrite.

Molly only wanted to protect her family—her life. There are only a few days left. We won't ruin it for her now.

This is the closest I'll ever come to telling the truth to an outsider. Simon was innocent. If you hear anyone claim otherwise, then they don't know what they're talking about.

SIMON

Lucinda and I know where you were going now," I say. "We know what happened."

I'm standing by the window and talking to Tilda again. The morning sun shines over the park where Erika and I walked in the rain.

You had something special. I could tell that you loved her

It sounded so naïve back then. But maybe that was all she could offer me. Did she feel bad? I think so.

But I don't forgive her. She didn't have to make the choices she made. During those minutes when she was driving to North Gate, she could have stopped herself and asked herself what she was doing. So many hours and days, when she was using Tilda's phone to trick everyone who was worried about her.

Erika sent me the koala.

"We're not going to tell anyone, except for my moms, that it was Molly," I continue.

Some kids run across the street outside my window. They're chasing one another. Shouting loudly, joyfully.

"I hope you understand. If you'd seen Molly yesterday ... She wouldn't be able to deal with it."

I've never heard anyone cry like Molly did in Lucinda's arms. She sounded like an animal.

We sat in the sofa near the stairs where Tilda fell.

Did it hurt? Did she have time to feel scared?

A woman steps out the front door on the other side of the street and calls the children to come in and eat.

"We'll let them live a lie these three days," I say. "And I hope Erika feels like shit."

Everyone who says they know what's best for me ... and think they're that much fucking better than me ... they're the worst ones.

"Stina is talking to Caroline and Klas now. She's going to say that someone came to the church and told her that your death was an accident. That this person panicked and hid you in North. I hope it will make things easier for them."

I take a deep breath before I continue.

"I don't know if we're doing the right thing. All I know is that I could never have done it without Lucinda."

Tears start to fall when I say her name.

"I think I love her."

And for a brief moment, just for half a breath, it's as if Tilda is here. It isn't quite a touch; it's more like someone is carefully moving the air across the skin of my back. Only a little more tangible than the feeling of being watched.

It's Tilda. I decide to believe that. And then she's gone. I wait, try to feel her again, but I already know she's not coming back. I turn around, but there's no one there. She's said goodbye.

NAME: LUCINDA
TELLUS # 0 392 811 002
POST 0051

I've dreamed about Tilda all night. The last dream was a real memory. She and I were Molly and Miranda's age. We'd watched a movie about two kids who got their parents to fall in love with each other, and we talked about doing the same thing. If her mom and my dad got married, we could be sisters for real.

We already knew that Klas and Caroline weren't in love anymore.

When I woke up, I wondered what would have happened if they'd divorced earlier. If none of the adults in these families had been hiding secrets.

It bothers me that we can't tell everyone how Tilda died and why. I want to silence everyone who said she was asking for it because she was an addict, because she was out of control. No one's asking for it. Tilda wasn't some bad girl who got punished for her sins. And she was, despite her secrets, more honest than most people.

I played Dad my recording of Molly. He's agreed that it's better not to tell anyone. At least he now knows, with 100 percent certainty, that Simon didn't do it.

I told him about the ADHD medication, too. He said he had his suspicions about which doctor "helped" Tilda with that.

I don't remember much of my other dreams about Tilda last night. They're only flashes. Tilda preparing for a competition. Taking water out of the bucket behind the starting block with cupped hands, splashing it over her body and bathing suit to lessen the friction. Rubbing spit into her goggles. Shaking out her muscles. Taking deep breaths.

Tilda taking a small gulp of pool water during warm-up when she thinks no one's looking. She did that before every race. Everyone was superstitious before the competitions. I always climbed onto the starting block from the right.

Tilda, who always wanted to be perfect.

She wasn't perfect. She was better than that. She was human. And if you're always trying to be seen as perfect, how are you going to be loved for who you are?

Tilda's last friend called me today. He wanted to hear how I was doing. We talked for a long time. He said he can see Foxworth in his telescope now. We talked about space, and what the chances are that someone or something out there finds out about our existence. He said that even if no one hears TellUs specifically, we've definitely left a mark. We are (were) a noisy species. Our phone calls and television shows and radio transmissions have been beamed into space for over a hundred years. And at the front of the line are the first radio broadcasts. If someone hears them, they'll be able to surf through our history on the waves, hear reports from the First World War, then the Second. Discussions and debates. Comedy and drama. Small and significant events. All the way up to this moment. "Our planet is like a bus full of really loud children," he said. "Pretty hard to ignore."

And he's right. It's going to be a cacophony of voices all making claims about what the world looked like and what made people tick. It's going to be full of contradictions. But maybe that's the thing. Maybe that chaos is the truest snap-shot of humanity. We're a pain in the ass.

Simon's here now.

He's asking me me to stop writing.

And I will.

SIMON

Lucinda smiles at me with tears streaming down her cheek. I sit down next to her on the edge of the bed and give her a kiss.

She looks tired. I haven't slept much, either. The moms finished the final bottle of wine, and at first, I thought I heard crying on the other side of the wall. Then I understood.

I try to shake off the thought. I don't want to think about Stina and Judette having sex. Not even my existence is proof that it's ever happened.

This morning they were wearing their wedding rings again.

"Have you told the aliens everything now?" I say with a nod to Lucinda's laptop.

She laughs and shuts it. "I can't tell them *everything*. But I've done what I could." She caresses the laptop with her fingers, dragging her nails across a sticker that's peeling at the edges. "Has Stina talked to Caroline and Klas yet?" she asks.

I nod and look out the window. The sun out there is blinding.

"It went well. But I don't know what they said. Stina is keeping it confidential until the end."

I turn toward Lucinda again.

"That it went well is all we need to know, I suppose," she says.

"Yes."

The weight of it hits me. No more mysteries. No more clues. Nothing we need to solve.

I guess she's thinking the same thing. It's already afternoon. Two and a half days left. Two sunrises.

I lie down next to her, catching a faint scent of detergent from the pillow.

"I saw the weather report this morning," Lucinda says. "They showed the forecast two days from now. And then ... nothing."

I move closer, feel the warmth of her body, focus on it until the wave of panic inside me recedes.

"They should tell us what the weather is like on Thursday," she continues.

"Just so we know what we're missing?"

"Yes. I'd actually like to know. I usually never care about the weather, but at least we'd know something about the day that never comes." She stops herself. "Is that weird of me?"

"No idea."

The day that never comes. The world that doesn't continue.

"The weather will be nice until the end, anyway. In case you were wondering," Lucinda says, and kisses me.

SIMON

H aven't you finished the sermon yet?" I ask when I come into the kitchen.

I add a *sorry* when Stina looks up from the computer and I meet her tired, bloodshot stare.

"I thought I just had a little polishing left to do. But now I want to delete it all." Stina rubs her eyes. "Who am I to lead people in that moment? Who is *anyone* to do it?"

This is a Stina I don't recognize; I've never seen her so resigned before.

"It'll be fine," I say, but it comes out sounding so flat that I immediately regret it.

"I don't know. I don't know anything anymore."

I stand behind her and give her a hug. She sobs softly, resting her cheek against mine, and puts her hands on my arms. It's almost as if we've switched roles. As if she's my child and I've got to comfort her.

I stay standing until she stops crying. Then I sit down opposite her at the table.

"Try it out on me, then," I say. "We can pretend that I'm someone you don't know. Now I'm entering the church. What do you want to say to me?"

Stina smiles, and wipes her eyes with the sleeve of her sweater. "I can't."

"You can."

She lets out a shaky sigh.

"The hardest thing is making everyone feel at home," she says. "The ones who believe and the ones who don't."

"Forget about the others. What do you want *me* to know? I mean, the me who isn't me?"

Stina looks embarrassed. She glances at her screen.

"I want you to feel hope."

"Good. So do I. But how do I do that?"

"By not being afraid. We can't do anything about what's happening, but we can trust in God to receive us. That's what I want to say, I suppose. That the end isn't the end."

"And if I can't believe in that? What do I do?"

"Then I at least don't want you to feel alone. We can't get past this moment, but at least we can get through it together."

"There you go," I say. "That wasn't so hard, was it?"

Stina smiles at me. Dries her eyes again. "Thank you."

"It's not for your sake, it's for mine. Lucinda and her family are coming to church, and I don't want you to embarrass me."

"I promise I'll do my best not to."

Judette comes into the kitchen. The timing is so perfect, I get the feeling she was eavesdropping from the living room. She sits down next to me.

"Emma wanted to play a board game tonight," she says. "What do you think?"

"I'd like to see Lucinda," I say.

Stina opens her mouth to object, but closes it again.

"I promise to stay at home all day tomorrow," I add quickly. "But I have to see her alone one final time."

Judette gives Stina a quick nod, then puts her arm around me, hugging me tightly.

NAME: LUCINDA
TELLUS # 0 392 811 002
POST 0052

D ad came home late last night from his final shift at the hospital. They don't really need doctors anymore. From now on, there are mostly volunteers who have chosen to stay behind to hand out medicine and food trays, watching over the sick.

See? I told you people can actually be good sometimes, too.

Dad and I stayed up and talked for a long time. We turned off all the lights except the Christmas star that's still hanging in the kitchen window.

Something happened. It's like we saw each other as people for the first time, outside of or apart from the roles we've had my whole life. We were Jens and Lucinda, not father and daughter. I don't know if you can grasp the difference, but it's enormous. Light-years.

I asked him if he'd dated anyone since Mom died. He said he'd had some brief relationships, but they were never significant enough that he wanted to introduce them to Miranda and me. I couldn't understand how he'd managed to date without me noticing anything. Apparently, they usually met during the day, while Miranda and I were in school.

We talked about Mom. I knew how they'd met—a New Year's Eve party at some mutual acquaintances' place during Y2K—but tonight he told me how she'd danced, what she'd been wearing, and that he'd immediately known he'd fall in love with her.

He told me what she was like. That she was effortlessly magnetic, but could make herself invisible when she didn't feel like talking to anyone. She hated the winter and black licorice, just like me.

He told me what it was like to plan her funeral while being terrified that he wouldn't be enough for his two kids.

I said he's been more than enough.

And I read him what I wrote to you in my ninth post here on TellUs. That was the first time he'd heard what it was really like for me when I got sick.

I cried in front of him for the first time since the diagnosis.

And I told him about Simon. I said I was happy. That might sound strange, considering I have approximately thirty-six hours left to live. But it's true.

I love him.

I love my dad more than ever, too, and Miranda.

And I love Tilda. Now that we know what happened, and I'm no longer busy trying to solve anything, my brain has finally started calming down, leaving some space for my feelings.

I'm off to see Simon soon. We're going to meet where everything began.

Tonight, you can see Foxworth with the naked eye.

P.S.: Dad and I decided we're going to join the service at the church. I'll get to be with both my family and with Simon.

I think it will feel good to be with other people.

Funny that *I,* of all people, should say that.

SIMON

This time, we've brought blankets and pillows. Lucinda's head is resting on my arm. We're lying next to each other on the swimming dock, looking up at the sky.

If it were cloudy, we wouldn't see it. But now it's sparkling over the treetops on the other side of the lake.

Foxworth. Our death.

I pull Lucinda closer and shut my eyes. Listen to the gentle splash of the water under the dock, the faint whisper of the wind in the trees, Lucinda's breaths.

"I wonder which star Tilda wrote about in her letter," she says. "The one that was forty light-years away."

I open my eyes. My gaze is automatically drawn to Foxworth. Am I imagining it, or is it shining more brightly than it did just a second ago?

"In forty years, they might see us lying here," Lucinda says.

I raise my hand, waving to our audience in the other solar system. Lucinda laughs, and waves, too.

"Maybe they'll see our first meeting," I say.

Lucinda raises herself on her elbow and looks at me. Her eyes shine in the dark.

"If it hadn't been for Boomer, you would have just pretended not to see me, right?"

"Yes," I confess. "I didn't know what to say to you."

"I just wanted you to leave." She leans her head against my chest. "I thought you were the kind of person who'd think you had to talk to me."

My fingers brush against her cheek. She pulls the blanket up to her chin.

"So we wouldn't be here now if it hadn't been for Boomer," she says.

"And if I hadn't been out running that day, despite my hangover."

"And if I hadn't walked all the way here, despite not having the energy."

A fish splashes in the water out on the lake. Other than that, everything is still. Can the birds sense it? They fly across the globe, follow the stars and the sun and the magnetic fields to find their way home. They have to notice the new star that shines more brightly than the others. They must know that something is wrong.

"What if we'd missed each other?" Lucinda says.

"We're together now," I say, and borrow Stina's words. "That's all that matters."

She lifts her head and kisses me lightly on the mouth.

"I probably would have hidden at home if it hadn't been for Tilda," she says. "She forced me back into my life."

I nod. Lucinda puts her head on my chest again.

A mosquito whizzes around my ear, drawn to the scent of our warm bodies, and I bat it away. It's the first mosquito I've noticed tonight. It really is fall.

"I think it would have rained the day after tomorrow," I say. "Perfect weather for staying in and watching a movie."

I can feel her cheek move when she smiles.

"Is that your prognosis?"

"Yes."

"What movie would we watch?"

I consider it. "Something decent. Not so terrible that we couldn't stand it, but not good enough that we'd care too much. It would be just the kind of movie you watch when you have all the time in the world."

"Plus, it wouldn't matter if we missed parts of it while we were making out."

"Exactly."

"And then what?"

"Sex."

"And then?"

"I've always wanted to go to Latin America."

"Same."

"Okay. Let's take a year off and travel around Brazil, Chile, Peru..."

"Imagine the amazing food we'll be eating."

"Yes. And how much we'll swim. We're going to spend the days on the beach."

"And get drunk at night. We'll celebrate over and over that I'm healthy again."

She caresses my chest.

"I want to see Dominica, too," I say. "Is it okay if we take a detour on the way home?"

Lucinda nods. "Of course. But after that, we need to take charge of our lives. I barely started high school."

"Are you going to keep swimming?"

"Yes, but I won't be on a team. And I'm going to apply to a new high school. An art school, I think. I'm only going to swim when I feel like it. And then I'm going to try to write a book."

I take her hand. Kiss the back of it. Continue to her fingertips. Down toward her wrist.

"What about you?" she asks. "What are you going to do when we get home?"

"First, I'm visiting Emma and my new godchild. And then I'm going back to school."

"You'll be done a year before me."

"Yes. But I have no idea what I want to be."

"You still have time to decide. Maybe you'll think of it when we're night-swimming on some Chilean beach."

"True."

"I like our future," Lucinda says.

"So do I."

Our mouths find each other in the dark. I curve a hand around her neck. Play with her short hair. She gets on top of me, pulling the blankets up around us both while Foxworth glimmers in the sky above us.

THE FINAL DAY

SIMON

t's still dark outside when a high-pitched whine wakes me up. I look up. Boomer's sitting next to my bed, licking his lips.

"Hi, boy," I say.

His tail pounds weakly against the floor a few times, but he keeps whining, fixing me with his large brown eyes. And suddenly, I remember. I pick my phone up from the floor.

It's six in the morning. I've only slept for a couple of hours. We have less than twenty-four hours left.

Panic grips me, making the muscles in my back contract, my skin tighten.

"What is it? Do you want to go for a *walk*? Do you need to *pee*?"

Boomer hardly reacts to the magic words.

I put my legs on the floor, and pat him on the head. Try to seem calm. He licks his lips again.

"Come," I say.

He lumbers after me out of the room. Emma and our moms are sitting in front of the television, Judette in her robe, Emma and Stina in the T-shirts they slept in.

A Catholic Mass is on the television. The cathedral is full of people, and everything is covered in gold and white and red. A choir of hundreds of children sings so beautifully it makes my chest ache.

"Sixty thousand people are there," Judette says. "There's at least sixty thousand more in St. Peter's Square outside."

The image transitions to the dome of St. Peter's Basilica. The sky is pale and cloudless. A soft yellow at the horizon.

Foxworth is clearly visible now. Notably larger than it was yesterday. My entire spine tingles. My fingertips prickle.

"Has anyone been out with Boomer?" I ask.

"We just went for a walk," Stina says.

"He's worried."

"It started last night," Judette says. "He was scratching at our door at three in the morning."

Boomer tilts his head to one side. His eyebrows draw together, as if he's trying to understand what we're talking about.

I sit down on the floor and pull him close. He sighs heavily and lies on his side with his head in my lap. The eye that stares up at me is so wide that the white is visible around the entire pupil.

The choir keeps singing. I try to breathe.

If only Foxworth had come at us from a slightly different angle. Or arrived a few minutes later, when the Earth had spun farther into space.

The floor sways beneath me. And my head is buzzing. It feels overheated, like my synapses are on fire.

"How are you?" Emma says.

I look up at her. I can't hide anything. I'm busy struggling for air.

"I'm having a panic attack."

Emma scoots down from the couch, sitting next to me.

"Don't fight it," she says. "That only makes it worse. It's not dangerous."

"I feel like I'm breaking."

"You're not. I promise."

"How do you know that?"

"I just know. Keep breathing."

She looks at me steadily. The simple fact that she doesn't seem concerned calms me. I focus on her gaze. Force air into my lungs. Emma nods encouragingly, and I take another breath.

I suddenly realize, with total clarity, what a good mother she would have been.

She puts her arms around me. I'm vaguely aware of Judette and Stina joining us on the floor. That they're holding us, too.

And I tell them that I love them. That I'm happy they're my family. I say I'm sorry we've had so many fights toward the end, and Judette says it's because we care about each other.

NAME: LUCINDA
TELLUS # 0 392 811 002
POST 0053

There's a saying I've always hated: today is the first day of the rest of your life!

It's supposed to mean that you can transform yourself, change your habits, make new and better life choices. Become an improved, happier version of yourself. Like you could erase everything that's happened to you by just *deciding* it. I had to hear it a few times when I was sick. Usually, the people who say it have no clue.

But today I'm beating them at their own game.

Today is the final day. *Period.*

And this is my final post.

I've been with Dad and Miranda all day.

Apparently, Dad got Grandpa to understand how video calls work so we could see each other when we talked with him and Grandma. (Not that Grandma said much. She mostly sat there and slumbered on.)

I'm taking a final shower in a few hours. Then we're eating our final dinner (three courses, another thing on Miranda's bucket list, even though Dad and I helped) and going to church. But first, we're watching the final sunset together in the garden. And we're saying goodbye to the house.

I wonder what Gill is thinking, if she's watching the live broadcasts from around the world. Naked hippies on the Canary Islands are preparing to welcome the comet. Tens of thousands of people have gathered on Gärdet in Stockholm. A group has occupied a pyramid in Cairo in order to divert the comet with the power of positive thinking.

Is Gill a little bit worried that she and the other comet deniers are wrong after all?

We have about nine hours left until it's all over.

I'm lucky. I'm going to be in church with my family and my boyfriend. And Mom and Tilda are in the cemetery. When Foxworth hits us, their ashes will mix with ours.

Don't tell anyone, but right now, it doesn't feel like it's all just going to end. I wouldn't call it God, or anything like that, but maybe there's a spiritual equivalent to all those radio waves being beamed into the universe. It seems unreasonable that eight billion lives could cease to exist in just a couple of seconds without leaving a trace behind. We'll still be here somehow.

But you and I have to say goodbye now. I've enjoyed writing to you. And now that I think about it, maybe we're not that different. Wherever you are and *whatever* you are, we were created in the same Big Bang, the one that kick-started this universe. We were connected in something that wasn't anything, and then suddenly became everything. So maybe there's a chance that you understand something of who I was.

And one day, we might be connected again.

Until then, thanks for everything.

— L

THE FINAL NIGHT

SIMON

P eople are squeezing into the benches, sitting in folding chairs and on the floor in the aisles, filling the balcony behind the pipe organ. Stina is at the front of the church. Standing up straight and confident, she leads us through the psalm:

Fair is creation, fairer God's heaven,
Blest is the marching pilgrim throng.
Onward, through lovely regions of beauty,
Go we to Paradise with song.

It's nearly time. We barely have a couple of hours left.

I hold Lucinda's hand tightly. She's on one side of me. Judette is on the other. I can see that Lucinda is miming the lyrics. She's not the only one who doesn't know the melody. Most of the people singing it are a bit older, but I grew up with this psalm; it carries memories of my childhood.

Ages are coming, ages are passing.

Outside the window, it's almost as bright as day. It's a world completely bleached of color. From the black sky, Foxworth glows like a white spotlight, like moonlight times a hundred.

The psalm is over. Stina looks out across the crowd. In the silence, barks can be heard outside the church. I try to make out if any of them is Boomer's.

We'll be right there, I think.

Stina agonized over what she was going to do with the

pets, but when people came rushing in, it soon became clear that all the dogs, cats, rabbits and guinea pigs wouldn't fit. And it seemed unfair to people with allergies to even try.

Stina talks about eternal hope, eternal life.

Emma touches a hand to her stomach.

Lucinda's dad tells Miranda to stop kicking at the benches in front of us.

Calm has settled over the church. I expected tears and hysteria. I wonder if more people feel the way I do. That there's something bigger than myself here. I don't know if it's God. Maybe it's just all the people here, the fact that we're sharing this moment.

We're one and the same. No one here is alone.

I wonder what Johannes is doing right now. We spoke for a long time today. They were going to have a party. Keep on dancing till the world ends. I hope they're at Vinterviken. That's where I want to picture him.

I wonder if Caroline and Tommy are with each other. If Ali and Moa are playing games in their dark cocoon. I wonder what's going on in the True Church, if Erika and Molly are there. Probably. I wonder what my family, the ones I've never met, are doing in Dominica. It's going to be 10:12 p.m. over there when Foxworth hits. I think about Micke. He sent his love to me when he and Emma spoke for the last time this afternoon. I think I understand him a little better now. He wasn't just rejecting Emma; he was also choosing to be with his family.

I'm so glad I never had to choose between my family and Lucinda.

"For I am convinced that neither death nor life, neither angels nor demons, neither the present nor the future, nor any powers, neither height nor depth, nor anything else in all creation will be able to separate us from the love of God that is in Christ Jesus, our Lord."

Stina asks us to find Psalm 256. There aren't enough books to go around. I angle mine so that Lucinda and her family can see. I know it by heart. It was my favorite psalm as a kid.

Don't be afraid, there is a secret sign, a name that protects you wherever you may land.

Lucinda gasps. Her eyes fill with tears.

Your loneliness has beaches into the light. Don't be afraid, there are footsteps in the sand.

"What is it?" I whisper.

"This psalm," she says. "They sang it at Tilda's funeral."

He loves you, he waits for you tonight.

"I like it better now," she whispers.

I squeeze her hand tightly. We cry together.

From eternity, he has chosen to meet you here.

The tears dissolve my final trace of resistance. I'm cracked open.

You're on your way. One day the night will turn white. One day and stars grow out of his embrace. Don't be afraid, there is a dark haven. You can't see it now, but you'll alight.

The song fades away. It's time for the Holy Communion. Stina reads the first prayer. Then we pray Our Father together, and she breaks the bread. When she says that anyone who wants to may approach, Lucinda and her family stay seated.

I bump against someone's legs as I pass. A toothless baby looks at me with wide eyes. Me and my sister and my mom walk up to my other mom. We stand in a semicircle with the others in front of the altar, which is also a semicircle, symbolizing the ones who came before us—the ones who are waiting on the other side to complete the circle.

It takes a lot of time for Stina to share the bread and the wine with everyone. She looks each of us deeply in the eyes when it's our turn. Smiles almost imperceptibly. I think she knows I'm proud of her.

And suddenly, there are only twenty minutes left. We're in a hurry, and Stina improvises. She says a final prayer of thanks. Blesses everyone in the church. The choir starts singing again. *You envelop me on all sides and you hold me in your hand.* Again and again. Stina leads them down the center of the aisle, encouraging us to join them. It's time to leave.

Lucinda's family has already reached the aisle and is waiting for us. Her dad is crouched down, his arms around Miranda. He kisses her again and again. I take Lucinda's hand. We follow the crowd.

I spot Amanda and her mom. We nod at each other. I think we say more through that nod than we could ever do with words. Everything is forgiven.

Judette and Emma are right behind me. Stina throws open the tall wooden doors before us.

It's so bright outside. It reminds me of finishing school before the summer, leaving the building. The vacation that stretched out before us always seemed endless.

"It's all right, Miranda," I hear Lucinda say.

Now I feel the fresh, cool air coming in from the outdoors. I drink it down while we walk on.

ACKNOWLEDGMENTS

Every book has its challenges, but this is by far the most difficult I've written yet. I definitely would not have made it without Ylva Blomqvist, my publishing star who lights up my sky more than any comet could. Also a big thank you to my editor Sofia Hannar, who extinguished grammatical errors and let me do rewrites up until the very last second.

Thank you Lena Stjernström and the rest of the team at Grand Agency, who held my hand when I thought this project would be my own personal Armageddon.

I would not have been able to write *The End* without beta readers who gave me wise feedback from different perspectives: Anna Andersson, Åsa Avdic, Sara Bergmark Elfgren, Helena Dahlgren, Daniel Di Grado, Moe Duke Bergman, Petra Flaum, Karl Johnsson, Jenny Jägerfeld, Judith Kiros, Sara Linderholm, Elin Lucassi, Hampus Nessvold, Mattias Skoglund, Erika Stark, Marcus Stenberg, Matilda Tudor, Rebecka Tudor, Carolina Wallin, and Pär Åhlander.

Big thank yous to friends, friends of friends, colleagues and strangers who helped me ask the right questions, and get the right answers. Every mistake is my own. I am so grateful that you so generously shared your time and knowledge with me: Astrid Avdic, Karin Bojs, Alexis Brandeker, Evan Matthew Cobb, Torsten Dahlén, Johanna Gustafsson, Stefan Hultgren, Torun Jämtsved Millberg, Sam Lang, Jens Lapidus, Christina Larsson, Åsa Larsson, Patrik Lundberg, Jerry Määttä, Elisabeth Nordlander, Patrik Olsson, Vicktor Olsson, Hans Rickman, Amanda Ringqvist, Sara Rörbecker, Alexander Rönnberg, Johanna Strandberg, Lone Theils, Anna Thunman Sköld, Maria Wahlberg, Katarina Wennstam, and Misse Wester. Special thanks to Emma Hanfot, who helped me with the medical stuff, and Gitte Ekdahl and Måns Elenius who helped me with everything from satellites to spores to railways, and read the text in different versions.

This book is for Johan, who I want to be with when the sky turns white.